BROKEN

MANHATTAN RUTHLESS

SADIE KINCAID

"We are all a little broken, it's the inevitability of a life well-lived."
Nathan James.

For my book lovers who want their book boyfriends to be a gentleman in the streets and a deviant in the sheets, I wrote Nathan James just for you.

All my love, Sadie x

PROLOGUE

My father pours six glasses of fifty-year-old Macallan and hands them out to my brothers and me. We stare out the window, watching the fireworks lighting up the night sky.

My youngest brother, Maddox, looks at his glass and swirls the amber liquid around the base like he doesn't know what to do with it. He's only sixteen, but I know for sure that's not his first drink.

Mason shakes his head and sighs. "Does anyone else feel like it's weird that it's just us?"

I nod my agreement. This house is usually so full of people, laughter, raised voices, and music, especially on New Year's Eve. But tonight there's only pain and silence.

"We could put the TV on. Watch the ball drop," my oldest brother, Elijah, suggests.

Drake shakes his head. "Nah. She used to hate that, remember? Was always convinced the time was off by a few seconds."

1

Mason laughs. "Remember how she'd always insist on using Great-Grandad's old Navy diving watch to determine when it was midnight instead?"

I frown. "Where the hell is that thing?"

Maddox reaches into the pocket of his jeans and produces the watch, his eyes wet with tears.

Mason knocks back his Scotch and jumps up from the sofa. "Jesus, it feels so weird without her here. Like this house has no fucking soul anymore. Let's get the fuck out of here and go somewhere."

Drake rolls his eyes. "Like where, jerkwad?"

"I dunno. A club or something. A place where there's life."

Maddox scowls. "And what about me, dickface?"

"Nobody is going anywhere," our father barks. "So quit your whining and drink your Scotch."

Mason sinks back down onto the sofa with a sigh. "Sorry, Pop."

My father knocks back his drink and stands in front of the window, ensuring he's in all our eyeline. He stares at the five of us. The James boys. Apple of our mother's eye. Dalton James has always been a giant of a man, formidable in business and ruthless in his quest to become the man his own father told him he would never be. He made his first billion by the time he was thirty-five. A loving, if strict, father. A man to look up to.

But now his shoulders are slumped in defeat. His suit, once finely tailored to fit the contours of his muscular physique, hangs loose around his shoulders. No less the man I respect more than anyone on this earth, but still a shadow of his former self.

He sucks on his top lip, the way he does when he's deep in thought or about to impart some of his legendary wisdom. "I have a piece of advice for all you boys. You live by this, and I promise that you'll never know a day's heartache in your life."

CONTENT WARNING

This is not a dark romance however it does have some emotionally charged themes which may be triggering for some readers.

The final trigger is also a spoiler, so if you prefer to go in blind then please stop reading now. However, if you feel that you need to be forewarned then this book contains discussion regarding the sexual assault/ suicide of a character not directly connected to the MC's. It also deals with pregnancy loss/ miscarriage.

Elijah stares up at him. "And what's that, Dad?"

The five of us wait for him to impart this particular nugget of wisdom.

He clears his throat, his deep gray eyes full of grief. "Never fall in love."

CHAPTER
ONE

NATHAN

My father tosses the glossy magazine onto the table. "Another one, Nathan?" he says with a heavy sigh.

I glance at the spread pages and the paparazzi snap of me and some socialite leaving a nightclub at 3:00 a.m. two nights ago. "At least I don't have my hand on this one's ass." A fact that she was particularly pissed about if I recall.

He shakes his head. "That is not the point, son. You're thirty-eight years old. When the hell are you going to grow up and take some responsibility for your life?"

I roll my shoulders and clench my jaw. Along with my younger brother, Drake, I own the biggest law firm in the country. While I specialize in criminal law these days, together Drake and I have brokered deals that earned my father's company hundreds of millions of dollars. I've always done all I can for my family. For my brothers. And he wants to preach to me about responsibility.

"You can talk, Dad. How many women have you fucked this past month?"

He scowls at me. "Your mother did not raise you to talk like that, Nathan. And I don't care how many women you hook up with, but at least be discreet about it."

I roll my eyes. "I don't see what the problem is. I'm single. These women are all consenting adults."

"The problem is, like it or not, you are this family's legacy. How do you think your mother would feel knowing you were dragging our good name through the gossip magazines the way you do?"

Anger bristles beneath my skin. "Don't use Mom against me."

"I will when it's goddamn true!" He bangs his fist on the table, his face turning a deep shade of red. I sink back in my chair and bite back the instinct to go toe to toe with him. He had a heart attack only four months ago, and he looks like his blood pressure is about to shoot through the roof.

Sucking on my top lip, I hold back all the things I want to say so I won't piss him off any further. He glares at me, the vein in his temple throbbing. Then he leans back in his leather wing-back chair with a sigh. "I understand you want to make your own way in this world. I said nothing when you went off and opened your own law firm instead of joining the family busi-ness. I kept my mouth closed when you recruited one of your younger brothers into the fold too."

I bite my lip before we get into the age-old argument about me corrupting Drake.

"I have no idea why you're so resistant to carrying on my name. Are you ashamed of who you are?"

I shake my head. "That's fucking unfair, Dad. Just because I didn't want to go into tech, you think I'm ashamed of my family?"

He nods to the magazine on the table between us. "Then

why else do you flaunt my name like this? This is not how a James man behaves."

"And how exactly should a James man behave, Dad? Like Elijah?"

He scowls at the mention of my older brother's name. "He understands duty."

"He's married to a woman who treats him like shit, and he's miserable as fucking sin."

My father shakes his head. He can't argue with that, so experience tells me he's about to try a different tactic. "I don't know how long I have left on this earth, son."

Oh fuck, here we go. "Will you quit with that? You're sixty-eight years old, not ninety. That's why Elijah and Mason took over the company. So you can start taking better care of yourself. Do that and you'll outlive all of us."

He stares at me, his gray eyes softening. We don't look alike; I got my coloring from my Spanish mother's side, but she always said I was still the most like him. I don't see it at all. "I don't want to outlive you all. But I do want to leave behind a legacy that I can be proud of. I want the James name to live on for centuries. And you, son, are my best hope of that."

Then you're fucking screwed, Dad! That's what I want to say, but I don't. "You have five sons. Why is this suddenly on me?"

"Elijah is stuck in that marriage whether she makes him happy or not, and we know she can't have children. And he's too loyal a man to ever leave her." He shakes his head. "Maddox lives with his head in the clouds, drifting from one city to another, refusing to commit to anything or anyone or do anything meaningful with his life."

"It's meaningful to him." I feel the need to leap to my youngest brother's defense. Like he hasn't dealt with enough shit in his life. He's earned the right to do whatever the hell he wants.

He snorts. "And then there's Mason." He throws his hands in the air. "There's no hope of him ever having kids."

"Well, that's a crock of shit. Gay people can and do have kids, Dad," I insist.

His brow furrows. "You know that's not what I'm talking about, Nathan. Can you ever imagine Mason with kids? It's just not in him."

I sigh because I figure he's right. "What about Drake? You haven't given up on him too, have you?"

He shakes his head. "Drake is too committed to his job."

It's my turn to snort. "And you think I'm not?"

"Drake works twenty hours a day, seven days a week. You're out every weekend, dating women and attending parties. Things come easily to you in a way they never have to your brothers, Nathan. You achieve the same results with half of the effort. You always have."

My hackles rise. "You're saying I don't work hard?"

"I'm saying you're incredibly gifted, son. Of all my children, you are the one who can have it all, and I refuse to let you squander the opportunity to carry on our family name. When I die and meet your mother on the other side, I need to be able to tell her that we have grandchildren. Can you not understand that?"

I blink at him, shocked. "So you want me to have a kid, is that it?"

"Two would be ideal."

"An heir and a spare, huh?"

His lip curls in a sneer. "Don't be vulgar."

"And when does this happen, Dad? I just knock up the first woman I find? Is that it?"

He shakes his head, his cheeks growing red again. "Of course not. You'll marry a suitable woman and then she will bear your children."

"Oh." I throw my hands into the air. "So now I'm getting married too?"

He glares at me, his jaw clenched tight. He's entirely fucking serious. "This is the one thing I'm asking of you, Nathan. The only thing I will ever ask."

I bark a humorless laugh. "Getting married and having a couple of kids is a pretty big ask, Dad."

Sighing, he runs a hand through his thick gray hair. "I always knew it would be you. You're not my firstborn, but you're the child I most see myself in. You were born lucky, son. Just like I was. You can take any situation and make it work. It's not like you're ever going to fall in love, so what are you really giving up? A couple years of meaningless encounters?"

"What if I don't want kids, Dad?"

He scrutinizes me with narrowed eyes. "Don't you?"

I swallow hard. Damn him. I've always been honest about wanting a family of my own, and now it's about to bite me in the ass. "Of course I do. One day."

"Then make one day come soon. While I'm still here to enjoy my grandkids. What the hell are you waiting for?"

"To find someone who wants to have kids with me would be a good start."

He gives me a triumphant smile. "Don't worry. I have that covered."

CHAPTER
TWO

MELANIE

"Tea, Melanie?" my mother asks with a saccharine smile as she holds the bone-china teapot aloft.

"No thanks, Mom. I better be heading home soon. I have an early start tomorrow."

Sunday afternoon tea at my mother's house is a torturous weekly affair. My penance for being such a terrible daughter— at least in my mother's eyes. She regards me with disdain. She hates my job, thinks it's beneath me. Well, not necessarily beneath *me* as much as beneath *her* to have a daughter who works as a veterinary nurse.

Her lip curls with the faintest hint of a sneer. "Bryce has something to discuss with you before you leave."

My heart rate kicks up a notch, and my eyes dart around the room. "Bryce is here?"

"He does live here, darling," she replies with a sniff.

I grit my teeth. "I know. He's not usually around is all." And that's exactly how I like it.

She gives the tiniest shake of her head, like she's dusting off any suggestion that my older brother isn't my favorite person in the world. He doesn't even make the top twenty. "Well, he has some good news for you. He's managed to perform a miracle."

A miracle? Has he had his own head surgically removed from his ass? Pressing my lips together, I stifle a snicker. I glance at the clock on the mantel and groan inwardly. I have plans with Tyler at six. He's going away tomorrow for eight weeks, and I want to spend every second I can with him before he leaves. But what my mother and Bryce want, they get.

I place my cup onto the intricately patterned saucer and drum my fingers on the table.

"Stop fidgeting, Melanie," my mother admonishes me.

I roll my eyes and blow out a breath. Thirty years old and still being chastised like a teenager. "Is Bryce going to impart this wonderful news any time soon?"

"He's a busy man. He'll be down when he's ready," she huffs.

Yeah, busy playing online poker or jerking off to cam girls.

I stare at the clock, watching the minutes tick slowly and painfully by while my mother and I sit in silence, waiting for her precious firstborn. Fifteen minutes later, he finally decides to grace us with his presence, strutting into the room like he's the king of the goddamn world. He's not even king of his own bedroom. Spoiled mama's boy.

He flicks his ash-blond hair out of his eyes and preens in the mirror before taking a seat at the table. I resist the urge to roll my eyes, not wanting to ignite his legendary short temper.

He puffs out his chest. "I've found a solution to our money problems, dear sister."

Not my money problems, jackass. *You* were in charge of the trust fund. *You* misused it and left our family almost broke. But I bite my tongue and smile sweetly. It's the only way to handle him and our mother. "That's good to know. I'm happy for you."

His right eyelid twitches. "It's not just about me. I'm doing this for all our futures. For you and Ashley too."

The mention of our younger sister's name makes annoyance prickle beneath my skin. He's never done anything for her other than screw her over. She almost lost her place at the college of her dreams because of him.

"I don't need money, Bryce. I'm happy at my job, and I love living with Tyler."

He snorts. "You're thirty years old, and you're happy living with our eccentric cousin?"

"If by eccentric you mean incredibly successful, gregarious, and funny, then yes, very happy, thanks." Bryce has always hated Tyler. He is faster, stronger, smarter, and better looking than my big brother, and that's always pissed him off. I suspect his use of eccentric is code for gay, because in addition to his many other flaws, my brother is also a raging homophobe. Not to mention the irony of a thirty-five-year-old man who still lives with his mother calling me out for living with my best friend, who just happens to be my cousin. Tyler and I were born on the same day and have been almost inseparable since.

Bryce's face twists in a sneer. "Well, this *proposal* is much more suited to a daughter of Luke and Miranda Edison."

The way he says proposal has the hairs on the back of my neck standing on end. "What exactly are you talking about? What does any of this have to do with me? I told you, I have no interest in the family money. Not that there's any left."

He raises his hand like he's going to smack me across the face for that last remark, but he quickly remembers where he is. My mother and her housekeeper are watching, and hitting his sister in front of them might just tarnish his good-guy reputation. No, he prefers to wait until we're alone for that. Not that I think my mother would even care.

"There's nothing left because our father made such poor business decisions," he spits.

Anger simmers inside me. That's a dirty lie, and he knows it. But I clamp my lips shut. I've been conditioned since I was thirteen to never question Bryce Edison. Placing my hands on my lap, I dig my fingernails into my palms and try to suppress the rage that wants to erupt out of me.

Bryce straightens his tie. "But *I* am about to fix all of that."

Well now I'm suspicious as hell. "How exactly?"

"I've arranged a match for you, little sister."

I frown. "A match?"

"Yes. A husband."

"A what now?" What the hell? My parents might have been rich once, and my mother comes from a long line of New York royalty, but we aren't living in a Jane Austen novel here.

"I've secured you a husband. A billionaire no less."

My god, he's entirely serious. "I don't want a husband."

"Did you not hear me? He's a billionaire, Melanie."

"I don't care if he's the king of England, I'm not marrying him."

He snarls. "You will do what is necessary to ensure this family's future, you ungrateful little bitch."

I open my mouth to reply, but no words come out. Instead, I blink at him in shock.

My mother turns to her housekeeper, who's hovering in the doorway. "Margarite. Please leave us."

Margarite dips her head like she's addressing the Queen and ducks out of the room.

"Mom!" I plead. "He can't be serious. I'm not marrying some crusty old billionaire."

Bryce places his hand on my thigh beneath the table and squeezes so tightly I know he'll leave bruises on my skin. I wince, which only makes him squeeze harder. My mother looks

13

away, like she always has. He leans forward, baring his teeth. "You will marry whoever the hell I tell you to marry, Melanie. It's your fault we're in this mess. You are the one responsible for our father's death. Or have you forgotten that?"

Tears blur my vision, and I shake my head. I hate him so much. His fingers dig in deeper, causing searing pain to lance up my thigh. "Now, are you going to keep your pretty mouth shut and listen to what I have to say?"

Tears run down my cheeks now, and I nod. "Yes."

He releases his grip and relief floods through me.

"Fortunately for you, my little Melanie," Bryce says, his tone resuming its usual creepy sing-song quality. My mother turns back to the table and watches our exchange. "Despite your *history*, I have managed to secure you quite the catch."

I swat away the tears from my cheeks. "Who?"

"Nathan James," he says with a smirk.

"Nathan James? The man who dates a different woman every week? The guy who works as a lawyer for the mob and is reported to have ice in his veins? You think he's a catch?"

"He's very handsome," my mother says coolly.

I blink at her. "Yeah, so was Ted Bundy."

"I had to do some persuading, but he's agreed to take you as his wife, and all he asks in return is that you deliver two heirs."

My throat squeezes shut. How can someone related to me be so cruel? "You know I might not be able to do that, Bryce. You know what happened in college."

His blue eyes are ice-cold as he glares at me. "Exactly. We know you're easy to knock up, little sister. And don't worry. I have a plan to relieve him of some of his millions without you having to have his kids first."

There are so many things wrong with what he just said that I don't even know where to begin. "And what if I don't agree to this? What if I don't want to *relieve* this man of any of his money?"

Bryce bares his teeth once more, looking like a diseased animal. "Then our mother will lose her home, and our little sister will have to drop out of that fancy college she's at and clean toilets for a living, won't she?"

There's nothing wrong with cleaning toilets, you entitled asshole.

"And it will all be your fault, Melanie. First you got our father murdered and then, when you finally have a chance to fix it and secure this family's future, you refuse." Bryce twists the knife deeper. "Surely you're not selfish enough to do that, are you?"

I would never do anything to hurt my baby sister. Ashley and Tyler are my world, and she's truly innocent in all of this. She still has two years left at Harvard, and tuition is expensive. I hate being backed into a corner, but he maneuvered me into one nonetheless. Like he always does.

"I'll think about it." I grab my purse and walk out of the room, and like I do every single time I come to this house, I wish my dad was still here. Because despite what Bryce would have people believe, he was a brilliant, kind man, and even if we were completely destitute, he never would have asked me to do this.

"We have a meeting with their lawyers on Thursday," Bryce calls after me. "I expect you to be there."

CHAPTER
THREE

MELANIE

Tyler stares at me wide-eyed from across the kitchen island, a large pepperoni pizza between us. "He wants you to what?"

"Marry some random guy and have a couple of kids." I throw my hands into the air. "Can you believe that?"

"Baby girl, I can believe anything of your brother. But damn!" He shakes his head and stuffs half a slice of pizza into his mouth.

"And I have no idea why this guy he set me up with would even want to marry me. He's like New York's most eligible bachelor. A confirmed playboy. And he's a lawyer for the mob who, if rumors are to be believed, has ice rather than blood running through his veins."

Tyler swallows and arches an eyebrow. "Is he hot?"

I toss my balled napkin at him. "That is not the point."

Grinning, he slowly nods. "So he is hot."

"His name is Nathan James. Google him and decide for yourself," I say with a shrug.

Tyler takes his phone from his pocket and taps away at it. "Holy fuck, Goose. This guy is fucking gorgeous," he announces only a few seconds later. "Have you seen that jawline? Wow! Come to Daddy."

I walk around the island and peer at the picture of my alleged husband-to-be wearing a tuxedo. He isn't smiling at the camera. In fact, he's scowling at it, like he's pissed about having his picture taken, but I have to agree with Tyler. He is hot. If you like grumpy, arrogant assholes—which I certainly do not.

Tyler stares at the image, practically drooling. "He looks like he could play Henry Cavill's hotter brother in a movie about hotshot lawyers who play rugby in their free time."

I roll my eyes and try not to laugh. "That is oddly specific."

He blows out a breath. "I mean, I'll marry the guy if you really don't want to."

I bump his shoulder with mine. "Pretty sure you're not his type, Mav."

He sighs dramatically and scrolls to another picture, then shouts, "Holy shit!"

"What?" I peer over his shoulder, but he clutches the screen to his chest and looks up at me.

"Did you know he has four brothers, and they're all insanely hot?" He holds the phone out, and I examine the picture of Nathan standing with his brothers and father at some charity gala last year. "Even his dad is fuckable."

"Ty!"

"What?" He shrugs. "He is. Those are some good genes, baby girl. If you're gonna have a kid with someone, at least this guy pretty much guarantees beautiful babies."

"All babies are beautiful," I remind him.

His nose wrinkles. "Nuh-uh. Remember when Ashley was born? She looked like one of those troll dolls."

"She did not!" I suppress a giggle. "She was adorable."

"Yeah, she is now. But damn, she was an ugly baby." He grins at me.

Glancing at his phone again, I take in every detail of the enigmatic Nathan James. "He is very handsome. So you see why I wonder what the hell he's agreeing to marry me for? He must have some hideous secret."

Tyler wraps an arm around my shoulders. "Are you shitting me? You are smart, kind, beautiful, and funny, and he'd be damn lucky to have you. You're the whole deal, baby girl." With his free hand, he scrolls through more pictures. "Not like these fake-ass models he's always pictured with."

"Yeah, not making me feel better, Ty."

He kisses the top of my head. "You're the best person I know, Melanie Edison, and don't you ever fucking forget it."

FOUR

NATHAN

"Jesus fuck, Nathan." My oldest brother, Elijah, shakes his head after I finish recounting what our father said to me earlier this morning. I left out the crap about me being the only one of us capable of having it all. What a load of shit.

I take a sip of my beer and signal the waitress for three more. "Yeah, you see what happens when you two fucks don't turn up for Sunday brunch."

"Sorry, bro," Mason says sheepishly. "I had a hell of a date last night."

I roll my eyes. "I thought you were dating the catalog model. Carter, was it?"

"Nah." He shakes his head. "That kind of fizzled out. You know I like to keep my options open, and besides, he was way too clingy for me."

"Yeah, way too pretty too," Elijah adds. Mason and I stare at him with matching grins on our faces. "What?" Elijah blinks at us. "I can appreciate a man's good looks. He just didn't seem

19

your usual type is all. You usually go for guys a little rougher round the edges."

"Mmhmm, the rougher the better." Mason licks his lips.

I roll my eyes, feigning my disgust, when I'm only jealous that my little brother isn't jaded by the endless monotony of making the same small talk with a different person every week all in the hopes of a good fuck. And even that is losing its appeal.

"Shall we get back to my problem?" I remind them.

They mumble their agreement as the waitress delivers fresh beers.

"So he's already got this wife picked out for you?" Mason asks.

"Yeah." I nod, recalling how ridiculous the conversation was. "He even has a meeting set up with her family lawyers for Thursday."

Elijah frowns. "Jesus fuck, Nathan!"

"Yeah, you already said that, asshole," I say.

"I know, but I think it's worth repeating." He's rarely this animated, and his reaction reassures me that our father's proposition to me earlier today was as outrageous as it seemed.

I take a long swig of my beer. "So what the fuck do I do?"

"First, who is this chick?" Mason asks.

"Well, she's a *woman*, and her name is Melanie Edison."

Elijah's eyebrows shoot up. "Luke Edison's daughter?"

I nod. "The one and only."

Mason grins. "She was two years below me in high school. My buddies all thought she was hot."

She doesn't have much of a social media presence, and the few pictures I did find online were from various animal rights and environmental charity functions. She appears to be impeccably turned out—brunette, curves in all the right places, a beautiful smile—but the photos gave the impression that she hated the camera. I sure know how that feels. There was no hint of a smile in the posed shots, but a couple of candids showed her laughing. Those were the ones that intrigued me most. "She's still hot," I tell them. "But that's beside the point."

Mason's brow wrinkles like he's deep in thought. "I heard she works as a vet's assistant or something now."

I nod. "Yeah, that matches what I found. She volunteers for a shelter too."

Mason nods. "That rings true. She was always fundraising for the local animal shelter in high school."

Elijah takes a swig of his beer and nods approvingly. "Seems like she's a nice person, then. At least there's that."

Mason sucks air through his teeth. "I'm sure I recall something about her dropping out of college to do a few months in rehab. Not that it makes her a not-nice person, and that could have just been a rumor."

I nod my agreement. "Yeah, she took a year off, and all the reports I found alluded to rehab." I spent four hours after I left my dad's house researching all there is to know about her. She has a college degree from Ohio State, has an unhealthy obsession with jelly donuts, lives in the meatpacking district with her cousin, Tyler, and has a twenty-year-old sister who's currently studying at Harvard. Melanie Edison is an interesting woman. Not half as interesting as her brother though.

Elijah's brow furrows. "So Dad wants grandkids. A legacy. But what does Melanie Edison get from this?"

"Um. She marries a handsome billionaire, fuck-knuckle," Mason retorts.

Elijah shakes his head. "She works as a vet's assistant."

"Veterinary nurse," I correct him.

"Okay, but I dunno." He shrugs. "Doesn't seem like the kind of job a gold digger would have. And what's Dad thinking? I could see why he might set you up with some heiress or socialite, but a veterinary nurse?"

I sigh. "Technically she is an heiress, there's just fuck all left of Edison Holdings to inherit, and the old man was fond of her father. Seems he bumped into her mother and brother at some event, and they got to talking. Turns out their company's failing and they're looking for some investors."

Elijah groans. "He's not investing in their company, is he?"

I shake my head. "He made it clear that's firmly off the table. But a marriage into the James family lends their failing business credibility, and it offers a level of assurance—accurate or not—to potential investors."

"So that's what her family gets out of it, but what about her?" Elijah asks.

I shrug. All my research led me to the same conclusion Elijah just made. She lives a modest life and hasn't taken any share of the profits from Edison Holdings for the past eleven years, so I can't imagine she's suddenly decided to marry for money. "I dunno, buddy. Maybe she wants kids and is fed up with the dating pool. Or maybe she wants to give up work and be a stay-at-home wife."

Mason peels the label from his beer bottle and stares at me. "So you're considering this thing?"

I draw a breath through my nose. There's no denying that the relentless dating is wearing thin, and even the inevitable sex at the end of those dates is no longer enough to get the blood pumping in my veins the way it used to. I think about my mom and what a wonderful grandma she would've been, and how my dad is desperate to know he has someone to pass his company down to after his sons. I'm not getting any younger. I feel like I've dated almost every unmarried woman in the tri-state area, and not one of them has held my attention long enough to get past a fourth date. What the fuck do I have to lose? "Enough to go to this meeting on Thursday and check out Melanie Edison and her motivations in person, yeah."

Mason snorts a laugh, but Elijah pats me on the back.

I take another swig of my beer and wonder why I didn't order something stronger. "I'm gonna have Drake come with me."

"Probably a good idea," Elijah says. "Contracts are his forte."

I'm inviting him because he's as good at reading people as I am, and maybe for a little moral support. I arch an eyebrow at Elijah. "You're saying they're not mine?"

"You thrive in the courtroom, Nathan. You always have. Center stage is where you and Mase are at your most comfortable. Contracts are a backroom job for guys who love details, like Drake and me."

Mason nods his agreement. "Hey, speaking of brothers, has anyone spoken to Maddox this week?"

An unexpected wave of sadness hits me in my chest, and I clear my throat. "I spoke to him a few days ago, why?"

"Just checking. He said he was headed to Florence last I spoke with him, but that was over a week ago. He didn't answer my call this morning. You think he's okay?"

I nod. Maddox is known to go off-grid for days or even weeks at a time when the mood strikes him. "Yeah, he said he was good. But he changed his mind about Florence and he's in Berlin now instead."

Elijah whistles. "That kid sure gets around. Lucky bastard."

"Yeah," I mumble, even though we all know there is nothing at all lucky about our youngest brother.

CHAPTER
FIVE

MELANIE

"Bye, Cass. See you tomorrow." My colleague and I part ways and I head for the subway. My feet ache, protesting every step I take, and I contemplate getting a cab but they're so expensive. Tyler does me a solid letting me live in his gorgeous apartment for barely any rent, so I'm able to afford the occasional luxury, but I decide against it and keep walking. The sight of the familiar car up ahead makes me groan. I wish I could turn and walk—no, run the other way, but he's already jogging toward me.

"What do you want, Bryce?"

He pulls a fake sad face. "I wanted to apologize for how I acted the other day, sis. I was stressed and ..." He flicks his hair out of his eyes. "I'm really worried. About Mom. About Ash."

Then stop gambling and making terrible business decisions, Bryce! That is exactly what I should say, but seventeen years of conditioning are hard to break. Bryce is a bully and a coward, and he will never change.

"Let me give you a ride home." He smiles with all the charm of a cobra.

"It's fine. I can take the subway."

His demeanor changes in an instant, and the smile turns to a snarl. "Don't make a scene, Melanie, and get in the fucking car."

With a roll of my eyes, I do as he asks. It's easier than arguing with him. He always gets what he wants anyway, and he has ever since we were kids. I shrug off my jacket and sink back into the passenger seat of Bryce's BMW. At least his fancy car is comfortable.

He's been driving for a few minutes when he brings up the real reason he showed up. "Did you give any more thought to my proposal?"

That word sends a shiver down my spine. He makes it sound so creepy. "To marry Nathan James and have his babies?" I snap.

He sighs and shoots me a sympathetic look, which I can only assume is fake because he has the emotional intelligence of pond scum. "Look, I know I might not have sold it very well, but this doesn't have to be a long-term thing. If we play our cards right, you can be divorced within a year. Two at most."

"And how will that help the business, Bryce? Nathan James is a hotshot lawyer. So is his brother. Even if he weren't, his family has a team of lawyers. You think they aren't going to have a cast-iron prenup?"

"Course they will." He snorts. "But we'll insist on a morality clause to protect our family's good name."

My brow pinches in a frown. "A what?"

"A morality clause. It basically means that if he does anything to tarnish your good name, then you can walk away with a pile of cash."

"What the hell could he do to tarnish *my* name?" I snap,

reminded of the rumors he and my mother spread about me when I took a break from college. At the time I was too broken-hearted to see how ridiculous their scheme was or how fucked up it was that they thought the rumors were more palatable than the truth.

"It's mostly used for cheating spouses," he says, giving a dismissive wave of his hand.

"But he might not cheat, especially if he has one of those clauses in the prenup. He's not stupid," I insist. I guess I don't like the idea of my husband cheating, even if the marriage is fake.

He gently squeezes my thigh. "Then, my dear sister, we make him cheat."

I blink at him. "Make him cheat?"

"Melanie, darling, no offense but you aren't his usual caliber of woman," he says with a cruel sneer, and in my mind's eye I see myself punching him in the mouth. "All we have to do is present him with a beautiful woman he can't resist, and I'm sure he'll take the bait."

I press my lips together, offended on so many levels that I can't think straight. "Like a honey trap?"

"Exactly."

"No, Bryce. *If* I agree to marry this guy, I am not going to encourage him to cheat on me. Why the hell would I even do that? It's crazy."

"He's going to cheat anyway, Mel. But this guarantees us evidence of his crime."

I fold my arms across my chest. "How can you be so sure?"

He glares at me. "Because he's Nathan James. Do you have any idea the type of man he is? He dates a different beautiful woman every week. Supermodels. Actresses. Whores. He's also a lawyer for the Irish Mob and the Cosa Nostra, and fuck knows who else. He is not a good man. And so what if we take some of his millions? It's pocket change to a man like him."

Turning away from him, I stare out the window. One minute Bryce is telling me what a catch he found for me in Nathan James, and the next what a terrible man he is. I don't know which is true, but I do know that Bryce doesn't really care. He'd marry me off to Lucifer himself if he thought he could make a quick buck out of it.

"You know this is the right thing to do, Melly," he says, his tone much softer now. The use of his childhood pet name for me makes bile burn in my throat. "For Mom and for Ashley."

For Ashley, yes. Not for Mom. And definitely not for Bryce. But my little sister's fate is unfortunately tied to theirs, and until she can stand on her own two feet, it's up to me to take care of her. Because there's nobody else to do it.

"Will you at least come to the meeting tomorrow?" he asks, his tone dripping with nauseating sweetness.

I wipe a stray tear from the corner of my eye.

"Melly?"

"Yes! I'll go to the damn meeting."

CHAPTER
SIX

NATHAN

I stare out the window at the retreating back of my date, looking at the same ass that captivated me two weeks ago when I first met her at the gym. So why is it doing nothing for me now? The doorman of her building nods in greeting and opens the opaque glass door for her. Before she steps inside, she spins on her heel, a scowl twisting her pretty features as she flips me the bird.

I snort a harsh laugh, impressed by her fire if nothing else. Her contempt is no less than I deserve after the terrible end to our already disastrous date. I wince at the memory of her on her knees, her lips wrapped around my shaft as she sucked me off. Or at least she tried to before I stopped her mid-act. Not that she wasn't eager or exceptionally talented in the art of giving head, but when she fluttered her eyelashes at me, her dark brown eyes wet with tears, it should have made my cock twitch and brought me closer to the edge. Instead there was nothing. And when I pulled her head back and told her to stop, the look

28

of pure shock on her face made me wonder if it was the first time she'd ever been rejected in her life.

The fact that I wasn't able to get close to finishing was no surprise to me though. My last few dates have ended in a similar unsatisfactory way.

"Home, sir?" My driver's familiar voice pulls me out of my thoughts.

After checking to make sure my date is safely inside her building, I lower the partition until I'm staring at the back of Teddy's head. "Yeah, home."

MY YOUNGER BROTHER paces the length of my office, his hands stuffed into his pockets and a frown furrowing his brow as he digests the information I've just given him about Melanie Edison and her family.

"Thanks for flying in to do this, Drake."

He stops in front of my desk. "Anytime. You know that."

I roll my neck and flex my shoulders, but it does little to ease the pent-up tension in my muscles.

Drake tilts his head and watches me with curiosity. "So, how serious are you about this meeting today? Is this just to appease Dad or are you actually considering this proposal of his?"

Taking a seat behind my desk, I run my tongue over my bottom lip and consider my answer. "I'm actually considering marrying this woman and having a couple of kids. Is that insane?"

He rubs a hand over his jaw and presses his lips together before he sits opposite me. "I wouldn't say it's insane, but as to whether it's right for you ... I guess it depends on your reasons.

Are you only doing this because Dad asked you to, or is there something in it for you? Something you actually want."

I recall my date last night and how bored I was listening to and rehashing the same old stilted conversation. And how the inevitable hookup that usually follows was as unappealing as the plain salad my date ordered for dinner at the finest steak house in Manhattan. "You know, even a couple of months ago, I would've said there was nothing in it for me, but lately ..." I glance at the painting on my office wall, a constant reminder of all the perfect summers we had as kids. Our dad teaching us to swim, and our mom cheating at volleyball and loudly proclaiming her innocence when anyone called her on it.

"And now?" Drake prompts me.

I run my tongue over my teeth. And now what? "I don't know, Drake, but I do know that the endless stream of women doesn't do it for me anymore. Meaningless hookups feel empty and ..." I shake my head, unable to explain it, even to myself.

"So you're looking for more? A relationship? That's understandable, but that doesn't mean you have to marry some random woman Dad picked out for you."

"But I don't want the whole falling in love bullshit that goes with a relationship, Drake. That's not for me, and it never will be. So maybe this is the way. If Melanie Edison and I are compatible enough, why not try it the old man's way? Because the idea of another year or more in the dating pool trying to find someone to marry and have kids with, not to mention managing all the expectations about not falling in love, exhausts me just thinking about it."

Drake rolls his eyes. "Your entire love life exhausts me. I don't know how you do it."

I shrug. "Yeah, well, maybe I won't be doing it for much longer."

He barks out a laugh. "Okay, so you do this instead. What

exactly is the plan here? You meet this woman and if you don't hate her on sight, you're going to go through with this?"

I narrow my eyes at him. "You say that like you think I'm not going to be able to read her. I'll know if we're compatible or not after five minutes, and you know it."

"I'm not doubting your people-reading skills, bro. But this is your life, not a case. You're going to tie yourself to this woman for life if you have kids together."

"I know, Drake. But this kind of arrangement ..." I blow out a breath as the realization hits me. "It makes sense for someone like me. I have absolutely no desire to do the whole love and romance thing, but I do want kids, and I want to have them with a woman I can trust and respect. And I'm sure I can work out whether Melanie is worthy of both those things by the end of the afternoon. So yeah, maybe a marriage that's also a good business arrangement is right for me."

Drake folds his arms and gives me a single nod of his head.

"So you're with me on this?"

"Always, brother."

The door to my office opens, and my secretary pops her head inside. "Your guests are here, sir. They're seated in the boardroom as requested."

I nod my acknowledgment, and she disappears from view.

Drake arches an eyebrow at me. "Time to meet the potential in-laws."

I stand and fasten my suit jacket. "Let's do this."

Drake stops outside the door to the boardroom with me behind him, his fingers grasping the handle. He flashes me a smirk over his shoulder. "You nervous?"

I scowl at him. Has he forgotten who he's talking to? "No, of course I'm not fucking nervous."

He chuckles. "Just checking."

We step into the room and are immediately greeted by a

man I recognize as Bryce Edison from the pictures I found online. He sweeps his blond hair out of his eyes before extending a hand. Drake shakes it while I look past him at the man I assume is their family lawyer, until my eyes lock on the only person in this room I have any interest in talking to besides Drake.

She stands facing the window, her back to the room, and is wearing a white blouse tucked into a black pencil skirt that perfectly showcases her hourglass figure against the backdrop of the city skyline.

"Miss Edison," I say, and she spins around, her eyes flickering to Drake and her brother before finding mine.

She takes a few steps toward me, her hips swaying slightly with each one. "Mr. James." Her voice is calm and clear, but I don't miss the way her left hand curls into a tight fist at her side or the soft pink flush at the base of her neck. She offers me a soft smile, and that's when I notice the striking green of her irises. She's much more beautiful in person than in the pictures I saw of her.

I take a step toward her, and now we're only a foot apart. Her breath hitches, drawing my gaze to her neck. The slender curve of her throat thickens as she swallows, and her body's reaction to my close proximity has my pulse spiking.

"Melanie, come sit," her brother orders, his nasally tone severing the connection between us. I'm immediately tempted to tell him to shut the fuck up and then, more importantly, to ask him who the hell he thinks he's talking to, ordering her to sit like a dog. Until I remember that she's not mine.

Not yet.

CHAPTER
SEVEN

MELANIE

There are so many voices talking at once, all of them speaking legal jargon that I barely understand, and my head is starting to spin. Bryce and our family lawyer talk the loudest, demanding to be heard.

I rub my temples and screw my eyes closed. When I open them again, Nathan's dark stare greets me from across the expanse of the boardroom table. "Give us the room," he says, and his low, commanding tone makes the hairs on the back of my neck stand on end.

I hear Bryce snort, but I'm unable to tear my gaze from the man directly in front of me. "I don't think that's going to happen," Bryce says, not bothering to hide the disdain in his tone. I'm not sure if it's for me or Nathan James—probably both.

Nathan still doesn't look at my brother when he calmly repeats himself. "Give us the room."

In my peripheral vision, I see his brother gathering his papers from the table and pat Nathan on the back. "Let's give them a few moments alone," Drake says, his tone as commanding as Nathan's.

With a grunt, Bryce pushes back his chair and stomps out of the room behind Drake and our lawyer, leaving Nathan and me alone. The room is silent, and the tension grows thicker with each passing second. Nathan leans forward and rests his clasped hands on the table. With narrowed eyes, he searches my face, and the heat of his gaze makes my heart rate spike and my insides flutter.

In such close proximity, there's no mistaking his dominant presence. Also no mistaking that he's far too handsome to need to find a bride this way. Something must be wrong with him. What if he's actually gay and all those women he's been photographed with were an elaborate smokescreen? Maybe I'm supposed to be his beard. That would certainly explain a hell of a lot.

I press my lips together and maintain eye contact even as my legs tremble.

"Why are you doing this, Miss Edison?" he finally asks, his voice thick and dark like rich melted chocolate.

"Because it's good for our families," I say, repeating my well-rehearsed mantra. The one I've been telling myself every moment since I first entertained the notion of marrying this man to secure my family's future.

He gives a subtle shake of his head. "No. That's why your family asked you to do this. But what exactly do *you* get out of it?"

I blink at him, entirely unprepared for his question. This was supposed to be a contract discussion between lawyers, not an examination of why I'm agreeing to this archaic proposal. "How about you tell me what's in this for you?" I challenge.

"The respectability of a wife from a good family. An heir or two," he replies, deadpan.

"I'm pretty sure you could get any woman you want, Mr. James, so why not find someone the old-fashioned way? And marry for ... you know, love?"

That earns me a sarcastic snort, and I frown. "You don't believe in marrying for love?"

"Do you, Miss Edison? Because if you have any romantic notions about marrying for love, perhaps this arrangement isn't for you, after all."

I clear my throat. Damn smartass. I can see why he's such a good lawyer. "Just because I believe that people *can* marry for love doesn't mean that's what I want."

"So what do you want, Melanie?" That's the first time he's called me by my first name, and the sound of it on his lips makes heat bloom across my chest.

"I want my family to continue to prosper and for my father's legacy to go on. I want my children to have a good life."

He leans back in his chair, eyes narrowed as he runs a hand over his square jaw. "But what about *you*?"

I swallow hard. What the hell does it matter what I want? He goes on staring at me, waiting for a reply to the question that I don't have an answer for. Because it's never about me, only about what's best for the family. I shake my head, unexpected tears burning behind my eyes.

"It's not a difficult question," he says, his tone clipped now like I'm annoying him.

I feel hot. My pulse races. I want to get out of this room.

"Melanie." His tone is authoritative and commanding.

"I just want some peace, Nathan. I want to go to work and do the job that I love, then come home and not have to worry about my little sister's college tuition or whether my mother is going to lose our family home because my brother is an idiot." The words pour out of me, and my cheeks heat with shame at my outburst. I probably screwed everything up. I press my palm against my flushed face. "I'm sorry. I didn't mean … My brother is a very good businessman."

"Do you think I'd enter into this arrangement without doing my homework on your brother? I'm well aware he's a weekend in Vegas away from losing what little is left of your family fortune." He drums his fingers on the table. "And I appreciate your honesty."

I blink at him. He knows we have barely any money left, but he's still considering marrying me? Why?

"Is that enough for you to do this? Sign the rest of your life —or at the very least the next ten to twenty years of it—away just to keep your family happy?"

"I've spent the last seventeen years trying to keep my family happy, Mr. James, it's what I do."

He tilts his head, his eyes softening as they rake over my body. Then he sits forward again. "I need you to know that you still have a choice, Melanie. While I don't care about marrying for love, we will be sharing a life together. It would be much more tolerable if we could at least be friendly. If you resent me for this, we're both going to be pretty miserable, and I don't want my children growing up in a toxic household with parents who can barely stand the sight of each other."

Relief washes over me in a comforting wave. The fact that he's thought things through to that extent certainly makes me feel a whole lot better about this bizarre situation. "I don't want that either."

He nods like he approves. "Well, this is your opportunity to back out. If you don't want this, tell me now. You can walk out of here and never have to see me again. I'll tell Bryce that it was my decision."

I scoff. "He won't believe you."

He arches one eyebrow. "I can be *very* persuasive, Miss Edison."

I'm sure I see the corner of his mouth curling into the faintest hint of a grin, and I bite my lip to stop myself from grinning back. Whatever the rumors say about him, and despite what my brother says about the kind of man he is, Nathan James is a decent man in all the ways that count. And that's a whole lot better than I could have hoped for. "I want to do this."

He gives me another curt nod, the softness in his features already disappearing to be replaced by his effortlessly cool facade. "Good."

"But …" I wince when he frowns. "I won't give up my job. Even when we have kids, I'd like to work part-time when they're old enough. I figure you might want some trophy wife who spends her days doing nothing but look good for you, but I love my job. I think I'd go insane without it."

"You work as a veterinary nurse, right?"

"Yeah." I look down, avoiding his gaze. It's probably not the sort of job a successful billionaire wants his wife to have. At least that's what my mother would have me believe.

"I don't want a trophy wife, Melanie."

He doesn't? My heart skips a beat, and I look up at him, meeting his intense gaze once more.

"Just someone who's honest with me and will be a good mother to my children. Can you do that?"

"Yes." The answer falls easily from my lips. "Although I'd prefer we wait a while to start trying for a baby. Not a long time, but maybe six months? I assume we'll have to live together, and this is all moving so quickly already. I'd like to get to know you a little better before we …" My cheeks burn at the thought of having sex with this demigod. "Add a kid into the mix."

He sucks on his top lip like he's mulling it over. "I suppose a waiting period would also stop any potential rumors about us marrying so quickly because you're pregnant. So you can have your six months, and of course you can keep your job."

I nod my appreciation.

"Then it's agreed. We'll work out the finer details of the contract over dinner this evening."

My brow creases in a frown. "Dinner?"

He rolls his eyes. "Dinner. That meal people eat in the evenings."

"Can't we just do it here?"

He stands and fastens his suit jacket. "We could, but I'd rather not. And we need to have a handful of public appearances before we announce our engagement. I'll ensure there are photographers waiting outside the restaurant to capture our *date*."

I swallow the knot of anxiety that instantly balls in my throat. "Oh. I didn't ... I don't want this to be some kind of media circus, Nathan."

He licks his bottom lip. "Neither do I. But people will speculate about our engagement, and for appearance's sake, this needs to look like a real relationship. A few public dates are all that should be necessary. Then we can marry in private and announce our wedded bliss after the event."

"I guess you have it all worked out."

He leans forward and splays his huge hands on the boardroom table. "I don't believe in leaving anything to chance, Melanie." He stands straight again and nods. "I'll pick you up at eight. We're going to Leonardi's, so wear something appropriate."

I bite back the retort on the tip of my tongue. *Appropriate.* I'm well aware that it's the most exclusive restaurant in Manhattan. Does he think I'm going to rock up in jeans and a T-shirt or a minidress that will show off my ass cheeks? I'll show him appropriate. "Of course," I say softly, offering him a demure smile.

CHAPTER
EIGHT

NATHAN

"Would you like me to go up for her, sir?" my driver, Teddy, asks as he rolls the car to a stop outside Melanie's apartment building.

"No. I'll go get her myself if she's not here on time." I look at the bustling sidewalk, at the people hurrying to the places they're going, separated from me by the thick pane of glass, then glance at my watch. I left strict instructions that she be ready by eight, and she promised she would be. I contemplated sending her a dress to wear but figured I'd learn a little more about her by seeing how she chooses to dress for dinner at an exclusive restaurant.

A few seconds later, she walks out of the apartment building, and fuck me, she does not disappoint. Her long dark hair is pulled to one side, falling in gentle waves over her shoulder. Her elegant jade-green dress ends mid-calf, with a split exposing the length of her left thigh, showing off a small expanse of her tanned skin. The fabric clings to every inch of her curves like it was sprayed on her body, showing nothing and everything at the same time.

"This her, sir?" Teddy asks.

I clear my throat. "Yeah."

He jumps out of the car, and I watch her walk toward us, her hips swaying in a seductive rhythm with each sure-footed step she takes in her heels. I bite my lip and grunt, sounding like a fucking animal.

Their muffled voices reach me before the car door opens. She peers inside, flashing me a sweet smile like she knows I watched her approach and enjoyed every second of it. Then she turns back to my driver. "Thank you, Tedward," she says with a musical laugh.

He almost suppresses his smirk before he closes the door on us, and she takes a seat beside me, revealing that her dress leaves her back completely bare. An image of me sliding my hand inside the fabric to see if she's wearing panties flashes through my mind and makes my dick twitch in my pants.

"Tedward is lovely," she says, cutting through my inappropriate thoughts.

I lift one eyebrow. "His name is Teddy, short for Theodore."

"Yes, he introduced himself as Teddy, but he seemed to like Tedward just fine." She flashes me a wicked grin. "Anyway, is this *appropriate* enough for dinner?" She gestures at her dress, and I narrow my eyes at her. We haven't even pulled away from the curb and she's fucking with me already. This woman is a spitfire. Nothing at all like the meek woman who walked into my office with her brother today.

I make a show of glancing over her outfit, like I haven't already committed every detail to memory. "It will do fine."

She blows out a breath. "Wow, Mr. James, so smooth." Chuckling, she leans back against the seat.

"Have you been drinking, Melanie?"

She wrinkles her nose. "Not yet. Why?"

"Taken anything else to help get you through the evening?"

Her eyes go wide and her neck flushes a pretty shade of pink, and now I feel like an asshole. Nothing in the information I found about her from the past nine years would suggest she has an ongoing drug problem. That was a low blow.

She rolls back her shoulders and fixes me with a hard stare. "I guess if we're going to be married, you have a right to know about my past, Mr. James."

"Don't care about your past, just the now."

"Yes, well, let's just say my stint in *rehab* was greatly exaggerated. Yes, I have a glass of wine or three occasionally, and when my cousin, Tyler, manages to persuade me to go clubbing, I've been known to down a tequila shot or four. But I don't do drugs."

"Good to know. But you are acting differently."

She tilts her head. "Different good or different bad?"

I press my lips together, mulling over the question. "Good."

A smile lights up her face. "I crack jokes when I'm nervous." She shrugs. "And also, today in your office was kind of ..." She blows out a breath. "Weird. I get quiet when I'm nervous too."

"So you get quiet or you crack jokes? Which is it?"

She arches an eyebrow at me. "Depends on the type of nerves, I guess."

I run my fingertips over the base of her neck and down the exposed skin of her back, suppressing a smile when she shivers at my touch. "And what form of nervous are you feeling right now, Melanie?"

Her eyelashes flutter against her pink cheeks. "The first-date kind."

I shift closer. "Have you had many first dates?"

She grins. "Not as many as you, Mr. James."

I swallow a laugh at her snappy comeback.

"Yeah, I do my research too, Iceman."

Wincing, I suck in air through my teeth. I got that nickname in college, and it's followed me through my career. While I don't mind being known as a man with ice in his veins, it's still uncomfortable to be called that to my face.

She laughs softly. "It's okay, I get it. *Top Gun* fan, huh?"

I shrug. "Who isn't?"

She leans closer, and her breath dusts over my cheek, making my already twitchy cock stiffen. "I'll let you in on a little secret about me, Nathan. *Top Gun* is one of my favorite movies, and I always preferred Iceman to Maverick."

Closing my eyes, I draw in a breath, and my nose is flooded by her sweet scent. She's flirting with me, which I didn't expect at all. When I open my eyes a second later, she's smiling at me like she knows exactly what's happening in my pants right now.

I stretch my neck. If she wants to play, we'll play. "Would you like some champagne to calm those nerves of yours, Melanie?"

Her lips curve at the edges, and her bright green eyes sparkle. I'm ashamed when I examine her pupils for signs of drug use, but as I already suspected, I see none. So what the fuck happened between leaving my office and now to bring about this change in her? She's like a completely different woman. And while I liked the woman I met in my office, I must admit I like this one even better.

"Hmm. Yes, please, Nathan." I swear she fucking purrs my name, and all I can think about is how it will sound tumbling from her lips when I make her come.

CHAPTER
NINE

MELANIE

Iceman? Nathan James is hotter than the fiery pits of hell. I was too nervous to appreciate his fineness in the board-room earlier, but he's everything I've ever wanted in a guy —at least as far as looks go.

There's a reason almost every woman in this restaurant has cast an admiring glance his way tonight. He's tall, at least six-two at a guess. Broad too. His shoulders and biceps strain against the taut material of his shirt when he rests his arms on the table. His jawline looks like it was chiseled by the gods themselves—or rather, the goddesses like Aphrodite and Hera, who knew exactly what a fine-ass man should look like. He might be a cold-blooded shark in the courtroom, but sitting opposite me in this fancy restaurant while I try my best to find out what his buttons are and how to push each and every one, I swear his dark eyes are twinkling with barely suppressed mischief. The man has a deviant side, I can tell.

And while he's yet to crack a full smile, his lips do occasion-ally twitch with the hint of one. I guess Tyler was right, Nathan isn't the worst guy I could have been set up to marry, and I should enjoy this while I can because who knows if we will even make it down the aisle.

I PEER OUT THE WINDOW, envious of the couples walking hand in hand in the warm summer New York air. Dinner was delicious and delightful. Nathan was charming and surprisingly funny, and I must admit that I'm not quite ready for this night to be over. "It's such a nice night. Shame we couldn't have walked a little."

Nathan presses a button to speak to his driver. "Pull the car over. We're going to walk the last few blocks."

"Of course, sir," comes the reply. "I'll wait for you outside Miss Edison's apartment building."

We walk in silence, and despite the warm night air, I shiver and wrap my arms around my torso.

"Shit, you're cold?" Nathan shrugs off his jacket and drapes it around my shoulders. The residual heat from his body warms me all over, and I shiver for an entirely different reason.

"Thank you." I pull his jacket tighter around myself. "Such a gentleman."

He arches an eyebrow. "You seem shocked by this revelation, Miss Edison."

A laugh tumbles out of me, and I guess my amusement must melt the ice in his veins because he rewards me with a real, full-on smile that reaches his eyes.

"Oh, wow." I bump my arm against his as we fall into step beside each other. "You do smile."

He rolls his eyes. "Only when the occasion calls for it."

I stop walking and place a hand over my heart. "I'm so honored to be present for such an occasion."

He comes to a stop beside me, his dark eyes scrutinizing my

face, but the hint of a smile remains on his lips. "Why do I feel like you're constantly testing me?"

We discussed some of the legalities of the contract during dinner, but that discussion didn't last long. Most of our evening was spent getting to know one another, and it seems he got a pretty good read on me. "Maybe because I am. I mean, if I'm going to marry you, I need to learn some very important things about you. You know, to see if we're compatible."

"Oh?" His smile becomes a wicked smirk that turns my insides to Jell-o. "And what things do you need to know?"

I smile coyly and resume walking. "If you have a sense of humor. If you have good taste in movies, which we've already established that you do. You know, if you're capable of making a woman ..." Turning my face toward him, I lick my lips, and his eyes darken as he waits for me to finish my sentence. I suppress a grin and add, "Fluffy pancakes when it's that time of the month and she's craving sugar."

A deep, rumbling laugh rolls out of him. "Why do I feel like I'm getting schooled by a pint-sized siren?"

"You are getting schooled, Ice. But I am neither pint-sized nor a siren."

This time he's the one who stops, and his fingers circle my wrist, bringing me to a halt right in front of him. He steps closer, looming over me even in my six-inch heels. His eyes rake up and down my body, and the heat of his gaze scalds me. "But you are pint-sized, Spitfire. And you are most definitely a siren."

Staring into his chocolate-brown eyes, I swallow down the thick knot in my throat. This feels real when it's not. I can't recall the last time I had so much fun on a date, let alone a time when I wanted to kiss a man half as much as I want to kiss Nathan James right now.

He leans closer, his breath dusting over my forehead, and a

shiver runs the length of my spine. "Are you going to invite me in for a coffee?"

I glance around, surprised. The walk was so enjoyable that I failed to register we had reached my apartment building. I bite down on my bottom lip and shake my head. "I'm not that kind of girl, Mr. James."

His devilish eyes narrow before he unashamedly rakes them up and down my body. "Oh, we're back to Mr. James now, are we?"

Tilting my head, I hold his gaze and try to stop my legs from shaking. "Well, there are no cameras here. No need to pretend we're on a date any longer."

"Actually ..." He takes a half step forward, herding me back until I'm pressed against the wall and his body is only inches from mine. So tantalizingly close that I smell his masculine scent—cologne, whiskey, and fresh air—and it makes the spot between my thighs ache. "I think I saw some paparazzi right over there." He jerks his head backward, and I peer over his shoulder.

"Nope. You must have been imagining things," I whisper, my cheeks flushing with heat.

He shrugs. "I think you should kiss me anyway. Just to be sure that this looks like a real date to anyone who might see."

"The only person watching us is Tedward."

A growl rumbles in his throat, and he dips his head lower. His mouth is so deliciously close, and his lips dust my earlobe. "Then let's give him something to watch, Mel."

I swallow hard as my pulse races beneath my skin. I bet he's an incredible kisser. It would be so easy to say yes and let him press me against this wall and kiss me senseless. But that would only make things more complicated. I need to keep a clear head around him. This is a business arrangement, a fact he's made abundantly clear.

I can't get carried away with myself by thinking it's anything more just because his body provokes such an intensely sensual physical reaction from mine. That would be reckless. Especially since I'm only ninety-eight percent sure I'll go through with this wedding. I at least want the option to change my mind if I decide to, and if we have sex, I'm not sure I'll be able to maintain any measure of objectivity.

I plant my hands on his chest and press a soft kiss on his cheek. "Goodnight, Mr. James."

I stifle a chuckle at the frustrated groan that tumbles from his lips. But he steps back and gives me space. He really is a gentleman, huh?

"Thank you for your jacket." I go to slip my arms out of the silk-lined sleeves, but he encircles my wrist with one strong hand, sending pulses of electricity skittering up my forearm.

"Keep it. I'll get it back Saturday night."

I frown. "Saturday night?"

"Our next date."

I arch an eyebrow. "What if I already have plans?"

His lips twitch again with the promise of a smile that he refuses to deliver this time. "Do you?"

I fold my arms across my chest and scowl. "No. But that's beside the point."

He's already walking toward his car when he calls over his shoulder, "I'll pick you up at seven, Melanie."

CHAPTER
TEN

NATHAN

Holy fuck. My heart is about to burst through my ribcage with the way it's hammering in my chest. I sink back against the leather seat of the car with the scent of her in my nose and only the faintest taste of her on my lips from when they brushed her skin. Fuck me, I want more. So much fucking more.

And I know she wanted more too. I could tell from her blown-out pupils, how her breathing grew heavier whenever I got close to her, and the way her body instinctively leaned into mine. But now my cock is hard, and I'm left with nothing but the memory of her to keep me warm tonight. I've never had any problems getting women into my bed, and this feeling is both unusual and unwelcome.

I pull out my cell phone and tap out a text.

You fancy a nightcap?

Elijah replies within seconds.

> How was the date?

> Meet me at the bar and I'll tell you

> Amber's sleeping.

I sigh.

> I didn't invite Amber

I stare at the three dots, waiting for his response.

> I'll meet you there in half an hour. Is Mase coming too?

> He's on a date with that underwear model and I can guarantee his night will have a happy ending. Unlike mine

> Well, I would have said that about you before tonight.

I can picture the grin on my brother's face and roll my eyes.

> I'll see you at the bar

Already two glasses of Scotch in, I slide Elijah's drink across the table to him when he arrives. He takes a sip and eyes me over the rim of his glass. "So?"

"It was okay." I shrug. "Less painful than expected."

"Wow." He purses his lips and nods. "I see nothing but happiness in your future then."

Ignoring his sarcasm, I take a swig of my Scotch and savor the rich, smoky liquid burning my throat. "Well, we don't marry for love, right?"

Elijah snorts. "It sure didn't work for me." He downs his drink and signals the waitress for another.

"Anyway, I'm being unfair. As a *date*, it was good." Pausing, I stare into the bottom of my glass. "More fun than I've had at dinner with a woman for as long as I can remember."

"So why the long face?"

I shake my head and blow out a breath. "As a rule, the fun part of my dates usually begins after the dinner and conversation." At least that was the case until recently.

"Oh." Elijah laughs. "So you're pissed because she didn't let you fuck her?"

"No, buddy. I'm pissed because I wanted to fuck her. I went into this tonight thinking it would just be dinner, and she surprised the hell out of me."

"So she's going to make you wait a while, horndog. Is that so bad? And isn't it a good thing that you want to fuck the woman you're going to marry in a few weeks?"

"I really don't know, Elijah. Being attracted to her makes the whole arrangement way more complicated."

He frowns at me. "Or easier if you're going to have kids with her."

"I dunno." He might be right, but all the things I'm feeling right now are making me think I've bitten off more than I anticipated. "Anyway, she was different tonight."

Our waitress brings us each a fresh drink, and Elijah thanks her and slips her a twenty for her service. With a sweet smile, she flutters her eyelashes at him, but his attention remains on me. "Different how?"

"She was quiet today in the boardroom. Reserved even. Then tonight she was fun. Flirty. Feisty as fuck." A smile tugs at the corner of my lips at the memory.

"Maybe alcohol loosens her inhibitions?" he suggests.

"Obviously not enough." I snort, the buzz from the whisky

finally taking the edge off my frustration, and he laughs at my crass joke. "But anyway, it wasn't that. She had a glass of champagne and two glasses of wine over the course of three hours. It was more like she acted differently around her brother. I think there's something weird going on between them."

His lip curls in disgust. "Eww, bro!" He lets a bit of his old frat-boy self slip out past his usual reserved-CEO facade.

I give him a light punch on the arm. "Not that sort of weird, you pervert." He snickers, but the troubled look in his eyes makes me realize what a bad brother I've been lately. "How are things with Amber?"

He shakes his head, avoiding my gaze. His only response is a heavy sigh, and he takes another gulp of his Scotch. After a long pause, he lifts his head again. His eyes glisten with tears when they meet mine, and my heart breaks a little for him. I remember when he and Amber met in college, and although she never seemed right for him as far as I could see, I also recall how happy they were. But they haven't been anything close to happy for a long time now.

"I don't know how to fix it, Nathan. Every time I try, it seems to push her further away."

I give his shoulder a reassuring squeeze.

"So, maybe Dad was right about not marrying for love, huh?" He downs the last of his Scotch.

"So what you're saying is I should count my lucky stars that I'll never fall in love with my wife"—I sip my drink—"but the fact that her sass, not to mention her fine-as-hell ass, makes me as hard as iron is a major plus?"

Chuckling, Elijah raises his empty glass in a toast. "You've got it made, brother."

CHAPTER
ELEVEN

MELANIE

Nathan stands outside my apartment building, leaning against his black limo with his arms folded over his broad chest and his foot resting on the door panel. He's dressed in jeans and a navy polo shirt, and I swear he makes them look as tailored as one of his Savile Row suits.

I walk over to him with a spring in my step. It's a beautiful summer evening, and I'm going on a date with a handsome, brilliant man who makes me laugh even if he doesn't mean to. What's not to be happy about? I catch his attention and smile, and I don't miss the way his eyes rake hungrily up and down my body, taking in my bare tanned legs in my pink summer dress.

"Hey." My voice comes out in a breathy whisper that I was totally not expecting to sound as sultry as it does.

His eyes are dark and intense. "You look beautiful."

My cheeks flush with heat, not to mention that space between my thighs. "You look handsome."

He flashes me an arrogant half smile. Yeah, he knows he's

hot. I bet women have been telling him that every day of his adult life. He opens the car door. "After you, Miss Edison."

I climb inside, holding my dress at the back so I don't flash him my matching pink panties, and I'm sure I hear him mutter a curse under his breath.

"So where are we going?" I ask as I peer out the window. He sent me a text message earlier, but all he'd tell me about tonight's date was to dress comfortably. Comfortable to me means yoga pants and Tyler's old football jersey, but I figured that wasn't what he meant, so I opted for my favorite dress. Casual enough to wear to a ball game, but fancy enough for dinner.

"It's a surprise."

"Can you give me a clue?" I ask, fluttering my eyelashes.

"You'll love it," is all he offers.

Nathan wasn't wrong about me loving our date destination. I stand outside the entrance of Central Park Zoo with a huge smile on my face. "But it's after seven. I thought the zoo was closed."

He winks at me. "Not to us."

He holds out his arm, and I link mine through his as the zookeeper ushers us through the barrier. I guess money really can buy you anything.

"There's no paparazzi around here though." I glance at the empty pathways. I've been to this zoo plenty of times, but it's more peaceful and serene than I realized when nobody else is around.

"What about that guy?" Nathan jerks his head toward the snow monkey exhibit, where one of them watches us walk by.

I snort a laugh. "I think he forgot his camera."

He flashes me a grin. "I thought it would be nice to not have to worry about cameras flashing in our faces tonight."

"It's a perfect date. Thank you."

He looks away and clears his throat. "You're welcome."

AFTER WE'VE SEEN ALL the animals and watched the sea lions being fed up close, Nathan gets each of us an ice cream cone. We sit on a bench to eat, enjoying the last rays of the evening sun.

"So, Miss Edison, if this is a perfect date, tell me about some of your worst ones."

I press my lips together and search my memories. "Oh!" I turn to face him. "One time a guy took me to meet his mom on our first date. She cooked us dinner and sat at the table while we ate. That was awkward."

He shakes his head. "Wow. Someone needs to teach that boy some game."

"Well, not everyone is as blessed with game as you, Mr. James."

He arches an eyebrow. "You think I have game?"

"Oh, come on," I huff, rolling my eyes. "We're alone in the Central Park Zoo, watching the sunset and eating ice cream. If we were on a real date, I'd be riding you like a rodeo bull already. You know you have game."

He snorts, then coughs and wipes ice cream off his nose. "You'd be what?"

My cheeks burn. Did I really just say that aloud?

"Because I'm pretty sure this is about as real a date as it gets," he says in that low, husky growl he has that melts my insides like chocolate.

"I wasn't being literal. It was just a figure of speech," I insist. But heat is building in my core, and a dull ache thrums between my thighs. The thought of climbing onto his lap and pretending I'm a cowgirl is an entirely pleasant one. Desperate to change the subject, I blurt, "Anyway, tell me about your worst dates."

"One time a woman proposed to me before we even got to the restaurant," he says, deadpan.

I slap a hand over my mouth, worried I'll spit out the bite of ice cream I just took, and laugh.

"Another time, my date insisted on trying to impress me with her pole dancing skills but got a cramp while she was upside down, dropped onto her head, and gave herself a concussion. We spent all night in the ER."

"What?" The look on his face has me suppressing my snicker. "Was she okay?"

"As far as I know, her pole dancing career is over." He flashes me a wicked grin. "But yes, she made a full recovery."

"Okay, I can beat that." I wiggle on the bench and sit up straighter. "One guy I dated got his dick completely stuck in his fly when he used the restroom during dinner, and I had to take him to the hospital. I've never seen so much blood or heard a grown man make those kinds of noises before."

Nathan winces. "Ouch."

"I know, right. Then there was the time I was having sex with a guy, and he started singing "Yeah" by Usher when he was about to come." I thrust my hips forward and back and sing a line of the chorus to give him the full effect.

Nathan doubles over, clutching his stomach, and for a second I'm worried he has food poisoning or something, but his shoulders are shuddering, and I realize he's laughing.

I laugh too, not only at the memory but at the sight of the Iceman himself so undone. When he sits up, tears are streaming down his face.

"That is the funniest fucking thing I've ever heard." He wipes his eyes with the back of his hand. "Jesus, Mel."

I shrug. "I've had some crazy dates."

"Yeah, you win."

"Women always have worse date stories than men. I think it's probably because we have way more invested."

"What makes you say that?"

"When you go on a regular date, I bet your only real concern is where to go and whether the condom in your wallet is expired." He arches an eyebrow, and my cheeks flush again. "Although you probably never have a condom long enough to worry about it expiring."

His lips twitch. "I'm not sure if that's a compliment or an insult."

I roll my eyes and continue. "Women have to worry about all kinds of things. Should I wax? Do I wear the sexy panties or the ones that will hold in my stomach if we go for pasta? Is he going to think I'm easy if I put out? Will he think I'm a prude if I don't? Is he going to turn into an asshole if I run into a guy friend? Is he all about that possessive big dick energy, and if so, does he have the equipment to back it up?" I stop talking, aware I'm babbling and also guilty of stereotyping.

Nathan's dark eyes narrow. "Is he all about the *what*?"

"Um. Possessive big dick energy."

He rests his arm on the bench behind me, so close I feel the warmth of his skin on my shoulders. "And just what in the fuck is that?"

I sigh. "It's when a guy is all possessive and controlling or acts like an arrogant asshole. Basically, he acts like he has a huge dick. Big dick energy. It can be hot if done right and if he has the means to back it up, if you know what I mean?"

He shakes his head. "Had no idea that was a thing."

"Having a huge dick?" I snort a laugh.

His expression darkens. "If this was a real date, Miss Edison,

I would put you over my knee and spank your bratty little ass for that."

Oh, dear sweet mother in heaven. Nathan James is the epitome of big dick energy. I flick my tongue over my ice cream. "Shame it's not a real date then, Mr. James."

His eyes burn into mine, and he licks his lips. I see him clenching and unclenching his fist in my peripheral vision, like his palm is twitching to smack my ass. My core contracts with need because the thought of him doing that is way more appealing than it ought to be.

"We thought you might like to take one of these as a reminder of your visit." One of the zookeepers approaches, smiling and clutching a stuffed red panda. "With our compliments."

Damn my love for those cute little ginger bandits interrupting the moment. I force a smile. "Thank you so much." I take the toy from her and sit back against the bench while images of me bent over Nathan's lap race through my mind.

CHAPTER
TWELVE

MELANIE

> I assume you don't have any plans for 4th of July?

I roll my eyes at the text message, but I can't deny the fluttering in my abdomen whenever I see his name on my phone.

I type out a reply, a smile on my lips.

> And why would you assume that?

> Because I haven't invited you anywhere yet

Arrogant asshole! Two days' notice and he expects me to be free. But I'm still smiling when I respond.

> I actually have plans with two guys that night.

> For your sake I hope they're Ben & Jerry

I snort a laugh.

> That was actually funny, Mr. James. But no, I'm working at the shelter.

> That's a terrible plan

> I'll have fun. My friends Cesar and Potato are a blast.

My phone rings, and I giggle when a picture of Val Kilmer from *Top Gun* flashes on the screen. "Hello?"

"Who the fuck are Cesar and Potato?"

"A basset hound and a corgi. Two of the longest-serving residents at the shelter. They keep me company while I do my rounds."

"So you'll be alone there all night?" He sounds grumpy.

"No Cesar and—"

"I'm talking about people, Mel."

"There'll be a security guard there too."

He sighs. "Why the hell are you working on the Fourth of July?"

"Because nobody else wanted to. I don't get asked to cover often, so I like to do what I can when they do ask. So I'm sorry if you had plans for some Fourth of July date extravaganza to impress the paparazzi with. You'll have to wait until the weekend."

He hums, and I wrinkle my nose, my suspicion aroused. "What does that sound mean?"

He mutters something unintelligible, then sighs. "I have to go."

I can't help feeling a little dejected, even if I did just blow him off. But it was for a good cause. "Okay. I guess I'll see you some other time then?"

"Yeah," he says, but he sounds distracted. "Bye, Melanie."

He ends the call before I can reply.

~

"I'll be at the front desk if you need anything, Mel," the shelter's security guard says, before he takes a bite of his jelly donut.

"Thanks, Serge. Everyone's been fed and is settled. Meds have been administered. I'll go give some more cuddles in a few hours. We'll be fine in here watching a little TV until then, won't we, boys?" I give Cesar a scratch behind his ears while Potato scampers around my feet.

Serge licks the powder from his lips, gives a polite nod, and leaves the small office.

I sink into the armchair and eye the pink box containing my jelly donut. Potato barks at me as though he's eyeing it too.

"You know donuts are bad for you, right?" I tell him.

He barks and wags his nubby tail while Cesar curls into a ball at my feet. I pick up the TV remote and flick through the free cable channels. I'm still searching for something to watch when Serge pokes his head through the doorway.

"Everything okay?"

"Um …" He runs his fingers over his thick gray mustache. "There's someone here to see you."

I turn off the TV. "To see me?"

"Yeah. Told him you were working, but he's quite insistent."

I roll my eyes. Please don't let this be Bryce. "Did he say what he wants?"

Blue eyes twinkling, he smiles. "Judging by the giant picnic basket he has with him, I'd say he wants to bring you dinner."

Definitely not Bryce. That familiar fluttering feeling swirls in my abdomen, but surely it isn't Nathan. There's nobody to see us here. Nobody to report our *date*. Well, except for Serge, who doesn't even know what social media is. And Cesar and

Potato, but I already know from experience they're entirely trustworthy—they know all my secrets and haven't told a soul.

"Shall I let him in? It's against protocol to have overnight guests, but I don't see why he can't stay for dinner."

Too stunned to speak, I nod. Surely it can't be him. But who else? Tyler's still out of town, and nobody else knows I'm here. "Yes, please let him in."

After Serge leaves, I go straight for the mirror and smooth down the flyaway strands of hair framing my face. I wasn't expecting company tonight, and I'm wearing my comfy yoga pants and an old hoodie of Tyler's, both of which are covered in fur, so I'm not exactly dressed for it either.

Potato woofs at my feet. "I know, little buddy. He's going to take one look at me and wonder what the hell he's marrying."

"Actually, you look kind of cute." Nathan's deep voice fills the room, and my stomach flips. I turn to face him, and my heart almost stops. His strong jaw is covered in a thicker coating of stubble than usual, and he's wearing gray sweats with a fitted white T-shirt. Hot damn.

Cesar lifts his head, gives Nathan a cursory glance, and resumes his former position, but Potato jumps up to sniff at the basket in Nathan's hand.

Nathan scratches his reddish-brown head. "Don't worry. I brought something for you too." Oh, dear mother, he likes dogs. "Now, sit," he commands, and my disobedient little buddy flops down onto his butt.

I blink at Nathan. "He barely ever listens to anyone."

He shrugs. "Guess it's all in the tone."

He's not wrong. I'm pretty sure I'd sit right now if he told me to. Probably even kneel. I banish such thoughts from my head and cast my eyes back to the large picnic basket hanging over his arm. "Did you bring me dinner?"

He sets the basket down on the table. "I brought us both dinner. And your furry pals here."

Tears well in my eyes. "You brought Potato and Cesar dinner too?"

He nods. "And little extra treats for the others. I got dog and cat stuff, but I didn't know what other animals you had here."

I gape at him and try to stop myself from drooling. Surely this man is not actually real.

"Mel?" he says, and I realize I haven't spoken for at least a minute.

"But ... why? What happened to your Fourth of July plans?"

He arches an eyebrow. "She's standing right here looking at me like I've grown an extra head."

I blush bright pink. "It's just ... I wasn't expecting you. This isn't very public for a date."

"It's not a date. It's dinner." He winks at me, then opens the picnic basket and pulls out a small bottle of wine. He holds it up. "Alcohol-free because I assume you can't drink on the job."

I fold my arms over my chest and watch him. He assumes correctly.

"I didn't bring glasses though." He pulls out a clear plastic container that looks like it has chicken wings inside. My stomach growls.

"We only have coffee mugs if you don't mind drinking from them."

He nods, seemingly unfazed, and continues unpacking the basket. Potato sits at his feet now, patiently waiting for whatever delights Nathan has brought him. Even Cesar shuffles over, his nose in the air as he sniffs out his supper. I gawk at him. Nathan James, billionaire bachelor, spending his Fourth of July at an animal shelter with a corgi and a basset hound—and me. How is this even my life?

I LEAN BACK on the Formica chair and rub a hand over my stomach. Nathan's picnic dinner was wonderful: chicken wings, potato skins, barbecue ribs, corn on the cob, and cheesecake. I couldn't eat another bite if he paid me. "I am so full. That was all delicious."

Potato woofs his agreement from where he sits next to me, and Cesar remains lying on top of Nathan's feet. Suitably impressed with the gourmet filet mignon doggy treats, the basset hound has been glued to my husband-to-be for the past hour.

Nathan scratches the dog's head and smiles. "Do you ever think about taking these guys home?"

"Cesar and Potato?" I shake my head. "No way."

He frowns.

"I mean, when I first started here years ago, I wanted to take home every stray or abandoned animal that came through the doors, but it's impossible to do that. So we do as much as we can for them while they're here."

Potato jumps up onto my lap, surprisingly agile for an eleven-year-old. I pat his head, and he sits obediently with his tongue hanging out.

"But both Potato and Cesar here have been at the shelter for almost seven years. They came in together after their owner got too ill to look after them. Most dogs will get adopted within the first year, but not these adorable little guys. They were so close that we couldn't bear to separate them, and they had a few foster trials but always got returned. After the fourth time, the management team decided they wouldn't put them through it again."

Potato yawns and curls up on my lap. I cup my hand under

63

his butt to stop him from falling off. "Am I boring you?" I ask the dog.

"You're not boring me." Our eyes meet across the table.

My face heats, and that fluttering in my abdomen whenever I'm around him kicks up a dozen notches. I clear my throat. "This is their home now. They live here and get plenty of walks and affection from the staff. They seem happy. It would be cruel to take them away from this now."

Nathan nods. "That makes sense." I swear his voice alone could melt chocolate.

I pull at the collar of Tyler's hoodie, suddenly feeling very hot. "Did I already thank you for dinner?"

His genuine smile is beautiful and disarming. "You did."

"It was a wonderful surprise. The best Fourth of July I've had for as long as I can remember," I admit.

His eyes narrow. "Yeah. Not exactly what I had in mind, but it's been nice."

I tilt my head, drinking in every detail of him. "May I ask what you did have planned?"

He looks up at the ceiling and hums.

I lean forward. "What?"

He looks back at me and sucks air through his teeth. "A private yacht on the Hudson. I had a section closed down for us. Fireworks. A Michelin-star chef."

"Hold on. Back right up." I hold up my hand. "You had a section of the *Hudson fucking River* closed down for us? Who are you? Bruce Wayne?"

"Oh, Spitfire, I can do things that would make Bruce Wayne look like Peter Griffin."

My laughter makes Potato jump, and I gather him into my arms and press a kiss on his head while he grumbles his displeasure.

"But who needs yachts and fireworks when we can drink

64

zero-alcohol wine from coffee mugs with your furry buddies, hey?" Nathan's brown eyes twinkle, and heat rushes between my thighs. This man is perfection personified. How the hell am I going to survive this arrangement without completely falling for him?

"The yacht and fireworks sound amazing too though."

He reaches across the table and brushes his fingertips over the back of my hand. "Some other time."

A knock at the office door has Potato jumping from my lap and barking. A second later, Serge opens the door. "Almost time for my evening rounds, Mel."

"Thanks, Serge."

He nods and ducks out again.

Nathan arches an eyebrow at me. "Was that his polite way of telling me I have to leave?"

I nod. "I'm sorry. We don't usually allow visitors."

"Don't apologize. He told me I could only stay for a couple of hours." He checks his watch. "Which means my time is up in three minutes."

I stand and attempt to brush Potato's fur from my pants. "I had a lovely evening. Thank you so much for everything." I start to pack up the leftovers.

Nathan pushes back his chair and helps, but when I go to put them in the picnic basket, he stops me. "Leave them in the refrigerator. Serge might like some dinner later."

"That's really kind of you. I'm sure he will."

We both close the lid at the same time, and our fingers brush. Electric sparks skitter up my forearm. "I wish you could stay," I whisper.

"Me too, Spitfire."

He picks up the basket and cups my jaw with his free hand, rubbing the pad of his thumb over my lip. "Are you free next Friday night?"

I take a breath, my heart stuttering in my chest. Next Friday? Not tomorrow? That's over a week away.

"I have to go to Chicago on business tomorrow, and I won't be back until next week," he says, and I wonder if he can read every thought on my face. As silly as it seems, I'm going to miss him.

"Yes, I'm free."

He winks. "Then it's a date, Miss Edison." He bends down and presses a soft kiss on my forehead. I lock my knees to keep them from buckling and try not to drool as I watch him walk out of the room.

CHAPTER
THIRTEEN

NATHAN

T glance at my cell phone on the desk beside me and suppress a smirk when I see her text message displayed on the screen.

> Is this a joke? Are you seriously choosing my clothes for our date?

I clear my throat, and my secretary looks up from her legal pad. "Excuse me, Helen. I need to deal with this."

She offers me a brief smile and places her pad and pen in her lap while I type out a reply to Mel.

> It's a gift. You know what a gift is, surely?

> It feels like a possessive, big dick energy move to me.

I suppress a laugh. Our last two dates play on a highlight reel in my head, and we didn't even so much as kiss. But fuck, I wanted to kiss her. I wanted to take her back to my place and fuck her until neither of us could walk.

So she thinks I have big dick energy? Well, she's sure right about one thing. I almost type that but refrain from being so crass. I picked the dress out especially for her, and it will look goddamn incredible on those killer curves.

> Have you even looked at the dress?

> That's not the point.

Helen taps her pen on her notepad, a subtle reminder that we're supposed to be going over my calendar for next week. I hold up a finger, letting her know I'll be just another minute before I send my final reply to Mel.

> Tonight will be a special occasion. I wanted you to have something special to wear. If you don't love it, don't wear it. I'll send a car for you at eight

I place the phone back on my desk, screen down so I'm not distracted by her reply when it inevitably comes through, and give my full attention to Helen. I already have way too much shit to do today without being distracted by a text argument with my wife-to-be—as much as the thought of doing that gets my blood pumping.

I CAN'T FAIL to notice the admiring glances Mel attracts as she winds her way through the crowded restaurant toward me. A group of men at a nearby table look her up and down when she passes. Annoyance stabs my gut, but she doesn't even glance in their direction. Her eyes are fixed ahead. On me.

I grin when I catch a glimpse of the blood-red fabric molded to her body like a second skin, accentuating the curve of her hips, and I'm practically salivating at the thought of how delectable her perfectly rounded ass must look in the clingy fabric. I knew that color would look incredible on her, but the fact that she's wearing a dress I picked out stirs the possessive animal inside me. I pull out her chair and kiss her cheek when she reaches me. The scent of her sweet floral perfume fills my nose and makes my mouth water. My hand skims over her hip, my lips linger on her skin a little longer than necessary, and I feel her cheek heat beneath my touch.

I clear my throat, breaking the connection that sparks between us. "You look beautiful, Melanie."

She absent-mindedly brushes the fabric covering her abdomen, and her sparkling green eyes meet mine as she mouths *thank you*.

Once we're seated, I take a moment to appreciate her captivating beauty. She wears minimal makeup and no jewelry aside from a pair of diamond earrings. Her thick dark hair is styled so that it falls in cascading waves over one shoulder again, exposing the soft skin of her slender neck. An image of me sinking my teeth into the creamy flesh there makes its way into my consciousness, and I mentally check myself. "I see you decided to wear the gift?"

Her cheeks flush pink. "Well, it is a beautiful dress. Thank you."

"You're welcome."

Her eyes rake over my features like she might read what I'm thinking by my expression alone. She won't. "Did you choose it yourself, or ..." She chews on the inside of her cheek.

I arch a brow. "Or?"

"Or did someone pick it out for you? A woman, perhaps?"

I pour her a glass of the Chardonnay I ordered when I

arrived and fight to hold back a satisfied grin. I have no idea why this woman makes me want to smile so goddamn much. It's unnerving. "Melanie, are you jealous?"

"No," she retorts, a little too quickly. "But I'd like to know if it's you who has such exceptionally good taste, or if you have some poor ex-girlfriend who dresses your dates for you."

She is jealous. Why does that make me so fucking happy? "I picked it out for you. I saw it in the window at Barney's and thought it would be perfect for you. Is that acceptable, Miss Edison?"

Her lips twitch. "Very, Mr. James."

Her eyes light up when I wink at her, but the moment is interrupted by the waiter coming to talk us through the specials.

"So what's the occasion?" Melanie asks, placing her soup spoon on the table beside her bowl.

I take a sip of my wine. "Any time I see you feels like a special occasion, darling."

She rolls her eyes and snorts a cute-as-hell laugh. "Nathan. I'm serious. You said tonight was a special occasion."

The ring box in my jacket pocket feels like it's burning through the fabric of my suit. Some part of me wants to surprise her and see her reaction, but I have no clue why, seeing as this is merely a business transaction for her. And for me too—that goes without saying. I lean closer, careful to ensure nobody hears me. "I was planning to propose."

Her eyebrows shoot up. "Here? Tonight?"

"It's one of the most exclusive restaurants in Manhattan. It's known for being a popular proposal spot. Seemed like the perfect venue."

"I know that, but I guess I thought ..." Her slender throat thickens as she swallows.

I frown. Surely she's not having doubts now. "Thought what?"

She shrugs. "I dunno. It's a little cliché, is all. I figured you'd be more inventive."

"Well, maybe I would be if this was a real ..." Hurt flashes in her eyes, and I decide not to finish that sentence, and not only because some piece-of-shit paparazzi could be close enough to read my lips.

With a nod, she sits back in her chair, her demeanor prickly in a way it wasn't a few moments ago. "You're right. This is the perfect venue."

"If you'd rather ..."

Her features soften on a faint smile. "Ignore me. I'm holding on to schoolgirl fantasies of a dream proposal. Here is great."

I press my lips together and resist the urge to ask her about that schoolgirl fantasy. It doesn't matter. I'm not her fantasy, and I never will be.

No time like the present. I fish for the ring inside my pocket and drop to one knee beside her. She gasps and puts a hand to her chest, playing her part to perfection. I'm vaguely aware of the restaurant coming to a standstill around us, and the vibrant hum of chatter fades to a few whispered voices. Keeping my gaze trained on hers, I take hold of her left hand and open the box, revealing the four-carat diamond ring. It sparkles, reflecting light from the chandeliers above our heads,

"Oh, Nathan," she whispers. "It's beautiful." Her glistening eyes flicker between the ring and my face. She's either an incredible actress or she *really* likes the ring.

"Melanie Edison, will you marry me?" I can barely believe the words come from my mouth, and I hold my breath, seemingly along with everyone around us given the quiet that's now settled over the entire restaurant.

"Yes. Yes!" she squeals, wrapping her arms around my neck and pulling me close.

Applause erupts, and I press my lips to her ear. "They're all still watching. I think we should probably kiss or something."

"Put the ring on me first," she whispers back.

I slide the ring onto her finger and notice the way her eyes shine with what appears to be genuine delight as she inspects her hand. There's another round of applause and a few cheers. Then her eyes are fixed on mine, her hands are on my face, and everything else ceases to exist.

I kiss her, not because I'm supposed to, but because I can't wait another second to press my lips against the plump bow of hers. Can't stop thinking about how it would feel to slide my tongue into her mouth and taste her. And the second I do, I regret it. She tastes like wine and sweetness, of all the things I shouldn't want. She tastes like she's mine.

Her mouth is warm and inviting, and when I flick my tongue against hers, the sexy little moan she gives makes my dick stiffen. I tangle my fingers in the back of her hair and tilt her head to the angle I want, the perfect angle to tongue-fuck her right here at this table.

"Congratulations, sir. I hope you and your lovely fiancée enjoy an eternity of happiness together." The restaurant owner's voice has me pulling back, leaving her breathless and looking like she wants more. My eyes remain locked on hers while I thank Javier for his kind words and the complimentary bottle of champagne I hear him order for our table.

"I feel like everyone's staring," Mel says with a breathy laugh, her cheeks pink and her red lips swollen from my bruising kiss.

One glance around the room confirms her suspicions, and

the moment suddenly seems too intimate to share with the world. It shouldn't feel that way. This is business, nothing more. I chose this place because I knew it would be crowded, and I wanted strangers' recording and snapping this moment with their cell phones. I wanted photographers to be waiting outside for us when we left.

By midnight, news of our engagement will be splashed all over social media, and the trashy news sites and gossip columns will be throwing out wild theories about our courtship. That's all precisely what I wanted. I don't understand why it feels so wrong now. Why do I wish I could take her away from all the lights and noise and fakery and finish up that incredible kiss with nobody's eyes on us? With no sound in my ears except my heartbeat and her soft moans.

"Nathan." She giggles, breaking the spell she has me under. "As much as I enjoy the sight of you on your knees for me, are you going to sit back down?"

I stand, but before I take a seat, I clasp her hand in mine. Dipping my head, I brush my lips against her ear. "Don't get used to it, Mel. You'll be the one on your knees for me before too long."

Her breath catches in her throat, and when I take my seat opposite her, her eyes sparkle with mischief, her cheeks now as red as her lips. The image of her naked and on her knees with her mouth open while she waits for my cock sends white-hot pleasure searing down my spine.

"Your champagne, Mr. James," the waiter interrupts us, and I force the image of me coming down my fiancée's pretty throat out of my mind.

FOURTEEN

MELANIE

Nathan drapes his dinner jacket over my shoulders as we walk to the car, and I pull it tighter, enjoying the way his residual body heat warms me. The fabric smells of his cologne, woody and masculine, and being blanketed in his scent heats me up for an entirely different reason.

A guy steps in front of us, holding an expensive-looking camera in his hands. "May I get a picture of the happy couple?" he asks, his eyes wide and hopeful.

"Sure." Nathan slips his arm around my waist and pulls me into him. I lean my head on his shoulder and smile for the camera, playing up the part. There were half a dozen photographers waiting as soon as we left the restaurant, and I used the same pose for them. Although it's not all an act. I am happy. There are worse men I could have been asked to marry than the sexy-as-hell billionaire who, despite his ice-cold exterior, is warm when it matters.

And that kiss. Wow! If he's that good at kissing, I can't help but wonder how good he is at other mouth-related activities.

Because at some point we'll need to have sex, and experience has taught me that good kissers are generally good at all the other stuff too. Of course, I could be completely wrong.

"Thanks. And congratulations," the photographer says, pulling me out of my thoughts of hot sex with my even hotter soon-to-be husband.

Nathan murmurs something to the photographer and hurries us along to the waiting car.

As soon as Teddy pulls the car away from the curb, I let out a deep breath. This is the first time I've been able to think clearly since the whirlwind of the proposal.

I turn to face Nathan, who appears as cool and calm as usual. "That was some night. Were you always planning to propose? You could have given me a little more warning, dude."

He shifts in his seat, angling his body toward mine. "Would you have been anxious all day thinking about it?"

"Probably," I admit.

He winks, and dammit, it makes him look even sexier. "That's why I didn't tell you earlier."

"I guess proposals are supposed to be a surprise."

"Exactly. You played your part beautifully, by the way."

My cheeks heat, and I don't miss the smirk that elicits from him. "So did you, Mr. James."

Taking my hand in his, he examines my new jewelry. "Now that we're officially engaged, I think all this *Mr. James* business will need to stop."

"Aw." I jut out my bottom lip. "Maybe I'll just call you Iceman instead."

His dark eyes twinkle with devilish intent, and my insides churn. I have no idea how this man gets through the day without being constantly propositioned, with his chiseled jaw, broad shoulders, and smoldering eyes. "Nathan will do fine, Melanie."

I tilt my head and purse my lips. "How about I just call you Ice?"

His tongue darts out and he licks his top lip, those incredible chocolate-brown orbs never leaving mine. "Whatever you say, Spitfire."

Damn! What I wouldn't give for that tongue to ... I mentally shake my head. How is this even real? I'm actually going to marry Nathan freaking James, and right now, I'm not even a little mad about it.

NATHAN WALKS me to the door of my building like he did on our past two dates, but this time he doesn't say goodnight. He simply opens the door and follows me into the lobby.

"Um. Where exactly do you think you're going, Ice?"

"Tonight, I'll be walking you to your door, Spitfire."

"But why?"

"You're my fiancée now." He shrugs. "Seems like we should take this relationship to the next level, don't you think?"

My breath hitches, and my entire body feels like it's engulfed by flames. While the thought of him doing all manner of unspeakable things to my body is all kinds of hot, having sex right now will only complicate matters. I need to keep a clear head at all times, at least until we're married, because he already makes me feel like a giddy teenager. This thing isn't set in stone yet, and anything could happen between now and the wedding. I figure a man like him could have almost any woman he wants, and there's every chance he could stumble on a better alternative to me on any given day. The last thing I need is to be stuck dealing with a broken heart. So there can be absolutely no sex and no falling for him. Nil. Nada.

He slides his hand to the small of my back, and electric heat sears my skin there, sending a shockwave of pleasure through me. His lips graze my ear. "Relax, Mel. I mean walking you to your door. I don't expect to be invited in."

"Oh." I nod. "Good. Just so we're on the same page. Because that would only make things awkward and complicated right now, and who wants that, right?" I clamp my jaw shut, determined to cut off my nonsensical babbling.

His lips twitch. "I'm sure neither of us wants to complicate anything, Spitfire."

Oh, but yes, I do. I want you to complicate me six ways to Sunday. I bite my tongue to stop myself from saying that aloud.

When we get to my apartment, I awkwardly shift from one foot to the other. Not inviting him in feels weird after he walked me all the way up here, but if he steps foot inside that apartment ... well, I'm pretty sure all of my defenses are going to end up shot to hell because I'm already hanging by a thread.

"This is me." I jerk my head toward the door, then fish my key ring from my purse and twist it in my hands.

He edges closer, crowding me toward the door until my back is pressed against it. My pulse races. "I'm not going to ask to come in, Mel," he says, his voice low and husky. He plants his hands on either side of my head. "But I am going to kiss you again."

Biting my lip, I stare into his dark eyes. I feel like a kitten caught in the paws of a panther. When I don't offer any resistance, Nathan bends his head and seals his lips over mine. They're soft yet demanding, and my mouth yields to his in an instant. When he flicks his tongue against the seam of my lips, I part them on a throaty moan, allowing him entrance. He takes full advantage, deepening the kiss as he presses his body into mine and pins me to the door.

I fist my hands in his shirt, pulling him deeper, my tongue dancing against his while he takes what he wants, all passion and dominance. A groan rumbles through his chest and into my mouth, mingling with the desperate, needy whimpers he's pulling from my core. He rocks his hips into me, and his hard length digs into my abdomen. I rake my hands through his hair, but he keeps his firmly planted on the door beside my head. Needing some relief for the ache between my thighs, I grind against him and he grunts.

All too soon, he pulls back, leaving us both panting for air as we stare into each other's eyes. I'm seconds away from inviting him inside when he presses a gentle kiss on my forehead. "Night, Spitfire." With that, he turns on his heel and walks down the hallway.

I tip my head back against the door, sure of one thing. Nathan James is going to break my heart wide open. And I'm going to let him.

CHAPTER

FIFTEEN

MELANIE

"Have you seen these?" Bryce tosses a stack of glossy magazines onto the table in front of me.

I give them a cursory glance but don't need to look to see what's been printed. Tyler sent me pictures from various websites yesterday morning, along with three dozen scream-face emojis. It seems like everyone in the world is aware of Nathan and me getting engaged the night before last. All my work friends have called or texted, and I even got messages from a few old high school friends I haven't spoken to in years. At least the photographs are flattering, and objectively, we do make a cute couple.

Bryce's expression is full of unbridled glee. "This is perfect, little sister. The more publicity your relationship gets, the more the James PR machine will want to keep reports under wraps when your marriage ends because Nathan James is a cheating snake."

I roll my eyes. All he needs to do is rub his sweaty palms

together and he'd be a caricature of himself. "But he's not a cheating snake, Bryce."

He snorts. "Not yet."

"Maybe not ever." I shake my head and pour a cup of tea from my mother's favorite china teapot. She took to her bed fifteen minutes after my arrival for our usual Sunday tea, overcome with joyful delirium over the news of my engagement to a billionaire being splashed all over social media and the gossip columns.

Bryce shoots me a look of pure disdain. "You have so much to learn about men like Nathan James, little sister."

"Or maybe you're just too quick to judge everybody by your own low standards."

He lifts his hand, and I flinch, causing a dark laugh to tumble out of him. He drops his hand, and I wonder if he realized how bad it would look for me to be photographed with a black eye. Not to mention how my future husband would want to know where I got such an injury, and then this whole arrangement could come to a grinding halt.

"All I'm saying is that you're convinced Nathan will cheat on me and you'll be able to cash in on this morality clause, but he's not an idiot. If he agrees to such a clause, he isn't stupid enough to break it. And besides any of that, what if he's just not a cheater? Because if I'm honest, he doesn't strike me as the cheating type."

As I expected, that only earns me a condescending sneer from my older brother, but I'm not going to sit here and have him talk trash about a man who has only ever been a perfect gentleman with me. He seems honest and loyal, the exact opposite of a man who cheats on his wife.

He snorts. "You're wrong, Melanie. But even on the slim chance you're right and he does manage to keep his dick in his pants for a few months, that's why we're going to put temptation in his way."

I throw my hands in the air. "Are you talking about that damn honey trap idea again?"

"It's the perfect plan, Melly." He arches an eyebrow, and it makes him look like a Bond villain. "And if you're so sure he won't cheat, what harm could it do?"

"I'm not marrying someone in the hopes that he'll cheat on me!"

He practically doubles over with laughter, which is abruptly cut off with a mocking smile. "And what's the alternative, little Melly? That he falls in love with you, and you live happily ever after?"

I clench my jaw tight and mentally count to five. "No. But our reasons for doing this are sound. We both want children. And if you're right that me becoming Nathan's wife will save Dad's business, this marriage will secure Ashley's future, which is my primary concern. He's a good man, Bryce, and no, we might not have a happily ever after, but that doesn't mean we can't be happy. That doesn't mean we can't raise children together and be friends while we do it." I think of my own parents and how unhappy my father must have been in his marriage. "And you know what, that's more than a lot of people get."

He shakes his head. "You're so naive."

"Maybe so. But I'm in this for the long haul. So even if you do go along with your ridiculous honey trap idea, I wouldn't divorce him anyway."

My words are like a red rag to a bull, igniting his short temper. He jumps up so quickly that the French antique chair clatters to the floor, and he bangs his meaty fist on the table. "This is not up for negotiation, Melanie!" He grabs my hair and yanks my head back. Sharp pain sears my scalp, but I don't struggle. I've learned enough painful lessons about the futility of such an endeavor. "You will marry who I tell you to marry, and you will do whatever the fuck I tell you to, when I tell you to do it. And if that includes divorcing that arrogant prick, you damn well will. Do you understand me?"

I press my lips together, refusing to answer.

He pulls my hair harder. "Never forget that *you* are the reason we're in this mess in the first place. *You* are the reason Dad died. And if you don't use that pretty cunt of yours to do something useful for a change, our baby sister will have to drop out of that fancy college, and I'll marry her off to some billionaire too," he spits, his expression twisted with rage. "Now do you understand me?"

Tears burn behind my eyes, but I refuse to let them fall. "Yes, Bryce."

He lets my hair go, and I wince at the burning pain left behind. "Good girl. Now, let's have some tea." His gloating smile causes my stomach to lurch, but I merely nod and hand him the teapot.

CHAPTER
SIXTEEN

NATHAN

Elijah stuffs his hands into the pockets of his dress pants and stares at the painting on my office wall. "We had some incredible summers at that beach, didn't we?" He releases a wistful sigh.

I step up beside him. "We sure did."

He tilts his head to the side and narrows his eyes, like he's scrutinizing each beautiful brush stroke. "I wanted to take Amber there this summer. Show her where Mom was born, you know?"

"So why don't you?"

His tongue darts out, moistening his bottom lip, and he moves to sit in one of the leather chairs near the window. He blows out a breath. "She doesn't want to go. Said she couldn't be away from her friends that long."

I press my lips together and tip my face up to the ceiling, suppressing the words that want to roll off my tongue. I don't give advice. Wise men don't need it, and stupid men don't take it.

"I know what you're thinking, Nathan," he grumbles.

"You do, huh?"

He stares out the window. "I'm not going to divorce her."

"Why, Elijah? Neither of you are happy. And you're both young enough to find someone else."

His jaw tightens. "I don't want someone else. If I did, I wouldn't be this fucking miserable, would I?"

I shake my head and sit across from him. "Point taken."

Seemingly appeased by my response, he changes the subject. "Anyway, what's the news on your upcoming nuptials?"

"I was thinking the third of next month. That gives us a little over two weeks."

Elijah frowns. "I'll be out of town on the third."

"Shit. Can you get out of it?"

He shakes his head. "I'm the keynote speaker at some tech convention. Can you do a different date?"

I frown. "It's the only day that works with my schedule for the next two months, and I want to get this part over with. It sucks you won't be there, but it's not like this is a real wedding. I doubt Maddox will be there either."

"But who's going to be your best man?"

I roll my eyes. "I'm not having a best man. This isn't a real wedding."

He shakes his head. "You still need a best man."

"I'll ask Drake or Mase. Not like you would've been my first choice, anyway." I wink at him.

"You piece of shit." But he smirks at my blatant lie.

"Seriously, Elijah. This isn't a big deal to me. If it meant anything, of course I'd change the date and have you there, but it's a piece of fucking paper."

"You say that now, Nathan, but marriage means something

whether you want it to or not. This is going to change your life. Melanie's too."

I suppress a sigh. Not that you'd ever know it by looking at the grumpy bastard, but he's a hopeless romantic, and in that regard, we are nothing alike. "We're both aware this is life-changing, Elijah, but the wedding itself is merely a formality." Our conversation is interrupted by a knock at the door. "That will be my fiancée now."

I tell her to come in, and Elijah stands, ready to greet his soon-to-be sister-in-law. When she walks into the room a second later, the beaming smile on her face almost takes my breath away. I've seen her smile before, but this one makes her beautiful face iridescent.

Jesus. What the fuck is wrong with me?

She laughs and jerks her thumb toward the open doorway. "I just saw the cutest dog in the elevator," she says, by way of explanation. "He was wearing a tie. Like an actual necktie."

Elijah side-eyes me, then crosses the room and introduces himself. Still smiling, she shakes his hand and asks him if he likes dogs.

"Of course I do." He shoots me a bemused look and shakes his head. I can only shrug in response.

"You want coffee?" I ask her.

She slips off her jacket and nods. "Yes, please. And do you have anything to eat? I'm starving. Work was stupid busy today, so I didn't get a chance to have lunch."

"I can have someone go get you something. Or there are bound to be some jelly donuts hanging around somewhere. We had a board meeting earlier."

Her eyes go wide, and she licks her lips. "Jelly donuts would be perfect."

While I'm asking my secretary to take care of the coffee and donuts, Mel has an animated conversation with Elijah about the tie-wearing dog, and by the time I rejoin them, my older brother is staring at her with an expression of wonderment on his face.

Dammit, he likes her. All my brothers are going to like her, and my father will adore her. And while I should be thrilled with the knowledge that she'll be a hit with my family, it only reminds me of how much she's going to encroach on my life, and a part of me already resents her for that. And yeah, I'm aware how much of a giant fucking asshole that makes me.

Annoyed with my brother—and even more annoyed at myself—I snap, "Didn't you have someplace you needed to be?"

"What?" Elijah blinks at me before realization that I want him to leave dawns on his face. "Oh, yeah." He turns toward Melanie.

"It was lovely to meet you, Elijah," she says, flashing him another one of her killer smiles.

"You too, Mel. I look forward to seeing you again soon."

What the fuck? He's already calling her Mel?

He says goodbye to us both and walks out of my office, but not before he gives me a thumbs-up behind her back. I roll my eyes. My older brother's approval means that my fate is sealed. There aren't many people who can win him over in a matter of minutes, but then I guess there is something truly remarkable about Melanie Edison, although I can't quite figure out what that is. Nor do I want to admit that fact to anyone, myself included.

After Helen brings us coffee and a selection of donuts, Mel sits back in one of the comfortable leather chairs, chewing on her jelly donut and staring at my mother's painting while I grab the prenup contract for her to look over.

When I sit down, I bite back a grin at the blob of jelly stuck to her bottom lip. "You have ..." Instinctively, I lean forward and swipe it off her lip with the pad of my thumb and immediately regret it. Her pupils blow wide at my touch, and now I have jelly on my hand and no idea what to do with it other than push my thumb into her sweet mouth and have her suck it off.

I shake my head, trying to dislodge the image, but my cock is already jerking to attention at the mere thought of her tongue swiping over my skin. Instead I suck the jelly off my own thumb, and that doesn't make things any less awkward.

She bites down on her bottom lip, staring at me with those piercing green eyes, and now all I can think about is bending her over my desk and fucking her. What in the actual fuck is wrong with me?

I rock my head back and forth on my shoulders and blow out a breath. "You like the painting?" I ask, desperate to alleviate the mounting tension.

Her eyes crinkle at the corners when she smiles. "Yes, it's stunning. Did your mom paint it?"

"How'd you know?"

She rolls her eyes. "It's signed Verona James. Right there in the corner."

"People don't usually notice."

She shrugs. "Well, I have an eye for detail."

"Then maybe we should go over the details of this prenup," I suggest, sliding a copy across the table. "A copy has been sent to your lawyer too. And to Bryce."

I don't miss the subtle shift in her demeanor at the mention of her brother's name. "I don't need to see it. I don't really understand the legal jargon, and I trust our family's lawyer to look it over and let me know if I should sign."

I frown at her. "But this is your life, Mel, you should know what you're agreeing to."

"I do know. I'm marrying you. We're going to have two kids,

or we're going to try to, anyway. That's the only part I'm concerned about."

I run my tongue over my teeth. "This is for your protection as well as mine."

"What do I need protecting from?" She snorts a laugh. "I have nothing to offer other than what's sitting right in front of you."

And that is all I fucking want.

"So I have nothing to lose," she adds.

"This details how the custody arrangement would look if we divorce after we have children. How you and our children would be provided for."

She sits up straight. "But why would we get divorced? If this is a business arrangement like you say it is, why would that change?"

Is she really this naive? "Nobody knows what the future holds. I doubt many people go into marriage planning for a divorce, but we don't know how this thing is going to turn out. This is just like an insurance policy."

She licks her lips, her eyes darting between the papers and my face. "I want this to work out, Nathan."

"So do I, Mel. Let me talk you through the papers, then we can go get some dinner."

She looks down at her navy scrubs. "I'm not really dressed for one of your fancy restaurants."

She looks effortlessly stunning in anything she wears, and I would take her anywhere she wanted right now, but I don't say that. "Then we'll go somewhere unfancy then."

Her smile reappears, and whatever worries that were triggered by the prenup seem to have been appeased for now. We go through the document together. She'll get alimony if we separate, but it's not generous by any stretch. She doesn't get a claim to my penthouse, my business, or anything else, no matter how many kids we have or how long we're together, and she doesn't question any of it. I read through the morality clause that was added by her lawyer one more time—if she cheats, she doesn't get alimony, and if I cheat, I'll owe her fifty million dollars. Satisfied with the verbiage and the knowledge that I'm no cheat—never had to be and never will—I sign next to my name and watch as she does the same.

~

MEL TAKES a huge bite from her first slice of pepperoni pizza and licks the grease from her chin before flashing me a wicked grin that travels straight to my dick. Fuck me. It's been a while since I've gone so long without sex, and that must be the reason I'm constantly horny. But I swear this woman could make getting an enema look sexy. Now that I think about it ...

"I guess this isn't the type of place you usually eat?" she says, interrupting my thoughts about her ass.

I glance around the pizza place. "Actually my brother loves coming here so I've been a few times before."

Her eyebrows shoot up. "Really? Which brother? Not Elijah?"

I shake my head. "No. He's more a steak and fine wine kind of guy. Mason."

"Oh. You have four brothers, right? I'm looking forward to meeting them. Are they all as nice as Elijah?"

I wipe my chin with a napkin, unable to suppress my smirk.

"What?" she asks.

"Nice isn't usually the first word people use to describe him, that's all. He's not usually so ..." I search for the right word. "Pleasant."

The spot between her brows pinches in a cute-as-fuck frown. "He was lovely."

"Yeah, you seem to have made quite the impression on him."

She leans forward, her green eyes sparkling with mischief. "I guess I'm just wildly charismatic." She licks her lips again, and I have a vision of that tongue licking something else. "Some might say irresistible?"

Yes, you fucking are. "Don't push it, Spitfire," I say instead, and she rewards me with a sweet laugh that's like a punch to my gut. Why the hell do I have this much fun just sitting here talking to her?

"You mentioned you had some thoughts on the wedding." She expertly changes the subject before helping herself to another slice of pizza.

"Yeah, I'm thinking Saturday, the third, at my family home. No press in attendance, but my father will put out a full press release the next day."

She frowns again. "The third of next month?"

"Yeah. That gives you two weeks to move your things. I have a company that can take care of that discreetly if you want to get a jump on it beforehand."

"That would be great. It's just ..." She bites her bottom lip. "My mom and Bryce will be there, no matter the date. But there are only two people I really care about being there, and that's my sister and my cousin. It's just that Tyler's traveling for work, and I don't think his schedule will allow him to get back here."

I don't dare unpack what the hell that means about her relationship with her mom and brother. Not when we're having such a pleasant evening. "I just figured the sooner we do this, the better. I'm happy to give you your six months." I almost choke on those words because the idea of waiting another six months to fuck her is unthinkable right now. But six months to start trying for a baby doesn't have to mean six months to have sex. At least I hope it doesn't. "But I want this part done as soon as possible."

"I do too. But Tyler has been there for every important moment of my life."

"And he still will be. This is just the signing of another contract, Mel. It's not that big of a deal. Elijah won't even be there. Nor will my youngest brother, Maddox. The wedding is merely a formality."

I hate the look of hurt that flashes over her face. Fuck, I really could have worded that better. But it's the cold hard truth. This is a business arrangement. And like Elijah said, the fact that we get along and seem to find each other attractive is a major bonus. Our sex life should be decent at least, and that's a big part of the reason I agreed to the morality clause. I also believe that if a spouse cheats, the injured party should be compensated in some way.

But our mutual attraction and friendly conversations don't make this anything more than what it is. I don't do love and romance. Never have, never will.

Still, I find myself reaching for her hand and gently squeezing it. "Hey. I want to do this with you, Mel. But the wedding is only the starting point. What matters is what happens after, right?"

"Ty always says the bigger and fancier the wedding, the more miserable the marriage." She lets out a nervous laugh.

I think back to the over-the-top, grand affair that was Elijah and Amber's wedding, compared to my parents getting married in a tiny church in Valencia with six guests, and I couldn't agree more. "Seems like this Tyler is a smart guy."

Her eyes light up. "He is. He's my favorite person in the world. I can't wait for you to meet him."

I grunt a response, irrationally pissed that some other guy is her favorite person in the world. I guess she can read me better than I thought because she laughs again, louder this time. "You do understand he's my cousin and he's gay?"

"I didn't say anything," I insist.

Her eyes spark with defiance, and Jesus fuck, I want to put her over my knee right here at this table and spank her ass. "Course you didn't, Ice."

I roll my eyes. "Eat your pizza, Spitfire."

CHAPTER
SEVENTEEN

MELANIE

I watch my sister curl a lock of my hair between her fingers in the mirror, and we both stare at my reflection. Her green eyes, so similar to mine, twinkle with happiness. "You look so pretty, Mel."

I blow out a breath and glance down at my simple cream dress. "Thanks, Ash."

She takes a sip of her champagne and giggles. "And Nathan is so handsome."

"He is," I admit.

"His brothers too." She wraps an arm around my waist and rests her head on my shoulder. "Dad would be so proud to walk you down the aisle, you know?"

I place my hand over hers and smile at the image of my father in his tux that I conjure in my mind's eye. I haven't told my sister about the contract between Nathan and me. As far as she's concerned, we had a whirlwind romance and couldn't wait another day to get married. I couldn't burden her with the knowledge that our family business is in so much trouble.

Perhaps I baby her, but I love her so much, and she deserves all the opportunities our father would have wanted for her.

"Are you sad Ty's not here?" she asks, breaking my train of thought.

I shove aside a twinge of sorrow and keep my tone bright. "Yeah, but I'll see him in a few weeks. And you're videoing the whole thing to send him, right?"

"Of course." She rolls her eyes. "I'll never hear the end of it if I don't."

I laugh, but she doesn't join in. Instead she spins me around to face her. "Do you love him, Mel?"

"Yes." I lie with ease. Or perhaps I'm not lying. I know that I could love him if I let myself fall.

Her brow furrows. "Just know that you don't have to do anything you don't want. You're the best person I know, and nothing you do could change how much I love you."

I blink at her. Does my baby sister suspect that this isn't the fairytale I've tried to portray? Of course she does. She knows me and she isn't stupid. I take her hand in mine. "I do want to do this, Ash."

"You're sure?"

"Yes." I nod, and I realize I'm not lying this time. "And I love you too."

She downs the last of her champagne and wraps me in a hug. "I'm gonna need to hold on to you for at least another five minutes before we go out there and you become Mrs. Nathan James."

"I'll always be your Mel."

"Always, sis."

DALTON JAMES HANDS me a glass of Scotch as he sidles up beside me. "Here, you look like you could use one of these."

I offer him a grateful smile. "I sure could. Thanks."

"There's no need to be nervous. Nathan is a good man. He'll take care of you, and you two will have fine babies."

I look up into my soon-to-be father-in-law's gray eyes. There's a hint of sadness in them, but they're kind too. And suddenly there's a lump in my throat. "I wish my dad was here."

He nods stiffly and takes a sip of his Scotch. "Your father was a good man, Miss Edison."

"Please call me Mel," I insist.

He nods. "He would be proud of you, Mel."

Tears prick at my eyes. I'm not convinced that's true. What would he think of me marrying Nathan just to secure the success of the business and protect Ashley's future? Despite my intentions, I'm sure he'd try to talk me out of it. I can almost hear him: *Don't make the same mistakes I did, baby girl. Life is too short not to fall in love.*

"Welcome to the family, Mel," Dalton says, raising his glass in a toast.

"Thank you." I down the Scotch in one gulp, wincing as it burns my esophagus.

I can see Bryce approaching, and I roll back my shoulders. "Would you mind escorting me to my spot, Mr. James?" I ask before my brother can attempt to take that honor. Not that this is really walking down the aisle, but it's as close as I'll ever get.

"Now, if I have to call you Mel, then you gotta call me Dalton," he says, his eyes twinkling. Then he takes my glass and places it next to his on a nearby table. "And the pleasure would be all mine." He holds out his arm and I link mine through his.

Together, we make our way to the small archway in the garden outside Nathan's family home, where the official stands with my husband-to-be. Nathan is wearing a black tux, and I've never seen him look more handsome. An unexpected twinge of regret niggles at me, a wish that this was real. I wish he was actually mine.

I push those ridiculous thoughts to the back of my mind and fix a smile on my face. Nathan catches my eye and winks at me, and I remember why I'm doing this. He's a good man. We'll have a nice life. And even if we aren't soulmates, I'm sure we'll be lovers and good friends. And that's more than a lot of people get, right?

"Have I told you that dress looks amazing on you, Mrs. James?" Nathan hands me another glass of Scotch. Between his father and his brothers slipping them into my hand every ten minutes, I'm starting to feel woozy.

I look down at my cream silk gown. "Thank you."

He slips an arm around my waist and pulls me closer. "And I wanted to let you know that you've been incredible today. I know this wasn't the wedding you dreamed of, but we can make it a successful marriage."

Successful? What does that even mean? I want more than successful, but I swallow that thought down with a mouthful of Scotch.

He presses his lips to my ear, and his warm breath makes me shiver. "You think we should put some music on in here or something?"

I glance over the small gathering that consists of Nathan's dad, two of his brothers, Bryce, my mother, and Ashley. Not exactly party central.

I snort. "I'm not sure even music could liven up this party."

His lips move closer until he's almost nuzzling my neck. "Not even 'Yeah' by Usher?"

A laugh bubbles out of me. "You play that, Mr. James, and I'm filing for divorce."

His eyes darken as they lock on mine. "Actually I don't think I'll ever be able to hear that song again without being eaten up by jealousy."

I roll my eyes. "Stop teasing me."

"I'm not teasing. You're mine now, and that means all of you. I'll give you your six months, but then all bets are off." His voice is deep and low, and it rolls through my bones.

My heart stutters in my chest, but before I can remind him that the six months only relates to baby making, Ashley grabs my arm. "This house is incredible, Mel," she says excitedly. "Mason just gave me the tour. Please tell me we can spend the holidays here."

Nathan steps back, and my sister wraps her arm around me, giving me a tight squeeze. "I don't know, it depends on ..." I look to Nathan for an answer.

His eyes are still burning into mine. "We can spend the holidays here, if that's what you want."

Ashley squeals, and I'm glad my glass is almost empty when she jumps up and down while holding onto me. "I already picked out my room. Come on, let me show you." I offer my husband an apologetic shrug as she drags me away, and I swear I can still feel his eyes boring into me even when my back is turned.

CHAPTER
EIGHTEEN

NATHAN

D rake wraps an arm around my shoulder. "I think you need to take your wife home, brother."

I glance at Mel, who's wearing a grin while watching her sister carry on what looks to be an animated—if a bit one-sided—conversation with Mason.

I wince. Why am I so fucking nervous about being alone with her? Because I have no idea how to play this. We should have had sex before tonight and taken the pressure off, then this would be a whole lot less awkward. But this entire situation has been far outside my comfort zone. I've done my best to be respectful of her wishes to wait until after we got married, but now it's our wedding night and I want to consummate our marriage more than I've ever wanted anything. And given the way she was rubbing up against me earlier, I think she does too.

Drake slips away to talk to our father, and I watch my wife for a few moments. She laughs at something Mason says, and fuck me, but she looks so damn beautiful. Then her expression changes on a dime, and her gorgeous smile disappears. When I look to find the source of her mood change, I see Bryce closing in on her. She visibly bristles when he pulls up a chair beside her. What the fuck is their deal?

I march over to her. "Mel, it's time to go home."

She blinks up at me, her eyes full of trust and longing—either that or she's completely tanked. Or maybe I am. But I reach for her hand, and she curls her slender fingers around mine. After giving her sister a sideways hug and a kiss, she says goodnight to Mason, and with barely a nod to her own brother, she stands and allows me to pull her against me. I slide an arm around her waist, and her body molds into mine like it was made to fit there.

"Will you look after Ashley?" I ask Mason. The girl looks no more comfortable with her older brother than Mel did.

Bryce snorts, but he's too wasted to argue. I guess the half-dozen bottles of Scotch my father laid out for today got put to good use.

"Course I will." Mason gives me a reassuring nod.

Teddy's waiting outside by the car, and Mel cheers when she sees him. "Tedward!"

He beams at her, and I can't blame him. Her joy is fucking infectious. "Mrs. James," he says with a polite nod before he opens the rear passenger-side door.

Holding a hand to her mouth, she snickers. "Mrs. James."

"That is your name." I lightly swat her on the ass. "Now get in the damn car."

MEL SNUGGLES into me the entire ride home, her head tucked into the crook of my shoulder and her legs curled up on the seat. I try to stop peering down her dress and staring at her amazing tits, to stop fantasizing about biting into them like ripe, juicy apples, but I fail miserably. By the time we get back to

99

the penthouse, I'm harder than stone and so desperate to fuck her that I can barely think straight.

But one look at her face when the car rolls to a stop tells me she's way too drunk for anything like that. Teddy opens the car door, and I climb out, beckoning her to follow. She just smiles at me.

With a grumbled curse, I scoop her into my arms and carry her bridal style to the elevator, which I suppose is only fitting.

"You're so romantic," she says, her voice a soft purr.

"I am not. You're just too drunk to walk, Mrs. James."

Sighing, she rests her head on my chest. "I like the sound of that name."

Yeah, so do I. I rest my lips on the top of her head, inhaling the now familiar scent of her shampoo, and carry her to bed. Not to mine, as much as I'd like to, but to her own room. The one she picked out and the place she'll sleep every night. The realization that she won't be sleeping with me makes a lump form in my throat, but I swallow it down.

When I lay her on the bed, she flutters her dark eyelashes and wraps her arms around my neck. "It's our wedding night, Mr. James."

"I'm well aware of that."

"So ..." She sinks her teeth into her luscious bottom lip, and I have to close my eyes to stop myself from doing the same. "Aren't we supposed to do something? Isn't it true that a marriage isn't legal until it's consummated?"

I open my eyes and roll them at her. "Not exactly, Spitfire."

"I think it is, Ice."

"You're way too drunk to consummate anything."

"Am not!" She juts out her bottom lip, but then she scrunches her face and groans. "But your brothers and your dad and all that whisky."

"Yeah, I know. If I'd known you couldn't handle your liquor, I would have told them to take it easy on you."

She snorts. "I can drink you under the table, Iceman."

I press a kiss on her forehead and unwrap her arms from around my neck. "Yeah, sure."

She blinks at me, her eyes brimming with sadness. "I'm really not that drunk."

"Way too drunk for my liking, sweetheart." I brush a lock of hair from her forehead.

"I'm not too wasted to know what I want. I can give my consent."

I swallow hard. Holy Mother of God, give me strength. "Call me old-fashioned, but I'd prefer you remember our first time."

She hums and bites down on that lip again. My cock twitches, trying to break through the zipper of my tuxedo pants. I need to get the fuck out of here.

"Can I at least kiss you?"

I close my eyes and stifle a groan. "Sure."

She giggles. "There are three of you. Which one should I kiss?"

I sigh. "The middle one, Spitfire."

She pushes herself up to her elbows and presses a soft kiss on my lips. Her taste is all Scotch and sweetness and sin, and I'm desperate to slide my tongue inside her mouth and kiss her properly. Aching to take what's mine. But I pull back, leaving her gasping and me leaking precum into my boxers.

"Can you at least stay until I fall asleep?" she whispers, nestling into her pillow.

Fucking hell. I'm gonna need the patience of a goddamn saint tonight. With a groan, I fall into bed beside her and roll onto my back. Snuggling against me, she rests her head on my chest and murmurs, "Goodnight, husband."

"Night, Mel." I choke out the words while my cock throbs

painfully in my pants. It doesn't take long for her to fall asleep, and as easy as it would be to let myself doze off right beside her, I roll her off me. She mumbles a sleepy protest, but she doesn't wake.

I crawl off the bed and stare at her for a few moments. Her chest rises and falls to a steady rhythm, and the contented smile on her face has me smiling back. I contemplate taking her dress off so she'll be more comfortable, but I don't trust myself to have my hands on her when I'm this hungry to fuck her.

That's exactly why I can't stay. If I do, I will definitely wake her in the night and convince her to let me bury myself inside her. And that contented look on her face right now, the one she never seems to have when she's around her brother, lets me know that she trusts me. Whether she has reason to or not, she does. And to my surprise, that's worth more to me than the brief, albeit sweet, relief—not to mention immense pleasure—that would come from sliding inside her.

With one more glance at her sleeping form, I switch off the light and head to my own room, resigned to spend the night tossing and turning to visions of her coming undone beneath me.

CHAPTER
NINETEEN

MELANIE

Nathan is fastening his cufflinks when I walk into the kitchen.

I blink at him. "Are you working today? It's Sunday." *And also the day after our wedding.*

He nods. "I got a call from the police station. A new case."

"So, you're going to get him out?" I assume it's a guy, anyway.

He winks at me. "Wouldn't be a very good lawyer if I didn't."

I shift from one foot to the other, feeling incredibly awkward. Snapshots of last night flicker through my head. Me with my arms around his neck, asking him to ... My cheeks flush with heat. "What did he do?"

"Something that got him arrested," he says cryptically, before pulling on his suit jacket.

I rub my throbbing temples, and he shoots me a sympathetic look. "There's fresh coffee in the pot and Tylenol in the cupboard above it."

"Thanks. I'm sorry I got so drunk."

He huffs a laugh. "There's no need to apologize. My brothers are pretty forceful with the Scotch."

"Yeah." The memory alone is enough to make my esophagus burn, and I rub at my raw throat. "What time will you be back?"

He shrugs. "Hard to say. Depends on what's waiting for me when I get to the station."

Regret punches me in the gut. Is this what my life is going to be like now? Me alone in this giant penthouse while he works? I guess I should have known that it would be. It's not like we're a real couple. He wouldn't even have sex with me on our wedding night.

"Why don't you hang out with your sister?" he suggests.

"Her flight was at eight. She has to get back to Boston this afternoon."

He sucks on his top lip. "Hopefully, I won't be too long and we can grab an early dinner."

My enthusiastic nod comes embarrassingly fast, and I want to kick myself for being so eager.

But if he notices my enthusiasm, he doesn't pass comment or react at all. With a single nod in my direction, he's gone.

See ya later, Ice.

I GLANCE at the clock again, like it will somehow be earlier than when I checked a few minutes ago and not almost 9:00 p.m. Nathan still isn't home, and maybe if it weren't so late, I wouldn't feel like a complete fool for sitting around this penthouse all day like a good little wife, waiting for him to take me to dinner.

The headache I've been suffering from off and on all day

104

makes a reappearance. Damn Nathan. He could have at least called or sent a text. Although I guess it's my own fault. He's been perfectly clear from day one what this is between us. And just because he can be charming and sexy when he wants to be, that doesn't change our arrangement.

I scroll through channels on the TV until I find a cheesy eighties movie. Exactly the kind of movie Tyler and I love to watch. I lie on the sofa, head snuggled into the cushions, and try to forget about Nathan and what a huge mistake I might have made.

"Hey, sleeping beauty," Nathan's deep, soothing voice rouses me from sleep, and I wake to find him standing over me.

"What time is it?" I rub my eyes and sit up.

"A little before midnight."

I blink at him. "So where the hell have you been?"

His handsome face furrows in a scowl. "Working."

I scoff. "Until midnight?"

"Yes, Mel. I'm sorry if my working hours don't fit your schedule."

I jump to my feet and tilt my chin up. "And I'm sorry that you'd rather spend your time with some criminal than take your wife to dinner the day after our wedding," I yell.

His entire expression darkens. "Are you fucking kidding me? You knew what my job was about. And this"—he waves a hand between us—"doesn't come before that. I've had a fucker of a day, and I don't need to come home to you bitching at me about not being here."

Tears sting my eyes, but I refuse to give him the satisfaction of seeing me cry. "I'll remember my place in the future, sir."

I spin on my heel to walk away, but he grabs my wrist and spins me back to face him, bringing my body flush against his.

His body heat penetrates the thin fabric of my dress, and my heart races.

He snarls. "Don't with the smart fucking mouth, Mel. Not tonight."

We glare at each other, both our chests heaving. He closes his eyes, his nostrils flaring as he inhales a breath.

With him no longer staring at me, the connection breaks, and I wrench my arm from his grip. "Don't worry. You won't hear from my smart mouth again."

I walk away, and this time he doesn't grab me back, but he calls after me. "Mel!"

Without turning around, I snap, "I'm going to bed."

CHAPTER
TWENTY

NATHAN

Jesus fucking Christ, I'm such an asshole. Today was a giant bowl of dogshit served with a side of ass, but that doesn't give me an excuse to treat her that way. Especially not after I forgot about our dinner plans. And even worse, I forgot to take two minutes from my day to let her know I'd be back so late. And now she's pissed at me, and I feel like a dick for yelling at her the way I did.

The truth is I like her smart mouth, but when I came home to find her asleep on the couch, all my frustration melted away. She looked so peaceful, so beautiful. And then I woke her up, and well ... Fuck. It all went to hell again from there.

Rubbing a hand through my hair, I sigh and head down the hallway after her. I knock on her door, but she doesn't answer. "I'm coming in, Mel, so if you're naked in there, you have about five seconds to stop me or put some clothes on."

I count to five, and when I don't hear from her, I push open the door. She's lying on the bed, the soft glow of the bedside lamp illuminating her face.

She sniffs. "What the hell do you want?"

I sit sideways on the foot of the bed so I'm facing her. "You think we could try this again?"

Her only response is a snort.

"Hey, honey, I'm home." I swear the corners of her lips twitch. "I'm sorry I didn't make it home for dinner. I'm even sorrier that I didn't call or text you. And I have no excuse other than I'm not used to having to tell anyone where I am or what I'm doing."

"That's not—"

"I already said it wasn't an excuse, Spitfire." I nudge her foot with my hand. "I also had a hell of a day, and when I saw you lying there, I ..." I swallow, because she doesn't need to know how I felt. And she's too pissed at me to hear me, anyway.

She rubs her foot on my hip. "You what?"

I crawl up the bed and lie next to her, thankful for the opportunity to lie down. "I forgot about dinner, Mel. I'm sorry. When I'm working, especially on days like today, I forget about everything but the job. But I understand that I'm not an island anymore, and I will try to do better."

She shifts onto her side, her lashes wet with unshed tears as she blinks at me. "You said that when you saw me lying there, but then you didn't finish your sentence."

I swallow. "I was relieved to have someone I could talk to after my shitty day. But then you reamed me out for doing my job and ... I guess not everyone understands what I do."

She places her hand on my chest, right over my heart. "I'm sorry, Nathan. I want to understand though. Help me to understand."

I let out a sigh. "I'm tired."

"Then just tell me about your shitty day. Please."

I lace my fingers through hers and press a kiss on her knuckles. I can't tell her the details of the guy who's been arrested for murder after some piece of shit raped his sixteen-year-old daughter so violently that she'll never be able to have children. How I spent most of my night trying to find her somewhere safe to stay because I can't get her dad out of custody until he's arraigned tomorrow. And I can't tell her how guilty I felt leaving him behind bars for the night. And maybe the story I'm about to tell her isn't mine to tell either, but it won't get me disbarred, and it had such a profound impact on my life that it feels like it's part mine.

I take a deep breath. "My father was furious when I told him I didn't want to go into the family business, but I've wanted to be a lawyer for as long as I can remember, and I couldn't see myself doing anything else. So I appeased him by going into corporate law, and I enjoyed it."

Pausing, I look at her. She motions for me to continue.

"After our mom died, Maddox got himself a girlfriend. Yasmin. My father hated her. She had bright purple hair and a lip ring. She was from a poor neighborhood, and he was convinced she was a bad influence on his son. The two of them were constantly getting into trouble, but they were sixteen. It was probably just normal teenage rebellion, but the more my father told Maddox she was bad news, the more he pushed the two of them together."

Mel gives a knowing nod. "Teenagers, huh?"

I nod. "They weren't great together. They broke up every couple of weeks, but it was like they were addicted to each other. I guess she was good for him in some ways though. She helped him through one of the hardest times of his life. But this one night, he took her to a party some of his football buddies were throwing. Being a football star, he always hung out with an older crowd, and there was beer and weed. Yasmin kissed some guy, and she and Mad had a huge fight. She told him to leave, so he did ..."

The heaviness of the memory threatens to crush me, and I let out a deep sigh. Mel keeps her hand on my chest and continues listening patiently. "That night three guys at the party raped her. She was in really rough shape."

Mel gasps, and her eyes fill with tears. "Oh, that poor girl."

"Mad blamed himself. He went with her when she went to the cops and pressed charges. Our dad offered to pay for an investigator. He'd heard rumors that Yasmin wasn't the first girl this had happened to. But Yasmin's dad was a proud man. As far as he was concerned, we were no better than the rich pricks who'd violated his baby girl. Mad even offered to pay, and I guess Yasmin would have let him, but her dad insisted she not take a penny of his money."

I pinch the bridge of my nose and suck in a breath. "They had hotshot lawyers, of course, who did their best to not even let it get to trial, but she ..." A lump wells in my throat, and I have to swallow before I can continue. "She was so fucking brave. And they eviscerated her on the stand. I went with Mad every day, and she sat there like a warrior while they fucking picked her apart."

Mel sniffs, wiping her cheeks with the back of her hand.

"The prosecutor did a fucking terrible job. The entire investigation was so goddamn inept, I suspect he was paid off. Or he was a misogynistic prick who subscribed to the whole 'she was asking for it' rhetoric that's still way too prevalent in our justice system."

"That's so wrong," Mel whispers.

I lick my lips, and the weight of all the guilt and shame of how we all let her down washes over me in a wave, threatening to pull me under. "She killed herself before the trial was over."

Mel lets out a loud sob. "Oh, Nathan."

"They were acquitted and ..." I press my lips together and stare at the ceiling.

"And then what happened? Where are they now?"

"Dead. Yasmin's dad shot two of them the day after they were acquitted. All he did was try to get some justice for his baby girl, and the DA went after him way harder than he did the three guys who raped an innocent teenager. I begged him to let me defend him. Even though I was in corporate law, I knew enough to do a better job than what I'd seen done for his daughter, but he refused. He's serving two life sentences now. After that I switched to criminal law. I wanted to even the playing field for people like Yasmin's dad."

"But I thought you only represented rich people? How is that balancing the playing field?"

I frown at her.

"I'm not trying to be an asshole. You're like the best criminal defense lawyer in the country. How can someone with no money afford you?"

"I'm fortunate enough that my defense clients pay me well enough that I can take on more pro bono cases than most without relying on my father's fortune to subsidize our firm. There are cops at every station in the city who know me and the type of work I like to take on, so they call me when they get a case like today's."

"So did he do it? The guy whose case you took on today?"

"It doesn't matter to me."

Her brow pinches in a frown.

"The world isn't black and white, Mel. No such thing as inherently good or unequivocally bad. I might respect the law because it's my job, but the law and justice are often two very different things. What if it was Yasmin's dad? And her family who needed looking after today?"

She rolls her lips together before offering me a single nod. "Then I'd say it doesn't matter to me either. You're doing the right thing."

I close my eyes and finally let the weight of the day leave me.

"I'm sorry I didn't give you a chance to explain."

"Don't be. I enjoy coming home to be reamed by my pint-sized siren."

She laughs softly, and her breath dusts over my cheek. "I guess we both need to figure out how to fit into each other's lives without driving each other crazy, huh?"

"It's only our first day, and look at us now. I think we're doing pretty good."

"Yeah." She closes her eyes, her hand still on my chest. "What happened to the third guy? If her dad only shot two of them?"

I swallow. "He died a short time later." I don't tell her that he was murdered, or how, because that's definitely not my story to tell, and thankfully she seems too tired to ask. A few moments later, her breathing evens out and she's asleep again. Instead of getting up and going to my own room, I watch her sleep. And that's all I do for the next several hours—watch her chest rise and listen to her soft breaths in the quiet room, and I've never felt closer to anyone before in my life.

TWENTY-ONE

MELANIE

It's been a little over two weeks since our wedding, and despite our shaky start, we've settled into something of a routine. Nathan's working hours are pretty much the same as mine, so he and Tedward drop me at work most mornings and often pick me up after. We flirt, and electricity sizzles beneath my skin every time our hands or arms brush. I constantly wonder whether I should just go for it and kiss him, but I always stop myself just in time. I'm sure he must feel the sexual tension simmering between us too—at least I hope it's not all one-sided. But if he does, he still behaves like the perfect gentleman.

Tonight, Nathan's driver picked me up alone after work, and the smell of garlic and tomatoes greets me when I walk inside the penthouse, making my mouth water. I head to the kitchen to find Nathan standing at the stove, dressed in gray sweats and nothing else. Now my mouth is watering for an entirely different reason, and I take a moment to drink him in.

I could tell from the way he fills out his designer suits and shirts and the feel of his solid chest beneath those clothes that he had a good body. But in the flesh ... Damn. And I only have a view of his back. Muscles ripple across his broad shoulders as he stirs something in the pot.

By some miracle, I let go of the doorframe and don't fall over. "You're home early," I say in a breezy tone, despite the way my legs are shaking.

He spins around, and I grab onto the counter for support. Those sexy gray sweats hang low on his hips, revealing a set of chiseled abs beneath his defined chest. I allow my gaze to drift lower—to the area which gray sweatpants were specifically designed to accentuate, and nobody will ever convince me otherwise. Yeah, just as I suspected, he has a huge appendage.

I quickly avert my attention to his face, but I'm not quick enough. He smirks at me, his dark eyes flashing. Dammit.

Fortunately, he's too much of a gentleman to point out the fact that I was very clearly just eye-fucking him. "My trial finished early, so I decided to cook dinner."

"It smells delicious. What are we having?"

"Paprika chicken and patatas bravas."

I lift my eyebrows. "Sounds fancy *and* delicious."

He shrugs, turning back to the stove. "It was a recipe of my mom's."

"She was Spanish, right?"

"Sí. My father met her in Valencia."

I perch myself on a stool and watch him cook, noting how at ease he seems in the kitchen. "Do you speak Spanish?"

"Sí, señora. Pero solo cuando estoy enojado ..." He winks at me.

Wow. Does he have to be so perfect at everything? "I have no idea what you just said, but it sounded hot."

His laugh is comforting but sexy, and heat blooms in my chest. "I said. Yes, but only when I'm mad or ..."

"Or?" I press my lips together.

He glances over his shoulder. "I'm sure you'll figure it out soon enough." His growly tone makes my core contract with need. I can't help but wonder what he didn't say and whether that has anything to do with the sudden spike in sexual tension in the room.

"You're in a very good mood, Mr. James. Did you win your trial?"

He remains focused on the food. "I always win, Spitfire."

I roll my eyes. "Of course you do."

THE HEAVENLY FLAVORS OF GARLIC, tomatoes, and paprika burst across my tongue as I savor the first mouthful of potato. I'm pretty sure I moan when the hint of spice kicks in. "This is absolutely incredible."

Nathan offers me his usual half smile in response.

I pop another cube of potato into my mouth and chew. "Are you just naturally good at everything you do?"

He arches an eyebrow at me, and I feel the flush creep over my cheeks. "I guess you'll have to wait and see, Spitfire."

Holy fuck. I'm not sure how much longer I can put up with the constant flirting before I end up throwing myself at him. "I mean you're an amazing cook," I add, trying to keep the conversation about the delicious food.

"My mom taught all of us boys to cook. She said it was an important life skill."

"Mmhmm, she's not wrong. How old were you when she died?"

A muscle in his jaw ticks. "Twenty-six."

"I'm sorry. It sucks to lose a parent."

He nods his agreement and tops up our wine glasses. "You were thirteen when your dad was killed?"

I swallow down a knot of guilt and sadness. "Yeah."

"That must have been rough on you all."

"It was. Ash was only three, so she doesn't even remember him. At least I have lots of memories, although sometimes I wonder if that makes it harder, you know?"

"I do."

"But if I had to choose, I'd rather have the memories and the pain of losing him than not remember him at all. I feel bad for Ash that she'll never have that."

He takes a sip of his wine and eyes me over the rim of the glass. "Is that why you're so protective of her?"

His question blindsides me. "I don't think I'm overly protective of her. She's my baby sister." I hear the defensiveness in my tone, but he's touched a nerve. I don't want to think about my overcomplicated relationship with my family right now. Or ever, if I can help it.

His eyes narrow, and he sets down his glass. "It's not a criticism, Mel. But when I asked you why you were marrying me, one of your reasons was you wouldn't have to worry about your sister. I get the sense you've always been the one to look out for her, that's all."

I stare into his deep brown eyes and wonder how a man who's known me for such a short time can understand me better than my own family—with the exception of Tyler. "I guess. My mom was never really hands-on. It was always my dad who was good with the parenting stuff. And then after he died, she kind of fell to pieces, and Bryce—" I swallow the lump in my throat. "I guess he took over for Dad in her eyes, and what little love she had in her heart, she reserved only for him. It felt like it was me and Ash in our own little world a lot of the time."

He nods, his jaw ticking, and I wonder what's going through his mind.

"So yeah, I guess I'm overprotective of her because there was no one else around to keep her safe."

"And who protected you, Mel?"

I frown. "I didn't need protecting like she did. She was a baby."

"You were only thirteen. Still a child yourself."

I'm blown away by his insightfulness. I feel like he can see me in a way nobody else can. "I don't know. Tyler when he was around, I guess. We were both kids, but we looked after each other. His mom was our dad's sister. She was never around much, and he practically lived at our house, but Bryce stopped him from visiting after Dad died. He's never really liked him."

Nathan's expression darkens. "So you lost your dad and your best friend around the same time?"

"I still saw him every day at school, but yeah, I guess I kinda did."

He tilts his head, and his eyes burn into mine. "I guess now I know how you became such a spitfire."

Regret and loneliness overwhelm me at the memory of my teenage years. Being stuck in that house with Mom and Bryce, feeling invisible and alone. It's no wonder I fell head over heels with the first guy who showed me anything akin to kindness when I went to college. But those memories are even more painful, and I almost choke on their bitter aftertaste. "It must have been fun growing up with four brothers," I say, desperate to change the subject.

He gives me another half smile. "You could call it that. I'd call it chaos."

"You're close to all of them though?"

He nods.

"Even Maddox?" I know he hasn't seen him for a long time, and after what he told me, I haven't pressed for more details on why his youngest brother left.

Sorrow washes over his face, but it fades as quickly as it appeared. "Yes. Especially him."

"I hope to get to meet him some day."

He nods, but that quiet grief returns to his eyes. "I'm sure you will."

WITH THE DINNER dishes washed and dried, I lean against the kitchen counter and watch Nathan put them away. His strong forearms and the powerful muscles in his shoulders flex as he moves deftly around the kitchen. I lazily drink him in, no longer attempting to hide it. If he's going to walk around this penthouse shirtless with the body of a demigod, he brings it all on himself. And it's not like I don't see the way he looks at me. The way his eyes darken when I'm wearing anything remotely fitted, and the way his gaze lingers on my ass and boobs when he thinks I'm not looking.

When he's done, he walks over to me with that sexy-as-hell half grin on his face. "You enjoying yourself there, Spitfire?"

I sigh. "I mean, I was."

He gives a single shake of his head and takes another step forward until our bodies are tantalizingly close and his eyes are locked on mine. "Looking at me the way that you do is going to get you into a whole mess of trouble someday, Mel." His voice is low and husky, and it melts me to my core.

I tilt my head to the side, my gaze remaining fixed on his face even as his rakes up and down my body. "Maybe I could use a little trouble."

He sinks his teeth into his bottom lip and tips his head back on a groan. When he looks at me again, his eyes are blazing with so much fire that my breath stutters in my throat. He bends his head, his lips dangerously close to my ear. "I bet you could use so much more than a little trouble, Spitfire."

He slides one hand to my hip, his fingers digging into my flesh in a bruising grip. A shiver of anticipation runs the length of my spine. I place a hand on his chest, my fingertips flexing over his solid pecs. His lips brush mine, and I whimper, acutely aware of the ache between my thighs at the mere memory of this man's kiss.

He takes a half step closer, and our bodies are flush. Heat coils in every cell of my body. His breath is warm and heavy on my lips as he continues taunting me with the promise of his kiss. I tangle my fingers in his hair. He grunts and rocks his hips, pressing every solid inch of himself against my abdomen.

I gasp.

"You feel what you do to me?" he groans.

I jolt when vibrations shudder through my hip. With a grumbled curse, he looks down, breaking the spell between us as he fishes his phone from his pocket.

He holds it to his ear, his hand still on my hip and his impressive erection still pressed against me. "What?" he barks.

I can hear the muffled voice on the other line but can't make out what they're saying.

"Right now?" Nathan sighs. "Then have the jet ready."

He ends the call and lets out of a string of curses. "I really have to go."

"Right now?"

He licks his bottom lip. "Believe me when I tell you that I know this is the worst timing in the history of the world, but I've been expecting that call for weeks. I'm—"

"Don't say you're sorry. This is your job." I step back, taking some much-needed air and space from his dizzyingly impressive erection.

His grip tightens on my hip, and he yanks me back so our chests collide. "Don't."

"Don't what?"

His expression is pained. "Don't pull away from me."

So many emotions shuttle around my body, and I don't know how to process them all at once. What I do know is that I need to get the hell away from him before I lose myself. I suspect that once we cross this line, I will fall for him completely. And I'm going to fall hard. "You're the one who's leaving, Nathan."

His jaw ticks, and I hold my breath. *Oh, fuck it! Just kiss me and tell me you'll be back soon.* He does neither. He takes a step back. "I'll be gone for a few days. Will you be okay here alone?"

I draw in a shaky breath. "I'll be fine."

Clearing his throat, he takes another step away from me, putting enough distance between us that I can no longer smell his cologne or feel the heat from his body. "Well, this is your home now. If you want to invite some friends over, you don't need my permission." He scrubs a hand through his hair. "I probably won't be reachable, so if you need anything, Teddy will take care of it."

A knot of sadness wells in my throat, and tears sting my eyes. Why do I feel so rejected by a man I just pushed away? Because he didn't pull me back. He'll never need me enough to pull me back. "When will you be home?" I ask, in spite of myself.

He shakes his head. "I don't know. A few days. I have to go pack."

Then he walks out of the kitchen, leaving me aching and needy, and most of all, feeling invisible and alone.

CHAPTER
TWENTY-TWO

NATHAN

My fingers twitch against my palm as I ride the elevator to my penthouse after a long three days away. Relief at being back washes over me and takes me by surprise. I never usually care about getting home. I've always been equally comfortable in hotels as I am in my own apartment, but the need to get back to New York as quickly as possible was never far from my mind this entire trip. Maybe it's because of the way we left things. Another moment and I would have had her naked and pinned to the kitchen counter.

I should have fucked her on our wedding night. Then the precedent would have been set, and we wouldn't have settled into this bizarre limbo where I'm not sure if I'm allowed to fuck her or not. She's my wife, right? Sex was always on the table because we're going to have kids. But each day that passes without us having sex feels like another step further into friends territory, and I find myself completely unsure of how to make a move on her. Like I've lost every bit of game I ever had.

Maybe I should simply ask if I can fuck her. Or kiss her and hope it leads to more.

I lick my lips, my dick twitching at the thought of my hands on her. This morning, I sent a text and told her I'd be home tomorrow, but my business wrapped up earlier than expected. I was unable to stay away for a second longer than necessary, so I had the jet prepared early.

While I have zero desire to examine why I couldn't stay away, I recognize that there can be only one explanation—she's five foot four and has the most incredible green eyes I've ever seen.

Her infectious laugh drifts down the hallway, and I curse under my breath, hoping she doesn't have a friend over. I want her all to myself, even if it's only to argue with her.

"Right there, baby girl?" The deep, masculine voice makes the hair on the back of my neck stand on end.

She releases a long, satisfied moan. "Yeah. Right there."

What in holy fuck? I stalk toward the den, my heart pounding in my chest and adrenaline pumping through my veins. I'm going to tear his fucking head off, whoever the fuck he is.

He grunts, like whatever he's doing takes effort, and she moans again. "You're so good at that."

Motherfucker! My hands curl into fists at my sides, and when I walk into the room, all I can see is the side of the asshole's head as he holds her ankle in the air. I snarl, snatching his attention. "You want to get your hands off my fucking wife?"

"Nathan!" Melanie shrieks, bolting upright. She blinks at me, her mouth open. "I thought you weren't getting back until tomorrow."

Yeah, no shit. A growl rumbles out of my chest as I cross the room. The asshole drops her foot but doesn't look the slightest bit uncomfortable that I've just caught him doing fuck knows what to my wife.

Melanie scrabbles to her feet, and only when she stands do I see that she's wearing pajamas, and one pant leg is rolled up around her knee. "This is Tyler."

I glare at him, and the cheeky prick has the audacity to smile at me. He's fully clothed too, so I have no idea what the hell they were just doing. "We haven't met." He holds out his hand for me to shake.

I glare at his outstretched palm. "What the fuck were you doing with your hands on my wife?"

Melanie covers her mouth but doesn't manage to stifle her snicker, and I train my glare on her. Does she think this is fucking funny? I guess the ferocity of my gaze stops her giggles in their tracks because her eyes widen, and she drops her hand. "Nathan, this is Tyler. My cousin. I told you about him, remember?"

I search her face for any hint of deceit. She's talked about him several times, but this giant tattooed fucker is not the man she described.

"Yeah, man. Sorry I couldn't make it to the wedding." Tyler stands tall, all six foot plus of him. He's as wide as a linebacker, but I'll still knock him on his fucking ass.

I bare my teeth. "What the fuck were you doing to my *wife*?"

He just stands there and fucking blinks at me, and I launch myself over the couch at him. He steps backward, an amused grin on his face.

"Nathan!" Melanie steps between us, her face a mask of horror. "I had a cramp in my leg. He was massaging it out. He's my *cousin*." She pulls a disgusted face.

I lick my lips and glance between the two of them.

Tyler holds his hands up in surrender. "Yeah, buddy. That is definitely not my deal." He laughs. Cocky fucker.

Melanie puts a hand on my chest, directly over my racing heart. "I get that must have sounded bad," she says softly, her lips twitching. "But I told you that he's a physical therapist. His hands are like a magician's. He was just getting rid of my cramp."

I narrow my eyes at her. Is she fucking with me? Her lips are still curling like she wants to laugh, but I'm sure she's aware that I'm seconds away from tearing Tyler's head off.

She tilts her head. "There's nothing going on here, I swear to you. He just got back in town, and I invited him over for pizza and movies."

"And even if she wasn't basically like my twin sister, I'm all about the dick," Tyler adds.

I shoot him a warning glare, but he merely shrugs. My pulse slows to a less alarming rate, and I direct my attention to Mel. "You were fucking moaning."

"Ugh. That's not your sex moan, is it?" Tyler balks, his face wrinkling with disgust. "Gross."

Her cheeks flush pink. "No, that is not my sex moan!"

Tyler arches an eyebrow at me. "Is it?"

How the fuck would I know? I pinch the bridge of my nose and close my eyes for a moment. This wasn't at all what I expected to come home to.

"Tyler!" Melanie admonishes him.

"What? He's gotta know what your sex moans sound like. Unless—" He gasps dramatically. "Unless you've been faking it!"

Melanie picks a cushion up from the sofa and hits him over the head with it. "I have not been faking. Now stop."

Laughing, he ducks away from her before she can land another blow. "Then why doesn't he know the difference between the sounds you make getting a massage and the ones you make getting your rocks off? Have you two not even ..." His mouth snaps shut, and he looks from me to Melanie with a wide-eyed expression. "Oh."

She closes her eyes and takes a breath, then fixes her gaze on me and shakes her head. "I'm so sorry. He's kind of a lot to deal with."

Tyler scoffs. "I'm a fucking prize." Then he snatches the pizza box from the coffee table. "But I think I'd better leave you two newlyweds to get better acquainted."

She rolls her eyes at him. "You don't have to go."

He grins and tucks the pizza box under his arm. "Clearly I do. Because there is some very *unresolved tension* in this room." He leans in and whispers the last part like it's a secret.

As he walks past me, he holds out his hand again. "Real nice to meet you, buddy."

Finally convinced that I walked in on something that sounded filthy but was in fact entirely innocent, I shake his hand.

"I'll call you tomorrow, Goose," he shouts over his shoulder on his way out the door.

I arch an eyebrow at Melanie. "Goose?"

She folds her arms over her chest, her eyes twinkling with mischief. "Your wife?"

"You are my fucking wife," I remind her.

She shrugs before grabbing the two empty soda glasses from the coffee table and carrying them to the kitchen island. I get the discarded pizza box and follow her, dumping it into the trash. She leans against the counter, observing me. "You seemed all kinds of jealous just then, Ice."

I close the distance between us, and she tilts her head back, giving me a defiant stare. "Well, I came home early from my trip and heard you moaning 'yeah, right there' to some guy. What the hell was I supposed to think?"

She crosses her arms. "Well, I'm not a cheater."

"Well, maybe if I knew what your sex moans sounded like, I would have realized that immediately."

"Don't feel bad." She grins. "Very few guys have heard my *actual* sex moans."

The thought of her with any other guy makes me want to punch a hole in something, but I swallow down the unexpected wave of jealousy because I'm having way too much fun playing with her. "Because so very few have agreed to sleep with you, or because they couldn't make you come?"

A laugh bubbles out of her lips, but she quickly composes herself and gasps, feigning indignation. "That was low, Mr. James."

"I can go lower."

She bites her bottom lip, her eyes raking over my face. "I bet you can."

I dip my head and press my mouth to her ear. "And I can guarantee I'd make you moan for real."

Her breath catches, and then she purrs. "A guarantee, huh? That's very bold of you."

"One hundred percent or your money back."

She laughs again, and the sound travels straight to my dick, making it jump in my pants. God, I fucking want her.

"I mean I'm intrigued, but ..." She tilts her head and flutters her eyelashes.

"But what, Spitfire?" I trail my fingertips over her collarbone, along the slender column of her neck, and suppress a satisfied smile when she shivers at my touch. My mouth waters. I want to touch her. Taste her. Claim her. Her breathing gets heavier, but she doesn't answer me. "How else are you going to prove to me that what you were doing on the couch with Tyler when I came in here was innocent? To avoid any further confusion, I think I need to know exactly what sounds you make when you come."

She moistens her lips. "You make it sound like it's a foregone conclusion that you could. I'm not built that way. It's not easy for me to ... *let go*."

I close my eyes and take a deep breath, inhaling her intoxicating scent. "How about I make you a once in a lifetime offer, Mrs. James. I'll give you one orgasm right now. No expectations, no strings attached. However you want it. What do you say?"

She presses her lips together like she's deep in thought, and my heart races while I wait for her answer. Finally, she offers me a sweet smile. "Yes."

CHAPTER
TWENTY-THREE

MELANIE

Nathan flashes an arrogant grin. Did I really just agree to this?

Yes. Yes, I did. Because the way he stormed in here a few moments ago calling me his wife, despite being possessive and asshole-ish, was spectacularly hot. And this thing between us has been brewing for weeks. We're going to have to have sex eventually if we're going to have kids, and if I'm honest, I assumed he would have pushed for it before now.

But this ... this feels all about me. I can count on two fingers the number of guys who were patient enough to make me climax, but if Nathan James does sex like he does everything else in his life, I'm willing to bet he'll refuse to give in until he makes it happen.

"How do you prefer your orgasms, Mrs. James?" He asks the question so casually while he rolls up his sleeves like he means business. The sight of his thick forearms render me mute until he tips my chin up with his forefinger. "Well?"

I blink at him. "What?"

"Would you like me to use my fingers? My mouth? Both?"

Holy shitballs. "I have no preference." That's a lie. I absolutely do have a preference, and it involves that wickedly sinful mouth of his, but admitting that is too embarrassing, plus I haven't showered since this morning. "Your call."

He hums appreciatively and rubs a hand over his jaw, his dark eyes sparking with devious intent. "Well, I definitely have a preference." He grabs me by my hips and lifts me onto the island. My breath stutters, and he's removing my pajama pants before I can form any kind of rational thought. I'm not wearing panties, so my lower half is bare, making me feel vulnerable and embarrassed. My skin flames with heat. This is Nathan James, and he's about to ... I really didn't think this through at all. He's dated the most beautiful women in the world. I bet they all waxed weekly and had beautifully landscaped lady gardens. Mine isn't exactly overgrown, but I am due an appointment.

Nathan grabs the stool beside him and, to my mortification, sits down between my spread thighs. He inches forward, his broad shoulders spreading my legs wider, then lifts my pajama top and trails his fingertips down my abdomen to the space between my thighs, his hungry gaze following in their wake.

Holy crap. "I haven't showered since this morning," I blurt out. "Tyler picked me up after work and I was so hungry and we were chatting and I just threw on my comfy pajamas and—"

"Jesus, Mel," he growls, before sucking on his lip and closing his eyes. I stare at him open-mouthed. Is this bad? Or good? "Lie back for me."

Heat floods my core so rapidly that my head spins. He places a hand between my breasts, gently pushing me backward, and I drop onto my elbows, my eyes still fixed on his face. But he doesn't meet my gaze. His focus remains locked on the spot between my legs like it's the most fascinating thing in the world. I'm hyperaware of how wet I already am, of how my arousal seeps out of me despite the fact that he hasn't even touched me yet.

"I have a waxing appointment next week," I whisper, my cheeks burning hotter than the sun.

He runs a fingertip through my center. "Your cunt is perfect."

Oh god, my what? Ordinarily I hate that word, but from his lips it sounds wicked and sinful and so hot I want to melt into the countertop. He slides his warm hands up my inner thighs, and they tremble beneath his expert touch.

He glances up at me. "Lie back and relax, Mel," he commands.

It's kind of hard to relax with your face inches from the most intimate part of me, Nathan. That's what I want to say, but instead I obey his command and lie down.

He growls. "That's my girl."

A whimper slips out of me, and I'm sure I hear him laugh. He presses my thighs down flat to the counter, and I actually feel a drop of arousal trickle out of me. I suck in a breath, torn between wanting to die from embarrassment and wanting to grind myself on his face. What is he waiting for?

"I can practically hear you overthinking," he says, and the way his warm breath dances over my wet flesh makes me shiver.

"I can't help it."

He presses a kiss to the top of my thigh. "What are you worried about?"

"I told you I haven't showered," I croak.

He kisses my other thigh. "I prefer it that way. I want to taste how your day's been."

Oh dear God in heaven. "What if I ... smell?"

He kisses me again, this time closer to my center. "You smell fucking incredible. My cock is hard just thinking about tasting you."

"Most guys I've been with have never made me come. It takes too long."

I'm rewarded with another soft kiss, and this time his nose brushes over my lips. "Eating pussy is one of the greatest pleasures in life, Mel. The longer I get to spend eating yours, the better."

Molten heat sears my core. "I need a wax."

"Your cunt is beautiful and pink and inviting. I'd put a picture of it on my desk in my office, but that would mean someone else might see it, and this ..." He trails his warm tongue from my opening to my clit, and my back arches off the countertop. "Is all mine."

"Nathan!" I pant, so desperate for more of what he just gave me, I'm pretty sure I'd do anything he asked me to right now.

He hums, and the sound vibrates through my flesh, shooting pleasure through my veins. "Jesus, you taste fucking delicious too, corazón." He flicks his tongue over me again, lapping leisurely at my wet center.

I can only moan as my thighs tingle and I inhale deep, soul-cleansing breaths.

He slides his hands around the backs of my thighs, pulling me closer, and although what he was doing already felt incredible, he takes it up a gear. He licks and sucks on my hypersensitive flesh, working his way from my entrance to the swollen bud of my clit, repeatedly bringing me to heights of dizzying ecstasy and then easing me back down before he does it all over again. And each time my need to come grows stronger. More urgent.

White-hot pleasure screeches around my body, searching for release. My head spins and my eyes roll back as I lose all sense of rational thought. I writhe on the countertop, begging and pleading with him to let me come, but the Iceman with the hottest, most incredible mouth I have ever known refuses to take pity on me. His murmured words of praise and encouragement only draw out my agony and pleasure into one long, seemingly everlasting moment.

I pant heavily as he eases me back down from the crest of another wave, knowing that I'm going to die when he finally lets me come. My soul is going to leave my body and forget its way back.

"Please, Nate!" I take one last shot at begging, but I'm unable to form the two syllables of his entire name.

He grunts, his fingers digging into the soft flesh of my thighs as he pulls me closer to his face, pressing me deeper into his eager mouth. Groaning, he feasts on me, sealing his lips over my clit, sucking hard and flicking the swollen bud of flesh with the tip of his tongue.

My entire body trembles. Every cell hangs on the precipice of an almighty explosion. I buck my hips, and Nathan keeps a firm grip on me, pinning me in place. I'm going to lose my mind.

Intense pressure builds in my core, snaking in my center and spreading between my thighs. I scream out a word that's unintelligible even to my own ears. When he grazes me with his teeth, I lose it. One explosion after another ricochets through me until they reach my aching center. And then something unfamiliar and euphoric happens—if I wasn't so high off this soul-altering, life-affirming orgasm, I might be mortified. My release rushes out of me like a river that broke its dam, soaking Nathan and the countertop and spattering onto the marble floor below.

"Jesus fuck." Nathan groans against my skin as he goes on sucking and licking me.

I shake from head to toe. My head is spinning. I feel like I just rode every rollercoaster at Six Flags on repeat for infinity.

Warm pleasure settles into my bones like an old friend. I gasp for breath, trying to suck in much-needed oxygen before I pass out.

And when I have the strength to lift my head, Nathan lifts his too. His fiery eyes burn into mine, and something passes between us. A connection that goes so much deeper than any I've shared with anyone else. Like it can't be broken.

Until he breaks it.

He wipes his glistening jaw, cleaning me off his skin. "Told you, Spitfire." Then he pushes back his stool, presses a single kiss on my abdomen, and walks out of the room.

I drop my head back, wincing as it hits the countertop with a dull thud. What the hell just happened?

CHAPTER
TWENTY-FOUR

NATHAN

Jesus fucking Christ on a motherfucking cracker. The blood pounding in my ears is echoed by the painful throbbing of my cock as I stalk down the hallway to my bedroom. I need to get away from her. Away from her sweet, addictive scent. Her supple body that responds to me like we've known each other forever. And definitely far away from her juicy, hot-as-hell cunt.

Why the hell did I do that? A quick finger-fuck would have gotten the job done much more efficiently, and I wouldn't have her scent and taste all over me. I glance down at my shirt, stained wet with her cum. Literally all over me.

I need a shower. An ice-cold two-hour-long shower.

Five minutes later, my cock is still harder than steel despite the cool water running over me. She's everywhere, invading every one of my senses. Her moans and desperate whimpers ring in my ears. All I can see is her incredible body spread open for me. I feel her under my skin. Smell her every time I take a breath. Taste her when my tongue brushes the roof of my mouth. She might as well have climbed inside me and taken up residence in my body.

I bang my fist on the tiled wall and mutter all the curse words I can think of. But it's no use, I can't shake her from my skin. I wrap my hand around the base of my shaft, squeezing tight until my eyes roll back and I feel some relief. If I leave this shower in the same state I walked into it, I can't be sure I won't go bang down Mel's door and fuck her where she stands. But I promised her one orgasm with no expectations and no strings attached, and that's exactly what I delivered.

I pump my cock, groaning as heat coils at the base of my spine. I try to think of anything but her, but there's nothing else in my head. My previous highlight reel has vanished. And I realize it's been absent for the past six weeks. Ever since I laid eyes on her, which I guess is a good thing. I am a married fucking man, after all. And those faceless women before her meant nothing to me. So I press my forehead against the cool tile and think of my wife. I imagine how good it will feel when I finally sink my cock inside her tight, wet cunt. How she'll scream my fucking name all over this goddamn penthouse. How I'll make her come so hard she'll forget any asshole ever put his hands on her before me.

I tug harder, and beads of precum weep from the slit of my crown. Mel is mine. All fucking mine. And I'll be fucked if I wait six months for the baby-making deal to kick in before I fuck her. She'll be lucky if she gets six more days before I claim her. With that thought, my climax washes over me like a tsunami, knocking the breath from my lungs. I rock onto the balls of my feet, my head spinning violently as endorphins flood my system and warm ribbons of cum streak over my knuckles.

I look down at the mess on my hand and wish my wife was in here with me to clean it up.

TAKING A SIP OF COFFEE, I stare out the window. Anything to avoid looking at the kitchen counter where I made her come last night. Not just come. She fucking squirted. All fucking over me. I bite down on my lip and stifle a groan because the memory is making my cock hard again, and I only just calmed him down. I haven't jerked off so much in the shower since I was a teenager.

"That was an asshole move you pulled last night."

Her voice startles me, and I spin around to face her. "What?"

She folds her arms across her chest. "You know what, Nathan."

I frown at her. "I really fucking don't."

She snorts. "Seriously. You ..." Her cheeks flush pink. "You did *that thing,* and then you just walked away without so much as a goodnight."

I guess I did leave her alone with a puddle of her cum to clean up. But if I hadn't, I would've fucked her right there on the counter and then she'd be way more pissed at me than she is right now. "I fulfilled our agreement."

Her eyes glisten with unshed tears. "You made me feel used and cheap."

Fuck. I sigh and shake my head. "I'm sorry. That wasn't my intention."

Her expression hardens as she steps closer, squaring up to me. "So what was your intention? Why did you run out of here like the place was on fire?"

Sure to god she fucking knows why. "You're a smart woman, Mel. I'm sure you can figure that out."

She blinks at me, confusion pinching her brow. "I d-don't ..."

I should walk out of here before this conversation gets any

more awkward and I end up admitting that I jerked off with the taste of her in my mouth and the scent of her in my nose. And how I came so fucking hard I almost blacked out. But dammit, this woman has me in some sort of chokehold. I close the distance between us but resist the urge to lift her onto the counter again and slide a part of myself inside her. Instead, I brush the pad of my thumb over her cheek. "I think you do."

She opens and closes her mouth, her frown deepening. "Well, I thought ..." She shakes her head, and the scent of her coconut shampoo fills my nostrils. My mouth waters to taste her again. "But no. You're not that much of a jackass to leave me like that to make me feel bad. At least you never have been before."

Her cheeks grow redder, and I cup her jaw in my hand. "So if I'm not a jackass, then why? Come on, smart girl, why else would I have needed to get the hell away from you last night?"

She stares into my eyes like she's trying to read my mind, and her pupils blow wide. "To um ... stop yourself from going any further?" she whispers.

"Bingo."

Her body leans closer to mine, and I instinctively edge forward too, as though we have some magnetic pull drawing us together. "B-but why didn't you want to ..."

I search her face. "Because I promised you no expectations. To have fucked you afterward, when you were on an orgasm high, would have been the exact opposite. Besides, I don't have any condoms here, and I know you want to wait to start trying."

She shakes her head. "I mean, I did. I do. Until we get to know each other. But I didn't think you'd want to wait that long to ... That's why I'm on the pill."

My cock twitches. "You're on the pill?"

She nods. "I should have told you. I'm sorry. I assumed ... But I thought we'd be ... and I just thought it would be easier than condoms." Her throat thickens as she swallows, and she looks down at the floor. "God, this is so awkward."

Cupping her chin, I tilt her head back up so I can look at her. "We haven't been great at communication, have we?"

She bites on her lip again. "No."

"How about we change that and be honest with each other about what we want from now on?"

"I'd like that," she says, her voice a sultry purr that makes my dick twitch again.

I close the distance between us until my chest is pressed against hers. An image of her hard nipples pressed against my skin makes me sway on my feet. "I'm sorry I made you feel cheap."

Her breath catches, and the blush on her cheeks races down her neck. I want to chase it with my tongue. I dip my head, dusting my lips over her forehead and inhaling the intoxicatingly sweet scent of her skin. The memory of her taste and the way she moaned my goddamn name slams into me. I want to taste her right now. I want to fuck her where she stands. I want to claim every single part of her.

My phone vibrates in my pocket, and I curse under my breath. I have a meeting that can't wait. I suppress a groan and step back from her, not missing the hurt look in her eyes when I do.

"We'll talk later," I tell her, resisting my desire to kiss her pink lips as she blinks up at me.

Reluctantly, I leave her standing alone in the kitchen.

TWENTY-FIVE

MELANIE

"Oh my god, Ty!" I throw my hands over my face, feeling my cheeks heat at the memory. "I practically asked him to fuck me, and he just walked out and left me standing there."

"He didn't say anything at all? Not even goodbye?"

Groaning, I flop down at his breakfast bar and unpack the sandwiches I picked up for lunch. "He said we'll talk later."

Tyler rolls his eyes. "So, he didn't just leave you hanging. He probably had some important billionaire business to attend to."

"Pretty sure everyone waits for Nathan James. He could have at least ..."

He flashes me a wicked grin. "At least what? From what you told me about what happened last night, he doesn't seem like the type of guy to *at least* anything. If ya know what I mean." He snickers. "I bet you won't be able to walk after the first time you two finally fuck."

I shake my head. "You're such a frat boy."

He tosses a grape at my head. "And you, baby girl, are blind."

I fold my arms across my chest and scowl. "Am not."

He steps around the kitchen island and slides his arm around my shoulder. "Are too. Even if we discount his whole *take your hands off my wife* routine, no guy eats your pussy that good if he's not into you."

I shrug him off. "What would you know about eating pussy?"

He tilts his head, eyes crinkling as he smiles. "I've been known to dabble occasionally. Besides, head is head. Nobody does it full gusto if they're not into the person they're giving it to. And from what you told me ..." He whistles.

My cheeks flame hotter, but the memory of Nathan making me come so hard that I squirted all over him and his kitchen floor makes me clench my thighs together. I didn't tell Tyler all the details, but I told him enough. "I'm sorry I told you that now."

His shoulders shake with silent laughter as he pours us each a glass of soda.

"What am I gonna do, Ty? I can't just keep waiting for him to make a move. I need to take back a little control here."

"So seduce him," he says nonchalantly, like it's the easiest thing in the world.

"And how exactly do I do that? The man is an ice machine."

Tyler laughs. "He wasn't last night."

I roll my eyes, but I can't argue. Nathan was straight fire last night.

Ty pulls my hair aside and drapes it over my shoulder, all trace of his previous amusement at my situation now gone from his expression. "He's just a guy, baby girl. Cook him a steak, wear some sexy lingerie, and he'll be putty in your hands."

Taking a sip of my soda, I stare at him over the rim of my

glass. I'm not entirely convinced that Nathan James is just like any other guy, but what have I got to lose?

~

I STEP out of the shower and reach for a towel when an ear-splitting alarm fills the room. I slam my hands over my ears. What in the bejeezus is that?

Oh crap, I smell smoke. Dinner!

I snatch my bathrobe off the vanity and wrap it around my wet body while hightailing it to the kitchen. Smoke billows out of the oven and the beeping grows more insistent. What in tarnation? I was only cooking potatoes. I grab the first thing I see, a dish towel, and pull open the door, coughing as smoke pours out. The smell of burnt cheese and cream makes me gag, but I swallow it down and pull out the tray.

Holy shit, that's hot! I let go and the tray hits the floor, splattering molten cheese and potatoes in every direction. I suck on my burned thumb. Why did I think this was such a good idea? I couldn't have just gone with a simple steak and fries. No, I had to get all fancy and try dauphinoise potatoes. Melted cheese drips down the glass door of the oven, and the marble floors are covered in a cream-and-cheese catastrophe. My hair dribbles water all over my face while smoke fills the kitchen, and the damn alarm threatens to make my eardrums bleed.

I look up at the source of the infernal noise and curse. It's at least six feet above my head, and I have no clue how I'm going to turn it off.

"What the hell?" Nathan strides through the smoke and opens all the kitchen windows before pressing a button on the panel near the pantry. The god-awful beeping finally ceases, but my ears continue to ring.

Coughing, I wave a hand in front of my face. "I'm sorry. I was trying to make dauphinoise potatoes, but your deranged oven hates me."

He eyes me suspiciously before glancing at the open oven door. An unidentifiable blob slides from the glass to the floor. "Maybe because you were using the electric grill and not the oven," he says, his voice strained with what I can only assume is suppressed laughter.

I throw my hands in the air. "Well, there are six dozen settings, and they all look the same. How many functions does one appliance really need to perform? Can't it just bake and roast like a regular oven?"

After grabbing an oven mitt from the drawer next to the stove, he picks up the tray of charred potatoes and scorched cheese and drops it into the trashcan, baking sheet and all. He turns and gives me his full attention, his lips twitching in a grin. "Cooking not really your strong suit, Mel?"

Pouting, I cross my arms over my chest. "Your fancy-ass oven doesn't make it easy."

He crosses the hazy room, although the smoke has started to clear, and rakes his gaze up and down my body. Thanks to my wet skin and dripping hair, the bathrobe clings to me, and he arches an eyebrow. "Were you making a special dinner?"

I clear my throat. "Kind of."

He cocks his head. "What for?"

I swallow. I'm such an idiot. "I, uh, thought it would be nice."

"And you were planning to dine in your bathrobe?" He's no longer bothering to suppress his amusement. Jackass.

I manage to tamp down the urge to stomp my foot. "No. I got out of the shower and the smoke alarm started going off. Then there was some kind of cheese explosion and ..." Embarrassed, I shake my head.

He presses his lips together and scans the room, surveying the carnage I've caused in his usually immaculate kitchen. My burned thumb throbs, and I suck it into my mouth again.

"Are you hurt?" His joking tone is replaced by concern, which only makes me feel like an even bigger idiot.

I hold out my thumb. "Just a tiny burn. I'm fine."

He takes hold of my hand and leads me to the sink, turns on the cold tap and lets the water run for a few seconds before holding my hand beneath it. "This should soothe most of the sting."

"I'm fine," I insist.

His brown eyes narrow. "When was the last time you let anyone take care of you?"

I blink at the unexpectedness of his question and answer honestly. "I can't remember."

He sucks on his top lip, his fingertips brushing over my palm as he continues holding my thumb under the soothing cold water. "Well, I appreciate the planning, even if the execution left something to be desired," he says, his lips curving in a way that makes me smile too.

"Yeah. Should have just stuck to steak and fries."

He places his free hand on his chest. "Now that *is* the way to my heart." He winks. "Or was it my pants you were trying to get into?"

My cheeks burn, and his eyes roam over my face and down to my cleavage. "Jesus, fuck," he mutters as he realizes his joke was spot-on.

I pull my robe tighter around myself, but it's too late because I already feel exposed and vulnerable.

He turns off the tap and inspects my thumb. Water drips from my hand onto his suit jacket, but he doesn't seem to care. "Feel any better?"

"A little, thank you," I whisper.

He keeps his eyes fixed on mine as he lifts my hand to his lips and presses a soft kiss to the dime-sized patch of pink skin. "How about now?"

Goosebumps break out along my forearms. "A little more," I croak.

Sucking my thumb into his mouth, he swirls that expert tongue over the pad, and I feel the effects in every part of my body. My lips part on a gasp, and he gives my burn another gentle kiss. His eyes are filled with longing as they sear into mine. "And now?"

"Better," I pant, my legs trembling.

He trails his free hand down the lapel of my bathrobe. "Are you naked under here, Mel?"

Molten heat fills my core. "Yeah. I just got out of the shower. I had a dress and some lingerie ..." I babble, wanting to face-palm myself for admitting that.

"I prefer the bathrobe."

"You do?"

He cocks his head to the side. "Actually, it's what's beneath it that I prefer." He tugs on the tie around my waist, and my robe falls open.

He sucks air through his teeth, his hungry gaze traveling lower. "Fuck me, you're beautiful."

The fire heating my cheeks races down my neck and chest. I shift from one foot to the other, and he smirks at me. "You were planning to seduce me with food and sexy lingerie, but you blush when I tell you you're beautiful?"

"I wasn't planning to seduce you," I protest.

His eyes twinkle. "No?"

"Well, no, I-I ..."

He wraps his arms around my waist. "So what exactly were you hoping for, Melanie?" His breath dusts over my forehead.

I press my lips together.

"Tell me, corazón." My breath hitches in my throat. One of my best friends in high school spoke Spanish, so I know the word means sweetheart in that context. I blink at him, wetness already slicking between my thighs. "What do you want me to do to you?"

I'm no wallflower. I've never had a problem asking guys for what I want, but Nathan James is intimidating, which is probably why he makes me feel more like a nervous teenager on a first date than a confident grown woman. Still, I take a deep breath and blurt, "I want you to fuck me."

He immediately lifts me, wraps my legs around his hips, and carries me a few feet to drop me down on the kitchen island. With deft, eager hands, he peels off my robe and explores my torso, squeezing my breasts in his palms and tugging on my hardened nipples. Moaning, I arch into the pleasure.

He hisses out a breath. "Fucking beautiful."

Threading my fingers in his hair, I pull his face to mine, but he dips his head and nuzzles my neck instead, biting and sucking while he spreads my thighs apart. And when his fingers slide through my wet center, I moan his name. The arrogant jackass laughs, and I hate myself for being so needy with him.

"I'm desperate to be inside you as much as you want me there, corazón," he growls, and that knowledge makes me smile.

"Then please," I whimper.

He dips one thick finger inside me, and my back bows with pleasure. "Jesus, you feel even better than I imagined you would." He groans. "You're soaked for me, little Spitfire."

He peppers kisses along my jawline while he fucks me with his finger, drawing a series of moans from my body. When he adds a second digit, my back bends, and I dig my fingernails into his scalp.

"I had to fuck my hand twice last night after only tasting

you. Once I bury my cock inside your tight little cunt, I'm going to be addicted. I'm going to fuck you every goddamn chance I get. I'm going to make you spill your cum on every surface of this penthouse. Are you ready for that?"

He twists his fingers inside me, and burning pleasure rockets through my core. "Y-yes!"

The animalistic sound he makes sends shivers of excitement and anticipation down my spine. Without warning, his fingers leave, but before I can protest, he leaps on top of me like a panther.

He pushes me down flat to the countertop and straddles me, making me gasp. Then he unfastens his belt and pants and frees his thick, incredibly impressive length. "I know I should take you to bed, but I can't wait another second to be inside you."

I pull him down on top of me, letting him know that the feeling is mutual. He climbs between my legs and nudges them apart before pressing the engorged head of his crown at my entrance. I hiss at the way it burns when he inches inside me and stretches me wide.

He stills his hips, his lips pressed against my ear. "You okay?"

"Yeah. It's just … you're kind of big," I admit, even though this man's ego needs no inflating, but he doesn't make any smug comments. Instead, he presses a kiss beneath my ear. "You can take all of me, corazón, but you just let me know when you're ready. Because once I'm all the way in, I won't be gentle."

I cling to him, and he rests his forehead against mine, his breaths labored and his muscles vibrating as he waits for me. The guttural sound he makes when I shift my hips has me suppressing a smile. Arguably one of the most powerful men in the entire country is trembling with the effort of not fucking me. It makes me feel like I'm made of granite. "I'm ready."

"Thank fuck," he grunts, sinking deeper inside me. The burning gives way to intense shockwaves of pleasure.

I wrap my legs around his waist, but he pushes them back down and fixes me with his fiery gaze. "No, corazón, you keep those beautiful legs spread as wide as you can for me," he commands in that low, distinctive growl that turns me to putty in his hands.

I sink my teeth into my bottom lip and nod while he pushes deeper. Euphoria races through my veins, and I let out a cry.

"You like that?" He pulls out and drives back in. "You like my cock filling your tight cunt?"

God, his filthy mouth has me purring like a kitten. "Uh-huh."

He presses a kiss on my forehead. "I'm going to ruin you, corazón. Every time you move tomorrow, you're going to feel me inside you."

"Please!" I claw at his suit jacket and suck in deep breaths as Nathan fucks me into the countertop. He was right about not being gentle, but I don't want that. I want this side of him. Raw and primal and unrestrained.

I look up at the ceiling and see us reflected in the polished chrome of the overhead light fixtures. Him in his suit and me sprawled naked beneath him, legs spread wide as he nails me into oblivion, and the sight alone is enough to make my thighs tremble.

Wetness slicks my thighs, and the sound of him driving in and out of me might be the hottest thing I've ever heard.

Nathan's lips are hot against my ear, his breath dancing over my skin every time he grunts and groans, only adding to the overwhelming sensations already swirling through me. "Such a good wife. You take my cock so well."

"Holy crap." My walls squeeze him, and my entire core feels like it floods with hot liquid pleasure.

"You think I can make you squirt for me again?" he asks with a throaty chuckle.

"I d-don't ..." I throw my head back, unable to finish the thought as my orgasm crashes over me, making every cell in my body melt into the countertop.

"That's my girl," Nathan grunts. He pins my wrists on either side of my head so he can rail into me even harder. Stars pepper my vision, and I can do nothing but lie here and take everything he gives me because I am completely obliterated. Boneless.

And when his hips still, he sinks his teeth into the base of my neck. I whimper his name and gasp for breath, my mind reeling with questions and emotions.

But one thought prevails—I want to be Nathan James's wife for real.

Forever.

CHAPTER
TWENTY-SIX

NATHAN

I wake the next morning with her warm body curled up against me. I've never been a cuddler after sex, but something about the way she's wrapped around me feels right. Banding my arms around her waist, I drop a soft kiss on her head.

She stirs, murmuring something in her sleep and rubbing her wet pussy against my hip. I bite down on my lip and grunt. My dick's already hard, and she's making it ache. I should roll her off me and go make coffee so we can have clear heads when we talk about what last night means for our relationship, but I can't tear myself away from her.

I rest my lips against her hair, and the scent of her coconut shampoo floods my senses.

"What time is it?" she mumbles.

I glance at the luminous clock on my nightstand. "A little after eight."

She sits up and rubs her eyes. "I have to get to work."

"Relax, corazón. It's Saturday."

She blinks, still looking adorably sleepy. "Oh, thank the lord. I'm still beat." She lies back down, her head nestled against my chest.

"Yeah, we stayed up pretty late, Spitfire."

I hear her swallow. "We sure did." She lifts her head and stares into my eyes. "Do you want me to go to my own room?"

I frown at her. "Fuck, no. Why the hell would I want you to do that?"

She shrugs. "I don't know. Last night was incredible, but this is ..."

I brush her hair back from her face. "This is what?"

"Waking up like this is intimate and ... well, it's more than sex."

"I sort of like it though. You?"

A smile spreads across her face, making her green eyes sparkle. "Yeah, I like it too."

I lick my lips and wonder if what I'm about to suggest is ludicrous, but the reality is that she's my wife. We live together, and we're going to have kids together. This isn't a big deal at all in comparison. "So how about you don't ever go back to your room?"

Her eyes widen. "You mean like ... stay in here? With you?"

"Well, you are my wife. I told you last night that once I fucked you there was no going back. I could definitely get used to waking up with you like this."

Her brow furrows. "I could get used to it too, but maybe that's what I'm afraid of."

I cup her jaw and tilt her head. "Why are you afraid of getting used to it, corazón?"

"Because this ... this thing between us, it's not real."

Lifting the covers, I glance down at my hard cock and our naked bodies covered in cum. "Looks pretty fucking real to me."

"I mean ..." She places her hand over her eyes, and her cheeks and neck turn pink.

"You mean that we started unconventionally and now we're acting more like husband and wife than you imagined we would?"

She drops her hand and nods. "I guess."

"How is that not a good thing?" I run my fingertips down her spine. "You said last night was incredible. We can have incredible every day and every night."

"Because it feels too good to be true."

I roll her onto her back, spreading her thighs with my knees, and rock my hips until I find a little relief for my aching shaft. Her pupils blow wide, and her chest rises and falls with each heavy breath. "I agree that *this*"—I grind myself against her—"does feel good, but it's definitely true, Spitfire. I'm constantly hard around you." I sink inside her soaking pussy. "And you're so wet for me."

She hisses as I stretch her wide and pushes her head back into the pillow. "Jesus, Nate."

"You see? So. Fucking. Good." I punctuate each word with a thrust of my hips, driving deeper inside her with every stroke.

"Yes!" Her nails claw at my back, her legs wrapping snugly around my waist, and I bury my face against her neck, inhaling her sweet scent while I nail her to the bed.

Her muscles clamp around me, squeezing me tight as I bring her to orgasm, and the way she moans my fucking name when she comes has me losing control right along with her.

We pant for breath as we come down from the high. "And you thought your body wasn't built like that, huh, Spitfire?" I growl in her ear. "I guess you just hadn't found the right guy."

Her lips curve in a grin. "I'd call you an arrogant jackass, but you're right."

"And not just come, I can make you fucking squirt."

She presses her lips together. "Yeah, that was definitely unexpected, Ice."

I run my nose along her jawline. "You think we can make that happen again?"

"I guess so. If you press all the right buttons."

I hum my approval. "Actually I think it was eating your buttons that did it."

She laughs. "You're so sure of yourself, Ice."

"I'm not sure how I feel about being the Ice to your Goose and Tyler's Maverick, by the way."

She curls her fingers in my hair. "I thought I told you that Iceman was always my favorite."

I rock my hips, my cock already hard again inside her. "Yeah?"

"Y-yeah."

"That's my good little spitfire." The need to claim her again burns in my veins. I'm fucking addicted to this woman.

CHAPTER
TWENTY-SEVEN

MELANIE

I discreetly pick at the lace trim on the tablecloth, wishing I was at Nathan's father's house rather than being forced to endure an afternoon tea with my mother and Bryce. He did try to insist on coming with me, but I suspect this is the last time I'll be coming here for a while given the conversation I'm about to initiate, and what I have to say needs to be said without my husband present.

"You're quieter than usual, Melanie," my mother says.

I shake my head. "Sorry, I was distracted. Did you say Bryce would be joining us?"

She sniffs. "He'll be down shortly."

Glancing around the room, I nod. The parlor has always been stifling. Even when my father was alive, this room was my mother's domain. *Don't sit there, Melanie. Don't touch that. Stop fidgeting.* I pull at the neck of my sweater, wishing once more I was with Nathan. Actually, anywhere but here would be preferable.

"You look tired, dear sister." Bryce's arrogant voice carries across the room. "Is married life wearing you out?" He snorts, and it makes my skin crawl.

"Actually, married life is great. Which is what I wanted to speak to you both about."

My mother blinks at me, her lip curled in a sneer, and Bryce snorts with disgust.

I clear my throat. "I know this marriage was—is a business arrangement, but it's working out better than I think any of us hoped. And I just wanted to make my feelings clear about the whole cheating clause."

Bryce rolls his eyes, but I continue undeterred. "Despite what you think of him, Nathan isn't a cheater. Your whole honey trap idea is ridiculous anyway, but it's not going to happen, Bryce. Promise me that you won't even think about doing something so stupid."

"And just what exactly qualifies you to decide that it's such a stupid idea, dear sister?" he spits.

"Because I know my husband. He's not a cheater."

He scoffs. "Then why are you so worried about trying the honey trap? If you're so convinced of his integrity, it won't matter. He'll say no, and there'll be no harm done."

"Just don't even try it, Bryce. I'm warning you."

He jumps to his feet and looms over me, his teeth bared and his body shaking with rage. "*You* are warning *me*? Don't forget who you're talking to, little sister."

My mother places a hand on his arm, and he sits back down. "This is the easiest way to get you out of this marriage, Melanie," she says softly, like she's trying to calm a skittish animal.

"I don't want out."

Huffing, Bryce crosses his arms.

"I love him, Mom," I admit. "And I think he might learn to love me one day."

154

Bryce's twisted laugh fills the room, and my mother shakes her head in dismay, her eyes full of pity. Like I'm some stupid little girl and not a grown woman who's perfectly capable of understanding when a man has feelings for her. "The business doesn't need money from a divorce payout. With Nathan and his father's contacts, you can get any investor you want. Hell, I'm sure he'd even loan you the money if the business really needs it. I could just ask him—"

Bryce crashes his fist down on the table. "You really are pathetic, Melanie. You think a man like that will listen to *anything* you have to say? All he wants you for is to breed you like a whore, and we all know he might never get to do that, don't we? You might be easy to knock up, but you're pretty damn useless at keeping those little bastards in there, aren't you?"

Tears sting my eyes, and I push myself to my feet. I have never met anyone so cruel in my entire life. "Promise me you won't go ahead with it, Bryce. Promise or I'll tell him about your ridiculous scheme."

He snarls, and spittle leaks from the corners of his mouth.

"Promise me!" I shout.

He glances at my mother, who gives him a single nod.

"Fine!" he barks. "But don't come running home to us when he finds out what a useless, needy little bitch you really are."

I'd rather die than come back here. "I won't. I give you my word."

As I walk down the driveway of my childhood home, I almost cry out with relief when I see Teddy waiting for me at the bottom.

He smiles, and I sniff and swat at my cheeks, hoping he can't tell I've been crying. "Tedward. What are you doing here?"

"Mr. James told me to wait for you. His father's driver can take him home."

As I get closer, Teddy's eyes fill with concern. "Are you okay, Mrs. James?"

"Yeah, I'm fine. Families, huh?" I say, forcing a smile.

"Do you need anything?"

I bite my lip and nod. "I could really use a hug."

Seemingly without a second's pause for thought, he steps forward and wraps his giant arms around me. I bury my face in his suit jacket. "Thank you, Tedward. Will you please take me home?"

"My pleasure, Mrs. James."

TWENTY-EIGHT

NATHAN

"Is everything okay?" I say into my phone after answering my driver's call.

I hear him take a deep breath. "I'm not sure, sir. Mrs. James just left her mother's house, and she seemed quite upset."

"Did she say what happened?"

"She said she was fine, but then she ... She needed a hug, sir."

I roll my neck and clench my free hand into a fist. I can guarantee her reaction had something to do with her asshole brother. "Bring her to me."

"She said she wants to go home, sir."

"You can get her here faster than I can get home to her. Bring her to me."

"Of course, sir."

I end the call and look up to find my dad and brothers staring at me. "Mel just left her mother's house upset. I told Teddy to bring her here."

My dad offers me a reassuring nod. "I'll set another place for dinner."

Elijah frowns. "Did he say what happened? Is she okay?"

I shake my head. "Teddy didn't know. She didn't say, and I know better than to push her on it. There's some weird dynamic there that I need to get to the bottom of."

Mason shivers. "Her brother gives me the fucking creeps."

"He's a dick," Elijah adds.

"Well, she'll be okay here with her new family," Dad adds, his gray eyes shining. "Maybe you should both stay over?" I don't miss the plea in his tone. He must be really lonely in this big old house without my mom and us kids. I get now why he's so desperate for grandchildren, and my heart aches for everything he lost when our mom died.

Stepping away, I dial Mel's number, and she answers after a few rings. "Hey, corazón, my dad and brothers are giving me shit for not bringing you here today. They miss you. We haven't eaten yet, so I asked Teddy to bring you here."

"Oh. I was gonna go home and have a nice long bath. I'm kind of beat."

"You can soak in the tub here. We'll stay over and watch one of those cheesy movies you like in bed. I'll make sure you're back in time for work tomorrow morning."

"Okay. That sounds nice." I can almost hear the smile on her face, and after I hang up, I spend a long moment thinking about how nice it will be to have a family dinner with my wife by my side.

～

"Wow!" Mel gasps when she walks into the bathroom. "That is a huge tub."

"Seems like a shame for one person to sit in it alone."

She folds her arms over her chest and smirks. "Aren't you supposed to be helping your dad with dinner?"

"Nah." I dismiss that with a wave. Elijah and Mason can handle it. "Tonight I'm only here to serve you, milady." I check the temperature of the water. Satisfied that it's exactly right, I shake the bubbles from my hand and turn off the faucet. "Your bath is ready."

"It looks incredible." A smile spreads across her beautiful face. She pulls off her sweater and tosses it onto the floor, and her bra quickly follows. After shimmying out of her jeans and panties, she adds them to the pile.

"Yeah, fucking incredible," I agree, my eyes roaming over every perfect inch of her naked body.

Her cheeks flush pink. She presses her lips together and shakes her head.

"You can't give me a sexy striptease and then shake your head at me for admiring the end result, corazón."

She laughs. "That was not a striptease."

"Looked like one to me. Now get your sexy ass in this tub."

She sashays over to me, kisses me on the lips, then climbs into the hot bubbly water. Lying back, she rests her head on the edge and closes her eyes. "Oh, this is so good."

After pulling off my own clothes and tossing them into the pile with hers, I climb in with her. She scoots forward without me asking, allowing me to slide in behind her. I wrap my arms around her and pull her back against my chest.

"Oh, now this feels even better," she says with a contented sigh.

I gather her hair in my fist and drape it over her shoulder before pressing a kiss on her temple. "Yeah?"

"Yeah." She sinks deeper into the water. "Did Tedward call you when I left my mom's house today?"

"He did."

"Traitor."

I dip my head and kiss her neck. "Part of his job is to take care of you, Mrs. James. What happened?"

"Just my brother being an asshole. I don't think I'll be going back there for a while."

Tension creeps into my muscles, and I band my arms tighter around her. "What did he do?"

"Nothing specific. He's just an asshole."

I have no idea why she's being so evasive, but I'm a patient man. "What about your mom? What did she say when he was being an asshole?"

"Nothing. She never does."

I rest my chin on the top of her head. "Has he always been an asshole to you?"

She spins around and straddles me. "Can we please stop talking about my brother?" She palms my already semihard cock, and it stiffens further in her grip. "I mean we're in this incredible tub. We're naked. You're hard."

"I'm always hard around you, corazón."

Her bright green eyes fix on mine, and I want to unpack the sadness in them, but she's closed off to me right now. She shifts her hips and lines my crown up with her pussy.

"I know exactly what you're doing, Spitfire."

She flutters her eyelashes. "And what's that, Ice?"

"You're trying to distract me so I'll stop asking questions you don't want to answer."

"And is it working?" she purrs, squeezing my shaft in her hand and making my eyes roll back in my head.

I bite down on my lip so hard I draw blood. "You know it is."

"I want you, Ice."

A growl rolls in my throat. "You've got me."

She sinks onto my cock, allowing me to fill her tight pussy inch by exquisite inch. I grab onto her hips, sinking my fingers into her flesh. She throws her head back and moans while her silky heat grips me tight. I swear I'm going to lose myself in this woman.

I hiss out a breath. "You're so fucking tight."

"You feel so good inside me, Nate. I ..." She sucks in a ragged breath. "Nobody has ever made me feel like this."

I bite down on the soft skin of her neck. "And nobody ever will, corazón. You're mine." I pull her down and thrust my hips at the same time, bottoming out inside her and making her cry out a strangled moan. "I'm going to fill your greedy cunt with my cum and then I'm going to eat it out of you."

"Holy shit!" Her inner walls ripple around me, milking my cock with hungry squeezes.

I roll her over me, rubbing her clit against my skin until she's mewling like my feral little spitfire. Her pussy grips my cock with a series of tight squeezes that has heat searing in my balls and fire burning my thighs. I hold her still and drive into her, causing water to splash out of the tub in waves.

My climax bursts out of me, and I sink my teeth into her skin as I pump every drop of my release into her wet heat. When she's teetering on the precipice, I pull her off me and set her on the edge of the tub, spreading her legs so I can feast on her dripping center. The taste of our release coats my tongue, making my heart pound in my chest. "Fuck. We taste so good, corazón."

"Nate," she whimpers, threading her fingers in my hair and riding my face. I flick her swollen clit with my tongue, and she comes apart for me, shaking so hard I have to work to hold her in place.

Lying back in the tub, I pull her to straddle me again and slide my tongue into her mouth, letting her taste how good we are together.

～

"I love dinner with your family." She lets out a contented sigh. "Can we do this more often?"

I press a soft kiss on her head while tracing my fingertips up and down her spine. She lies on top of me, naked and thoroughly fucked for the second time tonight. "We'll do it as often as we can, corazón."

She hums and presses her cheek into my chest.

"Now tell me what the deal is between you and your brother."

She tenses in my arms, but I only hold her tighter. "What do you mean?"

"You're always on edge around him. You bristle when he comes near you. Do I need to kill him?"

She pokes me in the ribs. "No!"

I give her another tender kiss. "So tell me."

She wriggles. "He's just not a nice guy."

"Yeah, I'm going to need more than that, Spitfire."

She lifts her head and stares into my eyes. "You really want to know?"

I arch an eyebrow at her. "You think I would've endured that awful movie about cheerleaders if I didn't want to talk to you after?"

She presses her lips together like she's trying not to laugh and then rests her head back on my chest. "He was always a bit of an asshole, but I never saw him much when I was a kid. He was always out with his friends. Then after Dad was killed—" She sucks in a shaky breath. "He said it was my fault. No, he convinced me it was my fault."

Anger vibrates through my entire body. "He did what?"

She shifts, and I allow her to roll onto her side and turn to face her. "We were all supposed to be at the beach that weekend, but my best friend Hayley was having a pool party for her thirteenth birthday. I begged and pleaded to stay home so I could go, but my mom said no. I threw an almighty tantrum." A tear leaks from the corner of her eye. "And Dad said I didn't deserve to go to the beach or the party, so we both stayed home. But the next day, Dad let me go to the party. I realized he scolded me for show and had always been on my side about the party thing. I swear he was always so understanding of teenage girl drama." A sad smile flickers over her face. "But if we had been at the beach like we were supposed to be, he never would have been home when those men tried to rob us. He'd still be alive."

I wipe the tears from her cheeks with my thumbs and cradle her face in my hands. "Jesus, Mel. You must know that doesn't make it your fault."

She sniffs. "But if I hadn't acted like a spoiled brat—"

Jesus. I could murder that prick with my bare hands for making her carry this guilt around all these years. "You were thirteen years old. Acting out is what you're supposed to do."

"I know that, but ... I don't know, Bryce made me believe it, you know? He's used it against me my whole life. And the truth is if it wasn't for me ... If we'd all gone along with Bryce's plan to go to the beach that weekend, my dad wouldn't be dead."

A spark of suspicion ignites. "It was his idea to go?"

"Yeah, he was so mad when Dad decided to stay home with me. He even tried to convince me to tell him that I changed my mind, but I was desperate to go to that party."

I band my arms around her and pull her closer. "And today?"

"He was just his usual asshole self. I doubt he could go a whole day without saying something cruel to me."

"Would you like me to have a word with him?" And by *a word*, I mean I'll break his jaw.

"God, no. Please don't. I'm fine, and I won't be seeing him for a while. I'd much rather spend time with your family."

"Your family too now, Spitfire."

She smiles, and Jesus fuck, it melts me. She calls me Ice, but all I feel is fire in my veins when I'm with her.

CHAPTER
TWENTY-NINE

NATHAN

I head for the office at the back of the Emerald Shamrock nightclub, looking for Shane Ryan, one of the four brothers who owns the club. He also happens to be one of my best clients.

He's perched on the edge of his desk, and he eyes me over the rim of his coffee mug when I step inside his office and take a seat. He places the mug down and jerks his head toward the coffee machine behind him. "You want one?"

I shake my head. "I'm good, thanks."

He sits behind his desk and leans forward, his hands clasped on the table in front of him. His huge biceps strain the fabric pulled taut over his arms, and I instinctively rub my jaw, recalling how he almost knocked me on my ass the last time I saw him. I've been on the receiving end of this man's right hook many times, just like he has mine.

"Haven't seen you at the gym for weeks, buddy." He arches an eyebrow at me. "Did I kick your ass a little too hard last time?"

I run my tongue over my teeth. "You fucking wish."

He laughs. "Congratulations on the wedding, by the way. That was … unexpected."

I shrug. "What can I say, I'm a hopeless romantic at heart."

That makes him laugh harder. "Yeah, right. You should bring her to the club sometime. Jessie would love to meet her." Jessie is his wife, and she's the reason I'm here.

I narrow my eyes. "And which club are you talking about?"

He smirks. "Whichever one you prefer, buddy."

As well as owning the Emerald Shamrock, the most exclusive nightclub in New York, Shane and his brothers also own a private members-only club. Some would call it a sex club, but it's much more sophisticated than that. "Maybe. We'll see."

"Well, let one of us know if you need a booth reserved."

An image of me fucking Mel in one of the private booths at The Peacock Club burns itself into my brain, and I shake my head to clear it. I never used to be distracted this easily.

Shane smirks at me. "Enough pleasure. I assume you're here to discuss business?"

"Yeah. I have something I need looking into. It's not urgent, but it's delicate. I can't trust just anyone with it."

He drums his fingertips on the desk. "You want Jessie to look into it?"

"Yeah." His wife is the best computer hacker in the country, possibly the world. There's no information this woman can't dig up, and she does it faster and cleaner than anyone I've ever known. And given the business I'm in, I've known a lot of people who offer those kinds of services. There's one guy in Los Angeles who comes close, but he lacks her finesse.

Shane's lips twitch in a smirk. "You do understand that I have *you* on a retainer, Nathan, and not the other way around. Seems like I'm the one working for you these days."

I hold his gaze, aware he's only half joking. I've requested his wife's services about half a dozen times in the past six months. And while Shane and I might be friends, he's still the head of the Irish mob, and I don't ever take his position in this city—or the things he's capable of—for granted. "First, I'm not asking you to do it. It's your wife whose services I require. And second, you're keeping your nose so clean lately, it's not my fault I have nothing to do for you."

He rubs a hand over his stubble, and his lips curve as he sighs. "What can I say? The love of a good woman does something to a man."

"Yeah. And I also know that your wife loves this sort of work, and that you and your brothers would do anything to make her happy, so it's almost like I'm doing you a favor if you think about it."

He chuckles. "You're a cocky fucker, and I like that. But yeah, she does love it, and it sure as hell keeps her out of trouble. And if there is one thing my wife is good at finding, it's fucking trouble." He shakes his head.

"This is nothing dangerous. I just need information on a murder that happened seventeen years ago."

His green eyes narrow. "And why is it delicate?"

"The victim was my wife's father. I'd rather not let anyone know I'm looking into it."

He gives a knowing nod. "I'll give her your number and you can tell her what you need. No sense in me continuing as the go-between if she's going to keep doing this kind of work for you."

"I appreciate that, Shane." I'm fully aware of the trust he's placing in me. The Ryan brothers might share their wife with each other, but they're notoriously possessive of her—bordering on rabid—when it concerns anyone else. "I wish she'd let me pay her for her time and effort."

He shakes his head. "I already told you, she doesn't give a fuck about money. Make a donation to charity instead."

"Yeah, I will." I know the perfect one, and she'll definitely approve because she helped bring down the fuckers who hurt the woman that set it up.

"So, your wife?" Shane asks, and my hackles rise.

"What about her?"

"It was sudden. I never thought I'd see the day you settled down. I guess I'm curious."

"She's one of the most incredible people I've ever met," I tell him honestly.

"I hope she brings you some of the peace you need, Nathan."

I frown at him. "You think I need peace?"

He sucks on his top lip for a second, then gives one firm nod of his head. "I think all men like us need peace. Not that we're ever willing to admit that until we find it."

"And who exactly are men like us, Shane?"

"Men who don't know we're broken until someone comes along and fixes us."

CHAPTER
THIRTY

MELANIE

I shovel a spoonful of cereal into my mouth as I scroll through the pictures Tyler sent me from his date at a miniature golf place last night. He's such a cliché. A smile spreads across my face and milk drips down my chin.

Damn! I wipe it with the sleeve of my pajama shirt, and that's when I see him leaning against the doorframe of the kitchen with his arms folded over his chest, looking sexier than any person has a right to look.

"How long have you been standing there?"

He grins. "Long enough to watch you inhale that bowl of Fruity Pebbles."

My cheeks heat with embarrassment. "I didn't get a chance to have lunch today because we were so busy. I thought you were working late or I would have cooked."

He crosses the room and leans against the countertop beside me. "We got everything worked out early."

"Have you eaten?"

He shakes his head. "But I see something delicious that I'd

love to devour right now." He dips his head and runs his tongue from my collarbone to my ear, making me shiver.

"You need actual food."

He slips his hand into my pajama pants. "I'll order us some takeout."

I arch into the pleasure of his fingers between my thighs. "I can cook us something."

He presses his lips against my ear. "I'd rather you spend the next half hour doing something else, corazón."

"Well, if you insist, Mr. James, sir."

He smiles against my skin. "That reminds me, we have an event to attend Saturday night."

Heat coils in my core as he continues toying with me. We've spent most of the two months since we got married in our own little cocoon, outside of work at least. I've been grateful for that, but there's no escaping who Nathan is and the circles he moves in forever. I knew this was going to be a part of our life at some point. "What event?"

"Some fancy dinner for my father's company. It's an investor thing, but he wants us there."

He slides a finger inside me, and I moan. "O-okay."

"Will you let me choose your dress?"

I narrow my eyes, trying my best to look indignant but probably failing miserably in my distracted state. "Why, you don't trust me to choose something appropriately fancy?"

"I trust you." He adds a second finger, and I have to wrap my arms around his neck to stop myself from falling off the stool with the rush of pleasure that engulfs me. "But I want to look at your ass all night in a dress I chose for you." He slides his fingers out of me and sucks them clean. "So?"

I bite my lip. "Okay."

"Good." Lifting me by my hips, he wraps my legs around his

waist and carries me to the bedroom. "I'm going to fuck that sass right out of you one of these days, corazón."

"You need to order dinner first." I flash him a wicked grin.

He keeps one arm under my ass and pulls his phone from his pocket with his free hand. "I can multitask."

"You're so clever," I purr.

He shakes his head, his eyes burning into mine. "You're about to be so fucked."

"Oh, I know."

CHAPTER
THIRTY-ONE

MELANIE

"Have I told you that you look stunning tonight, Mrs. James?" Nathan hands me a glass of champagne, and my cheeks flush pink at his praise. He told me before we left the penthouse, but I could listen to this man tell me how good I look all day, every day.

"Thank you." I flutter my eyelashes and run my free hand over his lapel. "I have to step up my game to have even a chance of competing with you in this tux, Mr. James."

His deep brown eyes narrow, and I feel like he's an apex predator and I'm his prey. Moving behind me, he glides one hand to the small of my back, then rests it on my hip. The other hand splays flat against my abdomen and pulls me closer. He places his sinful lips close to my ear, and his warm breath sends a shiver of pleasure down the length of my spine. A low growl rumbles in his throat as he kisses my neck. "You're doing such a good job of playing the perfect wife, Mel, but I hope you know that I'm going to fuck you like my perfect little whore as soon as I get you alone."

I blink at him in shock. Did he really just call me a—

"Nathan." A female voice cuts off the retort balanced on my lips. "It's so wonderful to see you."

Nathan holds his hand out in greeting to the older lady, leaving me missing the warmth of his touch. "Mrs. Gregory. It's always a pleasure. Have you met my wife, Melanie?"

I smile sweetly, playing the part of the devoted wife as I glance between him and the smiling lady with the white hair. She looks at the pair of us like we're royalty, or at least a celeb power couple. How smoothly he transitions from a filthy-mouthed deviant to the respectable Nathan James. It's astonishing.

"I don't believe I've had the pleasure." Mrs. Gregory offers me her hand. "And haven't I told you about calling me Elena? Mrs. Gregory makes me feel so old."

I take her warm hand in mine. "It's a pleasure to meet you, Elena."

Nathan's father sidles up to us, offers a brief greeting to Elena, then tells Nathan he needs him to meet someone.

Dipping his head, my husband dusts his lips over my ear. "I'll be back soon. Be good, my little siren."

I turn my attention back to Elena, who links her arm through mine and proceeds to give me the inside track on all the most notorious people in the room.

IT'S BEEN ALMOST an hour since Nathan disappeared with his father, and while I've had a lovely and incredibly informative time with Elena, I'm missing my husband and wondering where the hell he went. Making my way through the crowd, I scan the sea of faces until I spot him standing near the bar, talking to a tall blond woman. She throws her head back and laughs, revealing a set of dazzling white teeth behind full red lips. Then she squeezes his arm and takes a step forward, pressing her perky boobs up against his chest.

"Um, hi," I say when I reach them.

Nathan doesn't miss a beat. Slipping his arm around my waist, he pulls me to his side, and the blond steps back. "Deandra, this is my wife, Melanie."

She looks me up and down, her lip curled in the hint of a sneer. "I heard you got married. Such a shame."

I snort and wait for Nathan to tell her to go to hell, but the arrogant jackass only smirks. I'm sure this is the type of woman he dated before me. Impossibly beautiful and inherently confident. "Pleasure to meet you too, *Deirdre*. Enjoy yourself with *my husband*," I say with a saccharine smile before I shrug out of his grip and walk away to find someone who actually wants to talk to me.

I've only taken a few steps when he grabs me by the wrist and discreetly pulls me to his side again, heeling me like a disobedient puppy.

"Get your hands off me," I say through gritted teeth.

He ignores my demand and marches me out of the ballroom. As soon as we're in the quiet hallway, he releases his grip on me. "What the hell was that about?"

I open and close my mouth. "Seriously? She was rubbing her tits against you and then said you getting married was a shame, and all you did was smirk at her."

He pinches the bridge of his nose and sighs. "I didn't smirk at her."

I fold my arms across my chest. "Pretty sure you did."

"Okay, I smirked, corazón, but not at her. Not like that. Deandra is very well-known in these circles."

"What's that supposed to mean?"

"She hits on every man she talks to. Provided they're rich, of course."

"She was rubbing herself against you."

He shakes his head. "She stepped in for a hug, and I would have stepped back had you not arrived like my pint-sized protector to stake your claim." His lips twitch again. "Which was hot as fuck, by the way."

"I did not stake my claim."

His eyes roam over my body like he's not paying all that much attention to anything I say. "Seemed like you did."

Damn, he's infuriating! "You called me a whore."

Now I have his full attention. He glares at me, his brow furrowing. Then he grabs my arm and drags me into an alcove, maneuvering me until we're partially hidden by an antique suit of armor on display. "I did not call you a whore."

"You said—"

"I said ..." He hisses out a breath and yanks me closer until my body is pressed flush against his. "That I would fuck you like my perfect little whore. That's an entirely different thing, Mel."

I know it is, but I'm annoyed and on edge. I think about Deandra and the way she looked so good standing with him. "And have you fucked many whores?"

He rolls his neck and it cracks, making me wince. "If you're asking if I've ever paid for sex, the answer is no."

"Liar." I scoff, and it seems to snap something in him. Before I can blink, he spins me around to face the wall and pins me there, my cheek pressed against the cool brick as the warmth of his chest covers my back.

He catches my earlobe between his teeth and tugs gently, a low growl rolling out of him. He pushes his body into mine, and I'm pressed flat to the wall with no room to move. "Don't call me a liar."

"So you've really never ..." I suck in a breath. The weight of his body against mine has heat pooling in my core.

"I already told you I haven't." His hand coasts over my hip, down my abdomen, and between my thighs, where his fingers tug at the fabric of my dress. He hitches it higher until the thigh split moves and gives him access to my panties. "But I'm going to make you moan my name like I'm paying you to, Mel. Right here in this hallway. Maybe then you'll learn to curb this bad attitude of yours."

"I don't have a bad att—" The rest of the word is cut off by a groan because in one swift movement, he's tugged my panties aside and pushed a thick finger inside me.

"You're always so damn wet for me, Mel." He lets out a dark laugh, and his warm breath dances over the hairs at the nape of my neck.

"We can't ... not here ..." I gasp out the words, my body already sizzling with static electricity.

His lips brush tantalizingly over my skin, making goosebumps prickle out over my body. "I can do anything I want to you, anywhere I want to do it." He adds a second finger. My back bows, and his free hand goes around my throat, tipping my head back. "Can't I, corazón?"

"Y-yes."

He kisses beneath my ear, his body concealing mine as he works his fingers in and out of me. The fact that we could get caught at any moment only heightens all my senses, including the pleasure that is currently racing through my veins. "But never forget that you're *my* whore, Mel. I would never let anyone see you fall apart for me. That exquisite sight is only ever for my eyes."

I cling to his forearm, feeling the muscles flex as he works me expertly and effortlessly until I'm on the brink of a climax and whimpering his name. "Come on my fingers, Spitfire. I'm going to spend the rest of the night with your sweet cream all over my hand."

"Oh, god, Nate," I cry out, rocking my hips and chasing the release.

"I fucking know, corazón. Let go for me."

And I obey like a dutiful wife. My orgasm crashes over me in a slow-rolling wave, and only when I'm finished trembling in his arms does he spin me around and press his forehead against mine. "You still pissed at me?"

"No."

He gently kisses my lips. "Good girl. Let's go back inside."

CHAPTER
THIRTY-TWO

NATHAN

My driver opens the car door, and I guide Mel inside.

"Thanks, Tedward." She grins, and he smirks the way he always does when she calls him that.

"How long until we get home?" I ask.

"A little over an hour, sir."

I nod my thanks and climb inside behind my wife. As soon as I'm seated, I grab her by her hips and pull her onto my lap so she's straddling me.

She wriggles like I'm tickling her, and a musical laugh tumbles from her lips. "What are you doing?"

"There's not a chance in hell I'm going to last another hour without being inside you. You have any idea how hard I've been all night watching you in this dress?" I tug the fabric up to her waist.

"Nate!" My name is a feeble protest on her lips, and her hand is already on the back of my neck, fingers curling in my hair. "You chose the dress, so it's your fault."

I grunt in response and run my nose over the sweet-smelling skin of her neck while my hands glide over her body. Slipping my hand between her thighs, I groan loudly. "Your panties are fucking soaked."

She shifts her hips, pressing herself against my hand. "Also your fault."

The memory of her coming all over my fingers in that hallway makes my cock weep in my boxers. Finding the concealed zipper at the back of her dress, I tug it down, allowing the fabric to pool at her waist.

Moaning, she arches her back while I play with her pussy through her damp panties. I unclasp her strapless bra with my free hand, and it falls loose, freeing her perfect tits inches from my mouth. I suck on one of her hard nipples, sweeping my tongue over the hardened bud and making her cry out.

"I need you naked, Mel. Now," I growl, pulling her dress up and over her head.

"Someone might see us."

I turn my attention to her other nipple. "Nobody can see through these windows."

"What about Tedward?" she breathes.

"Not inviting him to join us, corazón."

She tips her head back on a laugh, and I graze my teeth along her throat. "I mean can he see us?"

"No." I bite down, and she whimpers, tugging my hair and grinding herself against my aching shaft.

I lean back and let my gaze roam over her incredible body. My god, she is fucking exquisite. I run my hands over her tanned skin, palming her tits and squeezing her supple flesh. She presses herself into me, arching into the pleasure.

I nuzzle her neck, teasing her with tongue and teeth while I slide my hand into her underwear. "Tell me why it is that I can barely keep my hands off you when you're near me."

"I don't know," she moans.

"You have some sort of hold over me that I can't break."

I sink two fingers into her tight channel and her back bows. She plants her hands on my shoulders, riding my fingers as I work them in and out of her.

"Nate," she pants, her pussy walls squeezing hard around my fingers.

"And nobody makes you come as hard as I do, do they, corazón?"

She sinks her teeth into her bottom lip and shakes her head. "N-no."

"I need you so fucking bad, all the fucking time. No one has ever made me as hard as you do. You know that?"

Her response is a whimper. With a growl of frustration, I fist my hand in her panties and tear them in half. She gasps, making her beautiful tits bounce. My patience gone, I tug open my belt and she follows suit, yanking on my zipper and sliding her hand inside my boxers. She wraps her fingers around the base of my shaft, squeezing and taunting me.

I press my lips to her ear. "Take out my cock and show me how you make yourself come, my little whore."

Her breath catches in her throat, and her chest flushes pink. Before she can chew me out for using that word, I palm the back of her head and crash my lips to hers, swallowing her sassy comeback. When she's pliant in my arms, I pull back. "Show me, corazón."

With hooded eyes full of desire, she grips my cock again and lowers herself onto my shaft. My eyes almost roll back in my head as her hot cunt fits snugly around me, wrapping me in her wet warmth. "Jesus fuck, Mel." I hiss out a breath.

"You like that?" She gives me a wicked grin and sinks down until I'm fully seated inside her.

I grunt. "You know I fucking do. Now show me how you touch yourself when you're thinking about me."

She slides her hand between her thighs and circles two fingers around her clit. I look down, watching her work herself over, and when she lifts her hips and sinks down onto me again, I almost lose my mind at the sight of my dick stretching her tight pussy.

"Look at us, Mel. Look how fucking well we fit together."

She looks down and mewls. "You feel so good inside me, Nate."

A loud groan pours out of me. "Yeah, I do."

Her fingers work harder, and she rocks her hips, chasing her release. My hands run over her back, her ribs, her hips, committing every inch of her to memory. "Make us come, corazón. I feel your hot cunt squeezing me. I want your cum soaking my cock."

"Jesus, Nate." She drops her head onto my shoulder, and her body quakes as she comes. The way she soaks me with her release and the sensation of her walls rippling around my shaft are enough to pull me right over that edge with her.

I dig my fingers into her hips, holding her still while I empty my load inside her, filling her tight channel with my release. My chest heaves as I pant for breath. I'm obliterated by my need to claim this woman over and over again until she craves me as much as I crave her.

She rests her forehead against mine, her hands clasped around the back of my neck. Our breaths mingle as we drink each other in.

"Wow, that was incredible," she says, breathless.

I run my fingertips down her spine, and she shivers. Pressing her supple body closer, I rest my lips on the slender column of her throat, and my cock twitches inside her. "*You're* incredible, corazón. I'm fucking obsessed with you. When I'm not fucking you, I'm thinking about fucking you. Either what I've done to you or what I'm going to do." I let the admission fall from my lips without stopping to consider what my declaration might mean for us. Because I need her to know, no matter what.

"I love being your obsession, Ice, and I love being the one who gets to unlock that fire in your veins."

I kiss her and band my arms around her waist, crushing her to me, and I keep her like that almost the entire way home. Her, naked and in my arms—exactly how I like her best.

CHAPTER

THIRTY-THREE

MELANIE

Nathan pops his head into the bathroom, startling me as I step out of the shower.

I grab a towel and wrap it around my body. "I thought you'd be home late."

He leans against the doorframe, a smile playing on his lips and his arms crossed over his chest, looking so sexy I could lick him from head to toe. "You're not happy to see me, corazón?"

I roll my eyes and step toward him. "Always, *light of my life*, but I haven't started dinner yet."

He tucks a strand of wet hair behind my ear. "My meetings wrapped up early. Remind me to fire the next person who schedules one on a Saturday afternoon."

I lean into him, and my body immediately responds to his solid warmth. It's been three and a half months since we got married, and our weekends together are my favorite part of every week. "I can do that."

"How about I take you out for dinner? I know a beautiful little Spanish place near Harlem."

My stomach growls loudly, and I stifle a giggle. "I guess that's a yes."

He hums his approval against my lips, then pulls back. "I'm going to take a quick shower. If you could be dressed by the time I'm done, that would be great."

I feign indignation. "Are you suggesting I take too long to get ready?"

"No," he growls, grabbing my ass. "I'm saying that you naked is a huge fucking distraction, and I want to take you out to dinner."

My face heats, and I bite my lip. "Well, I'll be dressed, but it will take me twenty minutes to dry this mane." I flick the ends of my hair.

He kisses me again and flashes me a wink. "As long as this sexy body is covered, I'll be okay." He stalks toward the shower and pulls off his clothes. I take a few beats to admire his muscular back before I force myself to leave the room, knowing if I stare at him any longer, I'll join him in that shower.

～

"THIS PLACE IS BEAUTIFUL, NATE." I shrug off my coat and glance around the restaurant. Although it's entirely indoors, it's decorated like a Spanish garden, and the soft flamenco music is interspersed with faint birdsong.

He pulls out my chair. "My mom used to love coming here. She brought us here all the time as kids."

I smile up at him, grateful for the piece of insight. He doesn't talk about his mom often, and I know it's a painful subject for him. A waiter comes to get our order, and without looking at the menu, Nathan orders a bottle of wine and food for both of us.

"Melanie Edison!" a loud voice calls out as soon as the

waiter drops off our wine, and I look up to see an old college classmate heading my way, a goofy grin on his face.

I don't even have time to look at Nathan before Craig grabs my hand and pulls me up into a hug. "What the hell, Melanie. I haven't seen you since—"

"It's great to see you," I cut him off before he can go any further.

He squeezes me tighter, and the strong smell of beer nearly knocks me out.

"Do you mind taking your hands off my fucking wife?" Nathan growls possessively.

My cheeks burn with embarrassment, and I try to take a step back so I can untangle myself from Craig's embrace, but he holds tight. "Craig, this is my husband, Nathan."

"Your husband, huh?" He looks down, flashing me a grin while still holding onto me before he looks over my shoulder at Nathan.

I glance behind me just in time to see my irate husband stand up, his shoulders rolled back and his jaw clenched. Again, I attempt to wriggle out of Craig's embrace, but he's so drunk that he hangs on like a limpet.

"If you don't take your hand off my wife's ass right now, I will break every bone in both goddamn hands."

I wrench myself out of my old college buddy's grip, and his eyes widen in shock. "It was nice to see you, Craig. You should go."

He blinks at me, then at Nathan.

"Craig, dude! We're leaving!" someone shouts from across the restaurant.

He glances in their direction before turning back to Nathan and me. "Nice to meet you too," he huffs, and goes to join his friend.

I sit back down, my neck and chest hot. "Why did you behave like that?"

Nathan sits too, a heavy scowl furrowing his brow. "Are you being serious right now?"

"Yes. He was just some guy from college."

"He had his hand on your fucking ass."

I roll my eyes. "It was my back."

His narrowed eyes pierce mine, and he shifts forward in his seat. "Pretty sure I know the difference between your back and your ass, Mel."

Tilting my jaw, I glare at him. So it's okay for him to have beautiful women hugging him, but when I meet an old friend there's an issue? What a hypocrite. "Pretty sure I know my own body better than you do."

He leans closer, his scowl deepening. "I wouldn't bet on that, corazón."

I swallow, my skin burning under the intensity of his glare. "He was drunk, that's all. I'm sure he didn't know what he was doing."

"So he did have a hand on your ass?"

I shake my head. "I never said that. He was an old friend, and you acted like a possessive jerkwad because he hugged me. Yet women are allowed to hug you, and when I question that, you ..." I suck in a ragged breath as I recall the night at the charity gala last month. Wet heat sears between my thighs.

Nathan circles his hand around my wrist. "I what?"

"If I recall correctly, you said something about *curbing my bad attitude.*"

His expression darkens, like he's remembering that night too. "And I'll do it again if I need to. Right here at this table."

My lip trembles, but I glare defiantly. "You wouldn't dare."

"I'd love nothing more than to put you over my knee and spank the attitude out of you, corazón."

BROKEN

"So do it," I challenge.

He holds my gaze for a few seconds, his lips twitching, before he releases my wrist and calls the restaurant manager to our table. I can only watch as they have a brief but animated exchange in Spanish, and I'm starting to worry it's becoming heated when the manager smiles and pats Nathan on the shoulder. With a polite nod in my direction, he walks to the nearest table of diners.

"What was that about?" I ask.

"Paolo is clearing out the restaurant for us."

I blink at him. "He's what?"

"He's asking all of these people to leave," he says matter-of-factly. "And then his staff will go home, he'll go to his apartment upstairs, and you and I will have the place entirely to ourselves."

I open and close my mouth, feeling distinctly like a goldfish. "You—what? You can't do that."

His eyes don't leave mine. "I just did."

"But ... these people are eating. You can't just toss them out in the middle of their meal."

His jaw ticks. "They'll be given twenty minutes to finish. Their checks will be taken care of, and their next visit will be free."

I gape at him. "That's going to cost you a fortune."

"It will be worth it, corazón." He checks his watch and smirks. "You have about twenty minutes until I get you alone."

I swallow hard. The threat in his tone is clear. He's pissed at me. We haven't had any serious arguments since the day after we were married, and I have no idea how he handles conflict. Although his reputation in the courtroom is ice, he's always been a blazing fire where I'm concerned, and something tells me I'm about to get burned.

After our food is delivered, I sip my wine and chew my pasta

187

until it turns to glue in my mouth. All the while, I watch Nathan calmly finish his steak and wish I had an ounce of his composure. My legs are shaking beneath the table, but it's not from fear. My blood sizzles with anticipation.

After the last customer leaves and the staff files out the door, Paolo bids us both goodnight and reminds Nathan to make sure he closes the door firmly when we leave.

Now Nathan and I are entirely alone, and although I won't meet his gaze, I feel his eyes on me as keenly as if they were flames licking my skin. My entire body thrums with nervous energy.

"Look at me," he commands.

I lift my head, allowing my gaze to travel up the thick column of his throat, the fine dusting of stubble that peppers his jaw, over his full lips, and finally to his piercing brown eyes. "What now?" I ask, aware my voice is barely a whisper.

His eyes darken. "Strip."

I blink at him like an idiot. The muscle in his jaw ticks, and I glance around the restaurant. It's now entirely empty, but the lights are still on—muted but still too bright for me to be thrilled about getting naked—and there are windows. Giant windows. And although we're tucked away in a corner and can't be seen from outside, it still feels very *public*.

"I said strip," he commands again.

My pulse hums against my pressure points. I tip my chin at him. "And what if I don't?"

The corner of his mouth curls, and he cups my chin in his hand, dragging the pad of his thumb over my bottom lip and making me shiver. "You know what edging is?"

I nod.

He keeps a firm grip on my face. "I will have your cunt aching and dripping for me before we leave this restaurant, corazón. And on the way home, I'll make you beg for the

188

promise of relief that I won't deliver. Then I will take my fill of your beautiful body over and over again until you're burning up from the inside out with the ravenous need to come. And tomorrow"—he presses a chaste kiss to my forehead—"I'll do it all again. So that by the time you go to work on Monday, you won't be able to think straight with the blood screaming in your ears and the throbbing between your thighs."

I swallow, my heart thumping in my ears.

"So don't make me ask you again." His tone is low and demanding, but I don't feel powerless here. Whatever else is between us, I know that I trust this man. He would never humiliate or embarrass me, no matter how pissed he might be.

Wrenching my head out of his grip, I stand and keep my eyes fixed on his as I reach for the zipper at the back of my dress. I slowly pull it down until the black fabric pools at my feet.

His face remains impassive. "Everything, corazón."

My fingers tremble on the hook of my bra, but I manage to unhook it and let it fall to the floor. Nathan's jaw is tight, his hands balled into fists at his sides. He's not as cool and calm about this as he's pretending to be. I make a show of hooking my thumbs into the waistband of my panties, swaying my hips as I peel them over my curves.

Growling, he leans forward in his seat, his eyes raking greedily up and down my body. A thrill of excitement runs through me. He makes no attempt to hide the effect I have on his body, and the knowledge that he wants me as much as I want him makes me feel sexy and empowered in a way I never have before.

I kick my panties off my feet.

"Keep the heels on." The deep timbre of his voice melts my core, and I press my lips together to stop myself from whimpering.

He trails his fingertips over the curve of my hip and skates them down my abdomen. His free hand rests on his thigh, and he clenches and unclenches his fist, just like that night at the zoo, as though his palm is twitching with the need to spank my ass. The thought of being bent over his lap and spanked makes liquid warmth seep between my thighs.

"You're so fucking beautiful, Mel." He grabs my wrist and yanks me toward him. I bump against his thigh and fall right over his lap, my ass in the air and my elbows on the bench. "But that's not going to distract me enough to spare your ass, corazón."

"Nate." I gasp out his name on a stuttered breath.

"Have you ever been spanked, Mel?"

"N-no," I stammer truthfully.

He runs his palm over my ass cheeks before squeezing one in a bruising grip, but it only makes me grind myself against his thigh. "I've been waiting for a reason to spank this ass since the first time you sassed me on our first date."

"I did not sass you," I protest.

A dark laugh rumbles out of him. "Yes you did, and you know it. From the moment you climbed into my car you were trying to push my buttons."

Okay, maybe that's true. I glance over my shoulder at him and arch an eyebrow. "Pretty sure you did some pushing yourself, Ice."

He delivers the first stinging slap to my ass, and I yelp in surprise more than pain. Surprise that I feel the ache leftover by his hand between my thighs rather than anywhere else. I hiss out a breath, and he spanks me again, a little harder this time.

Whining, I rest my head on my forearms and rub myself against his taut thigh muscle, stifling a moan at the delicious friction it provides my aching center. I need more. Lifting my hips, I push my ass into the hand rubbing over my tingling flesh.

He groans and spanks me again.

A keening moan is torn from my throat. "Nate, please?"

"You like being bent over my knee like this?" Smack.

"Yes," I cry out, and he delivers another blow.

I've never ached to feel him inside me more than I do right now. It's a visceral longing that comes from somewhere deep and carnal. This should feel so wrong, but in his arms everything only ever feels right. When he sinks two fingers inside me a second later, I scream his name so loudly that I'm sure people passing by on the street must hear me, but I no longer care. All I can focus on is Nathan.

"You're soaked for me already, corazón. I knew this would get you worked up." He spanks me again while he slides his fingers in and out of me.

"That feels so good."

"You look so good. Naked on my lap, soaking my hand with your juices."

Oh, dear sweet mother in heaven, that mouth!

Just when I think Nathan has me on the edge and can't possibly make this whole situation feel any filthier than it already does, he coats a fingertip with my arousal and slides it up the seam of my ass before pressing it against the tight ring of muscle. I almost freeze at the foreign sensation, but I'm too far gone. "Has anyone ever taken you here, corazón?"

"N-no."

He presses more firmly, and I tremble with anticipation, which he seems to take as an invitation to push the tip of his finger inside me.

"Oh, fuck." I squeeze my eyes closed as a violent tremor rockets through my body.

His groan is deep and low and full of satisfaction. "You're going to let me take you here though, aren't you?"

God, he can take me any way, anywhere. "Y-yes."

He glides his finger in and out of my ass while he keeps two more in my pussy. "Good girl."

A guttural groan rasps in my throat. I'm so close. "Nathan, please!"

Instead of taking pity on me, he removes his fingers. I whine at the loss of his touch, sinking onto his lap like I'm boneless. So he's edging me even though I did what he asked?

"Come here, corazón." His tone is soothing as he pulls me up into a kneeling position on the bench so I'm straddling one of his powerful thighs. He snakes one arm around my waist and uses the other to tangle his fingers in my hair and keep my head in place. "There's something unbelievably sexy about you being naked on my lap while I'm in my suit."

I roll my hips, and the hardness of his thigh between my legs makes pleasure curl in my center. "Yeah, you do seem to have a thing for that."

Nathan rests his lips against my ear. "You don't deserve to have me make you come."

I pout.

He trails his teeth and tongue along my jawline and down my neck. "But I'd like to see you make yourself come riding my thigh like that."

He sucks a hardened nipple into his hot mouth, and I moan his name, winding my fingers through his thick hair as I rub my aching pussy over him. Despite what he just said, he stokes my orgasm, squeezing my breasts in his huge hands and teasing my aching nipples with his delicious mouth until I'm on the edge of ecstasy. He grabs onto my hips, pulling me tight against his taut muscles and grinding his leg against my clit.

Unable to hold on any longer, I throw my head back as my orgasm washes over me. Warm and heavy, it takes me under with its intensity. And it's Nathan who brings me back, wrapping his arms around my waist and sinking his teeth into my neck.

When I can see again, I stare into his dark eyes, panting for breath.

Looking down, he smirks. "You've made quite the mess there, corazón."

I follow his gaze, and my cheeks burn with mortification at the sight of my arousal coating his expensive suit pants. His entire left thigh is covered in me. "I'm so—"

He squeezes my jaw and cuts off the rest of my apology. His dark eyes narrow, glimmering with a danger that makes me swallow nervously. "Don't you dare apologize for having any part of you on any part of me."

I press my lips together to stop myself from apologizing again.

"Get dressed, corazón. We're leaving." He lifts me off his lap, then uses his cloth napkin from dinner to wipe his pants and stuffs the damp material into his jacket pocket.

"That's theft." Flashing him a mischievous grin, I grab my panties from the floor.

"*That* is making sure nobody but me gets to touch or smell my wife's cum." With that, he lets out an animalistic growl.

I don't know if he's still mad about earlier, but even if he is, make-up sex with Nathan James will undoubtedly be even hotter than what we just did.

CHAPTER
THIRTY-FOUR

NATHAN

I've been feral with the need to fuck her since we were in the restaurant, but I've enjoyed teasing her too much to take her. Even in the car when she sat on my lap the entire ride home, I was too preoccupied with keeping her on the edge to do anything more than toy with her. But now, with the two of us alone in our penthouse, I'm going to claim every part of her.

We stare at each other, each of us panting with need, our breathing fast and hard.

She arches an eyebrow, knowing exactly how much I want her. Knowing what she does to me. In a single stride, I have one hand in her hair and one on her ass, and I herd her back toward the wall. A few seconds later, she's pressed against the plaster, and I'm grinding my aching shaft against her.

"Nate," she murmurs. I capture her mouth in a bruising kiss, unable to keep the animal inside me at bay for even a second longer. Yanking her dress up around her waist, I expose her thighs and run my hands up the supple skin to palm her ass. I lift her with ease, and she wraps her legs around my waist. Equally frenzied, she tugs at my belt and makes short work of unbuckling my pants, and then she's right where I want her, wrapping her slender fingers around my throbbing shaft. She squeezes hard, and I moan into her mouth, rocking my hips to find relief in the pressure of my body grinding against her.

She breaks our kiss and gasps. "Nate, I really need you."

I tug her lace panties aside and drive my cock inside her. She trembles, her head falling back against the wall, while I groan at the sheer relief that courses through me. "I know," I growl, nailing her to the wall with punishing thrusts as I bite a trail along her jawline.

"What were we even arguing about earlier?" she pants between breaths.

"Can't. Fucking. Remember."

She clings to me, her arms wrapped around my neck as needy whimpers and sexy-as-fuck moans pour out of her body, sounding like they're being dragged from deep in her core. It makes me drive harder, sinking so far inside her that I'm not sure I'll ever be able to pull free. She consumes me.

I dust my lips over her ear and bite down on her earlobe. "As soon as I'm done fucking you in our hallway, I'm taking you to bed and taking your ass, corazón."

Her green eyes go dark with longing. She bites on her lip and gives me a single nod. I bury my face in her neck and rail into her until she screams my name and I fill her with my cum.

MEL LIES BACK on our bed, her chest heaving with labored breaths. Holding a bottle of lube, I crawl over her and run my hand up her thighs, over her abdomen and breasts, and pause at her collarbone. "Are you nervous, corazón?"

The slender curve of her throat convulses. "A little."

I brush my lips over her jaw. "We don't have to do this tonight. We can wait."

She wraps her arms around my neck. "No. I want to."

"You're sure?"

She sinks her teeth into her bottom lip and nods.

"Turn over for me, Spitfire."

She does as I ask, turning her head to the side so she can watch what I'm doing. I open the cap on the lube and part her ass cheeks. "This will be cold," I warn her, and squirt a generous amount on her asshole.

She flinches, but then she moans when I massage a finger over the tight ring. I inch the tip inside her, and her sweet noises grow more insistent. "You like that, corazón?"

"Y-yeah." She pushes her ass back, and I reward her by sinking my finger in up to the knuckle. "Oh, Nate," she keens, pressing her face into the pillow and biting down.

I gently work my finger in and out of her until she's ready for another. When I add the second, she lifts her head and cries out my name.

"Still okay there?"

She nods.

"Words, Mel."

"Yes!"

Leaning over her, I rest my lips against her ear. "You're doing so well. Such a good girl letting me take your ass."

I work my fingers deeper, and tremors ripple through her body. "Please, Nate," she mewls.

My dick aches to be inside her. I can barely see straight with the strength of the need that courses through me. Sex has always been a big part of my life, but sex with her is other-worldly. I'm obsessed with the need to claim every part of her.

She lets out a long breath, her body sinking into the mattress, when I remove my fingers. I coat my cock with an excessive amount of lube, my hand slick with it as I tease her ass cheeks apart.

Falling onto the bed, I bracket her body with my hands and nudge the crown of my cock at her asshole. She whimpers. "I don't have to go all the way on our first time, corazón. Just as much as you can take, okay?"

Her cheek rasps against the pillow as she nods. "Okay."

I inch inside, breaching the tight ring of muscle with the tip of my shaft.

"Nate!" she gasps, her back bowing.

I rub a soothing hand over the small of her back, holding myself up on one forearm. "You still good?"

"Yes. Good."

"Good girl," I growl as I sink deeper. My eyes roll back at the way her muscles squeeze me. "You're so tight, corazón. You sure you're okay?"

"It feels so ..." She sucks in a breath. "Different but good."

I go on rubbing her back while I trail kisses over her shoulders. "You're doing so fucking well."

She practically purrs, and a smile spreads across her face. Dipping my head, I take her bottom lip between my teeth and tug lightly. "Next time we do this, you'll be on your back so I can look at your beautiful face while I fuck you."

I rock my hips, gently thrusting in and out of her. "Yeah?" she groans.

"Yeah. I can get deeper inside you that way too."

"How far inside me are you?" She gasps out the words.

I'm not even halfway in, but I don't tell her that. "Enough, corazón. Enough."

Burrowing my hand between her body and the mattress, I find her clit and circle the pads of two fingers over her slick bud.

She grinds herself against my hand. "Oh, Jesus, Nate."

"You gonna come for me with my cock in your ass, Mel?"

"Yes!"

I increase the pace of my thrusts, desperate to nail her to the mattress but careful not to push her too far. But with the way she feels around my shaft and the memory of what I did to her earlier in the restaurant, not to mention when we got home, I'm a few seconds away from losing myself in her.

"Come with me, corazón," I growl in her ear, increasing the pressure on her clit. Her muscles spasm around me, and the aftershocks from the rippling of her tight cunt vibrate through the tip of my dick.

She groans my name, her body trembling beneath mine as she comes for me, and the tremors of her body reverberate through me. I rock my hips, sinking deeper while she rides the high of her orgasm, and find my own release.

When I'm done, I rest my forehead between her shoulder blades, blowing out deep breaths and trying to calm my racing heart before it beats straight out of my chest.

"God, that was intense," she pants.

"It was amazing." I kiss her forehead and notice her wince when I slide out of her. "Did I hurt you?"

"No."

I push myself onto my knees. "Let's go get cleaned up."

She flips onto her back, her shining green eyes blinking up at me. "Can we just lie here for a little while first?"

"Whatever you want, corazón." I fall onto my back with a contented sigh and pull her into my arms, where she curls her slender body against mine. Forget just a little while; we can lie here forever if she wants to.

WE LIE IN THE DARK, showered and satisfied, but we're both fighting sleep. What happened tonight was so incredible, and I suspect we both want to bask in the aftermath a little while longer. She rests her head on my chest, and I trail my fingertips up and down her spine. "Are you sore?"

"A little, but it's a nice kind of sore, you know?"

"I should have taken it easier on you."

"No." She snuggles into my chest. "I told you, it's a nice sore. Like I can still feel you inside me."

My dick twitches, and I let out a groan. "Do you have to constantly make me hard, corazón?"

She laughs, and I can picture her rolling her eyes. "Everything makes you hard."

I resist the urge to swat her ass and instead band my arms tighter around her. "Everything about *you* makes me hard."

"Mmhmm, I like that."

"Being the first man to fuck your perfect ass was an honor. Thank you."

"Yeah." Her heavy sigh makes me frown.

"What's wrong?"

"I just realized I'll have no firsts like that with you."

God, she couldn't be more fucking wrong. She's the first woman I've allowed to sleep in my bed more than twice. The only woman I've ever lived with and allowed into every part of my life. The first one I'm unable to stop myself from thinking about all the damn time. She is my wife, and I never planned to get married. There are too many firsts to list, so I simply press a kiss on the top of her head and say, "You have all of my important firsts, corazón."

"I do?"

"Yes. Now get some sleep."

She nestles closer into me, letting out a contented purr. Closing my eyes, I drift off to sleep with thoughts of enjoying several thousand more nights like this one.

CHAPTER
THIRTY-FIVE

NATHAN

I return my phone to the nightstand and turn back to my sleeping wife, giving her my full attention. Her pink lips are slightly parted, and her dark lashes fan over her flushed cheeks. God, she is so fucking beautiful. I slide my hand over her hip, and her body instinctually melts into my touch. She fits against me like she was made to be here, her form carved to fit the contours of mine.

I must hold on a little too tightly because her eyelids flutter open. As soon as her eyes land on mine, she smiles. If I ever did actually have ice in my veins, that smile would melt it faster than ice cream in the sun.

"Morning," she murmurs.

I drop a kiss on her forehead and drink in her scent. She smells of perfume and me. "Morning, sleeping beauty."

She blinks. "What time is it?"

"Almost eleven."

Her hand flies to her mouth. "Nate! Why did you let me sleep so late?"

I shrug. "You had an eventful night, corazón. Plus, it's Sunday. We have nowhere to be except right here."

She murmurs contentedly and wraps her arms around my neck. "We can stay right here all day?"

I pull her closer. "We can." I think back to the text message I found from my father when I woke up. "But if you want to go out later, my dad invited us for dinner. Well, technically brunch and dinner, but I already said no to brunch because I have no desire to leave this bed for at least another hour."

She buries her face against my chest and purrs like a kitten. "An hour, huh?"

"Not for that, corazón." I glide a hand over her ass, and I'm relieved when she doesn't flinch.

"Shame." She giggles, snuggling closer.

I'm surprised at how much I enjoy doing nothing more than lie in bed with her in my arms. Sundays, when we get to sleep as late as we want and only do what we want, have become my favorite day of the week. "My insatiable little spitfire."

She hums like she's thinking. "If we can't have sex, can we have pancakes?"

"I'll make you pancakes, corazón."

"And can we go to your dad's for dinner too?"

It's become clear in recent weeks how much Mel loves spending time with my family, and they're obviously smitten with her too. Seeing Dad's smile reach his eyes the way it used to when my mom was alive is something I never thought I'd see again. "Yes, we can go for dinner." How could I ever deny her a chance to spend time with my dad and brothers, or them with her? Not only has Mel made my life richer, she's brought a happiness to the James family that I was beginning to think would elude us forever.

~

Mel climbs into my car, and I don't miss her wince when she flops down onto the seat with a thud.

I scramble in after her. "Fuck, Mel. Are you in pain?"

She shakes her head. "I just sat down a little harder than I intended."

I pull her into my lap and ignore her feeble squawk of protest. "You have to let me know if I'm ever hurting you."

Her green eyes soften, and her face lights up with a sweet smile. "I would tell you if it was something I couldn't handle. I promise you that I loved every single thing about last night. But the spanking and the …" She blushes. "Well, they were both firsts, so my ass is a little tender. That's all."

I search her face for any sign that she's uncomfortable now, but she seems to be telling the truth. "I find it hard to hold back with you. Last night was incredible, and I want to do it again, but if you're in pain—"

"I'm not in pain, Nate. Stop worrying about me. You seriously think last night wasn't incredible for me?" She presses her lips to my ear, and her warm breath dusts over my neck. "I came pretty hard."

A growl rumbles in my throat. "Yes, you fucking did."

She shoots me a saucy smile. "Exactly. So stop worrying." I reposition her so she's straddling me, and I can't help but smile at the way she shivers when I run my nose along her jawline. "How long until we get to your dad's house?" she breathes.

"Forty minutes."

She rolls her hips over me, making my cock stiffen. "Such a long time to sit in this car doing nothing."

I press a brief kiss at the base of her throat. "Actually, I have the perfect thing to keep you occupied for the next forty minutes."

A seductive smile curves her lips, and she tips her head

back. With a groan, I press my lips to the creamy expanse of her throat and allow myself a moment to feast on what she so generously offers.

CHAPTER
THIRTY-SIX

NATHAN

Mel's sweet-sounding laugh fills the car. "I'm telling you it's right."

Shaking my head, I stare down at the newspaper on my lap. "I'm almost certain the answer to thirteen down isn't cockblocker, corazón."

She trails her fingers over the two letters already filled in. "But it fits, see?" She laughs louder, and tears stream down her cheeks.

I can't help but smile at her infectious joy. "If I'd known you were going to be this much trouble, I never would have asked for your help."

Her laughter subsides, and she wipes the tears from her eyes. "Well, when you said you had the perfect way to spend forty minutes, I had no idea you meant completing the Sunday crossword."

"I'll have you know that the *New York Times* Crossword was an institution in our house."

She places a hand over her heart. "Then I'm honored to be a part of it."

Is she sassing me? I toss the paper onto the seat beside me and pull her into my arms. "So you agree that a crossword is the finest way to spend forty minutes on a Sunday afternoon?"

She presses her lips together and looks up, like she's taking time to consider her answer. "No," she eventually says.

"No?" I gasp, feigning indignation.

"I can think of way more fun things to do with you," she says with a sultry purr.

"Is that so?" I tickle her sides, and she curls herself into a ball on my lap, giggling uncontrollably and trying to barricade her torso with her arms.

Before long, I'm laughing along with her and wondering how the fuck I ever lived without this woman in my life.

∼

By THE TIME Mel and I get to my father's house, Mason and Elijah are already in the kitchen, bickering about how to make the best gravy.

They stop when we walk in, and both my brothers greet us with a hug. When the salutations are finished, Mason taps his mouth with a wooden spoon. "You know, I'm sure Mel can settle our Thanksgiving debate."

"No. Absolutely not." I shake my head. "You don't get to make my wife a juror in your annual mashed potato proceedings."

"What?" Mason feigns innocence with a dramatic shrug. "She's the perfect person to decide. She's never eaten with us before, so she has no idea whose mashed potatoes are whose. She has no skin in the game." He chuckles at his own pun, and I roll my eyes.

"Thanksgiving is only four weeks away and she'll be eating with us this year, so she should have a say in how the mashed potatoes are made," Elijah adds.

Mel looks between the three of us, soaking up every word with a confused smile on her face.

"It's ridiculous," I argue. "We're having mashed potatoes the way I always make them."

"Dad doesn't care one way or the other, and just because you and Drake like them that way doesn't mean we should all be subjected to your subpar potatoes. It's time for a revolution!" With a triumphant grin on his face, Mason hoists his spoon into the air. "And Melanie James shall be the one to lead us, heralding a new era of mashed potato splendor in the James household."

Mel snorts a laugh but quickly composes herself. Gripping Mason's elbow, she tips her chin up and smiles. "I'm in."

"Hell yeah!" Mason shouts.

I lift one eyebrow and stare down my little brother. "What if she chooses my mashed potatoes?"

He scoffs. "Never gonna happen."

I cross my arms over my chest and glare first at my brothers, then at my wife. "Fine. Bring it."

Elijah narrows his eyes and frowns at me. "No cheating. No giving her any signals or anything like that."

Mason nods. "Or any weird husband and wife telepathy shit."

Mel's laugh fills the kitchen.

I snatch the wooden spoon from Mason's hand. "And exactly what weird *telepathy shit* do you think we can do, numb-nuts? We're not twins."

Mason shrugs. "I don't claim to understand the intricate workings of married life. All I'm saying is don't try to sway her. I know you like to win by any means necessary."

"I don't need to cheat," I assure him.

Elijah puffs out his chest. "I will present Mel with her options. You two can stand behind her while she decides so there's no risk of foul play. Okay?"

"Fine," Mason and I say in unison.

Elijah guides Mel to sit on a stool with her back to Mason and me, then clears his throat. "You understand the gravity of the decision you're about to make, Melanie?" he asks, his tone all business.

She gives a firm nod. "I do."

He takes a breath. "Do we have lumpy mashed potatoes with skins, butter, and a little salt and pepper? Or smooth, no skins, with cream and just a dash of salt?" I scowl at the way he all but licked his lips when he gave her the second option.

She hums and takes the time to properly consider her options. Mason and I wait with bated breath.

"Definitely smooth with cream," she declares.

Mason roars triumphantly and jabs his finger into my sternum. "You just got schooled, son."

I drop my head into my hands. "Jesus, Spitfire. What the hell have you done?"

She spins around to face me. "Oh no. Was that not yours?" I can tell she's trying to sound contrite, but she can barely contain her laughter as Mason bounces around the kitchen like he just won the heavyweight title. He high-fives Elijah, and they both loudly declare their victory.

Mel wraps her arms around my waist. "I'm so sorry, Ice." She giggles.

Our father's loud voice cuts through the kitchen. "What's all this shouting about?"

Mason fist pumps the air. "We're having my mashed potatoes for Thanksgiving instead of Nathan's."

"No." Dad shakes his head. "Skin on with butter. Just like your mom used to make."

"But Dad," Mason whines. "You said you didn't care."

Dad shrugs. "That was only to spare your feelings, son."

Mel puts a hand to her mouth and stifles another giggle. Dad puts an arm around her shoulders and kisses the top of her head. "Lovely to see you, sweetheart."

"You too," she says, grinning up at him, and my old man smiles widely.

"Will your sister be joining us for Thanksgiving?" he asks.

Her smile falls and she shakes her head. "No, not this year. She's staying with her friend who'd otherwise be on her own, and they have plans to go to a concert. But she'll be home for Christmas. And I know she'd love to join us here."

My father gives her another brief squeeze. "She's more than welcome any time."

As soon as he's out of earshot, I pull my wife close and stare into her eyes. "I can't believe you didn't choose my potatoes, corazón. Your betrayal has cut me deeply."

A wicked grin spreads over her lips. "I'm so sorry." She flutters her eyelashes. "What can I do to make it up to you?"

"I'm sure I'll think of something," I say, squeezing her ass and arching my eyebrows.

"Come on," Mason groans. "Let the woman go so she can get a drink."

I tuck my face into her neck and smile against her skin. "I think my brother wants your attention. But remember … tonight, you're all mine."

After I lightly swat her ass, she plants a quick kiss on my lips and joins my brother at the bar.

As I set the table, I watch Mason teach Mel how to make a Mai Tai. Dad leans against the counter, chatting with them while Elijah finishes dinner. His wife rarely sets foot in this house anymore. Still, after twenty years, Amber doesn't look half as comfortable with my family as Mel does after less than four months.

She fits seamlessly into my life and into my family. Like she was always meant to be here. I offer my father a grateful smile. Without him, none of us would have her in our lives, and the fact that we could have been here today while she was someplace else—*with* someone else—is unthinkable to me.

CHAPTER

THIRTY-SEVEN

NATHAN

"How long will you be in Chicago?" With her head propped up on her hand, Mel leans on her elbow and traces her fingertips over my chest.

My gaze rakes over her naked torso, and I'm irrationally annoyed at the duvet for covering her up to her hips.

"Pay attention, Ice." Her admonishment is immediately followed by her beautiful laugh. She makes a V with her fingers and points at her face. "Eyes up here."

I look into her bright green eyes and grin. "But you're such a fucking distraction, Spitfire."

She rolls those pretty eyes. "Chicago? How long?"

Sighing, I lock my hands behind my head to stop myself from flipping her onto her back and fucking her again. "Three days."

She wrinkles her nose. "And you fly out tonight?"

I nod. "My flight leaves at seven."

"You're sure you can make it back in time for the Christmas

210

party at the shelter on Friday? It's the biggest fundraising event of the entire year, and they were stoked when I told them you planned to be there. You know, you're kind of a celebrity."

I love the way her eyes light up when she talks about the shelter. She doesn't get a chance to volunteer there as much as she used to now that we're married and I monopolize so much of her free time, but she still answers the call whenever they need her.

"Yes, I'll be there, corazón."

Her smile lights up her entire face. "Thank you. I can't wait for you to meet everyone."

"You look so fucking beautiful when you smile like that." I brush my lips over her cheek.

"Well, this smile"—she runs her hand down my chest and over my abs—"is reserved only for you."

"It better be." Her hand slips beneath the covers and I growl. I need to get showered and be out of the apartment in the next thirty minutes to make it to my 8:00 a.m. meeting. And once that meeting is over, I'm going to fire whoever arranged it. "You're going to get one of us in a whole lot of trouble if you move that any lower, corazón."

She presses her lips together like she's contemplating whether to continue, but her hand stills and she splays her fingers over my abs. "I wish you didn't have to go to Chicago later."

Dammit, so do I. I've never had a problem with our annual company meeting being held in Chicago every year. Until now. I make a mental note to talk to Drake about moving the meeting to Manhattan in the future. "Will you be good while I'm gone?"

Her eyes sparkle with mischief. "I'm always good."

Unable to keep my hands off her for another second, I flip her onto her back and pin her to the mattress. "Will you pretend that it's my fingers inside you when you get yourself off?"

"Always," she gasps, rocking her hips against my hardening length.

One look at the clock tells me I really don't have any more time to spare. I let out a frustrated growl that contrasts the gentle kiss I press to her lips. "I have to go." We both know I'm not only talking about my morning meeting, but also the trip to Chicago.

She nods. "I know."

After planting a final kiss on her hair, I tear myself away from her and head for the shower.

MEL PEELS off her coat and lets it slide down her arms to the floor, leaving her standing before me in her uniform. This woman somehow manages to make navy scrubs look like the sexiest clothing on the planet.

She bites her lip and flutters her eyelashes, playing coy. But I know exactly why she came to my office this afternoon, and I couldn't be happier about it. I'm harder than iron just thinking about her reason for being here.

"Come here," I command.

She takes two steps, her hips swaying seductively.

I shake my head. "Nuh-uh. Crawl to me."

She stops in her tracks and narrows her eyes, no doubt wondering if I'm playing. I'm not.

"Crawl to me, corazón. Show me how much you're going to miss me."

She pauses for a few more beats, but then she sinks to her knees, and my cock jumps in my pants. Her eyes never leave mine as she crawls to me, her hips and ass swaying like a pendulum—hypnotizing and alluring. I have never seen anything sexier in my entire goddamn life. She stops in front of me, and I grab her jaw, pulling her up so she's kneeling at my feet. A growl of appreciation rumbles out of my throat. "That's my good girl."

She licks her plump bottom lip, silently begging me to do the same. "What now, sir?"

Using my free hand, I free my cock from my pants and squeeze the base of my shaft. Sweet relief rolls through me, and I groan. "Seeing as you're already on your knees ..."

She slides her hands up my thighs, squeezing my tense muscles as she dips her head and licks the crown of my cock, cleaning the precum already beading there. Her moan is full of longing, and it makes me desperate to fuck her throat. Her hair falls in dark waves over her face, and I gather it in my fist at the nape of her neck. I don't want to miss a second of this particular show.

She trails her tongue up the length of my shaft, and my cock pulses, jerking at the sensation of her hot mouth on me. I run the pad of my thumb over her cheek, waiting for her to take all of me. I have limited patience when it comes to her and her body, but this is the last time I'll touch her for three whole days, so I want to savor every fucking second of it.

She teases me a little more, kissing my weeping slit before her tongue dances over my aching length. I growl in frustration, but it doesn't make her hurry, and I love that. She seems to know what I need without me ever asking. Our bodies are finely tuned to one another's, as though we've been doing this dance a lot longer than a few months.

When I'm on the edge of losing control and seconds away from driving my cock into her pretty throat, she wraps her lips around me and takes me inside her mouth, sucking greedily like she's as desperate to taste me as I am to be tasted. I tighten my grip in her hair, rocking my hips so I hit the back of her throat hard enough that tears leak from the corners of her eyes. I wipe them away and watch her suck harder and faster. Her needy little moans are muffled by my cock as she brings me close to the edge of ecstasy. My cock pulses in her mouth, so close to spilling my load down her throat.

"You take my cock so fucking well, corazón." My eyes roll back in my head as I get closer to the release she seems intent on denying me. Every time I get close, she eases off, pulling back and sweeping her tongue over me before I drive back inside her again. My frustrated grunts echo off the walls of my office. I've never allowed a woman to tease me the way that she does, but for some reason, I revel in the fight for control that we engage in during moments like these. Maybe because I like taking it back from her when she thinks she's won. The knowledge that I can take it at any time makes me feel invincible. It might be the hottest feeling in the whole fucking world.

Pushing her head forward, I force her to accept every inch of me. More tears leak from the corners of her eyes, and she draws a deep breath through her nose and swallows, gripping the tip of my cock in her throat and wrenching an earth-shattering climax from me. I roar out her name and hold her head still while I empty myself inside her.

Spent, I let my hands fall from her face and hair. She sits back on her heels, wiping my cum and her spit from her chin before she looks up at me with a triumphant expression on her face.

"You get so feral when I have my mouth on you, sir. I have no idea how you're going to cope without me the next few days."

I take a few seconds to catch my breath. "I think you're the one who gets feral, corazón. You're the one still kneeling at my feet after sucking my cock like my good little whore."

Her smile fades, and a look of hurt flashes in her eyes.

Tilting my head to the side, I study her beautiful face. "You still don't like me using that word?"

"I ... it's ..." Her slender throat thickens as she swallows, and her eyes glisten with fresh tears. She shakes her head. "It's not the word so much as ..."

I take her hand and pull her onto my lap. She straddles me, and I brush her hair back from her face. "What is it?"

"Given how we started, I think it feels a little too close to the truth." She tries to wriggle from my grip, but I band an arm around her waist and hold her tighter.

"How we came to be ..." I run my nose over her jawline and inhale her feminine scent as I slide my hand into her pants. "That was business. A mutually beneficial agreement for both parties." My fingers brush the soft lace of her panties, and her breath hitches in her throat. "But this ..." Tugging the fabric aside, I slide a finger along her slit and bite back a groan when I feel how wet she got sucking me off. I dip one finger inside her, and she arches into me. "This is personal, right?"

She sinks her teeth into her lip, but she doesn't answer.

I drive deeper. "Isn't it, Mel?"

"Y-yes," she gasps.

"No matter how we came to be here, you are my wife, and regardless of what I call you, or how often I fuck you like a whore when we're alone, outside of these walls, I will defend you and your honor with my dying breath. Do you understand me?"

She tips her head back, rolling her hips and grinding against my palm like she's chasing more of what I'm deliberately holding back from her. I add a second finger, and she mewls, still avoiding my gaze.

I fist my free hand in her hair. "Look at me when I'm inside you, corazón." Her eyelids flutter, and she fixes those hypnotic green eyes on my face. "Who are you?"

She drags her luscious bottom lip through her teeth before releasing it with a grin. "Your whore."

A growl rolls in my throat. "And?"

Her eyelashes flutter against her pink cheeks. "Your wife."

A possessive desire to claim her surges through my veins. "Exactly. You're my fucking wife." I slip my fingers out of her, and I'm unable to resist placing them straight into my mouth. Her taste floods my senses, and her chest heaves as she watches me, waiting for her reward for the sensational blowjob she gave me. I'll reward her so fucking hard she'll ride that high the entire time I'm away. I place her on the edge of my desk and take off her pants, removing her socks and sneakers too.

"This too." I tug at the collar of her navy tunic. "I want to see every inch of you." She lifts her arms in compliance, and I slide the cotton over her head and toss it onto the pile at my feet. Her bra joins the rest of her clothing, and I suck on each pebbled nipple before I sit down and take a moment to admire her almost-naked body.

Spreading her thighs wide, I place her feet on the arms of my chair and drop my gaze to the telltale creamy damp patch staining her navy cotton panties. I bite down on my lip, stopping a groan from tumbling out of me as I brush my thumb over the wet spot. "Yeah, such a whore for me, corazón."

She tips her head back, and the flush on her chest races up her neck until it covers her cheeks. "Nate," she moans.

"Don't mind me calling you a whore when I've got my hands on you, do you, Mel?"

"No." She bucks her hips, chasing the pressure of my fingers and the pleasure she knows I'm about to bring her. I scoot my chair forward and dip my head between her spread thighs, running my nose over her pussy through her panties and inhaling her sweet, musky scent.

"I don't usually eat at my desk." I look up at her and smirk. "But for you, corazón, I think I'll make an exception."

"Nate." Her pleading tone has my cock twitching to life again. I drag my teeth over the damp fabric and gently bite down on her clit.

She whimpers, and I go on teasing her through her panties, my tongue and teeth lashing at her sensitive flesh.

She places one hand on my head, threading her fingers through my hair and tugging at the roots. With the other, she attempts to pull her panties out of the way and tries to ride my face. I catch her wrist and hold it in place while I continue feasting on her through the damp fabric that separates my mouth from her. "Nate!"

I smile, glancing up at her. "This not enough for you?"

She shakes her head, tears streaming down her cheeks. "No."

Taking pity on her, I hook my fingers in the waistband of her panties. "Shall we get these off you?"

"Y-yes." Her fingers join mine, and she tugs at the fabric along with me. We get them off, and I return her feet to their position on the arms of my chair.

I run my pointer finger along her wet center, so pink and inviting and ready for me. Holding it up, I show her the arousal collected on the tip. "So wet, corazón."

She bites down on her lip. "Uh-huh."

I bend my head to the apex of her thighs and inhale. "And so fucking sweet."

"Please, Nate."

Fuck me, I love the way she begs. My tongue follows the same path my finger just took, and her creamy taste coats my tongue. I have no idea how I'm going to survive without this for three whole days when I can barely go twelve hours without a part of me inside a part of her. She tastes like she was made for me.

"Holy shit," she rasps, her tits heaving as she bucks her hips against my greedy mouth, and all thoughts of teasing her any further leave my brain in a rush. I eat her pussy like I'm a starving man eating his first meal in months, all tongue and teeth and lips, taking what I can from her, drinking in every delicious drop as I bring her to the edge of the abyss. Her legs tremble violently, thighs shaking as her clit pulses in my mouth like it has its own heartbeat. My cock is hard again, weeping and ready to take her as soon as I'm done with my feast.

I graze my teeth over her clit and rim the swollen bud of flesh with my tongue. Her climax spirals through her, tearing a guttural cry from her throat. She's still shaking when I stand, wrap her slender legs around my waist, and line the tip of my cock at her soaking entrance before driving inside her. Her teeth chatter and her head hangs back between her shoulder blades as she takes everything I give her. But it's not enough. I want her in my arms when she comes apart for me again. Pulling her up, I wrap my arms around her, banding her tightly to me. She responds in kind, clinging to me like she never intends to let me go. Pulling out slowly, I let her feel every inch she's losing, and she hisses out a breath.

I press my forehead against hers. "Will you miss me, corazón?"

"You know I will."

I do know that, and the knowledge burns through my veins, along with my need to own her. I sink back inside her, bottoming out in one smooth thrust. I don't want to leave her. Not for three hours, let alone three days. This right here is the only place I want to be for the rest of my life.

She claws at my neck as I fuck her on my desk, her sweet

cum spilling onto the solid oak and creating wet noises as I drive in and out of her, wanting this to last as long as possible, but also needing to fuck her harder than I've ever fucked her before. I want her to ache for me while I'm gone. The way that I'll ache for her. I want her to feel empty and lost without me inside her because that's sure as hell how I feel when I'm not with her. I'm feeling things for this woman I never thought myself capable of.

"Oh, that feels ... so good." Her head tips back on a scream, and her inner walls pulse tight around me as she comes again, milking my cock with hungry squeezes until I fill her with my cum once more.

My legs give out, and I sink into my chair, pulling her with me so she's sitting on my lap. "Come to Chicago with me," I pant.

She closes her eyes and shakes her head. "You know I can't. Work is especially crazy this time of year. We had three intestinal blockage surgeries today. I wish people would stop feeding their dogs the leftover turkey legs from Thanksgiving."

I suppress an annoyed sigh, and she curls a lock of my hair between her fingers. "But maybe next time, if you give me more notice?"

She's right. This has been planned all year, and I should have invited her way before now. But I don't usually have the luxury of notice in my line of work. Something about our arrangement will have to change because I need her with me. And once she's pregnant ... well, there's not a snowball's chance in hell that I'll be leaving her alone for days at a time. Which means something's gotta give. But that's a conversation for a different day. "I'll do my best to give you notice."

"And it's only three days. You'll be back before you've even had a chance to miss me."

Not fucking likely.

She stares into my eyes, and the deep green of her irises is obscured by her pupils. "I ..." Her slender throat convulses. Is she about to tell me she loves me? "I'll miss you though. Every second."

I nod and try to hide my disappointment that she didn't say those three words. Words that I'm strangely desperate to hear from her, but I don't say them to her either. Instead, I press my forehead to hers, and we sit in silence. Her naked, with our cum dripping out of her, and me wondering how the fuck I fell so hard and fast for a woman who was only supposed to be a business arrangement.

CHAPTER
THIRTY-EIGHT

NATHAN

Staring into my glass, I swirl the amber liquid around the bottom and think of Mel waiting at home for me. Sitting on the sofa in her favorite yoga pants and one of my sweatshirts while she watches some sappy movie. A smile pulls at the corners of my mouth. If I didn't have one last meeting tomorrow morning, I'd jump on the jet and go home to her right now. By the time I'd get back, she'd be sleeping, and my cock aches at an image of crawling into our warm bed, parting her thighs, and sinking inside her warm pussy.

"You want to join me for another one of those?" a sultry voice says in my ear.

I shake my head, not bothering to give the owner of the voice even a cursory glance. "No thanks."

"Aw, come on." She caresses my arm. "Not even just a little one?"

I shrug off her touch, looking at her for the first time, and hold up my left hand. "I'm married."

She glances around the almost-empty hotel bar. "Your

wife's not here though, is she?" She giggles and flutters her eyelashes.

"Doesn't make me any less married. Go bother some other guy and leave me the fuck alone."

She huffs dramatically and sashays toward the other end of the bar.

"She's in here every night looking for her next mark," the bartender says with a dry laugh as she picks up my empty glass. "Can I get you another?"

I should go to bed, but it's hard to sleep without Mel next to me these days. I can't remember a time in my adult life when I was dependent on another person for anything. A part of me hates the vulnerability of it, but for the most part, I like having someone to miss.

I guess one more Scotch won't hurt. It might even help me sleep.

JESUS FUCKING CHRIST. My pounding head drives me from sleep, and my aching eyeballs throb their protest at the sunlight streaming through the open blinds.

A sleepy moan echoes in my ears, and I close my eyes again. Someone is lying beside me. Instinct, or maybe it's simply the fact that I know my wife's body and scent so well, tells me it isn't Mel. Bile burns the back of my throat. I throw back the covers and jump out of bed, but the sudden movement only makes it worse, and I spew my guts out onto the thick gray carpet.

"Are you okay?" a woman asks.

I tune her out, hoping she's a figment of my imagination, and sink back onto the bed. My stomach rolls and my chest heaves, but I swallow down the urge to vomit a second time and swipe the back of my hand over my sweaty forehead.

"Can I get you a drink of water?" the voice asks.

I turn around. She's sitting up and the sheets have fallen from her body, exposing her breasts. I'm naked too. Motherfucking fuck. What the fuck is the bartender from last night doing in my bed?

"What the hell are you doing here?" I bark.

She pulls the covers over her chest, and her lower lip quivers like she's about to cry. "What? We ... well."

I jump up and pull on my boxers, which were hastily discarded on my side of the bed. My stomach rolls again. Please tell me we didn't ... "What happened? Did we—" I scan the sheets and floor for used condoms and don't see any, but I don't know if that's good or bad.

"We fooled around. You were too drunk to do anything else." With a huff, she climbs out of bed and gathers her clothes.

I close my eyes and try to piece together what happened last night. This is not who I am. I wouldn't cheat on my wife, not even if I didn't have the kind of feelings for her that I do. I'm not a fucking cheat.

Except a naked woman just got out of my bed, so what exactly does that make me? I bury my face in my hands and focus. I remember her pouring me a couple glasses of Scotch and telling me about her parents' ranch in Montana. I have a vague memory of laughing over a shared hatred for country music, but that's it. I have no fucking idea how we went from that to being naked in my bed together. No fucking clue at all.

"I don't remember anything," I groan.

"Really? Nothing? I mean, I know you were pretty wasted, but ..."

Sitting up, I scrub a hand through my hair and fight the constant urge to vomit while trying to engage the logical part of my brain to come up with a reasonable explanation that doesn't involve me cheating on my wife. She's fully dressed now, so I give her my full attention. "I told you I was married, right?"

She shrugs. "Married guys come through here all the time. Means nothing."

Rage simmers beneath my skin. I stand and take a step toward her. "It means something to me."

She fixes me with a glare. "It didn't seem to mean much last night, asshole." She snatches her shoes from the floor and, without bothering to put them on, storms out of the hotel room, leaving me standing here naked, about to pass out. My knees buckle, and I collapse onto the mattress.

I cheated on my wife. My sweet, caring Mel, who was waiting at home for me while I fucked around with some random bartender. What the fuck have I done?

I look around until I find my phone on the nightstand, and my heart sinks through my chest when I see her goodnight text. How the fuck do I tell her what I did? Despite how we started out, I know this will break her heart. It's damn sure breaking mine.

I suck in a deep, calming breath. I can fix this. I can explain that I got so drunk that I … that I what? I don't even know what the fuck I did with that woman. How far did fooling around go? Did I kiss her? What parts of her body did I put my mouth on? I lurch for the bathroom and barely make it to the toilet before I heave up the remaining contents of my stomach. When there's nothing left to throw up, I sink to my knees, press my damp forehead to the cool plastic seat, and pray to every entity I've ever heard of that I can find a way to make Mel forgive me.

CHAPTER

THIRTY-NINE

NATHAN

Elijah shakes his head, his brow furrowed as he tries to process the shitstorm I've just dropped in his lap. After canceling my meeting, I immediately left the hotel and asked the pilot to haul ass home. Within minutes of touching down in New York, I was on my way to my older brother's office. I needed to talk this through with someone before I faced Mel. And despite our differences, Elijah is the man whose opinion I trust more than anyone else's.

"So you got so drunk you blacked out?" he asks, his frown deepening.

"Yeah. At least I think I did." I pinch the bridge of my nose and try to recall more than the few little snapshots that came back to me when I was on the plane. Stumbling out of the bar. Me leaning against the wall in the elevator. Fumbling for my room key.

Nothing new appears. I still don't remember kissing her or touching her. I don't remember taking her clothes off, or my own.

Elijah shakes his head. "No."

I blink at him. I need his rational brain right now, not his denial. The time for unwavering brotherly support will come, but now's not it. "What do you mean, no?"

"Nathan, I've seen you drunk off your ass more times than I can remember, but you have never once blacked out. Last summer I watched you down a whole bottle of Johnny Walker Black in a matter of hours, and you still beat my ass at poker. You seriously think you blacked out after a couple of shots?"

My head is pounding too hard for me to make sense of what he's trying to say. "And? What the fuck does that mean?"

He sighs heavily, then picks up the phone on his desk and asks his secretary to bring him one of the drug tests they use to randomly test their staff.

"What the fuck. You think I was drugged?"

He hangs up the phone and narrows his eyes. "Seems more plausible than you losing your memory after a few glasses of Scotch, don't you think?"

I rub my temples, trying to alleviate the rhythmic drumming in my head, but it doesn't help. "But why the fuck would she drug me?"

He leans forward. "Did you check your wallet? Was anything missing?"

"I checked before I got on the plane. Everything was there."

He scowls. "She must have targeted you for a reason. It doesn't make sense otherwise."

My mind races with questions that I have no answers for, but my brother's suspicion ignites a flicker of hope. If I was drugged, that means I didn't knowingly cheat on my wife, no matter what happened with that woman. Maybe Mel will be able to forgive me. "How about we do this damn drug test first and then we can figure out who she was and why the hell she drugged me."

The door opens, and Elijah's secretary, Joseph, walks in. He hands him a white plastic envelope, sneaks a brief glance in my direction, then quickly leaves the room. My older brother clears his throat. "He signed an NDA," Elijah says when I stare at the door Joseph exited.

"What?" I shake my head, trying to clear it.

"If you're worried about him bringing us a drug test," Elijah adds.

I bark a humorless laugh and wince when it sets off the marching band in my skull. "I'm not worried about that. I'm worried about how the fuck I explain all of this to Mel." I glance at the plastic envelope in his hands. "Especially if that's negative. That would mean I cheated on my wife, Elijah."

"Don't get ahead of yourself." He hands me the swab kit. "Besides, I'd bet my Bentley you were drugged."

Scowling, I open the packaging and skim the directions. "I bought you that fucking car last year for your fortieth birthday."

"Then you know how much it means to me. Swab your cheek."

I rub the cotton end of the swab along the inside of my cheek and place it in the small container. "How long do these things take to work?" I glance at the indicator window.

"Just a few minutes." He holds out his hand, indicating I should pass him the sample. I have no idea what I'm looking for, so I hand it over. He stares at it, and I stare at him. Holding my breath, I feel like my world stops spinning on its axis while I await the results.

"Hmm," he finally says. "Positive for opioids and Rohypnol."

Both relief and fury rush through me, battling for dominance. "I was fucking roofied?"

"Yeah."

Sinking into the chair, I drop my head in my hands. "So

what the fuck did she do to me when I was unconscious?" Bile surges in my throat again.

"I can have her arrested for sexual assault within the hour. Did you stay at the Moretti hotel?"

I look up at him and shake my head. "I always stay there. But no. Not yet. Let me process. I need to speak to Mel and tell her, and then ..." The air leaves my lungs in a rush. It's all too fucking overwhelming to deal with right now. I'll get answers, I'm fucking sure of it, but right now I need to speak to my wife and tell her what happened. And hope that she knows me well enough to believe me.

I snatch the test off the table. "I need to go home."

"Nathan!" Elijah's voice is so full of concern that it irrationally annoys me. I don't need his fucking pity. "Let's talk this through. Let me—"

"The only person I need to speak to right now is my wife." I spit out the words, directing my anger at him because I don't know where else to put it. Other than on myself for being so goddamn stupid that I let myself get drugged.

He holds up his hands in surrender. "Okay. But I'm here if you need anything at all. Okay?"

Without answering him, I storm out of his office and head home with a churning in my gut that I have a horrible feeling isn't going away any time soon.

CHAPTER
FORTY

MELANIE

I bounce on my toes like an excited teenager about to go on her first date while I wait for Nathan to step off the elevator. I've missed him so much, which seems silly given that he's only been gone for three days, but any amount of time without him lately feels long and torturous. Smoothing down my dress, I think about the black lace I have on underneath and smile. I intend to welcome him home with all the enthusiasm of his own personal cheer squad.

The doors open and he steps out, and I let out an involuntary shriek as I bound forward and throw my arms around his neck.

"Mel." His voice is hoarse, full of pain, and I pull back and stare at his face. God, he looks awful. Pale and drawn. His eyes are bloodshot, and he has a thick shadow of stubble across his jaw, which usually only serves to make him sexier, but today it seems to make him look worn down.

"Are you okay? Are you sick?"

Shaking his head, he takes my hands in his. "Let's go sit."

My heart rate triples, and my legs begin to shake. "Why? What's wrong?"

He walks toward the den, leading me with him. "I need to talk to you about something."

"Okay," I whisper, afraid of what that something is given the haunted look in his eyes.

I take a seat on the sofa, and he sits on the coffee table in front of me, his hands clasped between his spread thighs.

He stares at me, and I swallow down a thick knot of anxiety. I have never seen this man at a loss for words. "Nate, what is it? You're scaring me."

"Mel—" His Adam's apple bobs. "I don't know how to tell you this, corazón, so I'm just going to come right out with it."

I nod, bracing myself.

"Last night at the hotel ..." He scrubs a hand over his jaw. "There was this woman. A bartender." I swear I see tears welling in his eyes. "I woke up in bed with her, but she drugged me, Mel. Elijah had me do a test. There were Rohypnol and opioids in my system."

He was drugged. How? Why would anyone—? Oh, god. My dear sweet Nate, what have they done to you? A strangled gasping sound comes out of me, and my hand flies to my mouth to stifle it.

He grabs my free hand, squeezing it in his. "She was in my bed, Mel, but I swear to you ... I swear I don't remember anything that happened. You know I would never cheat on you. Never."

Tears leak from the corners of my eyes, and his face falls. He thinks I'm upset with him when that couldn't be further from the truth. I shake my head. "I—I'm so sorry, Nate."

"You don't have to be sorry for me," he says, his tone soothing, like I'm the one who needs comfort when he's the one who was sexually assaulted. And I'm a hundred percent sure it was the work of my brother. "I don't know why the fuck she targeted me, but I'll find out." He presses his forehead against my knuckles. "I swear I never would have touched her, corazón. I had no idea what I was doing."

My stomach twists in a knot. I can't let him hurt any more than he already has been. He deserves to know the truth, even if that might spell the end of us. "It was Bryce." The words are a mere whisper, as though that will somehow make them less painful to both of us.

Nathan blinks at me. "What do you mean it was Bryce?"

Oh dear god, I'm about to break both our hearts. "He had this idea about a honey trap."

Nathan pulls back, his entire body rigid. "A honey what?"

My cheeks burn with heat and shame. "Th-the cheating clause. He had an idea to use a honey trap to get you to cheat, but I—"

"And you fucking knew about this?" Despite knowing I deserve it, I flinch at the harshness of his tone. I deserve far worse.

"In the beginning, yes, I knew he was thinking about it," I admit. "But once we were married, I told him it was a stupid idea. I pleaded with him not to go ahead with it."

"But you knew when I proposed to you, when I asked you to never lie to me? You knew that your brother was planning our demise all along? Just to get his hands on a few million dollars?"

Tears roll down my cheeks. "No. Yes. I never agreed to go along with his stupid plan. I just wanted to stop fighting with him, so I let it go. I was only trying to protect my sister."

He pushes to his feet. "Spare me the goddamn fake tears, Melanie. You fucking used me!"

I stand too and walk over to him, but he backs away. "I didn't want to use you, Nate. I never would. As soon as you and I started to ..."

"What?" He snarls. "Fuck?"

"No! As soon as I realized that we were in this for the long haul and that it wasn't some stunt, I knew I needed to make sure he wouldn't go ahead with it. That day when I left my mom's house so upset—when Teddy brought me to you, remember? I went over there, and I begged him not to go ahead with it. I made him promise, and he did. I swear."

He stalks closer and towers over me, shaking with rage. "You lied to my face. Not just before we were married but that day when I asked you what happened. You could have told me the truth."

I can't breathe. "I didn't want to lose you."

His face twists in a snarl. "You lied. You were going to use me for money."

I nod, shame-faced because those things are technically true.

"You sat back and let me walk into a fucking trap for some woman to drug me and do who the fuck knows what else!"

I shake my head, tears blurring my vision. "No. I had no idea he'd do that. I would never hurt you. He promised he wouldn't go ahead with it. And I swear I had no idea he'd go that far, Nate. All he said was he'd have a hot woman hit on you. That was it, I swear."

He scoffs. "You expect me to believe a word that comes out of your lying mouth?"

"Nathan. Please listen to me." I grab his arm, but he shrugs me off.

"You know what the worst part of this whole thing is, Melanie?" He spits out my name like it leaves a bad taste in his mouth. "The worst part is that I was fucking devastated when I thought I cheated on you. Thinking that I'd done something to hurt you caused me pain like I've only ever felt once before in my entire life. And it was wasted on you."

"No, Nate." I shake my head. "I'm so sorry."

"I don't fucking believe you." He grabs my purse from the small table beside the sofa and shoves it into my hands. "Get the fuck out of my house."

"Nathan, just let me—"

"Get the hell out, Melanie, or I'll have someone come drag you out of here." His vicious snarl makes the hair on the back of my neck stand on end. I swallow down the wail, filled with frustration and injustice, that wants to roar out of me and wipe the tears from my cheeks.

I did exactly what my brother wanted, and he still found a way to fuck up my life.

Nathan turns away from me, and my heart shatters into a million pieces that I already know can never be put back together.

CHAPTER
FORTY-ONE

NATHAN

I stare at the cell phone in my hand and try to remember if I called my brother or he called me. My chest is tight, my heart racing and lungs burning for oxygen, but I seem to have forgotten how to breathe.

I'm snapped back to reality when I hear Elijah's voice distantly yelling my name. I stare blankly at the screen for a long second, then hold it to my ear.

"She knew, Elijah," I rasp.

"Nathan, you're not making sense. What?"

"Mel fucking knew!" For lack of a better target, I direct my venomous rage at him.

"Knew what? About what happened in Chicago?"

Sucking in a series of deep breaths, I take a few beats to regain my composure before telling my brother all about my lying bitch of a wife and her family's scheme to fleece me for whatever money they could get their filthy hands on.

He's quiet while I purge the whole story. "So they set you up? Mel too?" he asks incredulously. "Fuck, Nathan."

234

I drop my head into my hands, not wanting to believe it myself, but she confirmed it with her own goddamn mouth.

"Nathan!" Elijah's voice rings in my ears. I assume he's been talking, but I didn't hear a word of it.

"I'm here."

"What do you want to do? We can have her and her brother arrested within the hour. The bartender too."

"No." I shake my head. "I need to know exactly what happened last night."

He lets out an exasperated sigh. "And how are you going to find that out?"

"I'm going back to Chicago to speak to the bartender, and I'm pretty sure the Morettis will be interested to know the sort of woman they're employing in their bar."

"Don't do anything stupid, Nathan."

I ball my free hand into a fist. Right now I could happily murder someone, but I force myself to close my eyes and think of my mom's painting hanging in my office, remembering the feeling of the sun of my face. My pulse begins to slow, and I take a deep breath. "I won't do anything stupid," I assure him.

∾

I HAVEN'T SLEPT in over twenty-four hours. Running on pure adrenaline, I glare at the woman sitting in front of me. Ariana Benjamin, twenty-seven years old. Worked here for two years. She's a single orphan with no siblings and no kids. No one to miss her if she doesn't come home tonight.

She glances at the door behind me, fear and worry etched all over her features. Yeah, she should be fucking worried, but not because of me. This hotel, the one I stay at every time I come to Chicago on business, happens to be owned by the Moretti family. They also happen to be Sicilian Mafia, my clients, and my friends. And this woman right here has fucked herself well and truly over by slipping a roofie into my drink while she was working at their bar.

The shock on her face when I walked back in tonight and escorted her to this office alongside hotel security was a sight to see. Clearly she thought I wouldn't suspect a thing. I wonder how many other poor fuckers she's done this to.

Her entire body trembles. "W-what do you want?"

"Right now, I am the only thing standing between you and your employers, Ariana. You do know who they are, right? What they do to people who fuck them over?"

Her slender throat convulses, and her wide, imploring eyes remain locked on the door.

I pull up a chair and sit. "I'll take that as a yes."

She gives a single nod of her head.

"Tell me what the fuck happened last night."

"I, uh—you got drunk, and we—"

I slam my fist onto the wooden table in front of me and snarl. "I will give you *one* more fucking chance to tell me the truth before I hand you over to the Morettis' men to do whatever the fuck they want. Now start from the very beginning. How do you know Bryce Edison?"

His name makes her blink rapidly. Her lips trembles, and her eyes fill with tears. "I met him here at the casino. I was paid to hit on a guy he was with. Afterward, Bryce figured out what I did and threatened to tell my employers what I was doing in their hotel. So he started blackmailing me."

"Blackmailing you how?"

Her cheeks flush pink. "At first, he wanted sex. But it was only when he came into town and that wasn't very often. But then he …" A tear runs down her cheek, and she swats it away and sniffs. "There was this guy he needed leverage on, so he asked me to drug him and then go up to his room and make it look like we'd slept together. I said no," she insists, swatting away more tears. "But he said he'd tell the Morettis that I'd been working as a honey trap in their casino, and I ..." Her eyes widen, and she shakes her head. "I had no choice. I know exactly who my employers are, Mr. James."

Keeping my glare trained on her, I refuse to show an ounce of compassion. But I bite my tongue and let her continue, resisting the urge to cross-examine her.

"I guess I should have left, but this is the best job I've ever had. It pays well and I have great healthcare. Besides, after I did it the first time, Bryce knew he was onto a good thing, and he threatened to tell them what I'd done if I left. I felt trapped."

I grind my teeth so hard my jaw aches.

"Then he asked me to do it again the night before last. With you." She sniffs, her dark eyes wide as she silently pleads with me.

When she doesn't offer any further information, I speak. "I'm still waiting for the part where you tell me what the fuck happened last night."

"Nothing. I slipped the drugs he gave me into your drink and then I helped you up to your room. You were out of it by the time we got there, and I had to call Bryce to help me lift you into the bed."

White-hot anger surges through my veins. "Bryce was here too?"

She nods. "He wanted to make sure I'd go through with it."

I snarl. "And then what happened? What the fuck did you two do to me while I was unconscious?"

"Nothing." She shakes her head. "I told Bryce to get out before anyone saw him up here. Then I took off our clothes and got into bed with you. I snapped a couple of pictures of me curled up next to you and waited for morning."

Jesus fucking Christ. Pair of goddamn snakes. "So we did nothing?"

"No! I know I'm a horrible person for what I did, Mr. James, but I'm not a ..." A sob catches in her throat. "I never would have done anything like that."

I roll my neck, trying to ease the tension solidifying my muscles. "And your other accomplice? The woman who hit on me at the bar?"

"Just some chick. I gave her a few free drinks and asked her to hit on you. She was more than happy to do it."

My temples throb. "Did you ever speak to Bryce's sister, Melanie?"

She blinks rapidly, her face a mask of confusion. "No. I didn't even know he had a sister. Why?"

I ignore her question. "So he never even mentioned her?"

She shakes her head, and a small wave of relief washes over me. But I quickly remind myself that it means nothing. Mel didn't have to speak to Ariana to have been involved.

I run a hand through my hair, and a heavy sigh pours out of me.

"What's going to happen to me now?" she asks, her voice small and quiet.

I fix my gaze on her face again. I've spent years in courtrooms and offices just like this one reading body language and facial expressions as well as inflections in speech, not to mention every other little tick that betrays a person when they're lying. And Ariana is telling the truth, I'm sure of it. The fact that she's another victim of Bryce Edison makes me feel a little sorry for her, but I refuse to let her know that.

"One of your employers is waiting outside to talk to you. If you're lucky, it will be Dante or Joey rather than Lorenzo or Max." Not that Joey and Dante aren't every bit as ruthless, but they are a little easier to reason with.

Her face pales, and she sucks in a stuttered breath. "Please, Mr. James," she begs. "I didn't mean to hurt you. Or anyone." Tears run freely down her cheeks.

I stand, brushing the creases from my suit. I need a shower and a long fucking sleep. "Yeah, but you did, Ariana."

I walk out of the room and straight into Lorenzo Moretti. He eyes me with concern, and I scratch my fingertips over the thick stubble on my jaw.

"Did you get what you need, compagno?"

"Yeah." I give him a brief account of my conversation with Ariana. "I know she fucked up, but it seems she was taken advantage of. I told her someone is waiting to talk to her. So she's fucking terrified right now."

He grunts. "She should be."

I glance back at the closed door. Her fate shouldn't matter to me, but it does. "What are you gonna do with her?"

He runs a hand over his thick beard and sucks on his bottom lip before answering. "She'll never work in this city again. Is that enough for you?"

Well, damn. Family life sure has mellowed my old friend. "Yeah, it is."

"And what about this Edison prick?"

I let out a long breath. A big part of me would enjoy seeing the look on Bryce's face when Lorenzo Moretti pays him a visit, but that's not how I handle my business. And this is way too personal to allow anyone else to handle it for me. "I'll deal with him."

CHAPTER
FORTY-TWO

MELANIE

I glance over my reflection in the bathroom mirror of Tyler's apartment. No amount of carefully applied makeup can hide the fact that I've been crying for the past two hours. I wish I didn't have the fundraiser tonight, but it's the one thing keeping me from finding my brother and wringing his neck.

I sniff, stifling yet another sob. *Pull yourself together, Mel.* It's not like what Nathan and I had was real. Not like he would ever truly love me.

Except it felt real. It felt better than anything I've ever had before. And even if it wasn't, he made me feel like it was. He didn't deserve any of what happened to him. Nobody deserves that, and the thought that I might have been able to stop it, or that I ever agreed to any part of it, is eating me alive. I can't get the image of him waking up confused and terrified with some strange woman in his bed out of my head. How he told me that it broke his heart to think he cheated on me.

My head drops, and a shuddering sob wracks my body. Every thought slices through my heart like a surgeon's scalpel. How could I have been so stupid to not have been honest with him from the start? It might have stopped him from marrying me, but at least he wouldn't be hurt. At least I wouldn't know the pain of losing him. Because beneath all the chatter and anger and questions racing through my head at a million miles an hour, that's the pain that beats the hardest inside my chest.

I had the most incredible man in the world.

And now I've lost him.

~

TYLER'S soothing voice fills my ear. "Oh, baby girl, I wish I was there right now."

I sink into the sofa in his living room and glance at his old football jersey sitting beside me. I run my fingertip over the letter M of his nickname, then pick up the jersey and press it against my face, inhaling his comforting scent. After fielding dozens of questions about where my husband was and lying to everyone about why he wasn't with me, I left the charity event early. Every time I heard his name was like a thousand needles skewering my heart. Even the cute rescue animals couldn't ease the overwhelming ache pulsing through my entire body.

"Your brother is a real piece of shit, you know that. I am going to kick his goddamn ass to kingdom come when I get back."

"No, Ty, you're not." He knows I abhor violence of any kind, and him getting in the middle of Bryce and me always bothered me. Tyler's had to stick up for me against my bully of a big brother for as long as I can remember, and I hate that he still has to.

"Then I hope Nathan uses some of his mob contacts to scare the living shit out of him instead then," he huffs.

"No," I groan. "That would be even worse."

"Someone has to do something about him, baby girl. He's ruined two people's lives, and for what?"

I rub my cheek against his soft jersey and close my eyes. "I know, Ty. And I'm sure Nathan will deal with him somehow. If he has any sense, he'll call the police, but I doubt that he will."

"Maybe he'll ruin him instead. Like financially. That seems more his style," Tyler muses.

"Yeah, and it wouldn't take that much effort. I'm sure he's already on the brink of ruin. Goddamn useless asshole."

Tyler snorts a laugh. "What are you gonna do now, baby girl?"

I choke back a sob. "I don't know, Ty," I reply honestly. "I feel so empty."

"Oh, baby girl," he says softly, and his compassion breaks me. My already shattered heart disintegrates in my chest, turning to a pile of ash as I press the phone to my chest. Loud, guttural sobs wrack my body. I hate that Nathan has been hurt because of me. I hate that I wasn't honest with him about Bryce's stupid plan from the start. But most of all, I hate my useless, waste-of-oxygen older brother.

When I press the phone back to my ear, Tyler is patiently waiting on the line. "I wish I could wrap you up in a hug, Mel."

I wipe the tears from my cheeks. "I wish you could too."

He sighs, and I love that he doesn't tell me everything will be okay or reassure me that Nathan will forgive me, because we don't know if either of those things are true.

I hear someone calling his name in the background and remember he's supposed to be working. "You go, and I'll call you later."

"I'm right here on the end of the line whenever you need me."

"I know."

"Love you, Goose."

"Love you too, Mav."

After we hang up, I stare into space and hold onto Ty's Maverick jersey, wishing with all my heart that I had my Iceman back.

I KEEP GLANCING at my cell phone on the coffee table, then at my coat hanging on the rack. I've been sitting on this sofa all night, wondering what the hell to do next. Drifting in and out of sleep with all manner of horrible thoughts swirling around my head. Do I call him or go confront him in person? But confronting him face-to-face would make me break my no-violence rule because I'm absolutely certain I won't be able to hold back from punching him in his fat, arrogant mouth. Or scratching his eyes out. Maybe both.

My heart is racing like a prize-winning stallion headed for the finish line, and my fingers tremble as I pick up the phone. I take a long, soothing breath and dial Bryce's number.

Waiting for him to pick up, I wonder if he knows what happened yet. Has Nathan already contacted him? Maybe he's in police custody? A few seconds later, he answers.

"Why are you calling me so early? It's barely seven," he barks.

"Why did you do it, Bryce?" I fight to keep the tremor from my voice.

He snorts. "Do what?"

His contempt shreds my last bit of restraint. "You know

what I'm talking about. You knew Nathan was traveling to Chicago for that meeting. You knew he'd be there," I screech.

"I have no idea what the hell you're talking about, little sister. And you'd do well to remember your tone when you're speaking to me."

"You'd do well to remember that I know exactly the kind of man you are, Bryce. I told Nathan about your ridiculous plan to trigger the morality clause in our prenup—"

"You did what?" he roars.

"I. Told. Him." I enunciate each word clearly.

"You stupid little bitch!"

"I'm stupid?" I snort a laugh. "You seriously think he's stupid enough to let you pull a stunt like that and not figure out something's going on? You have heard about drug tests, right? Exactly how loyal do you think this poor woman you roped into your scheme is going to be once Nathan gets a hold of her? Or reports you both to the cops for sexual assault?"

"You fucking told him?" he screams again. "If I go down for this, you're coming with me, Melanie. I'll tell everyone you were in up to your neck."

I let out a triumphant but hollow laugh. "So you're admitting it was you?"

He's quiet for a few seconds. "Fuck you!"

"I hate you, Bryce. I've always hated you, but this is unforgivable."

"If anything happens to me because of this, it will be on you, Melanie." His voice takes on a whiny tone now, and it makes my stomach roll.

He's such a manipulative little shit, and I can't believe I didn't have the strength to do this years ago. "You are dead to me, Bryce. You even come near me again and I'll go to the cops and tell them what you did to him myself. Do you hear me?"

The line goes dead, and I'm left holding the phone in my

hand, my chest heaving. An overabundance of emotions charge around my body, fighting for dominance. I close my eyes, trying to make sense of the thoughts racing in my brain, but there's no peace to be found. Everything is broken, and I don't know how to even begin to fix it.

FORTY-THREE

NATHAN

Two fucking days I've been scouring this city looking for this prick. Like I have nothing better to do with my time. I've barely eaten or slept since I got back from Chicago and Mel hit me with her little revelation, and work has been put on the backburner. My secretary is dealing with what she can in my absence, but I need to get back to the office as soon as possible. It's the only place where everything still makes sense to me. A place where I can have ice in my veins instead of the fire that's currently burning through them. Once I've dealt with this sack of shit, my life might get back to some semblance of normalcy.

Bryce Edison throws back his head and laughs at the blond sitting beside him. She flutters her eyelashes, pretending to hang onto his every word. And I have to assume she's only pretending because he talks nothing but shit. The fact that he's evaded me for almost forty-eight hours means Mel must have told him I was onto his fucked-up scheme. Which is only further evidence that she's a lying, scheming bitch too.

But the fact that he tried to dodge me tells me what a stupid asshole he is. Like there is anywhere in this fucking city, or the entire fucking country for that matter, where he could hide from me. If he'd done any homework on me, he would know that I have contacts everyfuckingwhere. As soon as he popped his little weasel-like head out of whatever hole he was hiding in, my sources were quick to let me know.

Which is why I find myself here, in a bougie little Italian restaurant in Hell's Kitchen, staring at the man whose life I'm about to ruin. I walk toward the table at the back of the restaurant, tucked away in a corner like he thinks that makes him less conspicuous.

The blond sees me first, and her eyes widen with confusion. I jerk my head toward the door. "Get the fuck out."

She pouts and looks at Bryce—who, upon hearing my voice, has turned an unnatural shade of gray. "Brycey, you gonna let him talk to me like that?" she whines.

He opens and closes his mouth. Pathetic piece of shit. I glare at him. "Bryce and I are going to have a talk, and I'm sure he doesn't want one of his whores to hear what I have to say."

"Get lost, Pammy," he snaps.

With a dramatic huff, she grabs her shiny pink purse and stomps out of the restaurant. I take a seat opposite him, and Bryce glances nervously around the almost-empty room.

"There's no help for you here, Brycey. Who do you think told me you were here?"

He swallows hard and shrinks back against the leather bench. "What do you want?"

"I want you to tell me what the fuck you hoped to achieve by having me drugged?"

He shakes his head vigorously from side to side. "I had no idea, I swear. It was all Mel's idea."

Unable to stop myself, I lash out and punch him square in

the jaw, causing his head to snap back. He wails like a fucking child, clutching his mouth as tears leak from the corners of his eyes. "Don't fucking lie to me, you useless prick. I know you were there."

He holds his hands up in surrender, his tongue swiping at the blood welling from the cut on his lip. "Okay, I was there. But it was Mel's idea. She wanted to fleece you for whatever cash she could, and I just went along with it."

Motherfucker. I could smash his head into this table right now and not bat an eye. But I ball my hands into fists and stop myself. Everything about him screams lies, and I need the truth.

I roll my neck. "So, that little bitch planned it all, yeah?"

He nods, his eyes flashing with unrestrained glee.

"So she must have known the bartender, Ariana?"

"Yeah. Mel was the one who got in touch with her. I've never even met her, Nathan. She gave her the drugs to put in your drink. Must have got them from work or something."

Fucking liar. I'm also pretty sure they have no need for Rohypnol in a veterinary hospital, but I keep that to myself and feed Bryce more rope to hang himself with. "So what was her endgame? Because that's the one thing I can't figure out."

Bryce leans forward. "Divorce you and get a huge payout, obviously."

Such bullshit. He lives and breathes the almighty dollar, but not his sister. Nothing about her involvement in this whole shitshow makes sense to me. "Obviously. So you have the pictures, right? Of me and Ariana?"

He runs his tongue along his teeth. "Yeah."

"And how much to get ahold of these pictures and make sure they never see the light of a courtroom?"

His eyes gleam with delight. "I'm sure we can come to some agreement."

"What about copies? How can I be sure no one else has them?"

"I have the only copies, and I'll destroy them. I give you my word."

I offer him a nod. Like I would believe a single thing that comes out of his mouth,

but for now I'll let him think I believe his bullshit.

"I hope so, because the last thing I want is for your bitch of a sister to get her hands on a dime of my money, and with those pictures as evidence, she could invoke the morality clause."

"Exactly. That's her intention anyway," he says with a conspiratorial grin.

I suck air between my teeth. Despite my anger toward Mel, the way he's trying to pin everything on her makes me want to rip his head from his shoulders more than anything he's done to me. "Except *you* have the photos, right?"

He blinks. "What?"

"You have the only copies. Not Mel."

"I-I ..." He pulls at the collar of his dress shirt, and a bead of perspiration trickles down his forehead.

"Almost like it was you who set this whole thing up and not her. Was the plan to blackmail me if she didn't accuse me of adultery? Because without her doing that, you have nothing. You do know that, right? You think I give a fuck if some pictures of a woman lying next to me while I'm asleep in bed are leaked, you stupid fuck?"

"I knew she was fucking useless," he spits, and for a second I wonder which she he's referring to, Ariana or Melanie. "All she had to do was let you fuck her for a few months and then do what she was fucking told. I handed her a fucking out and she throws it back in my face."

That was his chance to tell me that the photos show more

than Ariana said they would, but he didn't, proving she was telling the truth. Sitting back in my seat, I fold my arms across my chest while he spews a diatribe of venom toward his sister that further confirms she knew nothing about what was going to happen in Chicago. And while that makes me feel a little better, it doesn't change the fact that she lied to my face when we got married. Yeah, she might have changed her mind once we started fucking, but she married me with the intention of setting me up to cheat on her. All so she could divorce me and get her hands on a few million for this pathetic fuck.

And that's exactly what he is, pathetic.

Once he's finished with his little tantrum, I lean forward and plant my hands on the table in front of me, feeling calmer than I have in days. "You're over, Bryce. I am going to fucking ruin you. There won't be a single investor who will come near you or your company with a ten-foot pole. You are finished in this city. In this country. So enjoy your last few weeks as the big man living on whatever remaining dollars you've squirreled away because it's all about to come to a grinding halt."

If he had any sense at all, he would've saved some of the money he's stolen from Edison Holdings in offshore accounts, but I did enough digging into him before I married his sister to know he wasn't even smart enough to do that.

He opens and closes his mouth. "Nathan. No, please. We need investors. Our company won't survive." As I expected, the loss of status and privilege, only afforded to him by his father, is what hurts him the most. More than me beating the shit out of him. More than going to jail. It's the money he can't live without.

"That's kind of the point. And you won't be able to bleed the company dry," I say with a smile. "So like I said, enjoy the good life while you can, because I'm coming for you, Bryce."

His lip wobbles like he's about to have another epic tantrum. Having no desire to stick around and witness it, I offer him a final victorious wink and walk away.

Bryce is ruined; he's got nothing left. I got the truth. I won. So, why do I still feel like I lost?

FORTY-FOUR

MELANIE

I flop down onto one of the comfortable armchairs in the break room and sigh. Work has been ridiculously busy, but it's also the only thing keeping me sane right now. When my mind's not busy, it's filled with thoughts of Nathan. Even two weeks later, the look in his eyes that night when he told me to leave haunts my every waking moment. The fact that he was taken advantage of like that, that some woman drugged and touched him without his consent, makes anger and shame burn through my veins. I only wish there was some way I could make it up to him.

Gah! This is no good. I need to get him off my mind. Perhaps some mindless TikTok scrolling is just what I need. But my pulse quickens when I pull out my phone and see four missed calls from Ashley. I'm staring at the screen, running through all the worst-case scenarios in my head, when the phone starts ringing in my hand and her sweet face flashes on the screen.

My finger fumbles as I try to answer it as quickly as possible. When I do, heart-wrenching sobs fill my ear.

"Ash, what is it, honey?"

"Buh-Bryce said I have to l-leave college."

Rage sizzles beneath my skin. "He said what?"

After a long moment, her sobs subside, and she takes a deep breath. "He said that I had to come home because there's no money to cover the rest of my tuition this year. He only paid half and he was supposed to pay the rest, but he said he can't." She sniffs again. "He said there's nothing left."

Our older brother is the biggest shithead I have ever known. He could get that money if he wanted to. There's something left, or he wouldn't be driving around in his fancy cars and eating at the finest restaurants every week.

"How much is owed?"

"Forty thousand for this year."

I close my eyes and lean my head back. How on earth am I going to find that kind of money?

"I have a few thousand in savings. I could get another job, maybe ..." She trails off. "I dunno. Even if I can figure out this year, I have next year to think of. That's another eighty thousand."

I rub my eyes, and when I open them, I stare down at my hand in my lap. The answer to our problems is quite literally staring me in the face. It will break my heart to do it, and it will probably be the final nail in the coffin of my marriage. But Nathan's never going to forgive me anyway. I'll find a way to pay him back, even if it takes years.

"Don't worry about it, honey. I'm going to take care of it."

She makes a strangled sound like she's stifling a sob. "But how, Mel? Where are you going to get that much money?"

"I can get it, I promise. Just trust me. Everything will be okay, honey. If Bryce calls you again, ignore him."

She sniffs. "Thank you, Mel. I love you."

"Love you too, Ash." I hang up and prepare myself for what

I'm about to do. Bryce is doing this to punish me, and I can't let Ashley suffer because of my mistakes.

CHAPTER

FORTY-FIVE

NATHAN

I stare at the painting of the beach we visited every summer as kids. Every brushstroke is infused with love and joy and reminds me of a simpler time, despite the memories of Mom painting it between chemo and radiation treatments, her body growing frailer each passing day. The light in her eyes when she had a brush in her hands and paint smeared across her cheek couldn't be dimmed by even the darkest day. She finished it a few months before she died, and that beach is the last place I remember feeling truly happy.

Except that's not true.

I shake my head, not wanting to think about the last time I was happy. When she sat on my lap in this very office before I left for Chicago. When I almost told her how much I loved her.

My phone vibrates on my desk in front of me, and I answer it without glancing at the screen, thankful for any distraction I can get.

"Mr. James, it's Ernst. From Persephone's."

Why is a guy from a jewelry store I've only ever been into twice in my life calling me? And how did he get my fucking number?

Ernst clears his throat when I don't reply. "Pardon the intrusion, sir, but I have your number on file, and I thought, given that you and your family have been such good customers of ours, you might wish to know ..." He coughs but doesn't continue.

"Know what?"

"For some of our more exclusive, exquisite pieces, we offer a buy-back option, rather than having the piece be sold via another jeweler."

"So?"

He clears his throat again, clearly uncomfortable. "Your wife returned her engagement ring this afternoon."

I close my eyes and clench my jaw so tightly that a sharp pain radiates up to my temple. "For how much?" I ask through gritted teeth.

"You understand we can't offer market value, Mr. James."

"How much?" I bark.

"One hundred and sixty thousand dollars."

That's almost half what I paid for it. Fucking bitch! She sold our fucking marriage for a hundred-sixty grand. "Did she sell her wedding ring too?"

"No, sir. Just the engagement ring."

Yeah, I guess the wedding band would only be worth ten or fifteen grand, which is chump change in comparison. She'll likely hold onto that until she finds herself short of cash again. "I want it back."

"Of course, sir."

"And I'm not paying a dime over one-sixty."

"Of course not, sir."

I end the call and lean back in my chair, my heart pounding

in my chest and my temples throbbing. So she sold the ring, but for what? Because that amount of money isn't worth everything she put herself through by marrying me. Not worth giving up so much of her life for. I guess I have no idea who Melanie Edison is at all.

Rubbing a hand over my jaw, I blow out a breath before I dial my best private investigator. He's a hacker too—not as good as Jessie Ryan, but this is the type of information he specializes in getting. After a brief conversation, he promises to have Mel's financial records sent to me within a week.

Not that it will make any difference. Legally the money is hers to do with as she pleases, but maybe finding out what the hell she wants it for will make me feel less like going on a murderous rampage. Or maybe it will have the opposite effect. I guess we'll wait and see.

ONLY FOUR DAYS LATER, I'm staring at an email from my PI. He must have noticed that my work for him has dwindled and wanted to make a solid impression. I click on the link in his email, and the records fill the screen. She has less than two thousand dollars in her account. So where the fuck is my money? Glancing over her recent transactions, I see one payment to Harvard for just shy of forty thousand dollars and another payment to Ashley for the remaining one hundred and twenty grand Mel got for her ring.

And now it makes sense. Ashley has another year at Harvard, and if Melanie wasn't lying about her brother and the financial abuse, as well as the way he would use their sister to control her, then it adds up that she used that money to secure Ashley's future.

It doesn't change what she did. But for some reason, I feel

differently knowing that she used the money for someone else. That's the Melanie I fell in love with, not the woman who lied to my face. My chest aches with the weight of the emotions that rage inside me. I wish I knew which Melanie Edison was the real one.

CHAPTER

FORTY-SIX

MELANIE

T fish in my purse for my key to Tyler's apartment, juggling the bag of groceries in my other hand, when I hear footsteps behind me. The familiar heavy tread makes the hair on the back of my neck stand up.

With a thumping heart, I look over my shoulder and come face-to-face with my brother. "I have nothing to say to you, Bryce."

Grabbing my arm, he spins me around and slams me against the door, knocking the wind out of me and making me drop the bag of groceries.

Bryce's face twists into a vicious snarl. "Did you know we just lost our biggest contract? The only thing keeping us from going under? All the investors I had lined up won't even return my calls. All because you couldn't stick to the fucking plan. You ruined everything, you stupid bitch."

I square up to him, unwilling to play the role of dutiful little sister for a second longer. "There was no plan. You had someone drug and assault Nathan. You should be in prison. I

259

hope he presses charges and you end up there. You pathetic weasel."

He brings the back of his hand crashing down over my right cheekbone, and I stagger back, clutching my hand to my face. Tears prick at my eyes, but the sting of his blow hurts far less than the stark reminder that my brother despises me and always has.

He advances on me again and is about to wrap his hand around my throat when a deep voice booms down the hallway. "You lay another finger on her and you'll be taking a fucking leap out of that window, pissant."

I shiver at the tone and the familiar voice it belongs to but sigh with relief when Bryce backs away from me, fear etched all over his face now. Yeah, he's a big man hitting a woman, but he would never stand up to a man, and definitely not to Elijah James.

I rub my cheek and mouth a silent thanks to Nathan's older brother as he approaches. I have no idea what the hell he's doing here, but I've never been more grateful to see anyone in my life.

Bryce turns on his heel, his lips visibly quivering as he fights to maintain his composure.

Elijah bares his teeth like a rabid animal. "I suggest you get the hell away from her, and me, before I give you the ass-kicking you deserve."

My brother doesn't hang around to argue. Knowing he doesn't stand a chance in hell of even landing a blow, he darts past Elijah and runs for the stairwell. Coward.

Elijah scowls at my brother's retreating back, then returns his attention to me. "You okay, Melanie?"

Nodding, I absent-mindedly rub my cheek. "Yeah. Thanks to you."

He stoops and places the spilled groceries back into the

paper bag before handing it to me. I thank him again, and he stands in front of me, rubbing his knuckles. "Should have beat the shit out of him," he grumbles.

I don't argue, although I'm grateful he didn't. It would have resulted in yet another family drama I'd find myself in the middle of. "Why are you— What are you doing here?"

"I was going to leave this in your mailbox." He removes an envelope from inside his suit jacket. "But then I saw Bryce coming in here, and I ..." He licks his bottom lip. "Well, I guess I was right to check on you."

I blink at his outstretched hand, and my heart sinks. Surely that's not ... "What is it?"

"It was delivered to the penthouse. Nathan said you might need it."

I take it from him and glance at the postmark, sighing with relief when I see it's from Harvard. Probably Ashley's college tuition invoice. "You could have mailed it to me."

"Yeah, I could have." Elijah stuffs his hands into his pockets. "Maybe I also wanted to look you in the eye and ask if you knew what was going to happen in Chicago."

Guilt balls in my throat and tears burn my retinas. "I swear I didn't. And the fact that Nathan was hurt because of me will haunt me every day for the rest of my life. I'll never forgive myself for what that woman did to him."

His Adam's apple bobs. "She didn't do anything to him."

I blink at him, hoping I didn't mishear what he said. "She didn't?"

"Well other than drug him, which is still pretty fucked up. But that was it. She didn't assault him."

I suck in a breath as relief floods my body. While nobody has ever said the word rape aloud, that's exactly what it would have been, and knowing Nathan wasn't a victim of that makes me feel like a crushing weight has been lifted from my chest. "You're sure?"

Elijah nods. "Nathan spoke with her, and with Bryce, and he's one hundred percent sure."

"Oh, thank god. I appreciate you telling me that. Thank you, Elijah."

His dark eyes narrow with curiosity, his expression otherwise unreadable. After a few moments of silence, he tips his chin. "You should put something on that eye." Then he turns and walks away, leaving me standing alone outside Tyler's apartment.

CHAPTER
FORTY-SEVEN

NATHAN

I stare up at my older brother, barely able to comprehend what he just said. "You went to see her?"

"I delivered her the letter like you asked."

"I thought you were going to fucking mail it, Elijah. What the fuck?"

He sighs, running a hand over his thick beard and taking a seat opposite me. "I'm sorry if I overstepped, but I had to look her in the eye. After what she did ..." He blows out a breath. "She hurt all of us, you know. I trusted her too. I thought she was ..." He stops talking, and I'm grateful for no further reminders of what she was to me—to all of us.

But my heart constricts in my chest at the thought of him seeing her when I can't. *Or won't,* says a voice in my head, but I ignore it. "How was she?"

He avoids my gaze, the way he does when I'm not going to like what he has to say.

"How was she, Elijah?"

He sighs. "Bryce was there when I got there."

Fucking knew it. I snort. "They planning their next move, were they?"

"No, Nathan. He ..." He shakes his head. "He hit her."

A flash of anger has my blood boiling in my veins. My hands ball into fists. "He fucking what?"

"I saw him going into the apartment building, so I followed him. They were in the hallway. He called her a stupid bitch, and she said she hoped he'd go to prison for what he did to you. And he hit her."

Someone must have sucked the air from my office because I can't fucking breathe. I finally drag in a shaky inhale and will my racing heart to calm the fuck down. "He hit her?"

"Yeah. Right across the face."

A vision of him with his hands on her has that boiling rage about ready to burst out of me. "Is she okay? Did you break his fucking arm?"

"I told him to get the hell out of there. I figured you wouldn't want me kicking his ass while you're still figuring out what to do with him."

"That was before he hit my fucking wife, Elijah!"

He runs his tongue over his teeth, assessing me. We both know what I just called her, but neither of us are going to address that right now. And so fucking what if I called her my wife? It means nothing. Technically, she still is.

He clears his throat. "For what it's worth—"

I snarl. "Don't."

But he finishes his thought anyway. "I don't think she had any part in it."

I bang my fist on the desk. "She still fucking lied to me. She married me for my money." My heart splits in two. I could probably forgive both those things, but ... "She made me think that I fucking meant something to her." I can't forgive that. Not ever.

Elijah nods sympathetically. "I know, brother."

I put my head in my hands, wishing more than anything that I could forget everything about Mel and how much I still love her.

～

"This won't take long," I tell Teddy before I climb out of the idling car.

I stride through the building, adrenaline and anger pumping through my veins as I make my way to the top-floor offices of Edison Holdings.

I stride past the receptionist and walk straight into that smug fuck's office, ignoring the two people who run after me, shouting that he's on a call. Bryce looks up when I walk in, his tan face paling. I slam the door closed behind me and turn the lock, taking perverse satisfaction in making him tremble.

Stalking to his desk, I take the phone from his hand and end the call before tossing his cell phone on the floor.

"That w-was—"

"I don't give a fuck who it was, you piece of shit."

He straightens his jacket. "What do you want, Nathan? I thought we came to an agreement."

The anger that's been simmering in my veins since my conversation with Elijah earlier today boils over, and I launch myself over the desk, grabbing him by his throat and shaking him like a rag doll. "You don't have any sort of agreement with me, fuckface."

His mouth opens and closes, his lips trembling. I throw him back into his chair and pace the length of his office. I will fucking kill him with my bare hands if I don't get a handle on my temper, and even I couldn't get myself off a murder charge with a half-dozen witnesses outside.

I dampen my rage and adrenaline with cooling lungfuls of

air. And when I can look at him without tearing his head off, I sit down in front of his desk. He eyes me warily, his twitching fingers wrapped tightly around the arms of his chair.

I glare at his smug, entitled face and wonder how the fuck a good man like Luke Edison raised a piece-of-shit son like this one. "You know the people I work with, right, Bryce?"

He nods, his eyes wide and skin paler than chalk.

"You must also know that I could make someone as insignificant and pathetic as you disappear and not get my hands the slightest bit dirty. I've done it before."

His Adam's apple bobs as he swallows. "Yes."

I lean forward, placing my hands on his desk and glaring at him. "But for you, Bryce, I would gladly get my hands dirty."

He darts his eyes around the room like he's hoping someone might burst in and rescue him.

"If you *ever* touch a hair on her head again, I *will* make you my exception. There is nowhere you can run that I won't find you. And I will find you, Bryce, and I will crush every bone in your body to dust."

He stares at me, opening and closing his mouth like he's fucking mute. I grab his tie and pull him toward me. "Do you fucking understand me?"

"Y-yes," he sputters.

My eyes drift to the antique letter opener on his desk. Picking it up, I let go of his tie and grab his right hand instead, splaying it out on the desk in front of me.

"N-no." He shakes his head. "Please."

Ignoring his pathetic sniveling, I drive the sharp edge straight through his hand, pinning him to his desk. His mouth opens on a strangled scream, and I put a finger to my lips. "You don't want anyone coming in here, Bryce, because then I'd have to tell them all how you embezzled their pensions and all of your family's money. How you spent it all on whores and cards. And you don't want that, now do you?"

He presses his lips together and shakes his head as tears run down his cheeks. I tap the side of his face. "That's a good boy. Now stay the fuck away from my wife."

CHAPTER
FORTY-EIGHT

NATHAN

"Fuck me, I couldn't eat another fucking thing," Mason says with a loud groan, earning him a clip on the ear from our father, who he obviously hadn't realized had walked back into the kitchen.

"No cursing at my table." Dad takes a seat and promptly lights up a cigar.

"You're supposed to have given those up," Elijah reminds him.

Dad shrugs. "What's the point of living if you can't indulge in life's simplest pleasures, son? I have two vices, cigars and whisky, and I'm not about to give up either of them."

"Don't forget the women, Pop." Mason chuckles and receives a withering glare to go along with his sore ear.

Our dad sighs wearily, but he doesn't dwell on it any longer. Of all of us James boys, Mason is the one who can push him the most before he snaps.

"You had a heart attack, Dad. Those things aren't good for you," Elijah persists, but our father dismisses him with a wave.

"It's New Year's Eve. I have four of my boys here with me, and life is good. Can you at least let me enjoy my cigar in peace?"

I shoot my older brother a look, warning him not to press any further. Dalton James has been smoking cigars for over fifty years. A heart attack isn't going to stop him.

With a reluctant nod at me, Elijah turns his attention to our younger brother. "Drake, how are things in Chicago?"

Drake shrugs. "Same old, same old."

"You should come home," Dad says in a gruff tone. "You were only supposed to be out there for a year or two. Six years later and you're still there. Surely the office can run without you now?"

Drake bristles. "I like it there, Dad."

"You should be home with your family," Dad insists, blowing out a stream of cigar smoke.

I throw Drake a conspiratorial wink, and he rolls his eyes in response. It's good to be here with the four of them. My penthouse apartment has been feeling way too big and empty these past few weeks, which is fucked up given that I lived there alone for eleven years before Melanie Edison walked into my life.

"How are things with the Edison girl?" It's like my father can read my mind.

I seethe at the mention of her. "Her name is Melanie, as you well know, and things are exactly the same, Dad. She's a lying, soul-sucking bitch who will become my ex-wife as soon as possible."

"You've drawn up the divorce papers?" Drake asks.

"No. Not yet," I admit. I should have had them drafted the day I found out the truth about her, but I've been distracted. That's what I'm telling myself anyway.

My father's eyes narrow at me from across the table. "What's stopping you, son?"

I glare at him. "I've been busy. It's only been a couple of weeks. I'll handle it."

"I can handle it for you if you'd like?" Drake suggests.

I swallow the lump in my throat and shake my head. "No, it's fine. I'll do it myself." Having those papers drafted will make everything seem so final, and I don't think I'm ready for that quite yet.

"If you're sure." Drake eyes me with concern.

"I'll take care of it," I insist.

Our father snorts a laugh. What the hell is his problem? He's the reason I'm even in this mess. His need for a legacy fucked up my entire life. I was fine before, and now I'm walking around in some sort of fucking daze. He eyes me suspiciously. "Don't tell me you fell in love with the girl?"

I grind my teeth, and the muscles in my jaw tighten. We all fucking fell in love with her, but none of us are going to admit it. "No. I did not fall in love with her. I told you, I've been fucking busy."

"So get the papers drawn up and get this shitshow over with," Dad says, like it's that easy, which is bullshit. I know he's as hurt by her betrayal as I am.

"Why, Dad? So you can set me up with the next gold digger?"

The vein in his temple twitches, his face turning a deep shade of pink. I can feel my brothers' eyes on me, silently urging me to stop pushing him. Of all of us, I seem to be the one who's able to ignite his short fuse with the least amount of effort.

"Has anyone heard from Maddox lately?" Drake asks, swiftly changing the subject. Not that our baby brother is an easier topic for our father to handle, but at least it takes the heat off me, and for that I offer Drake an appreciative nod.

Elijah takes a sip of his Scotch. "I believe he's currently

headed to Tuscany. At least that was his plan when I spoke with him a couple of days ago."

"He should also be at home where he belongs," our father grumbles.

"Or maybe he should be out there enjoying his life while he's still young enough to do so," I snap.

That wins me yet another fierce glare before he shoves his chair back. "Elijah. Come take a walk with me. You can fill me in on the new Denver deal."

Elijah rolls his eyes at me but does as our father bids, and the two of them walk out of the kitchen, leaving Drake, Mason, and me alone.

"Do you actually want to serve her with divorce papers?" Mason asks.

I run my tongue over my bottom lip and stare up at the ceiling. "I don't fucking know."

Drake leans forward, his hands clasped on the table in front of him. "So there's a chance that you don't?"

"I guess that's what I don't know means."

Mason runs hand over his beard while Drake sits back in his chair and blinks at me. "Wow, bro," Drake says. "I assumed that after what she did, you wouldn't even entertain the idea of reconciliation."

I scowl at him. "Who said anything about reconciliation, asshole?"

He scowls right back. "So you don't want to divorce her, but you don't want to reconcile either? You're just going to leave yourself in some kind of limbo, not to mention her?"

I snarl. "You think she deserves any better than that?"

"No, I think that you do. Why torture yourself any further? If it's over, end it."

My pulse quickens, and anger fizzes in my veins. "Maybe it's not that fucking easy, Drake. Don't you think I want this to be over? Don't you think I wish every single fucking day that I didn't know what it was like to feel loved by her, even if it was all an act. If I could forget how good she felt in my arms, how her smile could make even the shittiest day brighter, how fucking good she tasted, I would do it in a heartbeat."

Drake opens his mouth to speak, but Mason puts a hand on our brother's arm, obviously making him think twice about whatever it was he was about to say.

"Whatever you decide to do, Nathan, we're here for you," Mason assures me, giving Drake a pointed look.

"We always have your back, bro," Drake adds.

A heavy sigh rushes out of me. "I know." I also know what I need to do next. Dragging this thing out is only hurting both of us, and as much as I want to hate Mel for what she did, I can't seem to find it in me. I make myself a silent promise that I'll fix it tomorrow.

But for tonight, I just want to sit here with my brothers and pretend that life is exactly like it used to be.

Tomorrow is a new year. A new start.

CHAPTER
FORTY-NINE

MELANIE

I pad along the hallway, fresh from my shower and planning to grab some snacks and watch TV in my room —which has pretty much been my evening routine for the past three weeks—when I hear a knock on the door. I'm not expecting anyone. Tyler stayed out last night with some guy he met at a New Year's party, and he already told me he won't be back until tomorrow. I pull my bathrobe tighter around myself as I head to check it out, wishing I'd put on my pajamas. I hope it's not my asshole brother. Although he's stayed out of my way since our encounter over two weeks ago.

I check the peephole, and my heart stops beating. Without thinking about why he might be here, I wrench open the door. "Nathan?" I manage to gasp, even with my heart caught in my throat.

He tips his chin at me. A light dusting of stubble covers his square jaw, and although it seems impossible, he looks more handsome than ever. Clearly our breakup isn't affecting him at all. "Can I come in?" he asks.

I step back, opening the door wider. "Sure."

He steps inside, and his masculine scent invades the space around me, bringing up a whole host of memories. I swallow down the regret that balls in my throat while he closes the door behind him. The soft click of the lock sends goosebumps prickling along my forearms. Being alone with him isn't good for my health.

Nathan's deep voice cuts through the silence. "Is Tyler home?" He looks past me, a frown furrowing his brow.

I fidget with the tie on my bathrobe. "No. He's out."

He continues to look past me, avoiding my gaze.

What is he doing here? "Did you want something, Nathan?"

His dark eyes finally burn into mine. He sweeps the tip of his tongue over his bottom lip, and my heart rate spikes. Without another word, he takes a few steps closer, and I feel the heat of his body in every cell of mine.

"Mel." My name is a pain-filled groan from his lips, and it feels like my throat is closing up. I can't do this.

Before I can take my next breath, he closes the remaining distance between us, and I find myself sandwiched between him and the wall. The solidness of his hard chest against mine and his breath dusting over my forehead cause a shiver to run the entire length of my spine. With his eyes boring into mine, he strokes a hand over my hipbone and along my ribcage, leaving a trail of fire in his wake.

My lips part on a gasp. I should tell him to stop, but I can't. Instead, I wrap an arm around his neck, tugging him closer. He kisses me. It's all-consuming fire and passion, and I'm powerless to stop him. Powerless to stop my heart from aching at the way his solid warmth envelops me and the memories of what we had. What we lost. Because he is everything.

I curl my fingers in his hair, and he groans into my mouth, pressing his hard length against my stomach. Heat floods my core. His kiss grows more fervent, his tongue lashing against mine as he takes what he wants from me. And I take just as much. I slip my free hand inside his jacket, skating it over the soft cotton shirt that covers his toned abs.

Breaking the kiss, he pulls back to stare into my eyes.

I blink, panting for breath. "Nate."

His hands slide to my hips, down my thighs, and before I can take another breath, he's yanking up my robe, exposing my panties. He runs his nose over my jawline while his hands move higher, dangerously close to where I need him most. "Say that again."

"Nate," I moan.

Using one hand, he frees his belt from its buckle and unfastens his zipper. "This whole goddamn building is gonna know my name by the time I'm done with you."

My breath stalls in my lungs, and white-hot anticipation spikes through my core. My fingers join his, fumbling with his pants. I reach inside his boxers and wrap my hand around the base of his shaft, and when I squeeze, he sinks his teeth into his bottom lip. His eyes roll back in his head, and his fingers dig into the delicate lace of my panties. The sound of tearing fabric makes me shiver with excitement.

After smacking my hands out of the way, he lifts me, his eyes still boring into mine as he wraps my legs around his waist and presses the crown of his cock at my entrance. My heart drums a wild rhythm, and aching need throbs between my thighs. I wrap my arms around his neck.

We shouldn't do this. I can't survive losing him again.

His mouth crashes against mine, possessive and dominant, and he drives inside me in one hard stroke. Pleasure laced with a hint of pain surges through my body, and I cling to him for dear life as he pulls out only to drive inside me even harder. Palming the back of my neck, he holds me possessively while his body crushes mine to the wall. His other hand roams freely, grabbing and squeezing the parts of me he can reach. He fucks me with brutal strokes, and it feels like a punishment, but I don't care. I want it—no, I need it.

"Holy shit!" Hot pleasure curls in my core, snaking through my limbs and weaving its way through every cell in my body. It's been too long since I've felt like this. Too long since my body has found the kind of euphoria that only he can bring me.

"You always took my cock so well, corazón," he whispers, his hot mouth pressed to my ear. His hand slides between us, and he pinches my clit, squeezing and rubbing while he goes on rutting into me like a feral beast. And I take it all, desperate for everything he can give me. Desperate for any crumb of affection or contact he offers, because I've been starved of him for far too long. And when my orgasm crashes over me like a tidal wave, he fucks me through it, burying his face in the crook of my neck and muttering Spanish curses. His hips still a few seconds later, and I know he's found his own release. I'm already anticipating the loss of him, and a whimper breaks free.

He slides his dick out of me and tucks himself back in his pants while I straighten my robe. He doesn't look me in the eye as he reaches inside his jacket and produces a folded envelope from the pocket. I swallow, tears welling in my eyes. *Please don't.*

He steps back, still avoiding my gaze, and hands me the brown envelope. "I want a divorce, Mel."

My fingers don't even feel like my own as they grasp the paper in a trembling grip. My lip quivers, and my throat closes over with the effort of holding back the sob that wants to pour out of me. But I won't give him the satisfaction.

He turns on his heel and walks out of the apartment, and only after the door closes behind him do I allow myself to feel the pain of what he just did. My knees buckle, and I sink to the floor, my back sliding down the cool plaster with a swish. Tears pour down my face, and my fractured heart disintegrates entirely, the pieces so fragile they would drift away on the slightest breeze.

I had the most perfect man in the world for me, and I let him slip through my hands. Now I'm left with only the soul-crushing pain of knowing that there's no chance of a future for us. Not after what he just did. He snuffed out the tiny flicker of hope that continued to burn, despite all the odds. And that's the cruelest cut of all.

CHAPTER
FIFTY

MELANIE

I gawk at the white stick in my hands, trying to convince myself that I'm seeing double for some reason and there's actually only one blue line staring back at me rather than two. Squinting, I peer more closely, and all my delusions fly out the window. How the hell I could have been so damn stupid?

I didn't register my missed period, assuming my cycle was messed up when I stopped taking my pill. And when I started feeling nauseated almost every hour of every day, I tried to convince myself it was food poisoning or a stomach bug. But now the evidence of my own stupidity is right here in my hands.

I sink to the floor of my bedroom and lean back against the bed. A fresh wave of nausea rolls over me, and I'm not sure if it's morning sickness or a result of coming to terms with my idiocy.

It's not that I don't want kids; I do. And at this point, the idea of being a single mom doesn't scare me. I have Tyler and Ashley and my friends, and I could make it work. It's the thought of telling Nathan that terrifies me. The fear that he will think this is some grand plan to trap him or extort some of his billions from him, when that couldn't be further from the truth. I almost wish this was some random stranger's baby instead, because then I wouldn't be forced to have the inevitable stomach-churning conversation with him.

Except in my heart I know that's not true. If there was one man in the world I would choose as the father of my children, it would be Nathan James.

If experience has taught me anything, a positive pregnancy test is only the first step. It doesn't mean I'm going to hold that child in my arms. But what if ... A flicker of hope sparks in my heart.

Regardless, keeping this from him isn't an option. Even if he ends up hating me, he deserves to know. I only hope he proves to be the good man I know he is and that he makes our child feel loved. Because as inconvenient as this pregnancy is, our baby is very much wanted. I place my hands over my belly, and a tear leaks from the corner of my eye.

"You're a little miracle, jellybean," I whisper. Then I pick up my phone and call the one man I know I can always count on.

Tyler answers on the third ring. "Hey, Goose," he says playfully, and I figure he has a guy with him.

"Can you talk?"

"To you? Always."

I take a deep breath and spit it out. "I'm pregnant."

"What?" he shouts. "Hold the fucking phone. You're what?"

"I'm pregnant, Ty."

I hear him blowing out a breath. "Give me one minute, baby girl."

There's a short, muted conversation between him and some guy before he returns to the call.

"I'm sorry. Did I spoil your date?" I ask.

"No. It was already spoiled. He didn't like *Top Gun*."

279

I gasp, feigning horror. "Not even the new one?"

"Nope. Can you believe it?"

"You sure can pick 'em." I laugh softly, thankful for my cousin and the way he's always there for me no matter what.

"So tell me everything, baby girl."

I take a deep breath and tell him everything about that night four weeks ago when Nathan broke my heart. I pour out my hopes and fears, and by the end of our conversation, I have a plan. I'm going to sign the divorce papers I haven't had the courage to look at since the day he gave them to me. My wish was that he'd somehow realize it was a huge mistake and change his mind.

But he's not going to, and me signing the papers will be proof that this isn't a scheme to get money from him. Then I'm going to march into his office and tell him I'm having his baby. He can choose to be involved or not. Either way, it doesn't matter to me.

Easy as pie. Right?

CHAPTER
FIFTY-ONE

MELANIE

I ignore the muttering and side-eye glances as I walk toward Nathan's office, stopping in front of his secretary's desk. I clear my throat, and she looks up at me, a sympathetic half smile on her face. I roll back my shoulders, trying to fake a confidence I don't feel. This all seemed much easier when it was only a plan in my head. The execution of it, however, is proving to be far more terrifying than I could have anticipated. I look Helen in the eyes. "I need to see him."

"He's not available right now."

I stay rooted to the spot. "I know he's in there."

"He's busy."

I wring my hands in front of me. "Please, Helen. It's important."

She smiles gently, and the pity in her eyes makes me want to cry. I ball my hands into fists, my fingernails biting into my palms as I try to stop myself from losing it in the reception area of Nathan's office.

"He has a meeting in ten minutes," she says with a tilt of her head.

"I only need five, but I need to speak with him." I guess she recognizes the desperation in my voice because she offers me another sympathetic glance and tells me she'll see what she can do before disappearing into his office.

Less than two minutes later, Helen ushers me inside. Nathan doesn't even bother to look up when I walk into the room, keeping his head bent over the papers on his desk. Narcissistic jerkwad.

My legs tremble with each step, and I take a seat opposite him while trying my best to forget the last time I was here and the things he said to me. What I almost said to him.

He still doesn't look at me.

I sigh. "I was told you didn't have much time."

His head snaps up, a scowl furrowing his brow. "What the hell do you want? If you're here to discuss the terms—"

"I'm not here about the divorce."

His eyes narrow, studying my face. "So what is it?"

Dear Lord, strike one of us down right now and save me from having to do this. I let out a shaky breath and fold my hands in my lap, squeezing them together to stop them from shaking.

"Melanie!"

I flinch at his tone, and I'm half-tempted to stand and walk out on his grumpy ass. He doesn't deserve to know. Doesn't deserve to share this with me, assuming by some miracle he wants to. But our child deserves a chance to know their father, even if that father is currently behaving like the world's biggest asshole. "Before I tell you this, I need you to know that it's not some move or a ploy to scam you. This is my life, and I'll be happy enough to walk out of here and never see you again, but ..." I suck in a deep breath. "I also believe that you have a right to know."

That scowl on his face deepens. "To know what?"

"That I'm pregnant."

His mouth opens like he wants to say something, but he's silent. The great Nathan James, lost for words. I bet that's a first. He sinks back in his chair and runs a hand through his thick hair. "How?"

I roll my eyes. "You need a biology lesson?"

His lip curls in a sneer. "You were on birth control."

"Yeah, when we were together. But the night you came to Tyler's ..." My voice drops to a whisper as the memory of that night slams into me. The hurt of him leaving feels every bit as raw now, even after four weeks.

"So you just stopped taking your pill?" He shakes his head like he doesn't believe me.

"Well I had no reason to remember to take it, and I had a few other things on my mind," I snap. "Forgive me if I wasn't prepared for you to come to Tyler's apartment just to get your rocks off with a goodbye-fuck before you threw divorce papers in my face."

His eye twitches, and he rolls his neck.

I blow out a breath. Anger isn't going to help this situation. "Like I said, I'm telling you because I believe you should know, but I don't want or need anything from you, Nathan. Truth be told, I'd prefer to do this alone than with someone who can barely stand to look at me. But *if* you want to be a part of our child's life, I won't stand in your way."

His Adam's apple bobs, and he fixes me with a steely glare. "And you're sure it's mine?"

He may as well have punched me in the gut. I reel backward, tears springing to my eyes as he rips a fresh slice out of my already broken heart. Mustering what little dignity I have left and willing my hormonal ass not to let him see me cry, I push myself up onto shaky legs. "Have a nice life, Nathan."

I spin on my heel and stride out of his office, slamming the door closed behind me.

CHAPTER
FIFTY-TWO

NATHAN

I rub my temples, my head throbbing and my ears ringing as I recall the look on her face when she walked out of my office. I'm such a fucking jackass.

"Here, looks like you need this," Mason says, handing me a glass of Scotch.

Ignoring the proffered glass, I drop my head into my hands and let out a heavy sigh.

The door to Mason's office opens, and I recognize Elijah's heavy footfalls as he crosses the room. "I'll take one of those," he tells our younger brother.

Mason pours him one, and Elijah sits on the leather sofa beside me. "So, what's the deal?" my older brother asks, cutting straight to the point the way he always does. "Or do we need Drake and Maddox to dial in?"

I shake my head. "It's not about business."

Mason snorts. "I figured that, bro."

I look up, glaring at him. "How?"

"Never in my life seen you this cut up over business." He shrugs and holds out the glass of Scotch, and this time I take it.

"So?" Elijah prods me.

"Mel is pregnant," I blurt, in the hopes that it will be less painful. It's not.

"Oh, fuck," Mason mutters.

Elijah knocks back his Scotch in one gulp. "How pregnant?"

I shake my head. "I dunno. Six weeks, I think. I'm not entirely sure how it works." Although I spent the last hour researching how many weeks pregnant she'd be given the date we had sex.

"You've been separated for two months," Elijah reminds me, like I'm not aware of that fact every second of every day.

"I know." I close my eyes and shake my head. "The day I gave her the divorce papers, we ..."

"You fucked her before you served her divorce papers?" Mason tips his head back and releases a dark laugh. "Jeez, bro, that's cold. Even for you."

"Fuck you," I mutter.

Elijah shoots our younger brother a warning glare. "And she told you this today?"

"Yeah, said she didn't want anything from me and she'd prefer me to not be involved, but she thought I had a right to know and I could be part of the kid's life if I wanted to."

He nods. "That tracks."

I scowl at him. "What do you mean, that tracks?"

He swallows hard. "She signed the divorce papers today. They were couriered to your office this afternoon. I asked Helen to let me break the news to you. I was going to tell you tonight. She's not contesting the divorce or the prenup. She's walking away without a dime."

Mason scoffs. "Yeah, because she's carrying his kid. Doesn't that guarantee her money?"

I turn my scowl on Mason now. Are we all as cynical as he is?

"That guarantees her child support, but that's for the child and not her. Certainly not for her family," Elijah clarifies.

Mason shrugs and downs his Scotch.

"The important thing is how you feel about this." Elijah rests a reassuring hand on my shoulder. "Do you want to be a part of the child's life?"

My heart feels like it's being squeezed in a vise. I stare into my older brother's eyes, and I swear I couldn't lie to this man if I tried. "Yeah."

He nods and raises his empty glass. "So you're gonna be a dad. We should celebrate."

"Yeah, well ..." I blow out a breath.

Elijah gives me a knowing look. "What did you do?"

"I asked her if she was sure it was mine, and she walked out."

Mason slaps his hand over his heart. "Ouch!"

"Will you stop?" I snap. "You're supposed to be making me feel better."

He pours me another Scotch and hands it over with a wink. "I am."

Elijah holds up his glass too. Mason refills it along with his own, then he holds it up. "To the first of the next generation, bro."

Elijah lifts his glass in a toast. "Congratulations."

I down my whisky, savoring the burn of the liquid in my throat.

Elijah wraps an arm around my shoulders. "She'll come around."

I sure fucking hope so.

. . .

Sitting in the back of my car on the way home from the office, I dial Mel. Like she has the past six times I called her, she sends me to voicemail. I curse under my breath and dial a different number.

"Nathan!" Her excited voice fills my ear. At least someone is pleased to hear from me.

"Hey, Jessie."

"Do you have another job for me?" she asks.

"Yup."

"Who is that, sweetheart?" Shane, one of her husbands, asks in the background.

"It's Nathan. He has another job for me."

I hear Shane's dark laugh. "Tell him I'm gonna put him on a fucking retainer if he keeps working you like this."

She giggles. "Did you hear that?"

"I did. And I'm sorry to take up your time, but this is personal, and I don't trust anyone else with it."

"Hey, you know I love to keep busy. So hit me."

I quickly explain that I need to know the details of Melanie's doctor's appointments. If Mel refuses to speak to me, I don't have any other choice.

"Let me get this straight," Jessie says, her tone showing no hint of the giggling, friendly woman who answered the phone. "You want me to invade your wife's privacy after you were a complete asshole to her?"

I wince. "I know. But I want to not be an asshole in the future. I promise I'm only going to be there for support, whatever form that takes."

"What if she doesn't want anything to do with you? If she did, she would have responded to your calls, right?"

I scrub a hand through my hair. "Jessie," I groan. "Come on. I know I deserve to suffer, but I promise you she doesn't want to do this alone. She's hurt, and that's on me, but I'm going to be this kid's dad." I swallow the lump in my throat. "Please?"

She sighs. "Fine. I'll get you the details of her next appointment, but after that you're on your own."

I thank her and end the call, but not before she makes me promise again that I will be less of an ass to my wife in the future.

FIFTY-THREE

MELANIE

"I wish I was there," Tyler says. "You shouldn't go to this thing on your own, baby girl."

I try to infuse my tone with confidence that I don't feel. "I'll be fine."

"That shithead should be going with you," he adds with a growl.

I sigh, not wanting to get into a discussion about said shithead right now. He tried to call me a few times after I walked out of his office four days ago, but he can go to hell. If he really wanted to be a part of this, he'd show his face and apologize for being such a giant dick. "I'll be fine. I'll call you later and let you know how it goes. Now I gotta go."

I end the call with Tyler and head out of the apartment building, trying to ignore the churning in my gut and the stream of negative thoughts racing through my head. *This time it will be okay. Third time's a charm, right?*

The sun is blinding when I step outside, and I shield my eyes from its glare, which is why I don't see him until I almost bump into him. He holds out a hand to stop me from colliding with his solid chest.

My heart lurches into my throat, and both relief and anger barrel into me, each fighting for dominance. I choose the latter. It's easier when dealing with him. "What the hell do you want?"

The arrogant asshole has the gall to gently grab my arm and flash me a smug half smile. "You have a scan today, do you not?"

I shrug out of his grip and glare at him, craning my neck to give him the full extent of my fury. "And what the hell has that got to do with you?"

He winces. "I'm sorry about what I said, Mel. That was a low blow."

"Damn right it was low, you conceited jackass." I try to move past him, but he blocks me, and the scent of his cologne makes my head spin. *Damn, did he always smell this good?* I shake my head to clear all the unwelcome thoughts that come with seeing him when I'm already so vulnerable. I hate Nathan James. "Get out of my way."

He grabs hold of my shoulders, and I'm forced to look at his handsome face. I stuff my hands into my coat pockets so I don't punch him in it. "I want to be there, Mel. At every appointment. I want to be a part of it."

I shake my head. "I don't need you."

"I know that. But you said—" His voice cracks. "Don't I deserve to be a part of our child's life?"

Our child. A sob wells in my throat, and I swallow it back down where it belongs. "No!" His eyes fill with sadness, and my weak armor cracks. "But our child does deserve to know their father, so ..." I shrug.

"So I can come with you to the scan?"

I nod but avoid looking at him. If I see the happiness in his voice reflected in his eyes, it will only break my heart more.

He steps back and opens the door of his car for me. I climb inside and lean against the door, trying to stay as far away from him as humanly possible. Once he's inside, the car pulls away from the curb. We spend a few minutes in awkward silence before I realize I haven't told him where my appointment is. I never told him I even had one. What the hell?

I turn in my seat and watch him stare out the window. So calm and self-assured, while I'm full of anxiety and fear. "How did you even know I had a scan today?"

He shrugs. "I'm a man of many talents."

"You must know that's a gross invasion of my privacy."

He gives me his full attention. "What else was I supposed to do when you wouldn't take my calls?"

"Because you acted like a giant asshole," I remind him.

He licks his bottom lip and closes his eyes, like he's trying to keep a lid on his emotions. "I'm sorry about what I said."

"Yeah, you already told me that." I turn and stare out at the people on the street.

"Why are you having a scan so early anyway?"

I press my lips together. Tears burn behind my eyes. I don't want to have this conversation. Not now, not with him. I hope my silence conveys that.

He presses me anyway. "Is it because there might be a problem?"

I swallow the lump in my throat and swat away the tear that rolls down my cheek.

"If there's something wrong, Mel, I should know. Let me—"

I cut him off before he can start playing the white knight. He does not get to be the hero here. "I lost two babies."

"Mel, I had no idea. I'm sorry." He reaches for my hand, but I yank it away.

"I don't need your pity."

He mutters something unintelligible, but I remain focused on the street outside and do my damnedest not to think about that time in my life. Thankfully Nathan doesn't push me any further, and we spend the rest of the journey in silence.

CHAPTER
FIFTY-FOUR

NATHAN

There's not much to be seen in the grainy image on the screen, but the obstetrician is smiling as she points out our baby, and the sound of the rapid heartbeat fills the small exam room.

But most of my focus is on Mel's face. Previously a mask of worry, it's now lit up like a Christmas tree. Her eyes shine with unbridled happiness, and I have never seen her look more beautiful than she does at this moment.

"You're six weeks and three days pregnant," Dr. Walker says.

"Wow!" I blink at the fuzzy image on the screen again. "You can be that accurate?"

"Sure can," she says with a smile, before she directs all of her attention to Mel again. "Because of your history, we'll schedule another scan at ten weeks and again at twelve weeks."

Mel nods her understanding, and Dr. Walker removes the wand and sanitizes her equipment while Mel cleans herself up. My hands twitch by my sides as I resist the urge to help her, but

I'm pretty sure she doesn't need my assistance to get her panties back on.

The doctor is making notes on her computer, and she glances up at Mel. "Remind me how far along you were with your previous miscarriages."

I watch my wife's slender throat thicken as she swallows. "Six weeks with the first, and sixteen with the second."

Holy shit. I know enough about pregnancy to know that sixteen weeks is pretty far along. No wonder she was so anxious on the drive here.

Dr. Walker hums, makes a few more notes, then gives us information on prenatal vitamins and care. I listen intently, swearing to myself that I will do everything in my power to make sure my wife and our baby are taken care in the best way possible.

WE'RE BACK in the car on the way home when I finally broach the subject of Mel's previous pregnancies. "How old were you?"

Her eyes fill with tears, and I want nothing more than to wrap her in my arms and take the hurt away for her, but I'm painfully aware that I have no right to do that anymore. "Nineteen."

Jesus fucking Christ. She was just a kid.

"You know that whole story about me leaving college because I had 'issues'?" She uses air quotes for the last word. "And everyone assumed I had a coke addiction?"

"Yeah."

"Not true. I got pregnant by my biology professor. My family couldn't bear the shame of it, so they allowed everyone to think that I went off to rehab rather than have anyone find out I was grieving for the two babies I lost."

"He got you pregnant twice?"

She nods. "The first miscarriage was early. Like six weeks, so they brushed it off as one of those things that just happen. But the second was at sixteen weeks and ..." She takes a breath before she continues. "Well, that's a whole lot different. And that's why they want me to have regular scans with this one." Her lip trembles, and I hate that she's having to relive those painful memories. I don't want to force her to talk about the pregnancies, so I focus on her college professor, who was a dick for knocking up his nineteen-year-old student.

"Did you love him? The father?"

"Yeah," she says softly, and I'm filled with burning hatred for the guy, and not because he probably took advantage of her, but because she loved him.

"What happened with him?"

"After the first time, we agreed to try again—"

"Even though you were still in college?" I frown.

She shakes her head. "I know it sounds crazy now, but after my dad died, I felt like I had nobody. I was mixed up. I was just looking for ..." She brushes a tear from her cheek.

She was just looking for someone to fucking love her.

"He was so sweet. So cool and mature, you know? I thought he was the most incredible person I'd ever met."

Of course he seemed fucking mature when you were nineteen. I fucking hate him.

"He sold me a future that seemed so much better than the one my mom and brother had mapped out for me. So, when he suggested we try again, it made perfect sense to me. We agreed I'd stay in college to keep up appearances and then drop out as soon as the pregnancy became impossible to hide."

"He sounds like a fucking asshole," I spit, unable to hold back and half expecting her to defend him.

Instead, she lets out a harsh laugh. "Yeah, he sure was."

"What happened between the two of you?"

Her beautiful face pinches in a frown as she stares over my shoulder. "After I lost the second baby, he blamed me. He said I partied too hard and hadn't taken good enough care of myself. I went to *one* party and had a single sip of wine." Another tear rolls down her cheek, and I go to wipe it away, but she roughly swats it away before I can. "We stayed together for a few weeks after that, but he kept getting worse with his bullshit about how it was all my fault. I couldn't deal with the grief, so I left and ..." She blows out a breath. "I went home and told my mom and Bryce, and they stirred up that stupid rumor about why I dropped out."

"And the professor? He just got away with what he did to you?"

"It's not like he broke the law or anything. Bryce and my mom wanted it all swept under the rug. I believe he was questioned by the dean about our alleged relationship, but he denied it all. He went on living his life like nothing had ever happened, and I was ..." She wipes her hands on her jeans. "No point reliving the past right now, huh?"

"Where is he now?"

"According to Tyler, who stalks him on Facebook, he's living in Ohio with his wife and two kids."

"You want me to take care of him for you?" I ask, only half joking. All she has to do is say the word. "Because I know people."

That gets me a soft laugh, and fuck me, but I love to see her smile. "I'm sorry I never told you, Nathan." I fucking hate that she calls me Nathan, but I bite back that particular retort. "It's just ... It hurts to talk about that with anyone, but I should have told you. I guess my mom and Bryce thought it was easier to marry me off if I was a reformed coke addict than someone who couldn't have kids."

I reach for her hand, and she doesn't pull away this time, so

I thread my fingers through hers and kiss her knuckles. Making a mental note to have Helen find the best obstetrician in the country, I silently promise to get her and our baby the best medical care money can buy. But I don't tell her that right now because I'm not sure if she'll view it as me overstepping, and I'm still on thin ice here. "You might have owed me a lot of things, Mel, but not that. And you can have kids, corazón. We're having one," I say instead.

She gives me a faint smile. "Yeah?"

"Yeah."

FIFTY-FIVE

NATHAN

I step into the reception area of the veterinary office, and I'm immediately hit by the smell of wet dog. The receptionist eyes me suspiciously as I approach with a pink bakery box clutched in one hand and a takeout bag in the other. When I reach the desk, it becomes clear that she's actually giving me the full-on stink eye. Her lip curls in a sneer. "Can I help you?"

I clear my throat. "I'm here to see Melanie."

She rolls her eyes and calls over her shoulder, "Mel, honey, your douchebag husband is here to see you."

Well, that explains the stink eye. A few moments later, Mel steps out of the doorway behind the receptionist, blowing her hair out of her eyes and wiping fur from her uniform. Her eyes bug out when she sees me. "Nathan. It's you ... I wasn't ..." She gapes at me.

I arch an eyebrow. "How many douchebag husbands do you have, Spitfire?"

299

The receptionist puts a hand over her mouth and stifles a snicker.

But Mel's face lights up, and her smile is worth being called a douchebag in front of a room full of strangers. She sidles up to her colleague and whispers, "You can't call him a douchebag, Cass. It's unprofessional."

Cass gives me once-over. "But he is though, right?"

Mel giggles, her bright green eyes fixed on mine. "Only very occasionally."

I shake my head. This woman drives me wild, and I have fucking missed having her in my life. "Are you free for lunch any time soon, Mrs. James?"

She smirks. "Maybe in about twenty minutes. You can wait out here if you like." She nods toward the seating area, which is full of wailing cats scratching to be removed from their boxes and dogs who either have ridiculous cones on their heads or they're showing off that they don't by licking their balls. All the human customers are gawking at me, the douchebag husband.

I blow out a breath. "Fine. I'll wait."

Mel bursts into a fit of giggles, but Cass opens the small half door that leads behind the desk. "Probably best you wait back here. Our clients adore Nurse Mel. One of them might just bite you on the ass if you sit out there."

Glancing back at the waiting area, I'm unsure if she's talking about the pets or their owners. I follow Mel down the hall, and she pops her head into an office. "Hey, Jake. That labradoodle came around just fine and is in recovery. Is it okay to grab my lunch now?"

"Whatever you want, Mel. Hey, I bought you some of that peppermint tea you asked for."

She thanks him and leads me into what's obviously their break room, stuffed with comfy chairs along with a small kitchen area. "Would you like coffee?" She examines a green box that's sitting on the countertop. "Or peppermint tea?"

I place the bag and the box on the counter. "Whatever you're having is fine."

She holds up the box. "Well, we don't have any decaf coffee in here, so I guess we'll go with peppermint tea." She fills an electric kettle, and I stuff my hands into my pockets because the urge to touch her whenever I'm anywhere near her is still too strong. "Did you bring us lunch?" She nods toward the bag.

"Yeah. Ham and swiss on rye."

"That's very sweet. Thank you." She licks her lips and stares at the pink box. "And please tell me those are jelly donuts in there."

"Not exactly, Spitfire." I flip open the lid and reveal a dozen ginger cookies.

"Mmm, cookies."

I take one out and hand it to her. "Not just any cookies. Cookies from the best bakery in all of New York."

She takes it from me, and her fingertips brush mine, sending an electric current along my forearm. Bringing it close to her face, she inhales. "Ginger?"

I nod. "My mom loved them. When the chemo made her sick, she said these were the only thing that helped with the nausea. I thought they might be good for the morning sickness."

She stares up at me, her eyes wet with tears that she quickly blinks away. "I'm sorry. I get emotional so easily these days." She sniffs.

I resist the urge to brush away the stray tear leaking from the corner of her eye. If I put my hands on her again, I won't ever want to stop. "I'm sure that's all normal, right?"

"Yeah." She wipes the tear away herself. "You'd better get used to another eight months of pregnancy hormones. You sure

301

you're ready for that?" She blinks up at me, and although it was supposed to be a lighthearted joke, we both know she's really asking me if I'm going to be there for her.

Unable to resist touching her any longer, I tuck her dark hair behind her ear. "Bring it on, Spitfire."

She smiles. That sweet-as-fuck, heart-melting smile. "Thank you, Nathan."

∾

WHEN I GET BACK to the office, a familiar face is chatting with my secretary, Helen.

"Sapphire, what the hell are you doing here?"

She tosses her long dark hair over her shoulder, her blue eyes twinkling. "I'm in town for the event on Thursday. Thought I'd drop by."

I ask Helen to rustle us up some coffees before I usher my old college buddy into my office. She takes a seat by the window, admiring the view for a moment before she turns her attention to me. "Congratulations on the wedding, by the way. I assume my invitation got lost in the mail." She smirks wickedly.

"It was a very intimate event. Only close family, and not even all of them were there."

She hums, eyeing me with suspicion, but she doesn't push, which I'm grateful for. "Well, I'm looking forward to meeting your lovely wife on Thursday. And I was hoping I could tag along with you guys. You know I hate walking into these things alone."

"What? Sapphire Huntington doesn't have a date? I don't believe it."

She rolls her eyes. "I've dated every woman in Chicago. Maybe I need to move back to New York."

"Pretty sure you've dated all the women here too."

She lets out a throaty laugh. "I was hoping your brother might be my plus-one, but he's not coming." She pulls a face.

"No. He has a huge case he's prepping for."

"He works too hard. I can't remember the last time we went out for a drink. I was so excited when he moved to Chicago, but he's nowhere near as much fun as you."

"Drake is a ton of fun," I insist, compelled to defend him. "He's just wrapped up in his work right now."

She rolls her eyes. "So can I be your third wheel or no?"

I clear my throat. "Actually, Mel won't be coming."

"Oh?" Her eyes narrow. "Trouble in paradise already?"

I glance down at my wedding ring, the one I still wear in the office. News of our separation isn't public yet, at least not outside of Nielsen's Veterinary Practice, and while I trust Sapphire, something stops me from telling her the truth. "No. She'll be out of town."

"So we can both go stag then?" Her eyes twinkle with mischief. "Just like college."

I pinch the spot between my brows. "Yeah."

"Great. I'll come by your place for a quick drink before we leave. We can catch up before we have to do the whole fake-smile thing all night."

I nod my agreement. It could be exactly what I need to take my mind off my pint-sized siren.

CHAPTER
FIFTY-SIX

MELANIE

"Have you eaten today? Taken your vitamins?" Nathan asks.

I roll my eyes, sinking my head into my pillow as I hold my phone to my ear.

"I'm sorry," he says with a heavy sigh before I can answer. "I'm not checking up on you, more like checking in on you."

"I know you are." It's kind of adorable how he's called me every morning and night since the scan two weeks ago. And I look forward to our chats way more than I probably should. What started as a check-in about my morning sickness and vitamins has turned into almost hour-long conversations where I run through my entire day. With Tyler out of town and Ash so busy with her studies, it's nice to have someone to talk to. They're the only ones who know about my pregnancy, and I won't tell anyone else until after my sixteen-week scan. "And yes, I've eaten and taken all of my vitamins."

"What did you have for dinner?" His tone has my toes curling with memories of how he would dominate my body. My skin flushes with heat.

"Um." I press my lips together.

"Tell me you didn't eat a jelly donut for dinner again, corazón?" That word slices a fresh welt in my heart, and tears prick at my eyes.

I blink them away and force out a laugh. "I did. Look, what baby wants, baby gets."

"I'm going to start having a chef deliver your meals if you don't start eating proper dinners."

I lick my lips. That doesn't sound at all unpleasant. "Like what type of meals?"

"Something nutritious. Like steak and dauphinoise potatoes, maybe?"

A hysterical laugh bubbles out of my lips, and he laughs too. "I made such a mess of your kitchen."

"Hmm. You sure did." His low growl turns my insides to jelly. Is he flirting with me?

I sit up, emboldened by unlocking this playful side of him again. "Hey, you know what I was reading about today?"

"What's that?"

I take a deep breath. "How some pregnant women get super horny."

He curses under his breath. "And are you?" The deep timbre of his voice makes heat sear between my thighs, and I clench them together. Well, I am now, Ice.

"Um. Kind of. Although I'm not sure that's entirely due to the pregnancy or whether it's remembering the dauphinoise incident."

He hums, low and sexy. "That was some night, huh?" His tone is softer now, and it's tinted with regret.

"It sure was."

His voice drops another octave. "So what exactly are we going to do about this situation, Mel? I mean, as the baby's father, I'm supposed to take care of all of your needs, aren't I?"

Damn right. But before I can reply, a soft voice calls out in the background. "Nathan, we need to leave if we're going to get there on time." My breath stalls in my lungs like someone just punched me in the solar plexus. He has someone with him? "Who is that?"

He clears his throat. "She's a colleague. We have a charity event to attend."

"Together?"

"Yes, together." He sounds exasperated now.

"Is she at your penthouse?"

"She's an old family friend, Mel."

So she is at his penthouse. I swallow down the giant sob that wells in my throat. God, I'm so stupid. Thinking he was flirting with me when he was getting ready for a date with another woman. I'm such an idiot. "Well, have a wonderful night," I snap, before ending the call and tossing my phone onto the bed.

"Asshole!" I shout, wishing there was someone here to hear me.

"Ow!" I yell, sitting up in bed and clutching my abdomen.

I blink in the dark room, trying to get my bearings, and another sharp stabbing pain lances through me.

No, please not again! I reach between my thighs and feel the warm wet patch on my pajamas. Tears leak from my eyes, and I turn on the lamp to see the blood on my fingers. No, no, no. This can't be happening. I did everything right. I took my vitamins. I didn't stretch too high or carry anything heavy.

"I did everything right!" I scream into the darkness. Pain and anguish crash over me in a long, never-ending wave, pulling me under until I can't breathe. Tears race down my cheeks, and I curl into a ball and sob, wrapping my arms around myself as I will my body not to betray me again.

CHAPTER
FIFTY-SEVEN

NATHAN

I end the call with a sigh, not bothering to leave a voicemail. Mel is pissed at me because of last night. Not that she has any reason to be. But I guess if I heard some guy in her apartment, I would have lost my shit and gone straight over there to find out what the fuck was going on, so I can't exactly blame her.

I'll go to her work during lunch and explain. It will give me a chance to make sure she takes a break and is eating properly too. I'd rather she didn't work at all right now, but I get that she can't—and won't—just up and quit her job. Plus, the doctor said there's no reason at all why she shouldn't work.

I glance at my laptop and then at the painting on my wall. It's my most treasured possession. I should keep it at home, but I spend more time at work than I do at my penthouse, especially now that Mel is no longer there. Her absence makes the place seem emptier than it's ever been.

I lean back in my chair and wonder what she's doing. If she

ate breakfast this morning, if she felt sick at all. Whether those ginger cookies I gave her are helping with her nausea. I hate that I only get to check in with her by phone, hate the thought of her doing this all alone. I should be there, holding her hair back when she's sick and rubbing her swollen feet.

Tyler will be home in a couple of weeks, and I guess she'll have him then, at least for a week or so before he leaves again. But I'm not sure if I feel better or worse about that. He'll be the one who gets to feel our baby kick for the first time and see her bump grow every day. The one who will hold her hand through it all. Envy burns through my veins.

She should be living with me, at least until she has the baby. Tyler is rarely ever home. She needs someone to take care of her. She needs me. The memory of our phone call last night plays on a loop in my head, particularly the direction it was headed before Sapphire interrupted.

I googled pregnant women being horny, and apparently it's a thing. I'll be fucked if I let anyone else scratch that particular itch for her.

The sound of my office phone ringing snaps me from my thoughts. I press the button, and Helen's voice fills my office. "It's someone from Jasper Hospital on the line, sir."

My heart rate doubles. "About who?"

"Mrs. James."

The breath leaves my lungs like someone sucked all the air out of them with a straw. I place my hand on the table, grounding myself to the solid wood, and stare at my mother's painting, hoping to channel some of the peace I usually feel when I stare at it. "Put them through."

A few seconds later, a doctor whose name I wouldn't remember if someone put a gun to my head tells me that Mel is in the hospital and that she lost our baby. I don't remember ending the call. I don't recall half of what she said. My soul cracks in two. She lost our baby. And she was all alone when it happened. Did she call out for me? Was she in pain?

Tears burn behind my eyes, and I rub my knuckles into the sockets. Tears won't help her right now. The only thing I can do is get to her as fast as possible.

∾

I RACE THROUGH THE HOSPITAL, frantically looking for the suite where my wife is lying all alone. When I get there, a blond doctor is waiting outside the door. "Mr. James?" I recognize her voice from the call earlier.

"Yes." I look behind her, through the crack in the door where Mel lies on the bed, curled in a ball.

"I'm sorry. There was nothing anyone could have done."

I blink at her. "But what happened? I spoke to her last night, and she was fine. How did she get here? Who brought her?"

"She came in a cab. She was already bleeding heavily, and she passed the embryo in the night. These things have no rhyme or reason, Mr. James. They just happen."

I glare at her, waiting for another platitude, but she doesn't offer one. Instead she gives me a sympathetic smile. "I'm so sorry for your loss. Your wife can go home when she's ready."

"So she's okay? Physically, I mean?"

"Yes. She should expect a little more bleeding for the next few days, much like a period, but other than that, she's perfectly healthy. I'm sure she'll be more comfortable at home."

I thank her and burst into the room. "Mel." Her name is a plea, but she doesn't look up.

Dropping to my knees at her bedside, I wipe away the tears streaming down her cheeks, but they're quickly replaced with fresh ones.

"I'm sorry," she whispers, and my heart fractures into a thousand tiny pieces. I would lay them all bare at her feet if I thought it would bring her any comfort.

"No, corazón. You don't have anything to be sorry for," I assure her, aware of the tremor in my voice.

She stares past me, unblinking.

I brush her hair back from her face and glance around the room. I fucking hate hospitals. Nothing good ever happens in them. "Let's get you home."

She goes on staring, and I place my hand on her cheek, rubbing the pad of my thumb over her soft, wet skin. "Mel. You want to get out of this place and go home?"

She sucks in a deep, rasping breath. "Y-yes."

"Good girl." I help her off the bed, then grab her coat and purse. "Tedward is outside."

She stands on shaky legs. "Can you take me to Tyler's?"

"Not a chance, corazón. You're coming home with me."

"I'll be fine. You don't need to take care of me."

Yes, I really fucking do. More than I've ever had to take care of anyone in my whole fucking life, I need to take care of you right now. I swallow down that retort. "There's not a chance in hell I'm leaving you alone right now, corazón. Now let's get the fuck out of this place." I slide my arm around her waist, and I'm relieved when she offers no further resistance.

Curled up on the back seat of the car, as far away from me as she could possibly get, Mel barely said two words during the car ride home. Does she blame me for what happened? She has every right to. I upset her, and then I hung up the phone to go to a fucking charity dinner. I never should have left her alone, not when she was carrying my fucking child, and especially not given her history. I let her down badly, and I don't know if I'll ever forgive myself.

When we get home, I pour her a glass of cold water and she drinks it all down. Then she stands in the kitchen, looking so broken and lost that I want nothing more than to wrap her in my arms and tell her everything will be okay. But I have no idea if she wants that from me. I have no idea how to comfort her when my own heart is so beyond broken that to even speak of what we've lost would render me a complete mess.

"I'm tired," she eventually says, her voice terrifyingly small and timid. "I think I'm going to lie down."

"Okay. You need me to do anything?" I wince at the sheer fucking ridiculousness of my question.

She shakes her head and drifts out of the kitchen without another word, like she's sleepwalking through the day and I'm not even here. As soon as she's gone, I sit on a stool at the island and rest my head on the countertop. I've never felt as utterly powerless as I do right now. Never in my life have I been so completely impotent, and I would give anything to take her pain away.

With nothing else to do, I wander down the hallway and stop outside her room, pressing my forehead against the door. Her low sobs break my heart anew. My fingers curl around the doorknob, and I contemplate whether to go inside or leave her with her grief. But I'm drowning here too, and she's the only person who has even an inkling of what this hurt feels like.

I push open the door and step inside, my eyes drawn to where she's curled up in the middle of the bed, her arms wrapped around her body, which shakes with the violence of her anguish. Wordlessly, I crawl onto the bed beside her and band my arms around her. She melts into me, laying her cheek on my chest and nestling into my body like it's the only place in the world she belongs. I hold her while she cries, her tears soaking through my shirt as my own silent tears drip down my cheeks, and I let myself grieve not only for the child we lost but also for the future that was only ours.

FIFTY-EIGHT

MELANIE

I open my eyes, blinking at the rays of afternoon sun glaring through the window. Pain washes over me anew, and my heart breaks all over again. I'm curled up on Nathan's chest, and my cheek is stuck to his shirt, which is soaked with my tears. I shift in his arms, and he mumbles something unintelligible.

I try to wriggle from his grip, but he bands his arms tighter around me. "Where are you trying to go?" he asks softly.

I sniff. "I-I soaked your shirt, sorry."

He presses a gentle kiss to the top of my head. "You can cry an ocean if you need to, Mel. I'll be right here."

I sniffle again. "I'm stiff. I need to move."

He hums but releases me, allowing me to roll onto my side. When he turns to face me, he brushes the pad of his thumb over my cheek. "I'm so sorry I wasn't there for you, corazón."

I shake my head. "It wouldn't have made any difference."

He swallows. "It would have to me."

"I did everything right. At least I think I did." I blink away another tear.

He cups my chin in his hand. "You did, Mel. You did everything. This is not your fault. Tell me you know that."

Logic tells me that's true, even if my heart won't let me believe that yet. "What if ..." My lip trembles.

He dusts his lips over my forehead. "What, corazón?"

"What if I'm broken?" The words leave my mouth on a sob.

He sighs, his warm breath dancing over my skin. "You're not. At least not in the way you mean. But we're all a little broken, Mel. It's the inevitability of a life well lived. And it's the pieces of us that knit back together that make us who we are."

I fist my hand in his shirt and bury my face in his chest once more. "Thank you for coming today."

"There is no world where I wouldn't be there for you and our baby. I'm right here and I'm not going anywhere, okay?"

I nod. But the reminder that there is no baby anymore makes tears burn my eyes again. This is the end of him and me for good, but neither of us wants to admit that right now. Because at this moment, we're all each other has.

"We slept through lunch. Let me make you something to eat."

"I'm not hungry."

He rubs a soothing hand along my spine. "Regardless, you're going to eat, corazón."

I grumble a feeble protest but don't resist when he takes my hand and pulls me up from the bed.

CHAPTER
FIFTY-NINE

MELANIE

The heated marble floors are pleasantly warm under my bare feet, unlike the wooden floors of Tyler's apartment. The smell of coffee makes my mouth water. Nathan is already at the machine, pouring himself a cup with his back to me. He's dressed in gray sweatpants and a tight-fitting T-shirt, and I lean against the doorframe, taking in him. He really is a good man. He was so sweet last night. After we ate dinner, we watched mind-numbing TV. I fell asleep with my head on his lap, and I'm pretty sure I woke up to him stroking my hair.

Then he walked me to my room, and I was so close to asking him to stay with me, but he kissed me on the forehead and wished me goodnight. It felt like asking him to spend the night with me, if only to have comfort from the warmth of his body next to mine, would be crossing a line.

He spins on his heel, and I clear my throat, pretending like I wasn't staring at him.

"Morning. Did you sleep?"

I nod and stretch. "I did. I forgot how comfy that bed was. It beats Tyler's old fold-out couch any day of the week."

He offers me a faint smile, and I ask, "Did you sleep well?"

"Not really, but that's nothing new." He takes a sip of his coffee. "You want a cup?"

"Yes please. Caffeinate me up." I sit on a stool and watch him fill a clean mug. "No reason for me to drink that decaf junk any longer, huh?" The swell of emotion takes me by surprise, and I swat away a tear that dribbles down my cheek, hoping he doesn't see. I'm not quick enough. The concern on his face makes me feel guilty for putting all of this on him.

He places the mug on the counter in front of me and rests his lips on the top of my head. "I'm sorry I can't seem to stop crying," I say with a sniff.

"You went through something horrific, Mel. You're entitled to cry as much or as little as you want."

I grab hold of his T-shirt and press my face against his chest, inhaling his comforting masculine scent. "Why us? Why couldn't I have kept this one?"

"I don't fucking know, corazón." He sighs. "I wish I did."

I look up at him, and the sorrow etched into his face makes my heart break all over again. "I know it was early, but I imagined what they'd be like, you know? Would they be super smart like you, or into animals and nature like me?"

He nods, his eyes glistening with tears. "I imagined too."

"You did?"

He brushes my hair back from my face. "Yeah. Whether I'd be going to dance recitals and little league games, or science fairs and debate competitions. Or all of the above."

My chest throbs with a dull ache. "I'm sorry we won't get to do any of those things together. You would have been the best dad."

A tear leaks from the corner of his eye, and it damn near

breaks me in half. He rests his chin on the crown of my head. "I'm sorry too, Mel."

I glance at the clock on the high-tech oven, the one that hates me. "Don't you need to get to the office? You told me you've been working Saturdays."

"Not today. I'm going to do a little work from home."

Nathan never works from home. "You don't have to babysit me, you know. I'll be fine."

"I know."

I take a deep breath. "In fact, I should probably get back home and leave you to your space. You know, in case your friend from the other night wants to visit again."

His eyes darken and his jaw clenches. "She's an old friend, Mel. I swear to you there is nothing at all between us. We were two friends going to a law society event together. I am not that guy."

In my heart, I know that's true, but it doesn't change the fact that I should leave. "I should go anyway."

A sigh rolls out of him, and he pulls back, gripping my chin and angling my head so I'm looking into his eyes. "Do you want to be alone right now?"

I don't, but I also don't want to be a burden to him. I say nothing.

"Tell me the truth," he pleads. "Because I sure as fuck don't want to be alone. But if that's what you really want, I'll take you back to Tyler's and I'll go stay with Mason or Elijah."

His admission knocks the wind out of me. I was sure he'd want to get as far away from me as possible, given everything that's happened between us. "I'd prefer to stay here with you."

"Good. It's settled then. When does Tyler get back?"

"Two weeks."

He wraps his arms around me and murmurs, "Two weeks then."

"Yeah, and then I'll be out of your hair for good."

CHAPTER
SIXTY

NATHAN

Two weeks. I have only two weeks to figure out whatever the fuck this thing is between Mel and me and what the hell I'm going to do about it. Because although her reason for being here is devastating, her presence in my life makes everything make more sense. I slept better yesterday morning holding her while she cried than I have in the past two months.

She puttered around my penthouse today, watching TV, reading magazines, and cooking us lunch while I caught up with important emails on my laptop. She's been in my orbit all day, and I've liked having her close by, but she left the den over ten minutes ago and hasn't come back yet.

I close my laptop and head into the hallway to look for her. When I get to her room, the door is open, and the sound of the shower running comes from the bathroom. The bathroom door is open, and I edge into the room and call her name.

There's no reply.

She showered a couple of hours ago, so her being in there

again so soon feels off. I ball my hands into fists and wrestle with my conscience. If she's simply taking a shower and I walk in there, I'll be invading her privacy. Even if she is still my wife and I've seen, touched, and tasted every inch of her delicious skin. But if she's upset, or something happened ... I'd rather ask forgiveness than risk her being upset and alone.

I walk into the bathroom and see her curled into a ball on the floor of the shower, her forehead resting on her knees as the hot water runs over her. A faint trickle of blood snakes its way from between her thighs and down the shower drain.

Anger at the universe, rage that she's having to go through this, swells in my chest. I swallow it down and step inside the cubicle, crouching down.

"Hey corazón."

She blinks up at me. "I-I—" A heaving sob wracks her body.

I sit on the floor beside her and pull her onto my lap, and the hot water runs over us both, soaking through my clothes.

"I st-started b-bleeding ag-gain. I thought the w-worst of it w-was done b-but—" She sobs.

"Shh," I soothe against her ear. "It's okay." I tell her this despite not feeling it. Right now everything feels as far from okay as it can possibly be. The feeling of powerlessness that pervades every part of my being is so acute that I taste it with every breath I take.

"I'm sorry, Nate," she whispers, nestling her head against my chest. "For ruining us."

I swear she just knocked the breath from my lungs. The blades of a thousand knives slice through my insides, and the swell of guilt and sadness that crashes over me makes my head spin. I hate that she carries so much guilt about everything. About us. Her family. The baby. "You didn't ruin us, corazón," I murmur, but I'm not sure she hears me over the sounds of the water and her crying.

CHAPTER
SIXTY-ONE

MELANIE

"Hi, Mel, how are you feeling? I called a couple of times, but you didn't answer. I figured you were still feeling sick as a dog." My little sister's excited voice fills my ear, and I choke back a sob. It's taken me four days to summon the courage to call her. How do I tell her she's not going to be an aunty after all? I guess the easiest way is to spit it out.

"I lost the baby, Ash." I say it quietly, afraid to say the words too loudly because they're too painful to remain in this room.

I hear her sharp inhale. "Oh, Mel. I'm so sorry." She sobs the last word.

"Yeah, me too."

"I'm coming home. I'll catch a bus tonight and be in New York by tomorrow."

"No, you will not," I insist. "You're not missing any classes."

She huffs. "I can catch up on classes. Tyler's away, right? I'm not leaving you on your own with this."

"I'm not on my own. I'm staying with Nathan for a few weeks."

"Oh." Her tone softens. I told her we separated but left out most of the details. My sister, being who she is, didn't press me. She knows I'll tell her when I'm ready. "What's that like?"

"It's okay, actually. No, it's good. He's been super sweet and supportive."

"As he should be." She snorts. "I'm still coming home."

I pinch the spot between my brows. "You will not miss classes and jeopardize your grades, Ash."

She sighs dramatically. "I know how much you've sacrificed to put me through college. I won't miss any classes."

I heave a sigh of relief. "Good."

"But I am coming home this weekend. I have a soccer game on Sunday, but I can get a train. Or I'll fly home Friday after class and catch the red-eye back on Saturday."

"You are not flying back here. Or getting on a train. You can't afford the fare."

"It's a couple hundred bucks. You worry about me too much."

No, you have no idea how little money there is. "Please listen to me. You need to save any extra money you have." I lower my voice to a whisper. "There's nothing left now. I paid your tuition and your rent, but everything else still needs to be covered, honey."

She sobs softly. "I hate the thought of not being there for you, Mel."

"Is that your sister?" Nathan's deep, soothing voice comes from behind me, and I spin around to see him leaning against the doorframe. I nod.

He crosses his arms over his chest. "When's she planning on coming back here?"

I blink at him while Ashley asks me what he's saying.

"Mel?" he prompts.

I swallow down the knot in my throat. "Friday night."

"Tell her I'll have the jet at the airport for her."

"What's he saying?" Ashley persists.

"You don't have to do that," I say to him, ignoring my sister.

He shrugs. "What's the point of having your own plane if not to use it?"

"Mel!" Ashley shouts.

"Nathan said he'll send the jet for you Friday night if you'd like."

She shrieks in my ear. "Yes! Yes, I'd like. And I can stay until Sunday morning if he can get me back here by noon."

"She has to go back early Sunday morning and be back by midday," I explain.

He nods. "That's fine."

"A private freaking jet. Oh my god." Ashley giggles. "And I'll get to see you."

"Tell her she can stay here," Nathan adds.

"Nathan said you can stay here too."

"Good, because there's not a chance in hell I'm staying with Mom and Bryce." She makes a fake vomiting sound.

"I guess I'll see you late Friday then." We say our goodbyes, and I hang up the phone before walking over to Nathan. "How long have you been standing there?"

"Long enough to hear you tell your sister not to come home because she couldn't afford to," he answers, deadpan. Then his expression softens. "Did you tell her about the baby?"

"Yeah. That's why she wants to come home. She said she can't stand me being alone."

He grunts, and a look of hurt flashes across his face.

"I told her that I wasn't," I rush to explain. "That I'm with you, and that you've been way kinder to me than I probably deserve."

He cocks his head, eyeing me with curiosity, and everything suddenly feels awkward and tense between us. I become aware of the closeness of our bodies. How a single step from either of us would have us flush against each other, and I want that so badly that I have to force myself to step back. I hate that I find so much comfort in the feel of his arms around me. I hate that I want so much more. That I want every part of him. Every night this week, I've lain awake, wanting to go to his bed and curl up beside him.

I've wondered how good it would feel to have his hands and mouth on me, and whether he could take away even a fraction of this bone-crushing despair I'm feeling, if only for a little while.

"Thank you for helping Ashley out, Nathan. It really means a lot to me." I stare up into his deep brown eyes.

"It's nothing," he says, his voice thick with emotion.

I shake my head. "Not to me." I press up onto my tiptoes, slide my hand to the back of his neck, and curl my fingers in the thick hair at the nape of his neck. Then I press my lips to his cheek, giving him the softest of kisses and inhaling his unique, comforting scent. A groan rolls in his throat, and I have to force myself to step back from him.

He's still staring at me like he's trying to see into my soul, and I feel the need to break the spell he has me under. I clear my throat. "I'll go start on dinner." With that, I retreat into the kitchen.

This arrangement is temporary. As soon as Tyler gets back, I'll leave this penthouse, and Nathan James will be out of my life for good. If I allow myself to fall for him all over again, it will tear me apart when I have to leave. And I'm not sure I'd be able to put myself back together after losing him a second time.

CHAPTER
SIXTY-TWO

NATHAN

Mel rocks on the balls of her feet as she stares at the elevator doors. She's been on edge all day, jittery and nervous, and probably excited too. From what she told me, she hasn't seen her little sister since Christmas, and I know how hard that must be because I know how much I miss Drake and Maddox even though I could technically go see them whenever I want. The memory of our miserable Christmas at my father's house, where the absence of both Mel and her sister was keenly felt by my father and brothers and me, leaves a bitter taste in my mouth.

I lean against the wall, watching her, my arms crossed over my chest. Teddy called less than a minute ago to say that Ashley was on her way up, and Mel practically bounced out of the den and down the hallway. I haven't seen her this animated since before she lost the baby, and happiness warms my chest from the small glimpse of the person she was before.

The elevator doors open, and Ashley bounds out and straight into Mel's waiting arms. She's basically a smaller, younger version of her big sister, with the same bright green eyes and long chestnut-colored hair. I watch the two of them embrace, and after a few seconds Ashley starts to cry, making me feel like a voyeur intruding on their grief.

Until now, the grief has belonged to only Mel and me. Sharing that with her has felt intimate and brought me comfort. Now she's sharing her grief with her sister, and while I know that's as it should be, it also makes me feel less needed.

It's late. I should head to bed and leave them to catch up without me watching over them, so that's what I do. And when I'm lying in bed, I realize that in all my thirty-eight years on this earth, I have never felt more alone.

MEL SITS cross-legged on the sofa in the den, coffee in her hands and stifling a yawn.

"Did you and your sister stay up late?" I ask, my tone full of concern despite my attempt to keep it light. But if she won't let me look after her, she needs to take good care of herself.

"Yeah," she says with a soft sigh. "I figure I need to grab onto all the sister time I can get before she goes back to Boston tomorrow." Sadness washes over her features, and I can only imagine how hard it is for her having Ashley and Tyler so far away all the time.

I clear my throat. "What do you two have planned today?"

She rolls her eyes. "Ugh. Ashley's favorite pastime —shopping."

I take a seat on the sofa beside her. "You don't like shopping?"

She wrinkles her nose. "Not really. I like shopping for a purpose, like if I need an outfit for something, but not just because. Ash, however, could shop all day, every day and never get bored of it."

I run a hand over my jaw. "So we need to create an occasion for you to shop for."

"Nah, I'm good."

"But if that's what it's going to take to make today more fun for you, how about dinner tonight? I'll take you and Ashley somewhere, and you can buy an outfit for that."

She shakes her head. "I don't want to go out."

"Fine. I'll cook dinner, but it can still be an occasion."

Her cheeks flush pink, and she drops her head, biting on her bottom lip. Now I feel like an asshole because I know her funds are limited. I take my wallet from my back pocket and pull out my black Amex card. "Take this and buy you and Ash whatever you want."

She blinks at me. "Are you serious?" Her accusatory tone makes the hairs on the back of my neck stand on end. "After everything that's happened between us—after what you accused me of—you think I'd take your money?"

I let out a heavy sigh. "Then take it for Ashley."

She rolls her eyes again. "She doesn't need your money either."

I bite back the retort on my tongue about her already having a hundred and sixty grand of it and slip the card back into my wallet.

We sit in awkward silence, and I'm about to fill it when she speaks. "That was very nice of you though. Thank you." She bumps her arm against mine. "But you know I can't take your money, right?"

"I know. It was a stupid suggestion. I just want you both to have a good day."

"We will." A faint smile lights up her face. "You don't need to spend a lot of money to have a good day shopping, at least not with Ash. You could come with us? She'll teach you the art of window-shopping."

Spending the day with her makes even that torture sound appealing, but I decline because she deserves some quality time with her sister. "As incredibly fun as that sounds, I think I'll pass."

She chuckles. "Yeah, I don't blame you, Ice."

My heart hammers double time in my chest at her use of that name. She must feel it too because her breath hitches in her throat.

"That shower is incredible!" Ashley's excited shriek pierces the air between us. She flops onto the armchair and starts running through her shopping itinerary, which she appears to have planned with military precision.

My cell phone rings, providing me with the perfect excuse to leave the room. When I see the name flashing on the screen, I realize my day is about to get a whole lot more complicated.

I wait until I'm out of earshot before I answer. "Hey, Jessie."

"Hi, Nathan. I have some information for you. Sorry it took so long, but you said it wasn't urgent and things have been hella busy around here." She lets out a breath. "Anyway, that was some rabbit hole you sent me down."

"It was?"

She laughs. "I haven't worked that hard for a long time."

"Shit. I'm sorry if it took up too much of your time." Until I saw her name on my phone a few minutes ago, I'd almost forgotten I asked her to look into Luke Edison's murder a few months back.

"Please don't apologize. I love this stuff. But accessing records from seventeen years ago isn't as easy as getting information on more recent stuff, is all. There were so many red herrings to follow. Whoever covered this up did a hell of a job."

My interest piqued, I head to my office and close the door. "Okay, give me everything you got."

"How's Mel?" Elijah places the tray containing our coffees and two bear claws on the table before taking a seat.

It's been over a week since she lost the baby, and we've settled into a routine where she watches god-awful TV or reads while I work on the sofa beside her. Each day I see a little more of her laughter and light. Having her sister home certainly seems to have lifted her spirits. "She's doing as well as can be expected, I guess."

He arches an eyebrow. "And you?"

I shrug. "I'm good."

"Don't lie to me, Nathan."

"What? I'm okay. I mean, it was … the baby was a part of her, Elijah. She lost a part of herself."

His brown eyes soften. "It was a part of you too."

I swallow down the knot of sadness in my throat. "I know. But I'm okay."

"And this thing between you and Mel?"

I frown. "What about it?"

He shrugs. "Seems like you two have been getting along well. Is she back for good?"

I shake my head. "Only until her cousin gets back to town next week."

He takes a sip of his coffee. "And how do you feel about that?"

"Jesus Christ, Elijah, is this some sort of therapy session?" I ignore the disapproving look from the woman at the table next to ours.

He rolls his eyes and leans forward, completely unaffected

by me snapping at him. "I fucking care about you, asshole. Sue me."

I snort. "If I did sue you, I'd win."

"Yeah, the Iceman is a real shark."

I roll my shoulders. "Yeah, don't forget it, buddy."

He smirks and gives me a pat on the shoulder. "Seems to me like the ice man has thawed for his veterinary nurse."

I grind my jaw and glare at him.

He cocks his head. "Touched a nerve?"

"Fuck you."

"Nice," he mutters.

"If you really want to be a good brother, you can come for dinner tonight."

His face becomes a mask of confusion. I think he's come to my apartment for dinner all of twice in the eleven years I've lived there. "Dinner? Why?"

"Mel's sister is staying with us until tomorrow. I have some news I need to break to them about their father's murder. It would make me feel a hell of a lot better to have someone there who will stop either of them from trying to slit my throat with a steak knife."

Elijah's brow furrows. "What have you found out about Luke Edison's murder?"

I check my watch and curse under my breath. I'm going to be late for a meeting if I don't leave now. "I'll fill you in tonight. You can be there at seven, yeah?"

He shakes his head. "I can't. Amber has a society thing she has to attend tonight. I'm supposed to go."

"You hate those fucking things. I need you there, bro."

He winces, and I know I'm asking a lot. His marriage is in big trouble, and him blowing off his wife and one of her fancy society events is likely to piss her off big time. But it's not like she's ever there for him when he needs her. "Can't you ask Mason?"

"Can't. He's dating some actor now, and he flew to London last night to watch him in a show. Drake has a deposition on Monday that he has to prep for, so he won't fly from Chicago for one night. And before you suggest Maddox, I have no idea where the fuck he is right now."

"So I'm your last resort?"

I shrug. "Kinda."

He snorts a laugh and shakes his head. He knows that's not true. "Fine. I'll come to dinner."

"Thanks, buddy. I really do appreciate it."

CHAPTER
SIXTY-THREE

MELANIE

"What time is dinner?" Ashley lifts the lid from the pan on the stove and peers inside.

Nathan shoos her away. "Seven."

She rests her hip on the counter and watches him chop vegetables. "And your brother's coming, right? Elijah?"

"Yeah."

She arches an eyebrow. "Does he look like you?"

Nathan shrugs. "I guess so. Why?"

Her lips twitch in a devious smirk. "Ashley!" I admonish her. "That's my husband you're flirting with there." I wince the second the words leave my mouth. Can I still call him my husband given that we're about to be divorced?

Nathan spins on his heel and looks at me with wide eyes. "Is your baby sister flirting with me?"

"Relax, Ice. She flirts with everyone."

His eyes crinkle at the corners. He grins at me, and I smile back. A wide genuine smile. Having Ashley here is good for us.

SADIE KINCAID

She's like a buffer tempering the constant tension that fizzles between Nathan and me. And right now, everything feels relaxed and—dare I say it—normal.

"Can I flirt with your brother then?" she asks Nathan.

"No. He's married too," he replies, turning his attention back to the cutting board.

"Shoot." My little sister pouts.

Nathan flashes her a grin and signals for her to pass him the head of broccoli on the counter next to her elbow.

Ashley asks him about his job and seems fascinated by the fact that he's worked with some of the most infamous criminals in the country. He answers her eager questions with patience. God, he would have made such a great dad. My heart aches, and I press a hand to my empty stomach, swallowing down the bitter feelings of regret now stirring.

Their chatter goes on in the background, and the normalcy of it soothes a little of the empty feeling inside me. For the first time in over a week, I actually believe that happiness won't elude me forever. There will be a rainbow after this storm. I simply have to be patient.

WHEN ELIJAH GETS HERE, Ashley rushes out to greet him, always eager to meet new people. When we've all exchanged pleasantries, we head back to the kitchen, and she pulls me aside. "He's even hotter than his brother," she whispers in my ear, giggling.

Like hell he is. "He's also way too old for you. And he's married," I remind her.

She spins around in front of me, sticking out her tongue. "Doesn't mean I can't admire the view."

I shake my head. Dinner is sure going to be interesting.

CHAPTER
SIXTY-FOUR

NATHAN

I clear my throat, and Elijah shoots me a concerned look, like he knows I'm about to toss a hand grenade into the middle of our pleasant dinner.

I direct my attention to Mel and her sister. "I have something I need to speak to you both about."

Ashley stares at me, her expression full of curiosity, but Mel's eyes widen, and I can feel the anxiety radiating from her across the table. I guess she can still read me better than I thought.

"There would never be a right time to tell you about this, but it's something you both need to know."

It's Ashley who speaks. "What is it?"

"It's about your father's murder. The men who were shot by officers at the scene, Wilson and Inglewood, are the men who murdered him, and it was a robbery that went wrong ..." I run a hand over my jaw. "But it wasn't an opportunistic crime. Bryce set the whole thing up."

Mel's hand flies to her mouth, her eyes filling with tears.

"What?" Ashley gasps. "How do you know that? I don't understand."

"When Mel mentioned that Bryce always blamed her for what happened and that it was his idea to go to the beach that weekend, it just didn't add up for me. I asked a hacker friend of mine to look into it. She found out that Bryce owed a lot of money to some very bad people. With no funds of his own left to access, Bryce recruited both Wilson and Inglewood to break into your house."

Mel speaks for the first time. "Nobody was supposed to be home."

"Exactly. They would have had the codes to the safe, and they would've walked away with close to a million dollars. But your dad was there—"

"Because of Hayley's pool party," Mel interrupts, and Ashley squeezes her big sister's hand.

"Bryce couldn't get a message to them in time to call off the job. They were raised by militia, massive conspiracy theorists, and refused to carry cell phones."

"So, Dad confronted them and they shot him?" Ashley says, her eyes wide in horrified fascination.

"Yeah, the ballistics report suggests that's what happened. But even though Bryce couldn't get through to Wilson and Inglewood, he did manage to contact one of his buddies from NYPD, Detective O'Grady, who made sure he was the first on the scene. When O'Grady found Luke had been murdered, he knew that the only way to stop Bryce's part from being discovered was to kill them both. He triggered the panic alarm, claimed he'd only just arrived when his colleagues got there and that he shot Wilson and Inglewood in self-defense. It was cast-iron."

Mel simply gapes at me, but Ashley lets out a low whistle.

"So how did your hacker friend get this information? And are you sure it's reliable?"

"I don't question her methods, but yes, it's reliable. I've seen the phone records between O'Grady and Bryce on the day of the murder. Four calls in the space of an hour, during which time your father was murdered."

Ashley leans forward, one hand still holding onto her sister's. "So what now? Can Bryce be arrested? Or this Officer Grady?"

"Unfortunately, there's not enough evidence to convict Bryce of conspiracy to commit robbery in any court. Wilson and Inglewood are dead. Officer O'Grady was killed about seven years ago. Ironically, he was shot in the line of duty while attending a robbery. And the men that Bryce owed money too, well they're not going to cooperate with any sort of investigation and implicate themselves or risk exposing their lucrative racketeering business."

"Fuck," Elijah mutters.

"Right!" Ashley agrees.

"So Bryce paid these guys off with our family's money as soon as he became the legal executor of Dad's estate and the CEO of Edison Holdings?" Mel asks, her voice little more than a whisper.

I nod.

"You know none of this surprises me even a single bit." Ashley shakes her head, her button nose wrinkled in disgust, but it's her older sister I'm more concerned about.

My girl wears her heart on her sleeve, and a full range of emotions plays over her face. Anger. Shock. Betrayal. Her eyelashes flutter, wet with unshed tears. Her fork clatters to the table, and she flees the dining room.

Elijah, Ashley, and I exchange concerned looks.

"I'll go check on her," Ashley says.

I shake my head, already pushing back my chair. "Finish your dessert. I'll go."

Ashley considers me for a second, seeming to wrestle with the idea of letting me comfort her sister, but she nods her agreement after a few seconds.

I find Mel in her room, sitting on the edge of her bed and staring into space. The door is open, but I knock on it anyway. Her head snaps up, and she swats at her cheeks.

"All I ever seem to do lately is cry," she says with a harsh laugh. "You must be getting fed up with seeing me constantly sniveling by now."

I sit on the bed beside her and bump my shoulder against hers. "I wish you wouldn't be so damn hard on yourself, corazón."

Sniffing, she shakes her head.

"I know it hurts, but I figured you both should know."

She presses her lips together and takes a deep breath through her nose. "Seems like the truth always hurts the most, right?"

I tuck her dark hair behind her ear. "Not always."

She turns and looks at me, her moss-green eyes glistening. "No, you're right. Lies hurt much more. Especially when those lies have become so ingrained in your consciousness that they're a part of you. They shape the person you are, affecting every decision you make."

I take her hand in mine, lacing our fingers together.

"He made me believe that my dad's death was my fault. I was thirteen years old, and he convinced me that it was my fault." A heaving sob wracks her body.

I squeeze her hand tighter, resisting the urge to offer to kill him and bury his body somewhere he'll never be found. I'll leave that for another day. Instead, I let her pour out the hurt festering inside her.

"He held it over my head every day of my life. It was why I could never cut ties with him. Why I agreed to all of his ridiculous schemes. Every decision I've made since that day has been influenced by the belief that my father was killed because of me."

She scrubs at her cheek with her free hand, and her gaze hardens. "I hate him, Nathan. I fucking *hate* him!"

Yeah, me too. "You never have to see him again, Mel. You can cut all ties with him, your mother too, if that's what you want. Or you can fuck with them both by taking everything they have. Tell me what you want me to do and I'll make it happen."

The way she looks at me makes my heart beat faster and my dick twitch in my pants. "You really would, wouldn't you?" Her face softens in a faint smile.

I'd do fucking anything for you. "You only have to say the word."

"I don't want anything to happen to them. I don't need that on my conscience. Besides, karma will get them in the end. But I do want to cut ties. I want my name removed from everything to do with Edison Holdings. Can that be done? So I never have to have anything to do with either of them again?"

I frown. Edison Holdings is her father's legacy, and just because Bryce has spent the last seventeen years bleeding the company dry, that doesn't mean it's irredeemable. "You sure? Because I can have Bryce removed as CEO, and we could appoint an interim—"

"No." She shakes her head. "I'm tired, Nathan. I just want to walk away. From everything."

Even me? That thought makes me stall for breath, but I don't voice it. What if she said yes? "Then I'll make that happen."

Her eyes shine, and she lets out a sigh. "Thank you for being such a good man."

She leans into me, and I wrap my arms around her, resting my lips on her hair. *A good man.* I've never considered myself one of those before. Ruthless in business and in my personal life, I've never cared what anyone thought of me, and that has served me well all these years. So why the fuck does her calling me that make me want to do everything in my power to prove her right?

CHAPTER
SIXTY-FIVE

NATHAN

I fucking love when she falls asleep on me while watching TV. How her soft pink lips part a little and she scrunches her cute button nose when she's dreaming. I love that when I came home from work today, she was here. Her presence pervades every inch of my penthouse—the lingering scent of her perfume, her books in the kitchen, the food she likes in the fridge, the stack of magazines on the coffee table. Even in my bedroom, the place she hasn't set foot in for months, she lingers there, and the memories of all of the nights she spent in my bed are starker now with her here.

I only have three more nights until Tyler comes back and she goes home, and I'm no clearer on what the fuck I want to do. No clearer on what she wants. We share this space like we're best friends, but the reminder that we were so much more than that is never far away. The chemistry is still there, and if I'm honest with myself, I would have had her in my bed by now if she wasn't recovering from a miscarriage. I would be fucking her every goddamn night and day.

Our divorce papers sit in the safe in my office, waiting for me to file them to make it all official. I guess I have three days to figure out if I'm going to. Or if she wants me to. I look down at her beautiful face. The lies she told me at the start of our marriage seem so far away from where we are now. And if she's telling the truth about her part in all that, those lies are insignificant compared to the hell we've endured the past couple weeks.

My phone vibrates beside me, Drake's face lighting up the screen. I answer with a whisper, careful not to wake her. "Hey."

"Hey, I have all that paperwork drafted. I'll email it over and you can take a look."

"Already? I only asked you this morning. Don't you ever take time off?"

He laughs. "You already know the answer to that, bro. Besides, it was an easy fix. Provided the current CEO agrees to the terms, nothing is contentious."

"Oh, he'll agree," I say with a low growl.

"Well, yeah. You got him trussed up like a Thanksgiving turkey." Drake laughs again. "You need me to do anything else with this right now?"

"No. I'm going to sit on it. Just wanted to have the option if we need it."

"Okay." Drake yawns loudly. "In that case, I'm gonna call it a night."

"Good night, buddy. And thanks."

He mumbles a good night and ends the call.

I brush a strand of hair back from Mel's forehead, and she smiles contentedly. I've missed that fucking smile.

But her eyelids flicker open, and the smile fades. My heart aches for her. It's like each time she wakes up, she remembers again, and I wish I could stop her pain. "Did I fall asleep on you again? I'm so sorry."

"Don't be."

She sits up and stretches. "I'll have to stop getting used to this. Tyler hates it when I fall asleep on him."

I don't want her falling asleep on anyone but me. A phantom clock ticks away the minutes in my mind, reminding me that I only have three more nights of her sitting on this sofa with me. Yeah, I need to figure out what the fuck I'm gonna do because I know exactly what I want.

I STAND on the front porch, waiting to be shown into the house, rolling my neck to ease the tension tightening my muscles. I tap my foot and grind my jaw. Is she fucking kidding me? I bang on the door again, and a few seconds later, a housekeeper answers.

"I'm here to see Miranda."

She blinks at me.

"I called ahead," I growl.

The housekeeper nods and allows me inside, leading me to a sitting room where Melanie's mother is perched on an armchair, sipping what looks like sweet tea.

She casts her eyes over me, not bothering to disguise her disdain, which is fine by me because I fucking hate her as much as I hate her son.

"Nathan James." She sneers. "To what do I owe this pleasure?"

I sit down in the armchair opposite her and brace my elbows on my knees. "All I want is the truth, Miranda. If you have a single ounce of motherly love for your daughter in your body, then give me the fucking truth. Did she know anything about what Bryce was planning? That he was still going ahead with his plan to set me up?"

She lights a cigarette and takes a long drag, her narrowed

pale green eyes scrutinizing my face. Blowing out a long stream of blue smoke, she crosses her legs. "Melanie wasn't involved."

"With any of it?"

She flicks the end of her cigarette into an ornately jeweled ashtray. "He told her about the honey trap idea before you two were married, but she wasn't aware of how far Bryce was willing to go."

The memory of that night in the hotel has rage simmering beneath my skin. "She didn't know he was planning to have me drugged?"

Miranda shakes her head.

I snarl. "Did you?"

She rolls her eyes. Of course she fucking did.

"Did she know something was going to happen in Chicago?" My heart stops beating while I wait for what feels like eternity. I believe Mel knew nothing about the drugs, but did she come to my office that afternoon knowing that her brother was setting me up?

She takes another long drag of her cigarette, her eyes boring into mine. "No."

I sink back into the chair, running a hand through my hair. Relief and regret roll in my stomach. Mel has been telling me the truth. In my heart I knew that, but I guess a part of me needed to hear it.

"A few weeks after you were married, Melanie told Bryce that there was no need to go ahead with his idea, and when he refused to back down, she begged him. He promised her he wouldn't go through with it to get her out of his hair."

"Did she tell him why she had a change of heart?"

Miranda scoffs. "My daughter always was a dreamer, Mr. James."

I clench and unclench my fists, barely able to contain my rage. "What did she say?"

BROKEN

She purses her lips, the fine lines around them becoming more pronounced on her otherwise taut, surgically enhanced complexion. "It wasn't so much what she said as the ridiculous notion that she had about the two of you."

I bare my teeth. "Which was?"

She rolls her eyes. "That it was love."

Love? I frown, and she laughs. "Silly girl thought the two of you were falling in love." She snorts. "Tried to convince us you'd loan us any money we needed if she simply asked you nicely."

I suck in a deep breath, so many feelings racing through my head, but there's one thing that I'm more sure of than I've ever been of anything, and Miranda should know it.

I stand and straighten my jacket. "It's a shame you don't have as much faith in your daughter as you do in your useless prick of a son, Miranda, because Mel was right." She tips her head, her lips set in a thin grimace as she glares at me. "I would do *anything* for your daughter. I would have even financed you and your bottom-feeding son. Looks like you backed the wrong fucking horse."

CHAPTER

SIXTY-SIX

NATHAN

She's sitting on the sofa reading when I get home, looking lost and lonely. Fuck, I want to wrap her up and protect her from every goddamn thing in this world that could hurt her. And I want to spend the rest of my life doing it. I can't let her go.

"Hey." I perch on the coffee table in front of her.

"Hey. Did you have a good day?"

"I did actually."

"That's good," she says, offering a feeble attempt at a smile.

"How do you feel about going out for dinner?" I check my watch. "I could get us a table at your favorite steakhouse."

She wrinkles her nose. "I don't really feel like peopling."

I drop to my knees in front of her. "Then I'll book out the whole place."

That at least gets me a flicker of a genuine smile. "That's such a Nathan James thing to do."

"I just want to see a smile on your face, corazón. Tell me what I can do to make that happen."

She presses her lips together like she's deep in thought. "Food is always a good start. But takeout would be more my speed, I think."

"Takeout will make you smile?"

"Not just any takeout. A pepperoni pizza from Jersey's, and also …" She sinks her teeth into her plush lower lip.

"Also?"

"An old movie on the sofa? With you actually watching rather than working?" She winces like she's asking too much, when it's not nearly enough. An image of us curled up on the couch with her nestled against me, both of us snuggled beneath a blanket, makes my cock twitch in my pants. "That's what you want to do tonight?"

She catches her bottom lip between her teeth. "More than anything."

Why the hell is that true for me too? Cuddling on the couch and eating greasy pizza isn't exactly me, but the thought of doing that with her sounds like heaven. "I have to send a few emails and take a shower. Can you order?"

Her eyes sparkle, and an actual smile flickers over her full pink lips. "And I get to choose the movie?"

I roll my eyes, feigning mild annoyance, but the truth is I'll do anything as long as it involves being close to her. "If you insist."

MY PULSE IS RACING as I dry off from the shower. We're staying in and eating pizza on the couch, so why do I feel like I'm fifteen and about to go on my first date with Cindy Green? She was the head cheerleader in high school, and it took me months to work up the courage to ask her out. She said yes before I even finished the question, and I've never felt that nervous around a woman since. Until now.

I walk down the hallway toward the sound of her voice. Is she only just ordering the food? No, I can smell pizza. A familiar voice joins hers, and my heart drops through my stomach.

What the fuck is Tyler doing back in New York already?

I make my way into the kitchen and see the two of them hugging. They part when I walk into the room, and Mel looks at me, tears glistening in her eyes. "Tyler came home early."

He spins on his heel. "Yeah. Thanks for looking after my girl while I was away. I can take care of her now."

I lick my lips and stare at the two of them. *She's* my *fucking girl.* At least I thought she was, but she's so goddamn happy to see him. Maybe he is the right person to take care of her. She married me out of guilt over her family and nothing more. She's already told me she wants to walk away from everything to do with them, and I can't help but think that includes me too.

"He brought up the pizza." Melanie nods to the box on the table.

"Great. You two should take it with you," I say, having to force the words out of my mouth.

Her face falls, and I want to kick myself in the ass for saying it, then kick Tyler out of my apartment, but my stupid pride won't let me.

"I guess I should go get my things then," she says quietly.

I don't answer her. Instead I glare at Tyler, the man responsible for ruining my fucking night, and quite possibly my whole fucking life.

Mel slips out of the room, and Tyler plants his hands on the kitchen counter, his lips pressed together in a thin line and his eyes narrowed with suspicion.

"You know I always respected you. Always thought you were this super smart guy who didn't give a fuck what other people thought of you, but I ..." He shakes his head. "Now, I guess I know better."

"What the hell are you talking about?"

He licks his lips and glances at the open doorway before turning all his attention back to me. "She's the best damn thing that's ever happened to you, Nathan. And I think you know that too."

My hands ball into fists. "Don't assume to know what I'm thinking, Tyler."

"Oh, I wouldn't dare." He barks a sarcastic laugh and sits at the island, then takes off his baseball cap and runs a hand through his hair. "You know, she always loved animals. Begged her daddy for a dog every single Christmas and birthday from the day she could talk. And when she turned thirteen, a few months before he was killed, he finally gave in."

Why the hell is he telling me this right now?

"But Mel didn't want no new puppy. Nope, she made him take her to the pound. And when we got there, she chose the oldest, ugliest mutt you've ever seen in your life. I mean this thing had a gray muzzle and one eye, but she insisted he was her dog. Now Mel's mom might be a stone-cold bitch, but Luke adored his kids. He didn't want his little girl getting attached to a dog that only had a little bit of life left in him. When he sat her down and explained that this dog likely only had a few years left at best, you know what she said?"

I suppress a sigh. "No."

"She looked him square in the eye and said, 'We could get a puppy who gets sick and dies or gets run over. Love doesn't care how much time we have. It just takes its happiness where it can find it.' And he got her that dog on the spot. She called him Floyd, and he was her best buddy for three years. He died a few days after she turned sixteen, and she was fucking heartbroken. Her mom told her she was stupid for getting so attached to something she knew was going to die, but that dog brought her happiness and comfort that can't be measured, and I know for a damn fact she still would have chosen him if she knew he only had three months left."

A knot of emotion balls in my throat, making it hard to speak, so when I do there's a distinct crack in my voice. "Cute story."

Tyler gives a single shake of his head and huffs a laugh. "The point is, Nathan, nobody knows what tomorrow's about to bring. You have to grab onto whatever little slice of happiness while you can, and you have to fucking live in it. If your relationship with Mel is truly over, yeah, you should absolutely let it go. Things die all the time, but killing them to stop them from dying is my idea of batshit crazy. So if you're only ending this with her in case it might cause you more pain later on down the line, well then, for all your fancy degrees and your razor-sharp brain, you're the biggest fucking fool I ever met."

He walks out of the kitchen, and I'm left staring after him with so many questions and feelings running through my head that I sway on my feet.

The sound of soft footsteps shakes me from my daze. A second later, she walks through the door, dressed in a sweater and jeans, her cheeks pink and her eyes red like she's been crying.

"Where's Ty?" she asks, her voice thick with emotion.

I shake my head. "I thought he went to look for you."

She glances behind her. "Maybe he went to the bathroom."

I walk around the other side of the island, my heart racing faster with each step I take toward her. She watches me, chewing on her lip and shuffling her feet.

I take a deep breath, remembering how excited she was just a half hour earlier at the prospect of watching a movie with me. Tyler's right—if life has taught me anything, it's that happiness doesn't always last, and we have to hold onto whatever slice we can get of it. "Stay, Mel."

She blinks up at me, and I take another step, closing the distance until we're only inches apart. "What?" Her voice is barely a whisper.

"Don't go home with Tyler."

"I d-don't understand. Like stay for tonight?"

I slide a hand to the back of her neck and stuff the other one into the pocket of my sweatpants to stop myself from picking her up, carrying her to bed, and chaining her to it. "No, not for tonight. Not to give me a kid. And not because you feel guilty or because of anything to do with our families. Stay for me. Because you are the only thing in this entire world that I cannot fucking live without."

Her lips part, but she doesn't speak. Her breath hitches in her throat.

"I love you, Mel, and I would die tomorrow if it means I get to love you for today."

Tears fill her eyes, and for a heart-stopping, world-ending moment, I think she's going to tell me that it's too late. "I love you too, Nate."

I move on pure instinct, crashing my lips against hers as I wrap my free arm around her waist and pull her body flush against my own. Sliding my tongue inside her mouth, I claim her, groaning with relief and desire, and the sound mingles with her whimpers. Her hands snake around my neck, fingers tangling in my hair and pulling me closer. She feels so good in my arms, but I need more. I'm done waiting. I want her more than I've ever wanted anything before.

"I guess I'm going home alone then?" Tyler's voice drifts through the room.

I stop kissing her, but I don't remove my lips from hers. "Get the fuck out of here, Ty."

He snorts a laugh. "Rude. Can I at least take a slice of pizza?"

Pulling back, I suck in a gulp of air. "Take the whole thing, just go."

I vaguely hear the sound of his laughter and the rustle of a pizza box before his footsteps disappear and it's just me and her again.

She tips her head back, teeth sinking into her lip and her green eyes twinkling. "He just took our dinner."

I plant my hands either side of her, bracketing her hips and pushing her against the counter. "Not my dinner, corazón."

She flutters her dark eyelashes, a smile lighting up her beautiful face. I should lift her onto the counter and take her right now, but it's been so long since I've touched her, and I need to take my time. Picking her up, I wrap her legs around my waist and carry her to the bedroom where I can take as long as I need to reacquaint myself with every delicious inch of her delectable body.

As soon as I get her into our bedroom, I peel off her clothes, kissing her skin as I expose it to the cool air. She shivers at my touch, goosebumps breaking out over her flesh.

"You're fucking perfect, corazón. Fucking perfect," I growl when she's naked, pushing her back onto the bed.

She watches me undress, her eyes hooded and her chest heaving with the effort of drawing air. I crawl over her, allowing my gaze to rake over every bare inch of her. She is so fucking beautiful. She wraps her arms around my neck, hurriedly pulling my face to hers, and I kiss her briefly, but her lips aren't where I want my mouth right now. I trail lower, dragging my teeth over her skin, and she arches her back, fingers threading through my hair as she moans my name.

I lick a path from her collarbone to her nipples, giving each one a gentle bite before swirling my tongue over the tip. Then I move lower, my lips barely leaving her skin. "I've missed this so fucking much, Mel."

"So have I," she moans, writhing beneath me. "I need you, Nate."

I spread her thighs wider apart and dip my head so her sweet scent fills my nose. "I know, corazón. You've got me."

I lick a path along her wet center and my cock weeps precum at the sounds my mouth pulls from her. She needs this as much as I do, which makes me all the more desperate to remind her exactly how good we are together. Swirling my tongue over her clit, I groan as her taste coats my tongue.

"You still get so fucking wet for me, huh, corazón?"

"Y-yeah." She bucks her hips, riding my face while I suck and lick her, moving up and down her soaking pussy before concentrating on her needy clit. I suck the swollen bud into my mouth and slide a finger inside her, and she comes apart, her legs shaking and her pussy walls contracting as she screams my name. And fuck me, I have missed hearing that.

I lick her through her climax, drawing out the waves of pleasure until her body stops trembling. Then I trail my lips over her stomach and back up to her neck before I settle between her spread thighs. With her hands clasped in mine and pinned above her head, I nudge my cock at the entrance of her soaking pussy and inch inside.

"Nate," she gasps, and I sense a hesitation in her voice, even with her head thrown back and tits heaving with each breath. I'm reminded of what her body's been through the past two weeks, and I pepper kisses over her throat. "Is this okay? Am I hurting you?"

She sinks her heels into the muscles of my ass and hisses out a breath. "Not hurting, but … I'm not on any birth control."

Jesus fuck! Why does that make me even more desperate to fill her with my cum? "I don't give a single fuck about that, corazón. Do you?"

She shakes her head, her bottom lip caught between her teeth.

I sink deeper and stare into her bright green eyes. "You want this?"

Her eyes roll back in her head. "Yes!" I seal my lips over hers and slide all the way inside her, filling up every inch of her hot, wet channel, and fuck me, but it feels like coming home. Bone-deep relief and pleasure roll through me, igniting a fire in every cell of my body while I slowly drive in and out of her, letting her feel every inch of me each time I fill her.

This is as far removed from fucking as things can possibly get. This is two halves of the same soul coming back together. This is me giving and taking every-fucking-thing we have left. She whimpers, her sweet sounds full of desperation as I take her slowly and deliberately, committing every second of this to my memory for eternity. Feeling every part of her body submitting to mine each time I sink inside her again. And when her whimpers turn to moans and her walls flutter around me, I roll my hips, sweeping the tip of my cock over the sensitive spot deep inside her that has her trembling in my arms and whispering my name like a prayer.

I'm on the edge too, but I need to give her more. Need to take more. Sliding out of her, I smile when she whines a protest, but I fill her with my fingers instead, moving down her body and feasting on her soaked pussy while I fuck her with my hand. She writhes beneath me, her body chasing another release that I'm desperate to give her. As if I can make up for all the time apart in one night. It might be impossible, but I sure as hell intend to try.

She comes for me a second time, her juices running down my palm and onto my wrist, and I lap them up, reveling in her succulent, addictive taste. I will never get enough of this. Of her. Of us.

I brush her hair back from her forehead, pressing a soft kiss on her lips and making her refocus on me. Her green eyes dark with desire, her cheeks flushed pink, and her pretty lips parted, she comes down from her climax. Without breaking our gaze, I slide my cock inside her once more, and her back bows.

"Nate!" she mewls, digging her fingernails into my shoulder blades.

I press my forehead against hers and fuck her slowly. "I know, corazón. I've got you."

Tears leak from the corners of her eyes. "You feel too good," she says, her voice hoarse. "Tell me we can have this forever."

She damn near knocks the breath from my lungs. I never want her doubting me—doubting us—ever again. I dust my lips over her ear. "I promise you forever and a day, corazón."

She rocks her hips and wraps her arms around my neck. "I'll hold you to that."

I go on steadily fucking her at a leisurely pace until I can't stave off my own release for a second longer. When I come inside her, filling her tight cunt with my cum, I damn near pass out from the rush of endorphins flying through my body.

But as incredible as it feels to be inside her, nothing beats having her curled up in my arms after. I order us another pizza, and we eat in bed, watching the cheesy romantic movie she chose. She falls asleep before the end, her head on my chest and her thigh draped over mine, her bare wet pussy resting on my hip.

I kiss the top of her head and smile. My wife. My every-fuck-ing-thing.

CHAPTER
SIXTY-SEVEN

MELANIE

The bed is empty when I wake. I run a hand over the cool cotton sheets and, noting the absence of warmth on Nate's side of the bed, swallow down the deep ball of sadness that wells in my throat. After last night, I thought ... The dull ache between my thighs reminds me that it wasn't a dream. It was all real. The things he said. The way he kissed me. Made love to me. Because what we did last night was not fucking.

I brush a tear from my eye and take a deep breath, ready to throw back the covers and climb out of bed, but the door opens before I can. Nate walks in carrying a tray and wearing nothing but those damn gray sweatpants, and I push myself up into a sitting position and switch on the bedside lamp. As he draws nearer, the smell of fresh pancakes fills my nostrils, making my mouth water.

Nathan sits on the bed beside me and places the breakfast tray, filled with pancakes, fresh fruit, and coffee, over my lap. A smile spreads across my face. "You made me breakfast in bed?"

He takes half a strawberry from the plate, pops it into his mouth, and winks at me. "I figured you needed some nourishment after I made you come half a dozen times."

I arch one eyebrow. "Actually, it was only five."

His lips twitch in a smirk. "Then I'll be sure to up my game for tonight."

I pick up a slice of banana and take a bite, eyeing the delicious stack of pancakes and hoping he's going to share them with me because they're almost as big as my head.

"That's not all I brought you," he adds, making me look up at his handsome face again. He reaches into the pocket of his sweatpants and pulls out a small black ring box.

Swallowing the banana, I glance between him and the box, my pulse spiking. I suck in a stuttered breath when he flips it open. Tears swim in my eyes. "M-my ring. How did you ..."

"The jeweler informed me that you sold it back to him."

Oh god. "I only sold it to—"

He pushes a strand of hair back from my forehead, and it's only then that I notice he's wearing his wedding ring again. Ever since the day he served me those divorce papers, I've kept my wedding band in my purse. "I know what you used the money for, Mel, and it's okay."

A wave of guilt rolls over me. "I'm sorry, Nathan. For everything. I—"

"I know." He dusts the knuckles of his free hand over my cheek. "And I know that you had nothing to do with what happened in Chicago."

Relief floods me, warming me from the inside. I stare at the beautiful diamond, hardly believing it's real. I loved that ring from the moment I saw it, but now it means so much more. "You got it back? For me? But we ..." I can't finish the thought.

"I never would've given it to anybody else, if that's what you're thinking. But I hated the thought that another person might buy it, and I guess I secretly hoped I'd be able to give it back to you one day." He slips the ring from the box and takes my left hand in his. "Mel, will you be my wife again?"

"I never stopped. Not for a single second."

The smile he gives me has a kaleidoscope of butterflies taking flight in the pit of my stomach. It lights up his entire face, making his eyes crinkle in the corners as he slips the ring onto my finger. "Perfecto como tu."

A giggle bubbles out of my mouth. "I love how you slip into speaking Spanish when you get all romantic."

He shakes his head, but his smile remains in place. "Eat your pancakes."

I lick my lips. "What if I'd rather eat something else?"

He narrows his dark eyes but spears a giant piece of pancake with the fork. "You need food. Now open."

I open my mouth, allowing him to feed me. The delicious, buttery pancakes flood my taste buds, followed by the sweet syrup, and I let out an appreciative moan. "These are so good. You should try some."

He leans forward and licks the residual syrup from my lips. "Mmhmm, delicious."

I roll my eyes. "You think you're so smooth, Mr. James."

"I'm smoother than fucking silk, Mrs. James. It's how I landed you, right?" He trails kisses over my jawline.

"Actually, I think you landed me with your huge ..." I sink my teeth into my bottom lip.

He arches an eyebrow at me. "Bank balance?"

I swat him on the arm and fake a horrified gasp. "I was going to say your huge—"

"Penthouse?" he offers.

I narrow my eyes. "No. Your giant-ass ego."

Laughing, he takes the tray off the bed and places it on the floor. Then he crawls over me, pulling me down the bed until

I'm lying beneath him and pinning my hands above my head. "I don't think that's what you were going to say at all, corazón."

"So what do you think I was going to say?" I breathe out the words, spreading my thighs wider to accommodate him.

He rocks his hips, rubbing his hardening length against the part of me that's already aching to feel him. "How about I show you?"

CHAPTER
SIXTY-EIGHT

NATHAN

My phone vibrates on the kitchen counter in front of me, and a text from Drake flashes on the screen.

> I'm outside. And I have cappuccino and waffles

Frowning, I text him back.

> Have you sent this to the wrong number?

> No, dude! I'm outside the elevator to your penthouse. Press a button and let me up

He's supposed to be in Chicago. What the hell is he doing here? I go to the intercom in the kitchen and check the screen, and sure enough there's my brother, a goofy smile on his face and a tray of coffee and a brown paper bag in his hands.

I press the button to allow him up, confused as to what's brought him all the way here but happy to see him. I grab plates from the cabinet, and a few moments later, I hear his heavy footsteps coming down the hall.

He holds up the paper bag and the tray containing three coffees. "Hey, bro."

"I love that you never visit empty-handed." He places his offerings on the island, and I wrap him in a hug. "But what the hell are you doing here?"

He cocks his head and winces. "I've been a shit brother. I should have been here for you, but that trial was ..." He blows out a breath. "I'm sorry about you and Mel. And about the baby."

"You couldn't be a shit brother if you tried, but thank you." I hug him again. "I'm fucking stoked you're here."

"Yeah, well Mase said Mel was staying with you for a while, but I wasn't sure if she was still here. I brought her a coffee and some waffles just in case."

Shit, Mel! I should go tell her we have company before she walks into the kitchen naked, which is how I asked her to dress for breakfast before she jumped in the shower ten minutes ago. Her footsteps coming down the hallway tell me I'm too late. I throw my hand over Drake's eyes, and he yelps in surprise. A few seconds later, Mel walks into the kitchen. Fortunately not naked, but she is only wearing one of my shirts, which skims her mid-thigh, and I hope to fuck she has panties on under there.

Drake jerks his head away from my hand.

"Drake!" Mel claps her hands together. "It's so good to see you."

I don't miss him taking in her outfit and side-eyeing me. "I brought waffles."

Her eyes light up. "Then I'm even happier to see you." She crosses the kitchen and peers into the paper bag before licking her pouty lips. I clear my throat, feeling strangely awkward. The last time I saw my brother, we were talking about divorce papers.

"I'm so sorry about the baby, Mel," Drake says.

Her eyes fill with sadness, but she smiles at him. "Thank you."

"Shall we eat?" I suggest.

"Please. I'm starving after ..." Her cheeks flush pink, and she presses her lips together. I'm almost certain she wasn't about to say anything about how hard I fucked her less than half an hour ago. It's pretty much all I've done since I put my ring back on her finger two days ago, but the memory alone is clearly enough to have her blushing like a virgin.

Drake smirks at me. "Did I come at a bad time, bro? Because I can come back later."

I roll my eyes at him.

"You're not interrupting anything, Drake," Mel says sweetly.

I wink at him. "Not right now, anyway."

"Nate!" Mel squeals, and her blush deepens further. Unable to resist making her squirm, I slip an arm around her waist and kiss her. Looks like all of my brothers will know we're back together by the end of the day.

AFTER WE FINISH the waffles Drake brought, he gets ready to leave. "I assume I'll see you both at Dad's for dinner later?"

I glance at Mel to gauge her reaction. I intended to spend the entire day alone with her, during which I would explore every single inch of her body. But her eyes are shining and she's grinning from ear to ear. It's easy for me to forget that from the age of thirteen on, she never had much of a family. It's also easy to take mine for granted.

"Sure, we'll be there later," I tell him.

Mel claps her hands and squeaks her delight.

Drake nods his approval and wraps his arms around my beautiful wife, giving her one of his infamous bear hugs. He whispers something in her ear that makes tears prick at her eyes, but the smile she's had on her face all morning grows wider.

After he leaves, I pull her in for a hug, desperate to touch her. She leans into me, her head against my chest. "What did he say to you?"

She laughs. "That's between me and him, Ice."

THE WAY my brothers and father fuss over Mel, practically ignoring me, makes me feel like I've brought a celebrity to Sunday dinner. But their joy, especially hers, keeps me from begrudging any of them for it. After chasing my brothers into the kitchen to fix drinks and check on dinner, Dad pulls Mel into his arms, squeezing her like he'll never let go. I watch the way she melts into him. My entire family fell in love with her the first time they met her, and I can't blame them.

When he pulls back, they both have tears in their eyes. "There are plenty of babies in your future. I can feel it." He gently wipes a tear from her face. "My Verona lost four babies before she had Elijah, and then she blessed me with five sons."

A lump forms in my throat. I had no idea they went through that.

She chokes back a sob. "Thank you, Dalton."

"No, thank you, sweet girl. You've melted this old man's ice-cold heart."

Drake sidles up beside me. "Well, fuck. She's got Pop wrapped around her finger. I haven't seen him smile like that since before ..." He doesn't need to finish the sentence.

I sigh with contentment. "Yeah, he's not the only one she's put a spell on."

"I see that, brother." He wraps his arm around my shoulder. "I'm happy for you."

A throat clears behind us. Drake and I spin around, and I blink at the sight that greets us, sure it must be a hallucination. I manage to find my voice. "Maddox!"

He drops his huge duffel bag onto the floor with a thud and rubs a hand through his shaggy beard. "Hey!"

Drake gasps. "Jesus Christ, Mad."

Our youngest brother shrugs. "I heard what happened. Figured you might need a hug."

"Fuck yeah, I need a hug." We both move at the same time, crossing the room and clashing in the middle, a mess of arms and shoulders as we grab onto each other. He smells of fresh air, peppermint, coffee.

"I'm sorry, bro." He bands his powerful arms around my back. "Elijah told me what happened, and it sucks."

I pull his face into my shoulder. "I'm so fucking happy to see you." It's been four years since Maddox walked out of this house with a promise that he'd never come back.

"Hey. He's not the only one who's missed you," Drake says, and I let Maddox go so the others can greet him.

I'm gawking at him when Mel curls her slender fingers through mine. "Is this your baby brother?"

"Yeah." I smile down at her.

"Is this the lady I've heard so much about?" Maddox asks, coming to stand in front of us.

"This is my wife, Mel."

"Mel." He pulls something out of his pocket. "I got this for you. It was blessed by a shaman. It's for fertility." He hands her a small wooden carving of the female form.

She takes it from him and holds it to her chest. "That's so sweet of you. Thank you, Maddox."

"Son?" our father croaks.

Maddox licks his lips, his dark brown eyes full of sadness or maybe regret. "Hey, Pop."

∾

"I REALLY LIKE STAYING HERE." Mel drapes her thigh over me and presses her body against mine. "It's so lovely seeing you with your dad and brothers."

I trace my fingertips up and down her spine. "I like seeing you with them too, corazón."

"And it was wonderful to meet Maddox."

I pull her tight, pressing a kiss on top of her head. Having Maddox home is the cherry on top of this already incredible day. Nothing could be better than waking up with my wife in my arms, having my ring on her finger, waffles with her and Drake, all rounded off with dinner with all the people I love most in the world. "I'm glad you two hit it off."

"He's so interesting. He has so many stories."

Yeah, you don't know the half of it. I keep that thought to myself. Not my stories to tell.

"And your dad was so happy to have him home."

"Yeah, we all are."

She yawns and snuggles into me. "I love you, Ice."

My heart feels like it's about to burst. "I love you too, Spitfire."

A little while later, Mel's breathing evens out, and I roll her off me and climb out of bed. It's unusual for me to struggle with sleep while she's next to me, but my mind won't stop racing with old memories. My brothers and me as kids. My parents hugging and kissing and laughing, so in love with each other. My mom's death. Maddox leaving.

I pull on a pair of sweatpants and walk over to the window, peering out into the darkness. Sorrow overwhelms me at the sight of my father sitting on the bench where he spent so many summer evenings with my mother. Seeing him there, all alone in the cold, has me pulling on a hoodie and sneakers and leaving my sleeping wife.

Cold air hits me like a wave of icy water when I step outside, and I head over to Dad and take a seat beside him. "What are you doing out here in the middle of the night? You'll freeze your ass off."

He tilts his face up to the night sky. "Just wanted some air."

"You okay?"

He closes his eyes and smiles. "Better than okay, son."

"It's good to have Maddox home."

His Adam's apple bobs. "It's better than good. I thought I might never see him again."

I squeeze his shoulder. "I know, Dad."

He turns to face me, his eyes wet with tears. "Him coming home, you and Mel back on track ... It's been a good day."

I lean back against the bench. "Yeah, it sure has."

"You love her, son?"

"With everything I have."

He pats my thigh. "I'm happy for you both."

"You're not mad I didn't follow your advice? To never fall in love?"

His laugh cuts through the quiet night. "When have you boys ever taken my advice? Besides, that was the worst piece of wisdom I ever imparted."

"Shouldn't you tell the rest of them that?"

He laughs again, crossing his legs and resting his ankle on his thigh. "They know, son. Just like you did, they know."

CHAPTER
SIXTY-NINE

NATHAN

She pours us each a mug of coffee and sets it on the kitchen island, bumping her hip against mine and giving me a huge smile that makes my heart skip a beat.

Jesus, who the fuck am I? Having this woman in my life has turned me into a goddamn Teddy bear, but I'm fucking here for it.

"Are you looking forward to going back to work today, corazón?"

She nods, her eyes shining with delight. "I am. They've all messaged me this morning being super sweet and supportive. We're getting jelly donuts for breakfast to celebrate my return." She bounces on her toes.

I rest my lips on the top of her head. "You and your jelly donut addiction."

She giggles. "I know. It's my one vice."

"Remember you need to leave early today. I already squared it with your boss." She sighs, and I put down my coffee and wrap my arms around her. "You don't have to be there if you don't want to be, corazón."

She looks up at me, her green eyes so full of trust and love. "But you think I should be, right?"

"I think it's probably good for you to get some closure. You have nothing to fear. If he even looks at you in a way that makes you the slightest bit uncomfortable, I'll break his jaw, then whatever other bone you'd like me to." I hate her brother, but I will always be grateful for the fact that he brought her into my life. So I will respect her wishes not to kill the piece of shit, even if I'm hopeful she'll change her mind someday.

"I'm not afraid of him anymore."

"No, because he's a fucking coward. And he'll get more than a letter opener through his hand if he ever lays a finger on you again."

She gasps, and I remember she doesn't know about that. Shit. "What do you mean? Did you ... Nathan." She admonishes me with a firm look.

I snarl at the memory. "Elijah told me what he did to you, Mel. He's lucky he's still able to walk."

She blinks. "But you and I ... we weren't even ... You did that for me?"

I brush back her hair and press a soft kiss on her lips. "I would die for you, corazón, so I'd sure as fuck kill and maim for you."

A giggle bubbles out of her and makes me smile. "I really shouldn't laugh at you stabbing my brother, but ..." She presses her lips together. "It's no less than he deserves."

I hum my agreement, dusting my lips over her jaw and down to her neck. She purrs contentedly, throwing her head back and allowing me full access to her throat. My dick stiffens in my pants, and she rubs herself against me. I growl with need. It's been three days since I asked her to stay, and I've barely been able to keep my hands or my mouth off her for a single second of them.

"I have to go to work," she moans.

I check my watch. "We have a little time. You'll be thirty minutes late at most." I trail my teeth over the sensitive skin of her neck and she shivers.

"I can't." She plants her hands on my chest like she wants to push me away, but she also grinds her hips over my aching cock. "It's my first day back."

"Maybe you should give up your job and become my twenty-four-hour fuck-toy. Always on call whenever I need you."

She laughs. "Or maybe you should be mine."

I nip at her skin. "If that's what you want, corazón."

"Mmm, tempting," she purrs.

With a deep sigh, I stop kissing her neck, give her a hard slap on the ass, and go back to my coffee. She grins at me in triumph, and I narrow my eyes. "Wait 'til I get you alone later, Mrs. James."

She flutters her eyelashes. "I can't wait."

MY SECRETARY POPS her head through the open door of my office. "Your guests are waiting in the boardroom, sir."

I dismiss her with a nod and take hold of Mel's hand, squeezing gently as she perches on the edge of my desk. "You ready, corazón?"

Her eyes shutter closed, but she offers a faint nod.

"I'm right here with you."

She opens her eyes and gives me a tremulous smile. "I know. I just hate being in the same room as them. Especially him."

"This is the last time you'll ever have to share the same air as either of them."

"You promise?"

I pull her into my arms and band them tightly around her. "I promise. We're going to have an incredible life, Mel, and they won't have any part in it."

She nestles her cheek against my chest. "I love you, Nate."

I rest my lips against her hair, and I'm cocooned by the smell of her coconut shampoo. The scent always takes my mind to our morning routine, when she showers and I put on a pot of coffee. It's one of the many simple daily routines that has become such an integral and gratifying part of my life. "I love you too, corazón."

She draws a deep, shuddering breath. "I guess we'd better do this."

We enter the boardroom together and, without saying a word to anyone, take our seats beside each other. Miranda sits across from us with her hands clasped in her lap and the faint hint of a smile on her face. To anyone who doesn't know about the cruel, spiteful woman beneath the mask, she'd appear demure and elegant. Bryce, on the other hand, bristles with impotent rage. His clenched fists rest on the boardroom table, the shiny scar on the back of his right hand making me smirk, but he keeps his gaze lowered, not daring to look at me or his sister. He no doubt recognizes how little provocation it would take for me to lean across the table and punch him in the mouth. And that would be the least he deserves.

Melanie rolls her shoulders back and defiantly tilts her jaw, but I know my wife well enough to feel the nervous energy radiating from her.

It's Miranda who breaks the silence. "May I ask why you've requested our presence here today, Mr. James?" She doesn't even bother to glance at her daughter.

I lean back in my chair, placing my hand on Mel's thigh beneath the table and giving her a discreet squeeze. "I think you'd be better off asking my wife that question, Mrs. Edison."

Miranda's lip curls, hinting at a sneer, before she regains her composure and angles her body toward Melanie. "Why are we here?"

Mel clears her throat. "There are going to be some changes at Edison Holdings."

Bryce speaks for the first time. "What changes?" He snarls. "The business is in a trust, and we're the trustees. You can't make changes without our consent."

Mel looks at me, her tongue darting out over her bottom lip. I nod, letting her know she's got this. I went over everything with her in detail.

"New trustees are being appointed. Elijah and Mason James," she says assertively.

"The fuck they are," Bryce snaps.

"Yes, the fuck they are, Bryce," she snaps right back. "Dad set up that trust to protect us all, but did you know there's a clause that allows the trustees to be removed or the trust dissolved if the trustees misappropriate funds?"

Bryce's brow furrows, but it's his mother who speaks. "You can't prove misappropriation of funds."

Mel plants her hands on the table. "Oh yes I can. Seventeen years of *business trips* to Vegas. All the brand-new, top-of-the-line cars that were purchased to transport Ash and me. When was the last time Ashley or I needed either of you to give us a ride anywhere?

"Both of you have proven that you're not fit to run Edison Holdings, and let's face it, there's nothing left in the trust fund to manage except the business, which is failing horribly. Paper-work has already been filed."

Bryce snarls. "We'll contest it."

A deep laugh rumbles out of me, and Bryce makes eye contact for the first time since I walked into the room. "You can try, dipshit. But the contract is very clear, and even if you had grounds to refute Melanie and Ashley's request to appoint new trustees, I would tie you up in court for the rest of your miserable life. By the time I'm done with you, you'll be sitting on a street corner, begging for nickels and dimes." His scowl deepens. "Alternatively, we could file criminal charges and have your ass tossed in jail for the rest of your life. Either of those options are fine with me."

"That won't be necessary," Miranda says, before her jackass son can dig himself into an even deeper hole. "What does this mean for Bryce and me? For the business?"

I lean back in my chair and allow Mel to deliver the wonderful news. "As you know, the business has operated at a loss for the past six years, but Nathan and I have looked at the books, and there's no reason it can't be turned around with a little hard work and common sense."

Bryce snorts, and I shoot him a warning glare that makes him clamp his lips together.

"A new independent CEO has been appointed. She's very experienced, and she's eager to explore some new ideas as well as—"

"So you just bring someone new into *our* family business and—"

I slam my fist onto the table, and Bryce flinches. "If you ever interrupt my wife again while she's speaking, I will punch your teeth down your throat. Do you understand me?"

His face turns an unusual shade of pale, and he nods. I offer Mel a smile. "Go on, corazón."

She smiles sweetly at me before turning her attention back to her mother and brother. "She has a lot of great ideas, and we believe she can turn the company around. Early projections suggest Edison Holdings could turn a profit again within two years."

"So your husband's brothers are the new trustees, and they ensure that you're the only one who benefits from the trust?" her mother asks, her tone dripping with disdain.

Mel leans forward, keeping her voice clipped and assertive. "That is not how trusts work, Mother. Managed properly, they benefit the people they were supposed to. Elijah and Mason have no need of anything from the trust. I don't need the trust either."

"Not now that you have your rich husband," Miranda taunts.

Mel's back straightens and her jaw tenses. "I haven't taken a cent from either of you in eleven years. I don't care about the money, Mom. But Ashley deserves it. She deserves to finish college and concentrate on her studies without having to take two jobs to make rent. *She* will be the beneficiary of the trust. Which is exactly how it should be."

"And what about us?" Bryce whines, like the pathetic man-child he is.

"Mother, you will be given a monthly allowance that will allow you to keep the house and maintain a certain lifestyle, although maybe a little more modest than you're used to, but certainly enough to be comfortable."

"And me?" Bryce says, his face turning almost purple and spittle flying from his mouth.

"You, my dear brother, will get exactly what you deserve." Melanie offers him a sweet smile, her hands clasped in front of her as she stares him dead in the eye. "Nothing."

Oh, I fucking love this woman.

Bryce opens and closes his mouth like a fish out of water.

"Relax, it's not like you'll be homeless," I offer with a shrug.

He pushes back his chair, looking like he's about to throw

an almighty temper tantrum. "You can't do this. I'm a beneficiary of Dad's trust too."

"Well we can always go with the other option, and you can enjoy free room and board for the rest of your life, courtesy of the United States government," I remind him with a grin. I fucking love watching him squirm.

Bryce is practically foaming at the mouth. He jumps to his feet, and his chair falls to the ground. My muscles tense. I am ready and willing to drop this piece of shit the minute he takes a step toward Mel. But Miranda stands too and puts a hand on his arm. "We're leaving," she says coolly. She's a shrewd woman, which means she knows they don't have a chance in hell of fighting this and that she's being afforded much more grace than she deserves.

I get to my feet, fastening the buttons of my jacket. "Before you go, there's one more thing."

Both Miranda and Bryce turn and glare at me. "Melanie is signing over her stake in the company to Ashley. You will no longer be a part of her life. Not ever. You hear something about our life that intrigues you, you fucking ignore it. You feel like reaching out to her and seeing how she is or if she can help you out of a bind, you fucking don't. You hear she has our child and you decide you want to play the doting grandma or uncle, you fucking forget about it. And if she ever has to hear from either of you again, I *will* destroy you both, and I won't lose a single second of sleep over it."

Mel stands by my side, exactly where she belongs, and laces her fingers through mine. With a final look of contempt, Bryce and Miranda walk out of the boardroom. As soon as they're gone, my wife lets out a long breath and leans against me. I wrap a steadying arm around her. "You were incredible, corazón."

"My legs were shaking the entire time."

"Nobody could tell. I'm glad I'll never have to go up against you in a courtroom, Goose."

She laughs, and the musical sound makes my pulse quicken and my dick twitch. I trail my fingertips down her spine and over her hipbone. She shivers at my touch. "Have you ever had sex in this boardroom?" she asks with a soft purr, catching me completely off guard. That twitch in my pants turns into something much more dangerous.

Never a man to mix business with pleasure, I have never in the seven years I've owned this building even considered fucking anyone in my boardroom. Now it's all I can fucking think about. "Not yet. Why, you have something in mind?"

She backs away from me, catching her luscious lower lip between her teeth. "Maybe." She keeps walking backward until she reaches the chair at the head of the table. Pulling it out, she takes a seat, a devious smile on her face and a wicked glint in her eyes. Her tongue darts out, moistening her full lips. "Crawl to me."

I cock my head, sure I misheard. "What?"

"Oh, you heard me, Ice. Crawl. To. Me."

I shake my head and suppress a laugh. "Oh no, corazón. That is not how this works."

She purses her lips, her eyes raking over my body. Then she stands and slowly peels off her pants and panties, kicking them off with her socks and sneakers. When she sits back down, she spreads her legs wide, putting her perfect pink pussy on display for me. Already glistening with her juices and begging to be eaten and fucked. "I said crawl to me," she repeats.

I blow out a breath, my eyes bouncing between hers and the space between her thighs—my nirvana. Running my tongue over my teeth, I will my dick to stop throbbing and clouding my senses, because I can't think straight. And surely that is the only logical explanation for why I drop to my knees in my own fucking boardroom and crawl across the room to her. The wicked smile on her face grows, and as I get closer, the scent of her arousal gets stronger, making my mouth water.

She practically purrs with delight when I reach her. I place my hands on the tops of her legs and skim my nose along the inside of her thigh. A deep growl rolls in my throat.

"Good boy," she says, and I nip at her soft flesh, making her yelp.

"Don't push me, corazón."

She threads her fingers in my hair and tilts my head up. "You look so good on your knees for me, Ice."

"I would spend every fucking day on my knees for you if you wanted me to," I tell her honestly. "Especially if it leads to eating this delicious pussy." I dip my head and lick the length of her wet slit, making her moan out my name. Flicking my tongue over her skin has her squirming and dripping onto the leather chair. I wrap my hands around the back of her thighs and pull her forward so her ass is perched on the edge of the seat, and then I eat her like I might never get the chance to again, sucking and licking and biting until she's begging me to let her come.

"Nate, please," she cries.

"Who owns this pussy, corazón?"

"You. Always," she whines, needy and desperate.

I look up, locking my gaze on hers as she fights to keep her eyes open. "You look so good when you beg for me."

She groans loudly, all frustration and desire. "Please!"

I chuckle, enjoying her pleading moans and whimpers as I remind her who's really in control here. And only when her legs are shaking and tears are rolling down her cheeks do I give her what she needs, flicking my tongue over her swollen clit until she squirts all over my face and my suit.

I sit back on my heels, wiping my mouth and taking a deep

breath as I look at her, practically boneless, sagging against the chair. God, she's fucking perfect.

Leaning forward, I press my lips to her ear. She clings to me, fingertips grasping at the lapels of my suit jacket. "Catch your breath, corazón, because I'm gonna bend you over this table and fuck you so hard that you might just regret making me crawl to you."

A smile spreads across her face. "Bring it, Ice."

Jesus, fuck! I love this woman more than life.

CHAPTER
SEVENTY

NATHAN

Ten months later
New Year's Eve

Stuffing my hands into my pockets, I look out over the New York City skyline. In the distance, fireworks light up the night sky, and I smile at how my brothers and I always insisted on shooting off the fireworks before midnight when we were kids. This is the first New Year's I haven't spent with my family. Well, *that* part of my family at least. I have a new one now.

Turning around, I watch her sleep. Although she's wearing nothing but a pair of panties, she's kicked off the covers, and her hand rests protectively on the swell of her belly. Our baby's due date was two days ago, but he's refusing to leave the comfort of his mother's womb. Stubborn, just like his dad.

I take off my pants and crawl into bed beside her, slipping my hand over her hip as I press my chest against her bare skin.

She shifts onto her back and lets out a sleepy sigh. "I fell asleep. Have I missed the ball drop?"

Dropping a kiss on her shoulder, I glance at the TV on the wall. "Not yet, corazón. We have fifteen more minutes."

"I'm sorry I'm the worst New Year's company ever this year."

"No." I kiss her again and rub a hand over her stomach. Our son kicks against it, and I smile. "You're the absolute best."

"You're so smooth," she purrs, pressing her beautiful ass against me and making my cock stiffen.

"You're a wicked little siren rubbing yourself on me like that."

She giggles. "Well, you did promise to take care of me after the movie."

"I know, but you fell asleep watching it." I nip her shoulder.

She rubs a hand over her abdomen before placing it over mine. "What can I say? Growing an entire human is a tough deal, Ice."

"I know, corazón, and you're doing an exceptional job."

"You think?" she whispers.

"I know." I trail kisses over her neck, and she moans. Taking my hand, she moves it down between her thighs. "Do you want me to take care of you right now?"

I tug her panties aside and her back bows. "Yes, please."

"My wife is such a needy little whore for me."

"Yeah," she breathes, rocking her hips to chase the friction of my fingers against her clit. I rub the pad of my middle digit over the swollen bud of flesh, and she whines—a sound full of need and desire. I ache to be inside her. Kissing her neck and shoulders, I tease her a little more, drawing out a series of whimpers and moans that have my cock weeping to take her. She groans when I stop, and I bite back a laugh. "You get so fucking desperate when I have my hands on you."

She doesn't even offer me any sass in return because she knows I'm right. I slide off her panties and toss them onto the floor. After rolling her onto her side, I hook her leg over mine, opening her wider for me. It's the most comfortable position to fuck her in while she's heavily pregnant, and it also gets her off quicker than any other. "But I'm just as desperate for you, corazón."

She giggles. "Oh, I know that."

I press the crown of my cock at the entrance of her wet channel. "You do, huh?"

"Yup. Admit it. You can't get enough of me, Mr. James."

"How much I want you has never been in doubt, Mrs. James." I slide all the way inside her in one slow, deep thrust, and her walls ripple around me, squeezing me and pulling me deeper. "I love fucking you." I grab her jaw and turn her head so she's looking up at me. I give her a gentle kiss on the lips as I pull out and sink back inside, making her moan into my mouth. "And I fucking love you."

"I love you more."

I shake my head. "Impossible." Then I seal my lips over hers again, kissing her with everything I have while I rock my hips and fuck her slowly. We only break our kiss when the faint noise of the TV in the background signals the ball has dropped.

She glances at the TV and then back at me, her eyes shining. "Oops, we missed it."

I drive in a little harder, and she gasps. "I didn't miss anything, corazón. Right here is the only place I want to be, and this is only thing I want to be doing."

"Me too."

I slip my hand between her thighs again, circling her swollen clit as I fuck her to a slow-rolling orgasm that has her whimpering my name and squeezing my cock so hard she tips me right over the edge with her.

I roll onto my back, and she turns around to face me, nestling into the crook of my shoulder as I wrap one arm around her. I press a kiss to her forehead. "I think we just started a whole new New Year's tradition, corazón."

"And what tradition is that?"

"I spend midnight balls-deep inside my wife."

She snorts a laugh. "That could be tricky at one of your family parties."

"I'll make it happen."

She yawns, rubbing her cheek against my chest. "I have no doubt you will, Ice."

EPILOGUE

MELANIE

One year later
New Year's Eve

Nathan wraps his arm around my waist. I smile up at him and ask, "Did he go back down okay?"

"Yeah. I think he just needed a cuddle from Dad," he replies, beaming. He's taken to fatherhood like he does to everything else—like he was born for the role. Seeing him with our son makes me fall in love with him a little more every single day.

He takes my hand in his and leans close, his lips pressed against my ear. "I believe we have somewhere else we need to be, Mrs. James."

I glance around the room, which is full of Nathan's family, along with Tyler and Ashley, who have been welcomed into the fold as warmly as I have. This is the annual James family New Year's party, and I'm pretty sure it's the only place we're supposed to be. "What are you talking about?"

He winks at me. "Oh, you know." Without waiting for my response, he pulls me out of the noisy party and guides me to a room a few doors down, pushing me inside.

I giggle as he closes the door behind us. "What are we doing in here?"

When he turns to face me, he has a wicked grin on his face. "Surely you're not forgetting our tradition, corazón."

My cheeks burn with heat. "Oh."

"Oh." His voice is a low, throaty growl, and he stalks toward me, already unfastening his belt.

"But our family is right down the hall."

He shakes his head. "Nobody will come in here."

I back away from him, fluttering my eyelashes as he follows me step for step. "They'll wonder where we are if we're not there at midnight."

He unfastens his pants. "Don't give a fuck."

I bump into the wall and gasp as the cool plaster hits the warm skin of my back through the thin fabric of my dress. "But maybe I do. I'll have to walk back in there with ..." I sink my teeth into my bottom lip rather than finish the sentence.

"My cum dripping out of you?"

My cheeks burn hotter.

He takes another step forward and presses me against the wall. "I thought you were enjoying the party. If you'd prefer, I can take you to bed and fuck you there, but then we won't be leaving it until morning. Your choice, but you're getting fucked either way."

I place my hands on his chest. "You're so sure of yourself."

"I told you where I'd be at midnight, Mel. Inside you. I can't go back on that promise now. It could be bad luck."

I wrap my arms around his neck and give a pensive nod. "I guess this has been a pretty good year. It makes sense to start this next one the same way."

His face breaks into a grin. "Exactly." He unzips his fly. "Take off your panties."

A laugh bubbles from my lips. "I can't."

His handsome face furrows in a frown. "Why not?"

I press my lips at his ear. "Because I'm not wearing any."

His animalistic growl turns my legs turn to jelly. "You are getting so fucked, Mrs. James." He hitches up my dress with one hand and frees himself from his pants with the other. My legs wrap around his waist, and he presses the crown of his cock at my entrance and sucks in a breath. "Always ready for me, huh, corazón?"

"Always."

He drives inside me, and I cry out at the exquisite feeling of being so full of him. "I'll make this quick and take my time with you later."

"I have to tell you s-something," I pant as he nails me to the wall.

He slows his pace and presses his forehead against mine. "Does it have anything to do with why you've skillfully avoided drinking a drop of champagne all night?"

"You noticed?"

He runs his nose over my jawline and presses a kiss beneath my ear. "I notice *everything* about you, corazón. When did you find out?"

"This evening before dinner. I was going to tell you sooner, but Drake needed to speak to you about something, and then everyone was always within earshot. I want to keep it between us for now."

He stares into my eyes. "You're making me a dad again."

I nod, unable to keep the smile from my face. "I sure am."

"You're so fucking incredible. I don't know what the fuck I ever did to get so damn lucky in life."

"You were born lucky," I remind him.

He shakes his head. "None of this meant anything until you. I would give it all up in a heartbeat as long as I had you and our kids, Mel. I mean that."

I place one hand on his cheek, and he presses his face into my palm. "I know you do." Then I squeeze my inner muscles around his shaft, and his eyes roll back in his head as he grunts out a string of obscenities. "But you don't have to give anything up. You can have it all, Nate."

He rocks his hips, and wet heat sears in my core. "I already have it all, corazón."

Yes, he does. And so do I.

NOT QUITE READY TO say goodbye to Nathan and Mel yet? You can get their exclusive bonus chapter Here

ARE you ready for the rest of the James brothers? You can preorder 3 of their stories now

Drake's story

Elijah's story

Mason's story

IF YOU'D LIKE to know more about Jessie Ryan and her four Irish Mafia husbands, you can find book 1 in their completed series here

Ryan Rule

And if you'd like to learn a little more about Nathan's friends, the Moretti's, the Chicago series is also available now

Dante

Joey

Lorenzo

Keres

ALSO BY SADIE KINCAID

Sadie's latest series, Chicago Ruthless is available for preorder now. Following the lives of the notoriously ruthless Moretti siblings - this series will take you on a rollercoaster of emotions. Packed with angst, action and plenty of steam — Order yours today

Dante

Joey

Lorenzo

Keres

If you haven't read the New York the series yet, you can find them on Amazon and Kindle Unlimited

Ryan Rule

Ryan Redemption

Ryan Retribution

Ryan Reign

Ryan Renewed

New York Ruthless short stories can be found here

A Ryan Reckoning

A Ryan Rewind

A Ryan Restraint

A Ryan Halloween

A Ryan Christmas

A Ryan New Year

Want to know more about the king and queen of LA, Alejandro and Alana, as well as Jackson and Lucia? Find out all about them in Sadie's internationally bestselling LA Ruthless series. Available on Amazon and FREE in Kindle Unlimited.

Fierce King

Fierce Queen

Fierce Betrayal

Fierce Obsession

If you'd like to read about London's hottest couple. Gabriel and Samantha, then check out Sadie's London Ruthless series on Amazon. FREE in Kindle Unlimited.

Dark Angel

Fallen Angel

Dark/ Fallen Angel Duet

If you enjoy super spicy short stories, Sadie also writes the Bound series feat Mack and Jenna, Books 1, 2, 3 and 4 are available now.

Bound and Tamed

Bound and Shared

Bound and Dominated

Bound and Deceived

ACKNOWLEDGMENTS

As always I would love to thank all of my incredible readers, and especially the members of Sadie's Ladies and Sizzling Alphas. My beloved belt whores! You are all superstars. To my amazing ARC and street teams, the love you have for these books continues to amaze and inspire me. I am so grateful for all of you.

But to all of the readers who have bought any of my books, everything I write is for you and you all make my dreams come true.

To all of my author friends who help make this journey all that more special.

Super special mention to my lovely PA's, Kate, Kate and Andrea, for their support and honesty and everything they do to make my life easier.

To the silent ninja, Bobby Kim. Thank you for continuing to push me to be better. And to my amazing editor, Jaime, who puts up with my insane writing process and helps me make each book better than the last.

To my incredible boys who inspire me to be better every single day. And last, but no means least, a huge thank you to Mr. Kincaid—all my book boyfriends rolled into one. I couldn't do this without you!

About the Author

Sadie Kincaid is a dark and contemporary romance author who loves to read and write about hot alpha males and strong, feisty females.

Sadie loves to connect with readers so why not get in touch via social media?

Join Sadie's reader group for the latest news, book recommendations and plenty of fun. Sadie's ladies and Sizzling Alphas

Made in the USA
Middletown, DE
23 July 2024